speak the truth

Volume One

Twoony

Speak the Truth Volume One

Copyright © 2012 by Twoony

All rights reserved.

Character Art by mailanoooo

ISBN (Paperback): 9798353886815

Second Edition

Imprint: Independently published

Dedication

This book is for all the fans who have supported Aron and Quinton's story for over a decade.
Thank you!

CHAPTER ONE

Never in my life have I ever been more embarrassed and infuriated at the same time. I'm not sure what I feel more; the painful humiliation or the raging anger within me. I am at such a loss for words that Langley has to speak for me.

"Are you deaf? Did you not hear who he is?" Langley is at a loss too.

His green eyes grow to the size of a saucer. His jaw can't stay closed, continuing to hang open even as he waits for an answer. Being a friend of mine for years, Langley has become accustomed to all those around me doing exactly as I say when I say it. I'm the Prince after all. With that title comes a few perks, like people listening to me.

If I say roll over, they roll over. If I say to speak, they speak and if I say to lick the dirt off the bottom of their shoes, then you bet your ass they will do exactly that, and yet, it seems someone has missed the memo.

"I heard," the demon-like boy says with onyx eyes that are deeper and darker than any abyss. His expression is that of utter boredom. He's acting like we just told him about the weather. "I just don't care."

Looking into black eyes filled to the brim with a confidence I cannot dream of possessing, I feel the fire in my stomach turn into a roaring inferno.

Who does he think he is to treat me in such a way? Does he not know what I can do to him? Getting him expelled would be easy. I could do it simply by suggestion!

The black eyed and even blacker haired boy gestures to an empty seat a few rows up. He says in a tone that clearly states his disinterest, "There's an empty seat there. Perhaps, if His Majesty wishes for a better spot, he should wake up earlier and get to class on time like everyone else instead of kicking others out of theirs like an immature brat."

The entire class gasps at his use of immature brat or maybe they're shocked from this entire situation. It isn't every day a person sees their future king being spoken to in such a way. Actually, it has never happened before. Never in my life have I been treated with such disrespect. To be honest, I don't have a clue how to respond. My brain ceases to function. It's burning with anger, with the need to slam my fist directly into his stupid pretty boy face.

To think this all started over a chair...

I woke up late, as usual. I always had this issue with waking up on time. It didn't take me long to dress, seeing as we had a uniform at Thorton's Academy. All I had to do was toss the blue uniform and tie on before heading off to my first class.

My short blonde hair always styled itself, so there was no point in messing with it. Luckily for me, our professor was not in class yet. On the board, he had written a curt note saying how he had forgotten something in his office and would return momentarily.

Not that I would have been in trouble for being late. I was sure he'd let me off the hook. This being my first day and me being, well, me. Langley happily offered me a good morning before I eyed the classroom for a spot.

I didn't want to sit in the back because I'd have a rough time seeing the board. There were a plethora of other students there as well, likely ones who had better eyesight or simply hated the idea of being called on so much that they would risk not seeing the board.

I didn't want to sit in the front either; the professor might pick on me. There was a perfect seat on the left side of the room near the window. The sun did not reach it in a way that would leave me squinting, and a pleasant breeze came from the open windows. However, someone had already discovered the seat and was sitting there.

Whatever. I'd just tell them to move.

I marched on over, head held high and Langley in tail. The boy didn't notice me standing next to him or, now that I think about it, he probably didn't care. His deep brown eyes that were borderline black, stared out the window. They didn't even turn to me when I cleared my throat.

"Hmm?" He hummed, still paying me no mind. It made my skin crawl.

"I want to sit here," I said, pointing at the desired desk. I let him off the hook since he clearly couldn't tell who I was by my voice alone. "Move."

I smiled and waited for him to do as I said. They always did. However, the boy finally looked at me with an expression of confusion. He raised an elegant brow and asked, "Why would I do that?"

"Because I said so," I replied, growing impatient.

Did he not know who I was? When I wanted something I got it, besides it was just a chair. He should move already so I could have it.

"And if I told you to jump off a bridge, would you do it?" he retaliated.

And that is basically how we ended up here. He made me look like a fool a bit more. I informed him of who I was, and he still insisted on insulting me and arguing. Perhaps I would not have been so angry about this entire ordeal if he hadn't spoken to me in such a way, but his arrogance pisses me off!

"You cannot speak to me like that," I hiss through teeth that have been clenched since the moment he opened his lips.

I'm the prince. Did his parents not teach him to respect the royal family?

"Oh, my bad," he says and, with a grin that only adds fuel to the fire, continues on. "Please come to class on time like everyone else, Your Highness."

"As if saying please fixes anything!" Langley hollers at my side. He seems as taken aback as me. He's never witnessed such disobedience either, and it's leaving us both annoyed. Langley is about to lean over and grab the demon when Professor Bennett arrives.

"Boys," Professor Bennett says, grabbing everyone's attention but mine and the demon sitting smugly before me. I continue glaring daggers at him and he's still smirking like... like... I don't even have a word for it!

"Is there a problem?" Professor Bennett asks.

"No," I hiss, wishing not to embarrass myself further.

I cannot believe I got into an argument over a damn seat, but it's this douchebag's fault. He is acting as if I'm not his future king and instead is treating me like some commoner!

Somehow, I make my way to an empty seat without stomping. He already called me an immature brat. Stomping will not disprove him. Not to mention I can feel his dark eyes watching my every movement to prove what he said to be true. I will not grant him the satisfaction.

"I'm glad you could join us today, Your Highness." Professor Bennett sends a smile in my direction, to which I cannot return. My blood continues boiling and probably will be for the next week. "I see you have already acquainted yourself with Quinton Underwood."

He gestures at the demon.

"Top of our class, top of the school, actually." Profess Bennett sends Quinton a proud smile. "Should you need any help and would feel more comfortable speaking with a student, then I would suggest you go to him."

The class erupts with giggles that Professor Bennett stares at oddly. One glare from me and everyone falls silent. Of course, they would giggle after what had transpired. I would rather drink orange juice after brushing my teeth than ask for that kid's help.

Top of the class, I should have figured as much. The confidence is practically seething out of his pores. I could cut the egotistical mist around him with a knife and serve it for dinner.

Sending a glare in his direction, I see that his attention is no longer on me but at the board. With his chin resting in the palm of his hand and his pencil hovering over his paper, he looks like nothing happened, like our argument was nothing to him.

My eye twitches.

How can he be so composed? There must be something wrong with his head. Is he not fearful of what I could do to him? I am the Prince of Gantia. I have the power to move mountains, crush cities, and demolish entire civilizations!

Ok, that's being overdramatic, but the point is that I have power. Crushing a pest like him is child's play for me, yet he doesn't look concerned at all.

I have never in my life been denied things I want. Normally I would not get so angry over a seat, but the way he acted like I was nothing made my blood boil. He spoke to me in such disrespect that I couldn't think straight, still can't think straight.

"I am so sorry, Aron," a voice says at my side that breaks me from my raging train of thought. Langley frowns as he, too, sends a glare towards Quinton, who still hasn't bothered to look over at us. He has to know we're staring.

"Quinton has always been a stuck up bastard, but I would never have dreamed he would speak to you in such a way. We'll teach him a lesson," Langley adds.

"Do it. I hate it when others do not know their place."

I do my best to forget about what happened by focusing all my attention on Professor Bennett's lesson. After all, this is my first day at school. I am now fifteen years old and Mom has finally talked Dad, the king, into allowing me to attend Thorton's Academy. To say I'm excited would be an understatement. I'm thrilled.

Being the heir to the throne, my father has always been rather protective of me. I was hardly ever allowed out of palace grounds, other than the political get-together that would further my father's popularity or the occasional fair, where father would shut it down and allow no others but the royal family and their bodyguards to attend.

I have no siblings as my mother is incapable of bearing anymore because of medical reasons. I am protected from the world for obvious reasons. Not everyone is kind, not everyone likes my father, which means not everyone likes me. Because of that, I am watched like a hawk.

The few friends I had when I was younger were children of our servants, who were more like forced acquaintances that would obey me rather than hang out with me. They were never a challenge in any games, always allowing me to win without much effort, always cheering for me while their eyes practically screamed that they didn't want to be within a five-mile radius of me. I would wave them off in the end, pretending to be mad to mask the pain and play alone. It was easier that way. If they weren't even going to give me a shot, then why even bother?

Then there were friends like Langley, kids of other political officials, who I saw on special occasions. Langley and I have seen each other more recently and will continue to do so, seeing as we are roommates now. He hasn't always been so kind to me either, though, once being like the other children who simply allowed me to do as I wished. He's much better now. Sometimes I clearly see the difference in our classes, when he backs down, when normally he would say something. It stings, but I've gotten used to the isolation.

I have been told that I have a serious issue with communication. I spoke my mind without thinking of the consequences. Of course I would. I was never taught otherwise. I grew up in a home where I got what I wanted, well most of the time. I suppose Dad spoiled me because he knew I hated being locked up in the palace all day. I was even homeschooled! It was awful. Not to mention I had to act properly and mature in front of the officials of the court. I could hardly ever act like a normal kid.

Unlike most children, who learned how to play sports and socialize with friends, I learned battle strategies and politics. While others learned to swim, I learned how to shoot a gun. While others learned how to make friends, I learned how to work a person politically. It was hell knowing that, no matter how hard I tried, I'd never be like anyone else, although I desperately wished for it.

No matter how much I begged to be put into school so that I could actually make friends, something that everyone should be allowed to do, Dad said no, but he said yes to me about everything else.

When I was seven, I insisted for Dad to buy me a replica of a knight's armor, of course, in my size. A week later, Dad and I had a matching set. We played together every evening, pretending to slay dragons and save princesses, and the occasional prince, for about a month before I moved on to something else.

When I was nine, I wanted a home movie theater, so my father tore down part of the castle that was hardly used and made one for me. He even got us early access to movies so we would see them before they even hit the theater. It was great to pretend like I was outside with everyone else watching movies when, in reality, the only one in the theater was me. At least I didn't have to share my popcorn.

Last year, I wanted a pond on palace grounds so I could go swimming or fishing. Not long afterwards, Dad knocked down a few trees and gave me exactly that. I even have a dock with a small boat.

I suppose that has made me have an issue with the word no. I'm so used to it always being yes that when it isn't, I'm not sure what to say or do. I have a feeling that this Quinton kid is going to be saying no to me a lot.

And I'm going to have to change that.

CHAPTER TWO

"Something wrong, Princess?" Quinton asks.

"Yes, remove your arm before I do it for you," I demand.

"No need to get snippy. I am only doing what the professor wants. It is not my fault you fight for shit." His hold around my neck tightens with each breath. I gasp for much needed air.

He does not need to hold on that tight!

Growling, I send my fist into his gut with enough force to release me. He stumbles prior to his foot hitting my chest. I don't know how he regained his balance before I could. I wasn't the one who had a fist shoved into their stomach.

I am not that smart, especially compared to Quinton, but I know I can pack a punch. Before Quinton can lower his leg, I grab his ankle. His eyes widen. I pull him forward. My fist decks him in the chin.

Snarling, he grabs my arm. I shout as he flings me over him. With a loud 'umph,' I fall back to the ground. I have time to blink before finding myself on my stomach, arms held behind my back by a pair of rough hands that can only belong to Quinton. From the corner of my eye, I catch his smug expression that makes my teeth grind.

"Ask nicely, Your Highness, and I might let up," Quinton teases.

I feel the rage inside me, the same rage I feel every time this prick is around. It's been two weeks since I started school. As I expected, Quinton has been a pain in the ass.

Two days after the chair incident, a few of my loyal followers paid Quinton a visit. I was shocked when the both of them returned covered in bumps and bruises. Quinton was fine, not a single scratch, other than the bruised knuckles that showed me exactly how they got those bumps and bruises.

Four days ago, I asked some upper classman to pay him a visit. I found the top students known for being the best fighters in the entire school. After all, Thorton is a school that not only teaches royals about politics, but also how to protect and defend themselves or others. We're royalty, after all. We get death threats daily. Me even more so. I can't count how many times letters have been hidden from me, emails, or even broadcasts. My parents don't want me exposed to the violence, though they know I'm going to have to see it, eventually. Being the next king comes with its disadvantages as well.

As I was saying, four upperclassmen went to visit Quinton next.

Quinton had a busted lip, a sprained wrist and a few bruises, while two of them were so bad they couldn't leave their rooms for a week. The other two were too scared to go anywhere near him. Smart and good at fighting? Is this guy an alien? He really pisses me off!

"Do you have any idea what I could have done to you?" I hiss, doing my best not to allow any dirt into my mouth. He presses so roughly on my back I am sure I will leave an imprint on the ground.

Quinton snorts. With a roll of his eyes, he says darkly; "Don't you mean what your father can have done to me? You can't do anything."

Quinton relinquishes his hold. I get up in a flash, sending my fist directly into his face, or at least I wanted to hit his face.

He moves in the knick of time, barely grabbing my wrist. Using the grip, he tosses me over his shoulder and onto my back again. I am prepared this time and send my legs up hard. He stumbles back before he can straddle me. The anger within me has erupted like a volcano.

"Shut up, shut up, shut up, shut up!" I scream and run at him at full speed.

My arms wrap tightly around his abdomen in a hope of knocking him over. His heels dig into the dirt, moving but an inch. Then I feel his elbow dig into my back with a force that brings tears to my eyes.

The pain does not make me let go. I pick him up and toss him to the ground with a force I didn't know I had. I am so pissed that I ignore the stinging of my back or the sudden loss of air in my lungs because of his knee burying itself into my gut.

I jump on him and throw punch after punch. He raises his arms, blocking each blow. He bucks me off the moment he gets the chance, then jumps up, only to have me running at him again.

I'm mad. I'm embarrassed. I hate him to my very core. Why would he say that? Why does he speak to me like that? Having someone look down on me makes my skin crawl. He's a piece of shit!

Suddenly, I am pulled away from Quinton. He has got a good enough hold on my sides to pull me away. I can't even take a breath before his fist is plummeting into my face.

A whistle blows seconds later. We're yanked apart.

"Boys!" Professor Yarley shouts, standing between the two of us with a stern expression.

I see now, after we've been torn apart, that I have done something to Quinton. I ripped his shirt to reveal that I was holding onto him with a grip that was already forming a gruesome bruise around his abdomen. I imagine the reason he nearly broke my nose with his previous punch is because he couldn't breathe while I was attached to him.

"You ass!" I scream, pointing an accusing finger at the still smirking brat. My other hand desperately tries to keep the blood from running into my mouth. "He could have broken my nose!"

"This is self defense class, but you two went overboard," Professor Yarley says. He eyes Quinton's stomach, then looks at me with an already bruising face and sighs. "It seems I can no longer allow you two to spar together. You don't seem to understand the word restraint. Come on boys, you both need to see the nurse."

"What do you want us to do about it?" Langley asks after my visit to the nurse.

He stares at the bandage across my face and the bruise that reaches from one eye to the next. I look like a truck hit me. Who knew Quinton could hit so hard? His fists are like rocks! Not that I didn't get him good either, but his wounds are hidden. Not fair.

"Nothing," I reply, trying desperately not to touch my face.

If my father finds out, he'll be furious. Probably even pull me out of school. I won't let that happen. I'm not getting stuck in that palace to wither away.

The nurse had insisted I call and inform my father of what had happened. I said to her I'm fine and she won't get in trouble. I'll make sure of it, which got her off my back.

Part of me wanted her to tell my father, though. I know exactly what he'd do. He would come storming down here in an instant. He would have Quinton expelled immediately, but would he come to think that being in school is bad for me? My previous thought of being taken away stopped me from allowing her to call. I've been here for a short while, and although Quinton bugs me to no end, I like it here.

I don't want to go back to being trapped in that box. I want to see new people. I want to talk with people my age. I want to learn about sports. I want to play sports! I want to learn how to fight by brawling with the other kids rather than an instructor. I want to make friends and enemies. Seems I already got one of those.

I want to do everything that normal people do. Even if I know, deep down, that will never happen. I'll always be treated differently, left out, but I should at least try, right? I need to stay in school.

And I also don't want to tell him because of what Quinton said. I won't go running to my father for help. If I'm going to get rid of this brat, then I am going to do it myself.

"What do you mean, nothing? Look what he did to your face!" Langley points at said bruised face.

I swat his hand away. Growling, I look over Langley's shoulder at the culprit across the room. To make matters worse, he continues sitting in that damn chair that made us fight in the first place. I think he arrives early to class just so he can grab it. What an immature sack of shit.

"I want to beat him myself," I say more to myself than Langley.

I want to prove to him it isn't only the king he should fear, but also me. I am the prince and I will teach him to treat me as such. He thinks he's better than me because he knows how to fight or because he's top of the class? I'll show him. I'll learn how to fight better than anyone else in the school! I will bring up my grades. I will crush him in every way possible.

Langley chuckles, which makes me send my glare to him instead. He frowns apologetically and answers my unspoken question. "I've never seen you so determined before to do something. It's interesting."

"You think my desire to crush someone to dust is interesting? What's wrong with you?"

"Shouldn't you be asking yourself that? The one who has a desire to crush someone into dust."

"Everyone has a worst enemy and mine is that thing." I point at the black-eyed demon across the room. As if he heard me, Quinton looks over and actually has the audacity to smirk upon seeing my black and blue face.

My hatred for him only grows. Can a person truly hate someone to this extent? I never imagined I would hate someone with a passion hotter than a thousand burning suns. It is to where the moment I see him, my blood boils. I wonder if he feels the same or does he find my existence as more of an annoyance than hatred?

Thinking that I mean so little to him pisses me off more. I want him to hate me to the same extent that I hate him. I want him to feel uncomfortable when I'm around. I want him to have to look over his shoulder at me. I want his teeth to grind when he hears my voice. I want to annoy him to where being in the same room drives him mad. I just want to piss him off as much as he does me!

Oh wow, I've got problems. I think I need a therapist...

Deciding it is best not to question my sanity, I try to come up with a plan to show Quinton how terrifying I can be. I obviously cannot win against him in a physical match. Sparring with my instructors has not taught me enough to take Quinton on, who clearly has more experience than me. That is to be expected though, since he's been at Thorton's longer than I have. I know he was showing restraint the last time or I would have had a broken bone within the first ten seconds of our wrestling. I am sad to say that physical violence is out of the question, for now. Give me a few more training sessions and I am sure I can beat him!

I need to get some dirt on him, find out his weaknesses. It should be easy enough for me. After that, I will devise the perfect plan to rid myself of the biggest pest of my life with my power, not my father's but mine.

CHAPTER THREE

"**S**o he is nothing more than a commoner. You know this is only making me hate him more."

Langley laughs. "I figured it would."

It's been a little over a week since the incident with Quinton. Langley and I have dug around to discover what we could do about the spawn of Satan. Sadly, I did not find out much about him. Every person I spoke to knew little to nothing about Lucifer-incarnate. Most said that he is quiet and keeps to himself. The few that knew things only knew that he is not a noble and that he spends most of his time studying in the library. He is as nerdy as I imagined him to be. Langley got more information on him than I did, so we met up today to speak about it.

"People know little about him," Langley explains. "He doesn't have any friends. His roommate says he keeps to himself. He's never even seen him play a video game or watch TV. Says he's always got his nose in a book."

I should have figured. He seems like the bookworm type. It should be a crime to be smart, strong, and good looking. Generally speaking. Girls flock to him like flies to a carcass. He must release some type of pheromone. It's ridiculous!

Why are so many people attracted to secretive men? Is it a fetish? I don't understand! He gives everyone the death glare whenever they come near. He's so cold-hearted he could stop global warming with a single look! Why can't he make himself useful and actually go do that? The polar ice caps are so far away that I would probably never see him again.

I smile just thinking about Quinton's long, and hopefully permanent, trip to the arctic.

"His roommate heard him call home once before and spoke with his mother, but it seems he doesn't do that often," Langley continues. "He tried speaking to him about his home life before, but he said he got stuffy and stormed off, insisting he never bring it up again."

So a home life he doesn't wish to speak of? I could try to dig deeper into that, see if that will ruffle him a bit. Let's see how he likes his parents being brought up, freaking jerk.

"He has excellent grades, always did; the best in our school actually and he's here on a full ride scholarship. If he doesn't place in the top five of our grade, he will lose his scholarship and have to go back to his old school."

My interest piques in the last sentence.

So, he has to keep his grades up in order to stay here. Interesting. I should have known that when the other students said he wasn't from a noble family. Commoners don't have the money to pay for the tuition here. Some of the cheaper books cost over $300. The uniforms are an entirely different story. Most people rather not touch that subject with a ten-foot pole. He'd have to have a scholarship or work three full-time jobs, live on the street and never eat in order to pay for it.

"He is in Dorm D then?" I ask, which causes Langley to nod.

There are four dorms all together. They have no special names, simply go by Dorms A, B, C and D. However, dorms A and B are for the elite of the elite, sons and daughters of nobles, like Langley and myself. In fact, I share a room with Langley. It is larger than the other rooms in Dorm C and D, I hear. We also have our own bathroom connected to our room with both a bathtub and shower, also something not in the other dorms. Dorm C is for those who are still high in the social rankings but not to where they are royal, more like sons and daughters of doctors and lawyers. Then there is Dorm D, for the kids who come in on scholarships or picked up through sports, academics, the arts, whatever.

It would be strange for me to go to Dorm D. It's on the opposite side of the campus from my dorm. I couldn't say something like I mistook it for my own. They look totally different. Dorm A and B are made to impress. They look more like mansions than dorms. Dorm D. Well, it looks like a dorm.

I suppose I could just say that I'm having a hard time in class and wish to speak with Quinton about tutoring me. It wouldn't seem fishy, seeing as he is the top student. But then what? I get into the dorm; knock on doors until I find his room and...what? Kick the shit out of him? I can barely take him on in training, so I know that won't work. Langley won't be of help either, considering he is worse than me. He can't fight for shit.

Scholarship. Scholarship. I have to do something about his scholarship. One can easily lose a scholarship, if their grades mess up a little. If he gets into too much trouble, he could get kicked out for making the school look bad. I would stick to fighting with him regularly as it would probably be easy, but seeing as I've already learned that fighting isn't the best idea, his grades are my only option to get what I really desire; his expulsion.

"We need to mess up his grades somehow," I say, my mind going over all the ways to do so.

What would be the most efficient way to take his mind off class in order for his grades to drop? What can we do to affect him in such a way that he loses his scholarship? Surely there must be something.

Langley hums to himself as he too tries to think of something. It takes the boy a moment before he snaps his fingers in realization, "Quinton's roommate says every night he goes out to the training yard for about an hour and a half!"

"So?"

What does training for an hour and a half like a damn overachiever have to do with anything? Seriously! Almost two hours!? Every night! He's a nut. He's definitely a nut, stupid over achiever. Does he want to make everyone else look bad? God, he's an ass.

Langley rolls his eyes. "We have over an hour to break into his dorm room, take all his studying material for every subject. We have that huge test in Professor Bennett's class in two weeks. It's worth twenty percent of our grade!"

"Could that work?" I ask, wondering if we would get caught.

Not to mention, will twenty percent really do that much? It's only for one class, and wouldn't it be weird if his stuff suddenly disappeared? What if he suspected us? There are cameras in the dorm hallways, too. We'd definitely get caught. I know I wouldn't get in much trouble, but I rather not have Quinton confront me about it.

Langley grins in a way I didn't know he could. He looks positively evil and, deep down, I am a bit proud. "Of course! I'll ask some guys to make a commotion outside of the dorm before we go in. That way, the guards will go out. They won't even see us sneak in. Besides, everyone bugs Quinton about his notes before a test."

"Really?"

"He's top of the class. His notes are guaranteed to get you an A! He'll just assume some desperate kids broke into his dorm and took his notes. He won't know that it was us. Besides, the guards won't go look over the tapes for the disappearance of a notebook. We just have to make sure not to take anything else or break anything." Langley points accusingly at me, making me flush a bit. I bite back a grin. "I'm serious, don't do anything."

"I wasn't planning to."

Ok, that's a lie. I had planned to mess his room up, break a few things, search for something that could embarrass him to no end! But my plan is ruined... I can still look around. Just don't break or take anything else. Even if this one test does not bother him too much, we can try messing him up more and more until he's too far gone to even help himself.

Langley is a genius. Even if we don't mess up his grades, we can at least screw up that test in Professor Bennett's class. I grab my friend by the shoulders and say, "I could kiss you right now."

"Though I am flattered, My Lord, please don't." Langley and I laugh.

This is perfect. If we pull this off, it could mess up his midterm as well! Langley said no one takes notes like Quinton does. Even if he asks around to borrow someone else's, I will make sure none of them hand it over. He won't have any studying material for the midterm! If he botches both tests, his grades will plummet.

I'm smiling just thinking about it. Oh, his face during those tests will be priceless. I can imagine it now, his brow furrowed in anger and confusion, his teeth biting at his lips in fear at knowing that his future is doomed!

I feel like one of those dastardly villains on TV, only a thousand times better because I don't go around telling everyone my plans.

"So when should we do this?" Langley asks, leaning over the table, seeming to be as excited about this as I am. I feel the table shaking from his constant jerking of his legs. Not that I am any better.

"First, we need to talk to Quinton's roommate to make sure he can get us in. You talk to some of the guys, see if they're willing to be a distraction." We wouldn't want to show up to find out that we can't get in, or worse, Quinton is there and discovers our plan.

Langley nods. "I have a class with him. I'll talk to him about it."

Langley speaks the next day with Quinton's roommate, who agrees to leave the dorm unlocked a week before the test. If Quinton asks about his missing material, then the boy can say he had forgotten to lock the door earlier.

We also get a few guys to agree to fake an argument outside the dorm in order to get the guards to leave. That way, we can sneak in. Usually the guards ask why you're there and to sign up under someone's name. Two people can sign up under someone's name. If we do that, then Quinton probably could put it together and realize what we had done.

Our plan cannot be in effect soon enough.

CHAPTER FOUR

"**S**houldn't I feel bad about this?"

"What?" Langley asks.

"Breaking into someone's room and taking their stuff. It should make me feel bad, right?" I ask because, honestly, Mother always told me not to steal. I never thought I would. Why would I need to? But as I stand before Quinton's room, I don't feel any guilt or regret. I want to get this over with, crush him into dust and part of me wonders if I've possibly gone mad. If so, it's not such a bad feeling.

I keep thinking of his expression when he's told to pack up and leave. The mere thought of his face scrunching up in pain and sadness brings me joy. Have I mentioned how much I hate him lately? Because I do.

"He's an ass," Langley replies with a snarl. "He deserves it."

And the boy pushes open the door, revealing the room.

It is a third the size of ours. My walk-in closet at home is probably bigger. Beds sit on either side of the room. Next to the bed, on the left, is a desk, right in front of the window, while the other desk is pressed against the wall just a few inches from the doorway. There are trunks at the end of each bed, a closet and a dresser. I see another door, slightly ajar, just enough to show a toilet and shower.

So it's true, Dorm D is nothing like ours. Seeing it makes me smirk, like I want to grab Quinton and show him my dorm that is a thousand times better than his and rub it in. Knowing him, it probably wouldn't bother him, but it would make me happy.

"Come on, the sooner we get out of here the better," Langley says, rushing over to the desk by the window. I follow him and the two of us dig around, grabbing notebooks and note cards.

"What about his books? They're highlighted, aren't they? He can retake the notes." I groan. Our plan isn't as perfect as I had thought.

Langley thinks it over a moment before answering, "We keep them in lockers at school, right?"

I nod. Everyone has their own locker, so we don't have to come running back to our dorms after every class.

"I'll ask around for someone to bust in, make it look like a prank. People have done it before." Langley hums to himself as he looks back at the other desk. "We better mess up his roommate's side too, so it doesn't look like we knew this was Quinton's desk."

As Langley pushes things around on the opposite desk, I think over what he said.

People have messed with Quinton before? What, like, teased him? Played pranks on him? Been mean to him? I can't imagine Quinton being teased. He's got a sharp tongue. He doesn't seem like the type of person to be pushed around by anyone!

Wait, aren't I trying to push him around? So am I not the only one? I know he's an ass, but people said he keeps to himself. I guess that doesn't mean people keep away from him, though. If anything, it puts a target on his back. People tend not to like those who stand out or are the least bit different. I've noticed no one mess with him before. We don't have every class together though, so it's possible that in other classes there are people messing with him.

Oh, whatever! He's a jerk. I don't care!

I shake all thoughts of pity for the jerk from my mind and continue on my search to find anything to destroy the douchebag. As I dig through his desk, I find... nothing, nothing interesting at all. He really is a bookworm because that's all I can find, book after book after book! They aren't even sketchy or something to laugh over. Why can't he be interested in something that I could show to everyone to embarrass him?

Most of the books he has are mystery or crime novels. He even has some autobiographies of cops who caught famous serial killers. I guess that is weird, but if I showed the girls this, they would probably swoon over him more, deciding that his interest in crime is because he wants to save the world or something.

I look under his mattress, in his trunk, in the closet, everywhere! I don't even find any porn! There are no family photos, nothing to embarrass him. What, is he not human? Part of me is actually a little concerned that he seems to have so little, nothing about himself. Don't most people have at least a family portrait? Maybe a picture of a pet or a friend? Quinton has nothing.

"There isn't a single thing in here other than his weird crime novels," I say around a pout. All that work for nothing. Well, not for nothing, even so, I wanted to find something! I'd be happy with a bad haircut from an elementary school picture!

Langley laughs. "We did what we wanted to do. Did you get his flash drive?"

I swing the small drive around my finger. "Yep! Maybe he has something on here?"

"Doubt it." Langley sighs. He turns to leave when my eyes fall onto something I had missed.

"Wait a sec," I say, scurrying over to Quinton's bedside.

I had looked under his pillow, but I hadn't looked in the case. Now I can barely see the edge of what appears to be a photograph peeking out from within. To make sure it's the only one, I pull the pillow out completely. Nope, there's only one.

"What is it?" Langley asks, his curiosity getting the better of him. He sits beside me and peeks at the picture, seeming as confused as I am. "Why is it..."

"Burned." I run my finger over the edge that flame has obviously singed away.

The face of a man has been removed. Beside him is a woman with breathtaking green eyes and shoulder-length brown hair. Her smile is dazzling. To be honest, Quinton looks like her. Holy shit, there is no way that's his mom! She's a total milf! How can the spawn of Satan come from such a beauty?

She smiles while holding tightly onto a young boy who has to be Quinton. I can't imagine there would be anyone else with eyes as black as that, although that smile of his is not one I've ever seen him wear before. It reaches from ear to ear. He actually looks happy, thrilled, in fact, to have the arms of his mother and the mystery man around him. I can assume the man in this picture is his father, but for all I know, it could be a brother or an uncle. Not that I'm curious or anything.

"He must really hate his dad to have burned him off this picture," Langley says, snatching it from my hold to examine it further. His mind must have concluded the mystery man to be his father as well. He flips it over to see nothing on the back. "Well, we learned he has daddy issues. Come on, let's go already."

"Yeah... ok..."

I can't help but wonder about the picture, though.

Was that man his father? Why was his face burned off when Quinton looked so happy to be around him? What could have possibly happened? I have been angry with my father before, but I've never burned him out of a family photograph. The thought has never crossed my mind; what could make a child do that?

I try to think of something that my father could do that would make me so angry. Nothing comes to mind. It makes me ask myself why Quinton would until I remind myself that it's none of my business and I don't care!

The two of us leave, our job done. I feel somewhat accomplished, having defeated my enemy. Ok, so I'm not for sure that I did, but come on, he can't be that smart. He has to study to get good grades, right? I'll be glad if it drops a letter grade. As long as he doesn't place in the top 5, my dream will come true.

Later that evening, I flip through pages of his notebook, shocked to find out that he really takes great notes. Things are so easy to read and understand, even his handwriting is nice, unlike my own that resembles chicken scratch. I feel as if I'm becoming smarter just looking over it all. He could sell this to kids! Why doesn't he? Probably wants to keep it to himself, selfish bastard.

Sighing, I push the notebooks aside. Langley said he would take them out to the trash cans later. We wouldn't want to get caught with them.

Sucks, I was kind of hoping I could keep them. I really could use them. I bet my grades will go from C's to A's if I kept the notes.

The small silver flash drive I took earlier sits before me, practically begging me to look at it. There has to be something on this. He is a teenage boy, after all. There has to be video games or porn. Something on here that shows he's human.

I plug it into my laptop. As expected, the flash drive appears with no cool name. Come on, everyone gives their flash drive a name. Mine is called Ozzie, not sure why. It looks like an Ozzie to me.

I open it, finding a few folders. The first is called 'School,' and of course it is full of his schoolwork, projects he has done, all perfect of course, and notes he has taken. There's nothing interesting. The second folder, entitled movies, is just that, full of TV shows and movies. So he is interested in TV after all? They, like the books, are all mystery, thriller and crime type shows with the occasional horror thrown in. It actually looks like a teenage boy's computer for a moment.

I will admit I enjoy some Criminal Minds. Oh god, we have something in common. No way! I'm never watching Criminal Minds again! Damn it.

The third folder, however...

I hesitate, my mouse hovering over the words 'Photographs.' A lump forms in my throat. For all I know, the pictures could be nothing more than a hobby. Langley and I didn't find a camera, but maybe he has one and enjoys taking pictures? At the same time, these could be family photographs.

Do I really want to do this? I mean... I want to get him out of this school, but to dig into his life like this is a bit. I would not want him looking through my photographs, especially if my family is in it.

Sure, everyone knows what my family looks like, but our personal photographs are our personal photographs. I don't want others to see. People deserve a right to their privacy. I don't want to be that jerk who invades not only someone's life but also their loved ones' lives as well.

I remove my hand from the mouse. I didn't realize I was sweating until I feel the dampness of my pants, where my hand now lays.

I can't do it. There's no way. That is going too far. I won't.

I quickly remove the flash drive and put it in the trash. If I look at it it'll only tempt me into opening the one folder I hadn't. I don't want to do that because I'm not that much of an asshole.

"Are you done with this stuff?" Langley asks, appearing out of nowhere. How long has he been in the room?

"Yeah," I answer. "Nothing interesting on the flash drive, either."

I bet there would have been had I opened the photograph folder. Maybe there would have been a picture of his dad in there. I guess seeing a picture wouldn't explain why he burnt one off. And why would he have a picture like that under his pillow if he had a folder of them on his flash drive?

I won't find out now. I don't need to know anyways! Who cares about him? He can do whatever he wants with his pictures. I don't care. I'm not curious at all.

Not at all.

CHAPTER FIVE

After speaking with Quinton's roommate, Langley and I discover we got away with sneaking in. Quinton returned to his dorm, found his things missing and, as expected, went to ask security if they had seen anyone come in. They said no. Quinton pushed it no further, telling his roommate that his missing notebook wasn't worth an investigation. It appeared he didn't have back ups because he hadn't seen Quinton studying over the last week.

He said nothing of Langley or me, so he must have assumed it was some kids with poor grades who needed his notes in order to pass. The next day, a few of the guys Langley and I spoke with broke into Quinton's locker and water damaged his textbooks to where they were unreadable. He got new ones, but none are highlighted or marked, so he has to start over from scratch.

Quinton sent me a glare during class that day. I assumed he would think it was my doing, but he had no proof, so he said nothing. Even if he proved who had damaged his books, it wouldn't have been me. Technically, I wasn't the one who did it. I simply suggested it and the guys did it for me. Seeing him glare at me like that sure brought a smile to my face, though!

I wake up the morning of the test feeling more excited than ever. This is the first time I've ever wanted to go to class knowing there would be a test. I want to see if our plan has worked. I want to see how worked up Quinton is going to be, looking at the test and realizing he doesn't know any of it. Ok, so he probably would remember some of it, but the panic of not studying accompanied by having not studied in a week will surely affect his grade.

I find myself in class almost ten minutes early on the day of the test, which is a miracle. I should get an award, but I don't exactly have the best reasons for being there, so I suppose an award would be a bad idea. There are four other people in the room, Quinton being one of them. I knew he had arrived early to take that seat in order to piss me off. Well, today he will be the one pissed off.

Grinning from ear to ear, I make my way over to him, ready to tease him about the upcoming test when...

"You're staring, Princess."

My eyes tear themselves away from the notes on his desk. Hell, he even has a stack of notecards full of information. They don't appear scribbled or half-assed either. They are proper notes that he took time to make. How did he get those? We took everything! I even got his flash drive! We got his laptop. His roommate told us he hadn't seen anything , so when could he have...?

"Just wanted to ask if you were ready for the test. It's worth twenty percent of our grade, you know," I say, forcing a grin in hopes to seem less suspicious or maybe that makes it worse?

My insides are churning. I can't believe he got notes! Who did he get those off of? I told everyone not to give him a damn thing. Not that he bothered to ask anyone.

"Shouldn't you be asking yourself that?" Quinton hisses, his eyes never leaving his note cards. His lips move as he silently mouths the questions and answers to each one. His dark eyes are so focused on the cards he doesn't notice me leaning in closer to see if the notes are really his or at least I thought he didn't notice.

"You're too close. Back up," he growls.

I snort. "Why should I listen to you?"

"You ask such a question, yet you order others and wonder why they do not listen. Are you stupid?" His voice oozes superiority.

My fist shakes with the desire to deck him. Not that it's a new feeling. I am surprised I didn't immediately punch him out of pure instinct alone.

"Is there a reason that you're such an asshole, or do you just like making others uncomfortable?" I hiss. He still hasn't looked at me. Damn it, look at me! It's like he doesn't even care that he's speaking to me, like I'm nothing to him. My biggest pet peeve is people not looking at me when they speak. It's common courtesy and I will admit I have my asshole moments, but even I look at someone when they're speaking!

The boy actually smirks as he replies; "I do get this fuzzy feeling in my stomach when I see you uncomfortable around me, kind of like I won a prize."

"You dick."

"Tsk, watch your language, Your Highness. Daddy would not approve."

Holy shit, it is hard not to hit him right now. Do not hit. Do not hit. Do not hit.

I take a deep breath. I did not come over here to fight with him. I came over to ask about the notes. I must know why my plan did not work, so in the future I can fix it.

"Where did you get those notes? Everyone's heard about those kids breaking into your dorm and taking them. You have back ups or something?" Maybe I'm asking too many questions. This could make me look suspicious, but I don't care. I want to know where we went wrong. I know we got everything!

Quinton scowls. His dark eyes finally remove themselves from his cards to fall onto me. I feel the heat from his glare, and suddenly, I feel like he knew all along that I had taken his notes. I don't know how to explain this feeling, like somehow he can see right through me. It's as if he's waiting for me to fess up... or maybe I'm crazy. How could he know?

"Why would I tell you that?" He says through clenched teeth. A lump forms in my throat. My hands shake. His voice is like a blade. "I hear you have a tendency to take things that belong to others."

"Aron!" Langley's voice pulls me away from Quinton, who is now back to eyeing his note cards one after the other.

It takes a moment for me to get my breath back. Huffing, I decide not to bother with him anymore. I don't want to mess up and end up admitting that Langley and I are the culprits.

"What... why does he have those?" Langley whispers once I am at his side. He eyes the notes suspiciously, probably also wondering if he had gotten them off someone. Those notes looked too elaborate, though, to belong to anyone else. He had to have back ups somewhere, but where? His locker? The guys found nothing other than his textbooks.

"I don't know, but I think he knows we did it," I mumble. Although Quinton's eyes aren't on me, I feel like he's still staring at me. My skin itches. It's weird. I suddenly have the desire to rub all over, to get his gaze off me physically, and it's almost maddening. Part of me wonders if that's what being guilty feels like.

"No way, how could he? No one would have told him."

"Whatever, even if he knew, he would have done something about it already, right?" I ask.

Langley nods. So what if he knows? Good, he should know! Maybe now he'll stop messing with me... why would he stop messing with me, though? Our plan didn't work. He had more notes stashed away somewhere. All I did was break into his room and take things he already had more copies of. Damn it, how else am I going to ruin his grades? If he has a shit ton of notes stashed away everywhere, this is going to be impossible.

I slam my fists against the desk, catching almost everyone's attention. I don't care though. I'm pissed.

"Aron, why don't we just give up? He isn't worth it."

"No way in hell!" I holler. People whisper until I shoot them all with a glare that clearly states I will throw them all into a dungeon if they don't stop. Wait, first I would need a dungeon. Whatever, I'll get one then!

Growling, I turn back to Langley. "He needs to know his place. He acts so cocky when he doesn't deserve to. I'm going to prove to him I can take care of my own problems."

Langley stares at me oddly, like he thinks I'm crazy. Maybe I am but... but I can do things on my own! I don't have to go to my dad for everything. I am the prince. I can fix my own problems. I can defeat my own enemies. I will think of this as my first battle and I will win.

CHAPTER SIX

"**W**hy are we doing this?" Langley groans, his chest rising and falling at a fast pace. He's out of breath. So am I. Sweat soaks his brow, same as mine. He's exhausted. I'm exhausted. Our legs feel like jello, but...

"Because that douchebag can do it, so can I!" I scream, ignoring the pain shooting up my legs. It's not only my legs that are in pain, though. My entire body is tingling with exhaustion that I can feel setting in further and further with each passing second. "Come on Langley, get up."

"Why am I your brawling partner? I suck at fighting!" Langley exclaims, but pushes himself up. He wobbles for a moment, seeming to be unsure if the ground is moving or he is. He holds up his fists, ready to block my attacks, but Langley really sucks at fighting.

"I need someone to practice with. I have to kick Quinton's ass!" I answer.

"Then ask Professor Yarley for some private lessons or something. I'm tired." The boy drops his fists with a sigh. His eyes are barely open, not that I'm any better. It's dark out now. Most of the dorm's lights are off, meaning about everyone is asleep, yet here we are training. "Seriously, you're letting him get too far under your skin, Aron. Forget about him."

My expression tells Langley that there's no way I am 'forgetting about him.' Forgetting about the biggest jerk to ever walk the earth is impossible. He makes me want to slam my face into a brick wall...or his. I would very much like to slam his face into one.

We failed at messing up his grades, so I have to go back to getting him in trouble through physical means. He can get kicked out for making the school look bad by fighting with the prince. Even if it isn't a physical one, if we angrily shout in class or something, it still looks bad. I have to do what I have to do in order to get him the hell out of Thorton's!

Sighing, I realize Langley isn't as determined in this venture as me. He is tired, so am I, so I decide to call it a night. We're both exhausted. It's not like I can get better overnight. It'll take time. I'll request private lessons from Professor Yarley tomorrow. It would be better if I had someone to spar with who is actually good at fighting.

Langley looks like a chicken with his head cut off when he fights.

"You said that out loud," Langley growls. "And I do not look like that! Take it back."

"Nope. You know it's true."

"It is not!"

It's strange. Normally I am the one to approach Quinton, but today, for some reason, I find myself face to face with him in the hall. People pass by, slowly, very slowly; to watch the train wreck they know is about to happen. Everyone knows by now that if the two of us are nearby, something is bound to happen. It's almost like a show to them they get regularly and they don't even have to pay for it.

Behind me, Langley is growling while everyone else is simply staring on, waiting to see what happens. They know it will be a fight, but watching a fight is still fun to them even if they know it will happen. The demon before me smirks as his eyes look over everyone before returning to me. I don't know what to expect...

"Getting private lessons now, are we, Princess?"

My eye twitches. How did he find out?!

"Good, a princess should always know how to defend themselves."

Fuck him.

The two of us are on the ground in a second. The hallway becomes an audience as they watch and cheer us on. He's winning...whatever this is, not that I'm going to give up because of that! As if I'd take it lying down. He may be winning now, but I can turn the rides and I will! I rather break every bone in my body than let Quinton take an easy win. I'm not going down without a fight!

We roll around on the ground, exchanging kicks and punches. Quinton has his arm around my neck in a second and a leg around my waist, keeping me on the floor. Langley jumps in at that moment and tries to pull the bastard off me.

Quinton's left fist, the one that isn't around my neck, hits the boy directly in the jaw, sending him into the wall. I take this moment, when he is more preoccupied with Langley than me, to push myself up, Quinton on my back. I stumble forward, both of us landing on the floor. The shock made Quinton loosen his grip and gave me the opportunity to get free.

I grab the boy by the hair and bring my knee into his chest, once, twice, he grabs my knee as I bring it up for the third time and flips me back onto the ground. I'm sure he would have continued using me as a punching bag had the professors not come out at that moment to pull us apart.

"What do you two think you're doing?" The teacher holding Quinton screams. One has their arms around me and a third is standing between the two of us, glaring not only at us but at the kids who have crowded around to watch us like we're a show. I suppose to them we are one. They all slowly scurry away, glancing back at Quinton and I to see a second longer but eventually disappear in hopes of not feeling the teacher's wrath.

Quinton's expression has gone back to being that of utter boredom, while I can't seem to keep the steam from blowing out of my ears. I pull my arm away from the teacher, rubbing my hand as I do so. Is his body made of rock, too? My fists never hurt so much.

"To the dean's office, now."

Quinton rolls his eyes but does as he is told. Sure, he listens to them. Stupid prick.

The two of us make our way to the dean's office with two of the three teachers with us. One is watching me; the other has his eyes on Quinton. I keep my eyes ahead of me because if I were to look at him, I'd probably jump at him again, the freaking jerk. I don't know what he's doing beside me, but I imagine it's not much, like he would show anything other than apathy.

We reach the office and take our seats before the dean. He's a chubby old man with a balding head that makes one want to tease him for the bright shine that could blind if the light hit it right. His eyes look over both of us before he asks, "What happened?"

"He's a dick, that's what happened," I reply, crossing my arms as I send a glare to the boy beside me. The bastard is sitting like he's royalty. He has one leg over the other and his hands are placed comfortably in his lap. Damn him! Trying to look better than me, I'm the royalty here!

Quinton snorts. "I'm sorry. I believe you were the one who tackled me. I was simply trying to make conversation."

"You called me a princess!" I shout back accusingly.

"Are you not one?"

"Fucking prick!"

"Boys," Dean Coyler sighs, rubbing his temple as he does. "I do hope this will not become a reoccurring thing- "It's already a reoccurring thing though. "We cannot have violence such as this in school. I am going to let you off with a warning, just this once. Do you understand?"

I roll my eyes. Sure, just this once, he says. I can tell by looking at him he has no intention of informing my father about this. His hands are shaking not out of anger but fear. If my father knew I had been harmed at school, he'd be furious. The dean would probably lose his job. He knows that. I know that. Hell, Quinton knows that.

The two of us nod, promise not to let it happen again, though we all know it will, and we are sent off to return to class...with escorts, of course. We're silent throughout the hall, though the tension between us says everything for us.

We are only getting started.

CHAPTER SEVEN

"Are you sure about this, Aron? Not many people stay over Christmas break." Langley is looking at me with a slightly confused and slightly worried expression.

"I'll be fine. Besides, I'm only staying here two out of the three weeks...as if my mom would let me stay here during Christmas." I send Langley a reassuring smile. He frowns, still unsure about leaving me alone on this campus for two weeks...well, not totally alone. There's still security, a few teachers and kids who stay. My parents wouldn't let me stay unless there was security so I'll be fine!

"I'm serious, it's all good!" I insist.

I don't think he's totally convinced, but after another moment or two of him eyeing me suspiciously, the boy sighs. He shakes his head but says his goodbye as he grabs the last of his luggage and heads off for the airport with most of the other students.

Christmas is finally here. It's cold outside. Snowy, white cyrstals cover everything. The halls and walkways are decorated with greens and reds. There are snowmen and Santas and elves in the windows. The trees are covered in ornaments made by the students and the largest Christmas tree I have ever seen sits in the courtyard. It's more beautiful than the tree my family puts up during Christmas. I love it.

And to think I have this all basically to myself.

There is a three-week Christmas break where mostly everyone returns home to see their families. Originally I too planned on heading home but...I have been locked up in that castle for so long that I feel that once I go in, I won't be coming out.

My parents weren't too happy when I told them I wouldn't be coming home until Christmas Eve, leaving us only a week of Christmas break. It took some convincing and a lot of begging, but they got over it, understanding that I wanted some space. Mother claimed by spring break I will probably be like all the other kids who wanted to run home the moment they got a chance. I didn't tell her I doubted that, but simply laughed and agreed with it.

By the second day of break, mostly everyone is gone. Security has lightened up and almost none of the students or teachers are left. I think I counted 5 other kids during breakfast this morning in Dorm A. Let's say there are as many as that in the other dorms that would mean there are only 20 kids on campus. Thinking of it being so dead, so quiet, is actually relaxing in an odd way.

It's so quiet it's unreal. No one is watching me, analyzing my every move. I feel this sense of freedom, like I can go running through the snow while screaming at the top of my lungs. I don't, but it's that kind of feeling. It's peaceful and calming. This was a good choice. I think I will be fine being alone for two weeks.

I decide to investigate the campus some more. Although I've been here half a year, I still haven't seen everything. Usually, once Langley and I are finished with class, we head back to the dorms or hang out with our friends on the courts or in the rec area. There are buildings I haven't seen, though I'm sure most of them are probably full of classrooms, but whatever, an adventure is an adventure.

As I expected, most of the buildings are offices or classrooms. Some are even closed off, probably to save on electric and heating considering there is no one inside. It was still nice to walk around, even with the cold nipping at my nose. The scenery is nice, with trees covered in white and shining crystals that sparkle with the sun's rays. I bury my face deeper into my scarf. Although my cheeks hurt from how cold they are, I am still not willing to go inside.

I don't like the cold, but I love winter. It's a time of year when everything is dead, yet it looks more beautiful than ever. Things have this almost healing glow that makes you stop, stare and admire that simplicity of nature and how beauty can be such a small thing.

It isn't until I can no longer feel the tip of my fingers, even with gloves on, that I finally force myself indoors. I make my way to the library for a book that I have to have read for English. It doesn't have to be finished until the end of January, but I might as well do it now when I have an entire two weeks to myself.

While walking through the halls, I come across a few other students. We stop, say hello, and have a little small talk before heading our separate ways. Most students are too nervous to spend more than a few minutes around me. They smile, laugh, talk, but I can see in their eyes how each word they say is phrased precisely. They don't speak their mind. Instead, they speak what they think they wish me to hear; they phrase things in a certain way that won't bother me like everyone always has and most likely always will. I sigh and shake that somber thought away.

I will admit it is strange being on campus when there are no classes, but I enjoy the silence. It's good to have silence every now and again. Everyone needs their space. Everyone needs time to themselves to just take a deep breath and relax.

The library doors are open, revealing the emptiness within. The elderly library woman is sitting at the front desk, her nose buried in a book. I'm not even sure if she notices me walk in. I'm ok with that as she's always kind of freaked me out, so I tiptoe past her as fast as I can.

"Now, where would it be?" I whisper to myself within the aisles. I don't really use libraries. I don't even know why I'm whispering no one is in here to disturb me anyway, except the elderly woman up front, but it's not like she's studying or anything.

Still, I stay silent as I search for my book. It's so quiet that I can hear myself breathing. Part of me thinks this is something out of a horror movie, a boy alone among the shelves, unaware of the danger behind him.

I peek over my shoulder.

Damn it, I'm freaking myself out. Now I only want to find the book and get the hell out. I'm giving myself the shivers. Sadly, the gods find amusement in my fear because I cannot seem to find this book anywhere. Another student could have checked it out already because they had the same idea as me...I should ask the clerk lady.

I step out of the aisles into the sitting area; ready to go to the front and ask where the hell this book is when...

"Why the hell are you here?" I scream, shattering the silence enveloping the entire campus. I actually cringe after hearing my voice echo throughout not only the library, but the halls. Wow, it is seriously quiet here.

The devil spawn looks at me with a sharp glare. I hear some 'shush', the sound too echoes in the library. I'm only assuming the library clerk made such a noise since I see no one other than Quinton and myself here. There are other sitting areas, but I doubt a student would 'shush' someone. Anyway, back to the problem here.

"What are you doing?" I hiss, trying my best to whisper, but with it being so quiet in here, I still feel like I'm making too much noise.

Quinton rolls his eyes as he flips another page of...of the book that I've been looking for! I should have known he had it. It's just my luck. My arch nemesis has the book I need. Of course he does. That makes perfect sense! I hate your world.

"Reading," he replies. Somehow, his voice is not as loud as mine. Of course it isn't because Quinton doesn't raise his voice. He always speaks slowly and precisely. He pisses me off. "This is a library."

"That's not what I mean." I look over my shoulder to see if the old lady heard me. I can't really see her from here, but when I don't hear her shush me again I take that as being allowed to speak. I hop onto the couch across from the boy. He still hasn't bothered to look at me and I'm half tempted to go over to him and force him to, but resist the urge to do so. "It's Christmas break. Why are you still on campus?"

"Why are you?" He asks.

"Don't ask me a question when you haven't answered mine."

"Why should I have to answer your question?"

I am going to have the word 'why' removed from the dictionary immediately. I cannot believe my two weeks of wonderful, calm Christmas break is going to be ruined.

Knowing that Quinton is still around is enough to ruin everything, even if I do not see him after today. I will know he's here and know that I could run into him, and that is enough to ruin everything.

Maybe I should pack up now and leave.

Huffing, I throw one leg over the other and cross my arms. Quinton has his nose buried in the book still. By the looks of it, he's over halfway done. I could ask him to lend it to me when he's finished...no, no, no, no, no! I will not ask him to lend me the book. Why would I ask him that? He'd say no, anyway.

"Could you lend me that when you're finished?" What the hell! Why...didn't I tell myself a second ago not to ask him that? There is something wrong with my mind and mouth coordination. I need to see a doctor.

Quinton's dark eyes finally take a moment to peer over the book at me. The way he's holding the book covers up half his face, leaving only his smoldering eyes visible. Having his eyes on me makes me squirm. Geesh, if he keeps giving girls looks like that, it's no wonder they fall for him.

Hold on, scratch all that. Dark, smoldering eyes? I'm nuts. I am serious. I need to see a doctor. I'm making an appointment as soon as I get back to the dorm. I have issues.

"You can read?" His voice is enough to tell me that behind that book he is smirking. His question makes my eyebrow twitch in annoyance.

"Yes, I can read. I can kick your ass too, pretty boy." Being around him makes me violent. I am not the type to throw my fists so much, but man, when I see him, I get the urge to pound his face in with a hammer!

Quinton, with a roll of his eyes, snorts. "You could try, Princess. Anyway, I'm nearly done. You can have it afterwards."

My anger dwindles down to a small flame. Did he just offer me the book? My shock must have been written all over my face because Quinton is speaking again, "You look more stupid than usual with your jaw hanging open like that."

I snap my jaw closed. The action makes him chuckle. The sound makes me shiver. It's strange to hear him chuckle like...like he is amused. Quinton doesn't get amused. He's always bored or annoyed...ok he's usually just bored. The only time he seems to be annoyed is when I'm around, which I am quite proud of, by the way. Hearing him chuckle, though, is such an oddity that I have no idea how to respond or react to it. It goes to show that he is human and, honestly, that freaks me out a bit.

"Uh...thanks...I guess."

"Hmm."

I'm not sure why I stay after we're finished talking. I somehow find myself watching videos on my phone, with my headphones in, of course, because I don't want to be 'shushed' again. Quinton says nothing, though. In fact, he doesn't look at me again until he has finished the book and gets up to leave, handing me said book before he goes.

"Make sure to get an ice pack," he says after tossing the book into my lap.

I jump from the ice pack landing on me before staring at him in confusion. "Huh?"

"A paragraph in and I bet your brain will be fried."

I really hate him.

CHAPTER EIGHT

I 'm thinking I should have gotten that ice pack. Half way into the book and I'm ready to give up. My head is pounding. It's been pounding since...actually, let's not talk about that. Isn't there a movie? I wonder if I could get away with watching it? I'm not sure if I can handle the rest of this book. How did Quinton read it so fast and with such ease? Why is he so bloody perfect? Ugh!

I decide to watch the movie. I am not a reader, never have been. I get bored a few paragraphs in. I am definitely more of a movie guy, although this book isn't really something I am into anyway, which means I won't be into the movie. I should at least try to watch it though, right?

Of course, ten minutes into the movie, my eyes are halfway shut. I have to drink two monsters and eat two six packs of Reese's to keep myself awake. I'm more the action movie type of guy. I can enjoy slower paced movies, but they have to be something that creeps me out, you know, like the ones based on real events that make a shiver run down your spine.

By the time the movie is over, I'm bouncing off the walls. It would be nice if Langley was still here. I need someone to calm me down. I can't even go shoot some hoops. I mean, I could, but it's not as fun by yourself, especially now that I've actually played with other people.

Back home the servants would play with me, but none of them knew how to. They always let me win too...not that the kids here don't either, but at least they try to put up a fight. Thinking about it is kind of pathetic. It's hard to know your true potential when no one ever shows theirs. How am I meant to get better if people don't try their best against me? I guess being a Prince isn't all perks.

I shake my head and decide to go on another adventure. I scurry around campus, searching for anyone willing to play a game with me. How come earlier I saw five kids at breakfast, around 9 at lunch and a few in the halls, yet now I can't find a single person! I suppose they could be in town, shopping or seeing a movie, but my father told me the only way I could stay over break is if I stay on campus.

Damn, what am I gonna do now?

Then it hits me. My grin actually hurts. It's so large.

There is no way Quinton is smart, attractive, and good at sports, right? No one is that blessed. I could get him to play a game with me, totally crush him and rub it in his face for the rest of his life! This is great.

I am pounding on Quinton's dorm room door in no time. If he is pretending not to be there, it will not work because I will stand here for however long it takes. I even scream when after five minutes there is no answer.

My screaming works. The door is flung open to show a very annoyed Quinton. It's weird seeing him in a pair of gray sweats that barely cling to his hips and a black beater that makes me wonder why the hell I ever fought with him. I've never seen him in such normal clothes that actually makes him look like a fellow 15-year-old of the male species. Who knew Quinton could be so normal?

Shaking my head, I tell myself not to stare at his muscles because...well, why would I be staring? I shouldn't be. That's just weird!

"What the hell do you want? And how do you know where my dorm is?" Quinton hisses. He isn't expecting it, so when I move forward into his room he stumbles back, allowing me access. A second doesn't pass before he points a finger at the door. "Get the hell out."

"Come on, we're arch enemies, so of course I know where your dorm is," I reply like its common knowledge. It should be. He should know we're enemies.

"People don't have arch enemies."

"Yes, they do."

Quinton rolls his eyes. As he's rubbing his temple, a vein throbs above his eye. "What do you want?"

"Let's go play some basketball." I send him an innocent smile. Oh, if only he knew I planned on crushing him like a bug and reporting to everyone in school how he cried and begged for mercy. I doubt he'll cry, but I can dream. Let a man have his hopes.

Quinton stares at me quizzically. Oh no, has he caught on? He cannot be that smart. Sighing, he pushes past me to take a seat at his desk. I gasp. How could he just ignore me like that?

"Come on, get changed, let's go!" I order, kicking at the back of his desk chair after each word. Quinton spins around and grasps my ankle. I yelp when he pushes me to the floor.

"Why should I go play a game with you?" Quinton groans, sending me a glare as he does. His face clearly states how much he does not like me being in his room. I grin. It feels great to piss him off. I love it. Perhaps this is how I should spend my next two weeks? Making Quinton's life a living hell while no one is around to stop me! Oh, the temptation is real.

I push myself into a sitting position. I decide to skip past trying to persuade him. I know how to get him to come along. Leaning back onto my elbows, I do my best to mimic one of Quinton's cocky expressions. It must work because his eye twitches. "Why don't you want to? Scared I'll beat you?"

He snorts. "A toddler could shoot better than you."

"It's ok to admit that you suck at basketball."

"I don't."

"Then prove it." I know I've caught him before he even gets up to grab a set of clothes. My grin cannot be any bigger. I amaze even myself with my skills of manipulation. I must have gotten it from my mother.

The two of us are silent as we walk side by side to the gym, which is a good five-minute walk away. Looking out of the corner of my eye, I see Quinton's eyes flicker with that teen spirit of competition. So he really is just another teenage boy, after all? I'll keep that in mind for future plans of embarrassment.

We make it to the gym. It's empty but unlocked. The keys for the balls are hanging on the metal doors as they always are. The two of us change before bringing them out and lowering one of the hoops.

"What are we playing to?" Quinton asks, winding his arms up. Of course, he'd be the type of guy to stretch before playing a game for fun. What an uptight ass.

"First to 20 wins." I don't want the game to be too short. This is meant to get some of my energy out. Plus, who knows, Quinton might be decent.

"You're going to cramp," Quinton says, pointing to me, who has already started shooting while he is continuing to stretch.

I roll my eyes. "Thanks mom, I'll wash behind my ears really well too."

The demon huffs but doesn't stop from stretching until he feels he has warmed up enough. Finally, if he didn't finish soon, I was going to start without him. I pass the demon the ball first, so I can see if he's actually any good.

The game begins.

Quinton is as fast here as he is during training. I thought with a ball in his hand and his attention on trying to score a few points, it might slow him down. I was very wrong.

His feet move at a pace I can hardly keep up with. I feel myself tripping over my own feet. I silently thank Langley and Professor Yarley, who have helped build up my stamina over the past few months. I am sure in a fight Quinton would still win, but right now he isn't using his fists, so I don't have to worry about them.

"Tired already?" He teases, noticing how my breath is already labored. I growl. He's breathing heavy as well, but seems much more composed than I am. "We only just started."

"Shut it!" I snap, trying to reach for the ball. He takes a quick step back, nearly sending me toppling over. During my trip up, he looms forward and past me. Desperately, I try to catch up, only to reach him a second too late.

Quinton jumps and sends the ball straight to the hoop. It doesn't even hit the rim, but makes a perfect 'swoosh' sound as it enters the net. I feel my teeth grind. This will not be as easy as I hoped, but there is no way I am letting him beat me.

The moment I get the ball, I'm moving. Quinton is quick, his eyes never leaving me for a second. It is the first time he has ever paid such close attention to me. During all our arguments, Quinton's eyes have always kept themselves on something else. I believe he did it on purpose to anger me. Don't most people dislike it when they are speaking with someone and their eyes are elsewhere? It shows that they are not interested or listening.

So now, feeling his full attention on me for longer than ten seconds...it feels strange. I'm shaking a bit. It has to be from the adrenaline... I fumble with the ball, giving Quinton the chance to snatch it from me.

I make myself a mental note after he scores another goal not to get caught up in him again. I will not make the same mistake twice. Right now isn't about how Quinton is finally looking at me. This is about beating him, putting him in his place, and I will not let anything stop me from doing that.

The game goes on, never losing its fast pace. Quinton is ahead of me by two points. If he makes this shot, I lose. I do not want that so, even with my legs screaming at me to let up, I jump to block his shot, knocking it off course. When I touch back down, I wobble, nearly toppling over. The action makes Quinton smirk.

"Shut up," I groan, going after the ball regardless of the exhaustion I am feeling. I definitely got my energy out.

"I didn't say anything," he says smugly, waiting for me to begin.

Sadly, I did not win this game. He beats me 20 to 18. I'm pissed my plan didn't work, but I feel accomplished having nearly won. It isn't so bad being only two points behind. It was a close game, and I was actually ahead of him a few times.

I face Quinton, who is breathing as heavily as I am. Thin lines of sweat roll down his face that he wipes away with the back of his hand. Seeing Quinton like this reminds me he really is a normal guy. Half of me expected him not to sweat at all or for his sweat to be green or something.

I'm ready to tell him it was a good game. I had fun...until he speaks.

"Was this another one of your schemes?" The boy asks, glancing at me from over his shoulder.

"Huh?"

"Hoping to beat me at basketball and tell everyone about it? You're predictable, Aron." His smirk sends a bolt of anger through me. I once again have the urge to hit him. Had he known this the whole time? He must have only agreed to come along because he knew my plan would be a failure. I cannot believe a guy like him exists. He's such an ass.

"Scheme? I don't need schemes. I can tell the guys as soon as they get back I beat you even if I didn't, and they'd believe me!" I shout in frustration.

Quinton turns to face me fully. His smirk falls and is replaced with the look he always wears, but his eyes are dark, darker than usual. I don't know what he's thinking. It's different, though, the expression he wears. It's minuscule, but I notice that there's something else even if I can't quite tell what it is.

"You won't." He says.

I won't, what?

"You won't tell them you beat me."

He didn't need to say that. I already knew I wouldn't.

CHAPTER NINE

I should, though. I should tell everyone that I kicked the shit out of him and beat him twenty to six! No one would question me...at least not to my face. Quinton will be put in his place. People will tease him for finally failing at something; even if they know deep down he didn't.

Why then; why won't I do it? Why won't I crush the bastard? I could spread all the lies I want, all the rumors that could lose him his scholarship. It would be so easy!

Staring up at my ceiling, I wonder if I'm being too nice. It's ok to lie about it, it's ok if I tell everyone I beat Quinton, and it's ok to spread rumors about him. He deserves it.

Honestly, I want to tell everyone, but I want to tell everyone the truth. When I beat Quinton, and one day I will, I want to tell everyone about it. Even if they all think I'm lying, I want to know I'm telling the truth. It doesn't matter what they all think as long as Quinton and I know it's true. I want to see his face when I beat him. Will he be sad, angry, shocked and confused?

I want to feel accomplished.

Groaning, I roll onto my side and stare off into space. I'm being stupid, but I guess I won't be telling anyone about our game. Man, I suck. What's so good about being the good guy, anyway? The villains are always the best. They have far superior wardrobes too.

The game was supposed to calm me down and ruin Quinton. Now I'm depressed. I think I'm going to go get hyped up on some more sugar now. It's better to be hyper with no idea how to calm yourself than lying around your room depressed about some stupid fucking douche bag who needs to have his head smashed in. Argh, he pisses me off!

Quinton, you piece of shit!

To make matters worse, I couldn't seem to stop running into him. Every day, for a week, I find myself face to face with the bastard. And no, it didn't happen just once a day, but more like a dozen times. We'd see each other in the cafeteria, in the library, on campus, in the gym, everywhere! To be honest, it isn't his fault or mine. There aren't many people on campus. We're here by ourselves and we are both going to the places where we could occupy ourselves.

Even so, can't he go somewhere else!

Isn't he a bookworm? Stay inside and read, ya nerd! Stop coming out, so I have to see your face. It drives me nuts. I want to pound his face in every time I see him. He always looks so smug, sitting on the couch like that with his legs over the other. His elbow on the armrest, propping his head up with his fist as watches something on his laptop. Every now and again his lip press together in thought, eyes widen in shock or interest and his hair keeps tickling his nose, making it wiggle in this chipmunk sort of-

"What do you want?"

Oh, he's talking to me. My expression must say I am not sure what he's talking about because he sighs.

"You're staring at me."

"I am not!" Because noticing that his nose occasionally twitches like a little baby squirrel or chipmunk is proof that you were obviously not staring at him.

Oh god, I can't believe I was staring at him! Stop it, Aron, stop it!

Quinton leans forward to pause whatever it is he's watching. He removes the earplugs from his ears as he puts his attention on me. "Why are you here?"

"It's the game room. Everyone is allowed here." I have the sudden feeling of déjà vu. Didn't I ask him that in the library last week? Heh, we're opposites from last time. Weird.

"Why would you be in the game room watching your, as you so put it, arch nemesis watch TV?" the son of Lucifer asks with one of his trademark blank expressions. His eyes show how curious he is, though. I can almost see the question marks dancing in his eyes.

He has a point, though; why am I here? Wasn't I complaining earlier about how seeing his face pisses me off? But here I am, watching him watch TV. I'm not even watching anything on the big screen anymore.

I look over to see that what I put on earlier has ended. Some show I don't know the name of is now playing. When did I start watching him? And when did he notice? I bite my lip as I suddenly feel warm.

"Uh…" I don't have an answer. I'm trying to come up with an answer, but even my bullshit one's make little sense. What am I supposed to say in this situation? Shit.

Quinton groans. Instead of waiting for me to respond, he plugs himself back into his laptop, losing himself once again into whatever he's watching. I'm curious, so I lean over to take a peek. It doesn't look familiar, some type of crime show or something.

"What are you watching?" I ask. Maybe I was staring at him earlier because I got bored with whatever was on TV. I probably looked over and started staring because I was bored and needed something to occupy me. That something happened to be Quinton. Yep, that's it. We'll go with that.

Quinton doesn't answer. I wonder if his show is too loud. He heard me earlier though, didn't he? Little shit is ignoring me. Growling, I yank one of his ear buds from his ear. The action makes him shoot a deadly glare at me.

"Don't touch my stuff," he says, to which I ignore.

I place the bud in my ear. It seems to be one of those crime shows. If it's like Criminal Minds, I'm sure I'll like it. I'm actually pretty interested in shows like that.

"You really like this crime stuff, don't you?" I ask, still watching the show. I'm totally lost, but from the looks of it, this episode is halfway over, so obviously I would be. "I see you with those mystery and crime novels all the time. You want to be like a cop or something?"

To be honest, I knew before I asked that he wouldn't answer, however; I did not know that he'd slam the laptop shut and rip his headphones from me. I am ready to give him a piece of my mind once again when he shoots up, and he's already halfway out the door by the time I spoke. "Hey! Hey, get back here! Quinton c'mere!"

"My life and interests are none of your concern," he hisses and, without bothering to look back, exits the room.

I'm left lost on the couch, staring at the exit he took, flabbergasted.

I don't see him for the rest of the break.

"Tell me sweetie, how are classes going? Have you made many friends? How about your grades? I could have looked, but I thought it'd be better to ask you about them. Oh! How is Langley? Is everyone treating you w—"

"Mom!" I grunt. If she holds me any tighter, I am going to die. "Can't breathe!"

"I'm sorry," she laughs, finally allowing me to take a breath of fresh air. "It's so strange not to have you here with me all the time. I've missed you so much. You look like you've lost weight. Are you eating enough?"

"One question at a time, dear, you're smothering the boy," Dad says, opening his arms for me to jump into. I don't care if I'm almost sixteen years old. I will hug my dad like I'm eight if I want to!

"We really have missed you, son," Dad says as he holds me as tightly as I do him.

"Missed you guys, too." I do mean it.

Mom may smother me and talk too much and Dad may be a little overprotective, but they're my parents and I love them. They treat me well. I know many people are not lucky enough to have parents as great as mine, so I appreciate them. I thank them and tell them I love them every chance I get. I imagine I always will. I suppose that also has to do with my family always being openly lovey.

Dad has no issue showing how much he loves Mom with constant hugs, kisses, and flirtatious remarks. I may grimace or gag at hearing it, but I enjoy seeing them so happy. Mom loves holding hands and cuddling with Dad, so physical contact with my parents never bothered me. Their lovey ways spread to me, so I'm used to it.

"Tell us everything!" Mom shouts, wrapping her arm around my own as she tugs me towards the kitchen for dinner.

I tell them almost everything. I leave out a lot about Quinton, simply stating that there's this smug guy in class who irks me a bit. Dad asked if I wanted him to be expelled, as I expected he would, but I said that it's fine. I should learn to put up with people who twist me the wrong way. He looked proud to have heard me say that and didn't push the matter. Had I told him everything that had gone on between us, I know for a fact Quinton would be gone in a second.

As tempting as that is...

"I'm glad you are enjoying yourself," Mom says after hearing my stories about school. "I remember high school, being young and in love."

Oh, no, not this again.

"Mom, please don't tell me the love story between you and—"

"When I met your father—"

I should never have come back.

After having to listen to Mom for an eternity about meeting my dad and how they fell in love, I thought I would prefer having my face smashed in by Quinton. It is beyond weird hearing how your parents hooked up. I do not need to know any of that! Gives me the shivers.

Somehow I make it to my room without vomiting my dinner all over the place. She has told me that story for years, but it still makes me queasy. It's not that I'm not glad that they got together, but she never leaves out my conception. No child should know the specifics of how they were conceived! She even told me the date they believed to be correct, June 3rd.

I vowed to myself that on that day, I will do nothing. I do not care if I get myself the sexiest girlfriend ever. I. Will. Not. Do. Anything on June 3rd. I am scarred for life because of her.

After a hot shower and some midnight reruns on TV, I finally fall asleep. My eyes feel heavy, body tired, and the bed feels more welcoming than it ever has. I never thought I would miss it so much. Maybe I should ask Dad to have it taken to my dorms.

Dorms. I wonder if Quinton is still at the dorms. He has to be lonely.

CHAPTER TEN

It's Christmas morning when I feel myself being tackled off my bed. With a loud shout, I, and whoever dared assault me in my sleep, tumble to the floor. The giggling is familiar. I can't seem to place it though I know I have heard it before.

"Good morning, sweetheart! Time to get up!"

Ah, it's Mom. I don't know how I couldn't recognize her immediately. Guess I am not fully awake, so my senses are for shit.

Yawning, I stretch out on the floor, still not bothering to get up, though. "Oo arlly..."

What did I even say?

"There is no such thing as too early on Christmas!" How Mom understood me with my face in the carpet I do not understand. Must be a mother thing. And how come she is the one waking me up? Aren't the kids supposed to wake their parents up on Christmas? Something is wrong here.

I stopped doing that when I was ten, after I realized that the presents really aren't going anywhere. I would go to sleep like I always did and wake up whenever my parents would tire of waiting for me. They are more excited about my opening of presents than I am. Must be another parent thing.

Mom ushers me to get ready. She even gets me out a pair of clothes while I'm taking a shower. Normally, I would toss what she picked out back into the closet and grab whatever I wanted to wear, but I figured it's Christmas; what the hell, I'll humor her. It's not like she picked out something weird like she usually does.

She sat out a simple pair of gray sweats and a navy hoodie. I throw both on and tiredly make my way down to our living room, where a sizeable amount of presents awaits me.

I smile upon seeing both my parents waiting for me on the couch. Mom giggles, holding out her camera like she always is on Christmas. She takes pictures nonstop on Christmas morning and always prints them out and add to her collection.

Dad is on the floor next to the presents, ready to hand them out to their proper owner. Christmas is a day where my dad has no work whatsoever. He doesn't read over papers or sign bills or read up on what is happening in the world. On Christmas it is 100% family time. We open gifts, play with them all-day and deep into the night. It's the only time of the year where such a thing like this happens. I really love Christmas.

It doesn't take us all long to rip into our presents. Mom gets a picture of me with each gift I unwrap. She does the same with my father. She then makes me take pictures of her opening her presents. There's a lot of them and it takes some time to get through them all, but exhaustion never sets in. We're having too much fun to be tired.

We have an amazing Christmas lunch, because I told them never to wake me up before 10 or I might die of sleep deprivation, before we spend the rest of the day together watching movies and messing with our new gizmos and gadgets. Dad got me a plane that I'm currently flying around the living room, paying no mind to what's on TV. Instead, I'm focused on the plane I have circling the chandelier.

"Honey, how do I change the background?" Dad asks, with his glasses perched on his nose.

"Oh my, you really are clueless when it comes to phones, aren't you?" Mom giggles.

I watch her try to explain to Dad how to work his new phone. He always had that stupid flip phone, saying he didn't need a new one because his secretary carried around all kinds of gadgets. We finally talked him into getting a modern phone so he can try to keep track of a few things himself.

I roll my eyes at the two of them. But the more I look at them, the more I wonder; what could my father do to make me want to burn him off a picture?

Ugh, stop thinking about it. Quinton is a pain in the ass. Why should I care? Why am I even thinking about that? How did it even come about?

I keep telling myself not to care, but I can't help but think about it. Not just the picture, but also about him.

What is he doing right now? Is he at the dorms? Did he decide to head home after all and visit his family? What is his mother doing? What about his father? Does he even have a family other than his mother? Is he opening his presents? If he's still at the dorm, did he even get any presents? Is he the type of guy to even celebrate Christmas?

Is he lonely?

Ah, I don't care; I don't care; I don't care!

Maybe I should have stayed?

Christmas break is over and I'm on my way back to school in a blink of an eye. Langley is there before me. The two of us talk about our break, he doing most of the talking since I didn't want to say much about my encounters with Quinton. I don't even want to imagine what sort of things he would say. I focus more on the presents I received as well as what my folks and I did, which was mostly spend time together.

"You going to do the same thing over spring break?" Langley asks as he looks for spots to place his new belongings. He got a pretty cool stereo system that we have hooked up to the massive 70 inch TV I got. Now we're just trying to make room for them. Maybe we should get a bigger room?

I shrug as I think it over a bit. "Probably. It was kind of nice being here on my own."

"That sounds like something Quinton would say."

I hit him for that.

"Ouch! I was kidding, geesh!" Langley rubs at the back of his head with a frown. He continues to try to push some more of his things out of the way while I am trying to hook everything up. I looked at the instructions earlier, but it's still difficult being so cramped back here while trying to see. "Did you run into him at all during break? He never goes home on breaks."

Good thing my face is behind the TV or Langley might have found out that I really ran into him, a lot, during the break. My cheeks feel kind of hot. Shit, I'm blushing, aren't I? Stay behind the TV, stay behind the TV! Why am I even blushing? I am half tempted to slap myself.

"Uh, yeah, once or twice. So he's never gone home, not even for summer?" I ask.

Ok, I am curious about his home life, just a little though! It's only natural to want to know more about your enemy, right? Right. I need to know his weaknesses and stuff.

"Mm, nope, not that I heard of." By the sound of Langley's voice, I don't think he finds my question weird, but that's not the biggest thing on my mind.

If Quinton doesn't even go home for summer break, then how long has it been since he's been home? We are sophomores, so that means it's been a year and a half since he's been home. Wouldn't he want to go home? Most people want to go home. They miss their own beds, their belongings, their friends...their family, even more so. Surely Quinton misses all that and wishes to see those who are important to him?

"You done back there yet?" Langley asks, peeking in from the other side.

I glance down, shielding my face from view in case my cheeks are still flushed. Nodding, I push myself out from behind the TV to admire our new system. I hope my face will cool and my thoughts go on hold, at least for now.

"This is awesome," Langley laughs, already digging through our countless numbers of movies for something to watch.

Good. I need to think about something else.

CHAPTER ELEVEN

I f looks could kill, Quinton and I would both be dead. Here we are at yet another argument revolving around his issue with authority and my issue with idiots who can't hear. Even with the time we spent together during Christmas break, it did nothing to fix our relationship. It is as it always has been and I have a feeling always will be.

"I got here first," Quinton claims.

"Yeah, well, I'm older than you, which means I was here first."

"That only means you were born first, stupid." Quinton's insults aren't even coming out as harsh as usual. I must really be getting on his nerves. That thought makes me grin.

"Let go," I demand.

"No."

Why are we fighting over a piece of cake again? Oh right, because it's Valentine's day and they only make this super deluxe, devil's chocolate cake once a year! I've never had it before. He had some last year, I bet, so I should have it! Jerk, let it go already.

I wish someone else had grabbed it so I could take it. Why does Quinton make everything so difficult? Can't he be like everyone else and do as I tell him to? Life would be easier for the both of us. Stop giving me some semblance of hope that I can be a normal person because we both know that isn't the case.

"Do I need to order you?" I ask, tugging at the plate the work of art is sitting on.

"It doesn't matter if you did. I wouldn't listen," Quinton says with a scowl. He tugs as well, pulling the plate back to where it had been previously. It was neither closer to him nor me but directly in the middle and at this rate, it will probably stay that way.

Fifteen minutes of our forty-five minute lunch has already been wasted in our tug-o-war. I think our fights no longer affect people. At the beginning of the year, we would have crowds around us whispering and gasping while now, after it's been over half a school year, it has become natural for us to fight. The crowds have dwindled down to only a few onlookers who giggle at the two of us before passing on.

We still have people staring, but now they are at a distance, not really as interested anymore. Unless one of us throws a fist, then the crowds are swarming again.

"Aron, you can have mine," Langley says, holding out his piece of cake he got before me.

I think Langley is growing tired of our antics as well. He has tried talking to me about it, but I always blow him off, insisting that I can't just 'forget about Quinton.' How can anyone forget him? He's the biggest asshole I've ever met! Besides, it would make it seem like I was backing down and I will never back down, especially from Quinton.

"No way! That's yours and this—" I pull hard, only to have Quinton step forward. He's so close now I can feel his breath on my cheeks. Being this close, I notice that he's taller than me by about two inches. He must have realized I noticed because he smirks.

Regardless of the height difference and how it actually bothers me a bit, I still spit out, "This is mine."

"This is annoying." He sighs.

For a second, I think that I have won this battle, that he is going to let go of this glorious work of art and be on his merry way. However, this is Quinton we're talking about. He makes nothing easy. He must make sure that he ruins everything and so, with no warning, he flips the plate in a second, sending the cake to the floor with a 'splat.'

The cake is ruined. If it had landed on the cake itself rather than the top where all the delicious icing is, I probably would have still eaten it. Gross? I think not! I would have cut the piece off that touched the ground, anyway. The icing is the best part, though! Without the icing, it's nothing.

"Wha...why would you," I can't even speak.

My cake! He ruined my cake! He is a hell spawn, because who in their right mind would destroy such a piece of art? It's cake for fuck's sake!

Shrugging, Quinton brushes past me. What he says next almost makes me believe that murdering him would be worth the jail time. "I don't even like chocolate."

"What?!" Langley is forced to hold me back.

We fought over that piece of cake for like 20 minutes when he doesn't even like chocolate! First of all, who the hell doesn't like chocolate? Chocolate is great. He is a nut. Second of all, why did he even try to take it if he doesn't like it? He only did it to mess with me, to piss me off. He calls me immature! Oh, right, sure, I'm immature, but I'm not the one who fought over a cake when I didn't even like chocolate cake!

I hate him. Holy shit, I hate him.

"It's fine, Aron, have mine." Langley hands me the plate that holds his. I, of course, want to try it so I decide that we'll split it. The cake was very delicious, but my own would have been better. The taste of victory would have sweetened the cake! But Quinton ruined it.

"Stabbing the cake will not help," Langley chuckles, watching me stab away at my slice of cake. Chopped up or not, the cake is still good. Besides, I need to stab at something or else I'm going to explode.

"Imagining it as his face helps!" I grumble.

"I really don't get you two," Langley sighs.

I look up at him, wondering what he meant by that. What is there not to get? We hate each other, so we fight. It's that simple. The boy waits to see if I catch onto what he means. When I don't, he shakes his head and adds, "There have been other people that you've hated and you always got rid of them within a week. Why are you going so easy on Quinton? Why do you purposely get his attention? Running into him in the halls, shouting about how he's a jerk in class. Why do you do it?"

For a moment, my mind is blank. Langley stares at me, waiting for a serious answer. Normally, I would probably laugh and say how he pisses me off, so I have to do it, but let's be honest, that's not the real reason. It's an excuse.

I try to think it over, to come up with something that makes sense. There are a lot of things, actually. Like I said earlier, he gives me this semblance of hope. I came to school wishing to be normal, though I know that will never happen. I will never be normal no matter how hard I try, but I wanted to at least get a little closer to normalcy. Quinton kind of gives me that. He doesn't back down like others do. He stands up against me. He speaks his mind to me and that—isn't that what normal people would do?

I don't know how to explain it to Langley, but the only thing that really comes to my mind is...

"Because he's brave."

Quinton is definitely very brave.

Langley looks confused. "I don't get it."

I don't really expect him to. I don't think many people would, but it makes perfect sense to me.

"I'm the prince, people, instead of respecting, fear me," I explain. "Others have said to me what Quinton has said, but they were always shaking with fear. Their eyes showed me how frightened they really were and it wasn't that I got rid of them within a week, they got rid of themselves. They gave up standing against me after some harsh pranks, but Quinton hasn't given up yet. Even after I sent guys to beat him up, even after we got into fights, and even with the threat of my father looming over him, he doesn't change his mind. He tells me what he really thinks about me, so...he's just different."

By Langley's expression, I can tell he still doesn't get it. Like I said, I don't expect him to. He isn't me. He may be a nobleman, but people aren't scared to speak their mind around him. Well, some are, but they're different from me. I walk into a room and immediately people try to befriend me, not out of respect but to protect themselves.

People figure it is better to be friends with the ones who hold the power than to be the enemy. Quinton isn't like that, though. He knows what I can do. He knows his life could be ruined because of me, but he rather be ruined than fake and that makes him different.

I don't want to crush him with the power that my father has. I want to crush him with my power, to prove to him that even if I'm not the prince, I would still win against him and that is why he is different.

I think if I were to have said that all aloud, Langley would think me weird. Many people would probably think that, but it's the truth. That is how I feel. It isn't weird to want to prove yourself, right? It isn't weird to want people to see that you are strong even without a royal title, right? That's normal.

Whatever, like I need anyone to tell me if my thinking is correct or not. If that's how I feel, then that's how I feel and nothing is going to change that!

CHAPTER TWELVE

"**D**amn it!" I scream. Pain shoots up my leg. I feel it pulsating. It's the strangest feeling in the world when you desperately wish to touch it, but know that will only make things worse. It's that type of feeling that makes your teeth grind and has you rolling on the floor in agony. "Damn it, damn it, damn it!"

"What the hell, Quinton?!" Langley screams as he shoves Quinton with a force that sends the boy toppling over.

I'm shocked to see him fall so easily because normally it takes all the power in me to move him an inch, let alone knock him over. And why are his eyes so wide like that? It's like he's seen a ghost.

"You fucking broke his ankle!" Langley shouts, kneeling to inspect my ankle that is continuing to throb terribly.

"No." I shake my head. It hurts, but I can still move it. I'm sure it's a bad sprain. We got into another fight as we usually do, but this time we might have gotten a little too rough. Neither of us has actually gotten injured to this extent, some bumps or bruises, but that's it. Damn, this really hurts. "I can move it b—Ah!"

I find myself scooped up from the side without warning. An arm is around my waist, basically holding me up as I hop on one leg. The world takes a turn for a moment. I have to blink a few times to realize I've gone from sitting on the floor to standing. I think for a second that it's Langley, but I hear him shouting behind me, which means the only other option is...

"Quinton, I am giving you ten seconds to let go of me before I break your fucking neck." My threat doesn't even make him flinch. Of course it wouldn't. My arms shake from the pain running up my leg that I'm not even sure if I could crush a bug with them right now.

"Be quiet," he orders.

I cock a brow and ask, "The hell is your problem? Where are you taking me anyway?! Seriously, let me go!"

He doesn't listen and I do not know why I tried ordering him. Quinton never listens.

We made it to the nurse's office in record time, even with me hopping most of the way. She doesn't seem at all shocked to see us. She shouldn't be. We're here all the time with bumps and bruises though this is probably the most serious.

"What happened this time?" She asks, rushing over to me once she realizes there is a reason I am not walking in here on my own.

Quinton places me on the bed. I hiss the moment the nurse touches my ankle. It already looks like it's swelling. To be honest, it resembles a balloon a bit. I actually feel like laughing at the sight. She apologizes as she examines my ankle, telling me that I have a bad sprain.

As I thought, it isn't broken. Quinton looks more relieved than I am. What? He thought if he broke it or something, I'd tell my dad and get him expelled?

"I am going to have to at least tell the Dean about this," the nurse says, looking between the two of us.

Quinton is too busy staring at my now wrapped ankle to really notice her. He's freaking me out with his staring. Say something, jackass.

"Yeah, sure, just make sure not to bother my dad," I order her like I've always done. Again, don't want him dragging me back home because I've gotten into some fights. I'm a teenager. We get into fights, so let me have a little normalcy in my life, thanks.

"Hey, hey, asshole," I call out to Quinton after a few minutes of his silent staring. It takes a moment, but he finally looks away from my ankle. His eyes are as dark and unreadable as always. "Your staring is creeping me out. Stop it."

"You will have to be on crutches," he says, his voice so soft I hardly hear it. What's up with him? He's acting weird.

"I know, thanks a lot." His shoulders tense upon hearing me. Now I notice he has his fists clenched at his side, like he's holding back or something. Holding back what, though? Did I hit him a little too hard? His brain must not be working. Normally at the end of a fight, he's insulting me about how bad I am, but he hasn't done that.

"What's up?" I ask, getting annoyed by his weird behavior. It's not like him and when he doesn't act like himself, I don't really know how to act either.

I hear Langley outside the nurse's office asking if he can come in. She must have told him no, that I needed rest or something because he hadn't entered yet.

"You're acting really weird. Did I hit you too hard or something?" I ask.

Quinton turns away from me with a snort. "I'm fine."

Before I can bug him more about his obviously not fine behavior, he leaves. I shout after him, ordering him to apologize or something, but he's out of the office in no time. Hell, I think he moved faster here than he has ever in our fights before. To replace him is Langley. He comes running in, sending a glare behind him at Quinton as he does.

"Your ankle ok?" He asks, taking a seat at my bedside. He examines the wrapped appendage with a concerned scowl.

"Just a bad sprain. I'm going to be on crutches for a bit until it's fine enough to walk on." Damn, that is going to be a pain. I should have ignored the pain and got a few more hits in on Quinton for this, that asshole. However, it's fine. I have injured myself before, broken my wrist once while climbing trees and sprained my other ankle when I was younger while playing baseball. Crutches are better than a cast, I guess.

"Tell me you're telling your dad about this. He could have broken your ankle," Langley huffs. He knows the answer before I tell him, though, which is probably why he's already glaring at me.

"No way." I shake my head stubbornly. "And it's not broken. Calm down."

"But he could have! Ugh, you—"

The rest of what Langley has to say is completely ignored, as I think over what he had said. He could have broken it.

Quinton acting weird earlier. Could it have been because he was... worried?

He reacted so fast to me being in pain. It was like he wasn't even thinking about anything other than getting me to the nurse as soon as possible. He practically carried me here, after all. He didn't even hesitate. He looked so shocked. He stayed while she examined me to hear the verdict and only left after he knew I was ok.

Was he worried that he had broken my ankle? Was he possibly feeling guilty? Or angry at himself for having almost broken my ankle? We've hurt each other before!

But I guess we have never broken bones. Blood has been drawn, but only from minor scratches that were made by our fists or us wrestling on gravel. Neither of us has been seriously injured and, I mean, I don't want to break his bones.

I say all the time I'd love to stab him or kill him or toss him off a bridge, but it's all only words. I don't actually want to do that. If… if I broke Quinton's bones, I think I would feel terrible. Isn't it natural to feel bad about that?

This is Quinton though. He's a selfish bastard. He doesn't care!

Maybe he cares because that bastard hasn't even looked at me for a week! And it's not his normal, "I'm better than you, so I'm not looking at you," kind of ignoring. No, it's something different. I could be wrong, but normally I feel his confidence oozing out of him and spreading through the room like a virus. Lately, he seems to be lacking.

Even after my many attempts at pissing him off, he hasn't retaliated like he usually does. I shout about how he's a total ass in class, yet he does not snort or comment on it. I run into him in the halls, only to have him maneuver himself to the opposite side. I poke at him with my crutches to be a pest, but he never says a word, simply pushes the crutch away or moves. It's strange. I don't like it.

It's bugging me in a way that I cannot tolerate. I don't know why. I should be happy that he's ignoring me. I should be glad that he moves out of my way like all the others. I should be happy that he isn't calling me a brat or childish, but I'm not.

Every day feels kind of boring. I didn't realize how much I spoke with Quinton until he stopped speaking with me. Though we share only three classes together, it feels like we see each other all the time and without him it's empty, dull.

I'm fed up with his weird behavior.

So, one evening after his rigorous training, I make my way to his dorm. I am determined to know what his problem is and to fix it immediately. We must have our normal banter or I'm going to go insane. It's strange seeing him back down and I'm kind of pissed that I'm pissed about that. Does that make sense?

I knock on Quinton's door, expecting him to answer, only to have his roommate appear.

"Uh, what are you doing here, Your Highness?" The boy asks. He looks up at me with slight concern and confusion. I dig through my brain for his name that has completely escaped me. Part of me feels bad for not remembering when I've spoken with him before.

"Is Quinton here?" I ask. Still cannot remember his name, though. I think it starts with a T.

The boy whose name I am now sure starts with T nods. "Yeah, but he's taking a shower."

I should have guessed that. I can hear the water running.

"Your name is Timmy, right?"

"Taylor."

"Ah, Taylor." Knew it started with a T! I get credit for that, right? "Would you mind leaving for a bit? Quinton and I need to have a talk."

Had it been anyone else asking, I'm sure Taylor would have refused. This is his dorm room, after all. Why should he leave? But since it's me, he agrees and quickly gathers a few of his things, books and studying material, I think, and vacates at the speed of light. I don't blame him. He probably thinks we're about to get into a fistfight that will destroy the dorm. That is possible knowing Quinton, but I'll try my best to avoid it.

I take a seat at Quinton's desk. It's as bland as ever. It's been months since I broke in here and it looks like he has done absolutely nothing. He should have a poster or some pictures up or something. His side of the room is so bland compared to Taylor's. At least Taylor seems to be a normal kid with posters of movies and music on his walls. His side of the room looks lived in while Quinton's is so pristine one would think no one lives there.

My walls are covered at home and at school with posters and even pictures. My desk has junk all over it, ranging from books and notes to little figurines and comics. Quinton's desk looks like some middle-aged, workaholic stick in the mud owns it.

His bed is even made. Who makes their bed anymore? I sure as hell don't. It's going to be messed up once you get back in it, anyway. What a weirdo...

"What are you doing here?" An all too familiar voice asks from behind me.

My eyes tear themselves from examining the lameness known as Quinton's room to Quinton himself.

How is it he's half naked and dripping wet, yet he looks as conceited as ever? If he were in my dorm room and I was soaked, in nothing but a pair of black boxers that leave nothing to the imagination, I know I'd feel self conscious.

"Nice to see you too," I say with a smile while desperately trying not to look anywhere but his face. It's a lot harder than I thought, or I'm willing to admit.

Quinton does not hide the look of annoyance on his face. He seems fine knowing that I am well aware of how much he doesn't want me here. "You didn't answer my question."

True, I did not do that. "And you aren't wearing any pants. Seems like we all have our little problems."

With a roll of his eyes, Quinton heads for his trunk. I stare out his window because I have no desire to see him and his basically naked glory walk by. I ignore the sounds of him redressing and focus all my attention on the outside world.

The clouds are nice today, fluffy and stuff.

A second later, Quinton finally has on a pair of sweats, which are still weird to see him in. In my mind, he wears suits even outside of school.

"Do you want something, or does the prince simply have so much time on his hands that he can go to another person's room and stare out their window?"

Why do I want to talk to him again? I should leave now and let what's been happening continue on. He's driving me up the wall and we've been talking for thirty seconds. How can a person even do that? He is maddening.

"I do have a reason for coming," I finally reply, reminding myself how boring it's been without our little quarrels, even if he is a total ass. Once you have something in your life for so long, it feels weird for it to be gone, even if I don't want to admit it. "I've come to discuss how you've been avoiding me."

"I'm not avoiding you."

Oh, come on, even I can tell he's lying. He can't believe I'm actually buying that, can he?

My expression must have told him exactly what I was just thinking because he sighs and says, "You should be happy about that."

"Yeah, well, I'm not." And I hate to admit it and I think Quinton is as shocked as I am about it because his black eyes, that are normally so hard to read, show surprise for a moment.

I clear my throat and make sure not to make any eye contact with Quinton as I say this because if I did, I know I would run out of here and pretend this never happened. "Listen, I... I don't know for sure if I'm right, so just listen and if I'm wrong, be a nice guy for once and keep your trap shut."

His expression tells me he definitely will not, but I go on anyway.

"I think you're feeling bad about my ankle."

He says nothing even after I wait for him to.

I take that as a right to continue. "You shouldn't. I was also hurting you. I mean, those guys sprained your wrist earlier in the year and we get into fights all the time. You shouldn't feel guilty about it because my ankle didn't break and I'm fine. We're both fine, so just stop acting so weird, ok?"

I really should have thought over what I wanted to say before I said it. I sounded so stupid. He's going to call me stupid, isn't he? I know it.

Or not because Quinton says nothing. I'm growing impatient with his silence.

Is that his way of saying, "ok I'll stop being a weirdo," or is he trying to tell me to leave? He's always been hard to read. He must be well aware of that too, so his silence isn't at all helping the situation. After my curiosity gets the best of me, I finally turn to face him to see that he isn't looking at me but glaring at the ground. Geesh, what did the floor ever do to you, bud?

"Quinton," I call out, wondering if I've angered him somehow. I can't think of what I said as something worth getting angry over, but who knows about Quinton?

"Hey, you ok?"

"Fine," he says through gritted teeth. "I'm fine."

"Like hell you are. You're sending your death glare at the floor. Usually it's at me. If you aren't glaring at me, it means something's wrong!" It's kind of scary when I can tell something's wrong. Doesn't that mean we've spent too much time with each other?

"I should have been able to hold back."

"Huh?"

Quinton still won't look at me. "I should have been able to hold back. Next time if I can't..." He doesn't have to continue for me to understand.

Even I get it now. He's angry with himself for not being able to keep himself from hurting me. Quinton, who is usually always in control of himself and those around him, is worried because, for once in his stupid life, he wasn't able to control himself. He thinks that if we were to fight again, he really would break a bone. I guess that is a concern. Sometimes the two of us get so caught up with wrestling that we forget what we're really doing, but...

"Stop being such an idiot!" I shout, making Quinton finally direct his glare at me.

I don't know if he's mad at me for calling him an idiot or shouting... or both. Probably both. He probably thinks shouting is childish.

"Shit happens, Quinton! Shit is going to happen, especially between us," I exclaim. "We're the only ones who can take the other on. What happened to the overly confident Quinton? I'm thinking you were just putting on a show for me."

The boy growls at my grin. He really doesn't like it when I bash in his confidence, does he? I sure as hell do. Seeing his face scrunch in anger like that brings me great joy.

"Get the hell out," he says, pointing to the door. "Now."

"What? Why? I thought we were having a moment!"

I know that I've got Quinton back to normal the second he grabs my collar and literally throws me out of his dorm room. Shouting as I hit the concrete floor, I roll onto my back and shoot a glare at Quinton, only to see him grinning back.

"See you tomorrow, Princess."

"Screw you! I never should have come over!"

Maybe I should have stuck with boring days. He really is such an ass.

CHAPTER THIRTEEN

"Does this look infected to you?"

"What happened to your knee?!" Langley groans while examining the black and blue sliced open knee of mine. I disinfected the wound and wrapped it moments after I got it, so I don't think it's infected, but a second pair of eyes is always nice.

"Ah, Quinton and I got into it again, this time outside on the concrete sidewalk. Not one of our best ideas," I mumble while inspecting the newest injury. There isn't any pus. I don't have a fever either. I'm sure I'm fine.

"Again? That's the second time you two have brawled this week," Langley grumbles. Langley's voice tells me he is getting annoyed with the battles between Quinton and I. Hey, we can't help it. It just happens. "Aren't you two going a little overboard? Try not to get expelled. We have a month left till this year is over."

Ah, yes, summer is drawing near. It's more like three weeks, which is, in my opinion, not long enough. Even after staying on campus over spring break, I still don't have the desire to return home. I tried asking Mom if I could stay here for summer break too, but she said hell to the no, or something along those lines. Now that I finally got myself out of the castle, I really want to stay out. It's not that I don't love going home, but each time I do, this feeling sets in that I won't return, and that bothers me.

I haven't really made any new friends to be honest, but Langley and I have gotten closer! I have been able to play sports with other kids, laugh and talk about random things with people my age. It's nice not always speaking of politics and work. It's nice to talk about dumb shit that has no point and not expect to be judged about it. Being around people my age is a blessing, and it relieves me. Hell, even being around Quinton is relieving in a way, a weird way, but relieving.

"I think we're trying to do it to make up for the 2 months we won't see each other," I explain, grinning.

We have to fight now because if we start at the beginning of the next year, the teachers will be fed up with us and actually punish us. I think they're all so tired of the two of us they've given up trying to prevent the fighting.

I can't believe it's been nearly a year since this began and I still haven't crushed Quinton into dust. Though, I have noticed that it has gotten easier to fight with him. I have been doing my best to train, to catch up with him, but he's always one step ahead of me. Still, sometimes I can see how shocked he is at how much I have improved since coming here. That's right, be amazed!

If only my grades could do the same. It isn't really a good thing for the prince to make straight C's except for gym. I got an A in that, woohoo! People expect me to ace everything. That's impossible. I'm not that smart. I wish there were more physical types of courses. My gym score proves I am a more physical being than a mental one.

If I were a mental one, then I would have been able to find more answers to the questions about Quinton. I never got the chance to ask him again why he refuses to go home during breaks. I can't really ask him why he burned a man's face off a photograph when he has no idea I even saw it. I've been trying to piece the puzzle known as Quinton together, but so far I've got nothing but the basic assumptions.

Hates his dad and doesn't want to go home? Abusive family, but that isn't always true. Sometimes it isn't abuse that drives a family apart. He could have abandoned them, cheated on his mother, or discovered an alien race that resulted in experimentation on Quinton, making him the unbelievable asshole he is today. Personally, I'm leading towards the last option.

But if any of those are true, then how come he doesn't want to talk to his mother? Why only speak to her once a week or less? Is he mad at her? What for? Is she abusive too? Then why does he have her photograph?

Too many questions with no answers. I doubt I ever will receive answers. I remember the last time I tried asking Quinton why he was here on break. He blew me off and stormed away before I got a chance to ask more. Even Taylor knows nothing about his own roommate. From what I hear, Quinton doesn't really talk to him and their evenings are spent with them studying or Taylor playing games on his own. I kind of feel bad for the kid, but he seems to be used to Quinton's naturally silent nature.

If I try speaking of personal matters again with Quinton, I'm sure I'll get the same results... or he'll be fed up with my asking and instead go for a physical approach. Either way, I won't get an answer.

He makes everything so complicated. Can't he just have a mental breakdown in front of me and spill his secrets out? He will probably get that stick out of his ass if he did. Keeping secrets is never a good idea. It puts stress on you and those around you, and Quinton is definitely stressful.

And I am not interested because I care or anything! No, it's because we are enemies and it is important to know your enemy, and the secrets they carry. I simply wish to know about him in order to defeat him. Yep, that's why.

"Do you have any plans for summer?" Langley asks, changing the subject from Quinton. I'm sure he's tired of talking about him. I have this nasty habit of grumbling about him and his 'asshole-ness' all day.

I shrug in response. "The usual, I guess. I'll still be forced to study and take lessons. Be locked up at home like usual. What about you?"

"My parents and I are taking a trip around Europe. We're leaving the day after I get home and won't be back till a week before school starts." His grin shows how excited he is although he's been to Europe I don't even know how many times. He has told me that Europe is his favorite place. He enjoys seeing all the old castles. Once he is back, I'll probably have to listen to him tell me about his trip before looking through hundreds of photographs. Not that I mind.

I've been to Europe before, but never for sightseeing. My parents and I would go for balls or to visit relatives. I was lucky to be allowed on the lawn, so going out onto the streets was definitely not an option. We may have gone out once or twice, but things were always closed off from the rest of the world. It isn't the same if you aren't surrounded by people, by life other than yourself.

Hopefully, my being in school will show Dad he can loosen up a bit. I'm sixteen now and it's not like I can't handle myself.

Suddenly, the intercom kicks on. Someone calls me to the office. I don't know what they want until Langley says that he got called in earlier to talk about his grades. I guess all the kids have to go over their yearly achievements. Great, just what I need; a disappointed teacher telling me I can do better.

I sigh and leave to see Professor Bennett where I know exactly what he will say, or at least the gist of it. It doesn't take long to reach the office. The guidance office is with all the other offices. They have their own building, containing the dean's office, along with all the professors and counselors. Being in there makes me feel strange, like everyone is watching me.

I scurry to my homeroom teacher's office, Professor Bennett. My hand rests on the knob, ready to burst in and apologize for my lack of greatness, then I hear Profess Bennett speak to another student.

"As expected, your grades are incredible. I have gotten nothing but good comments about you from the other professors. You are exceeding all our expectations. We are lucky to have you."

I have this nasty feeling that he's talking to...

"Thank you, Professor. I am glad I haven't disappointed you." Quinton. I should have known it was Satan incarnate the moment he said, 'your grades are incredible.' Of course they are. He's Quinton! If his grades weren't perfect, I'm sure he'd go nuts. Freaking overachiever.

"It is especially shocking for you. Who would have thought you'd do such a great job considering who your—"

"That has nothing to do with one's abilities," Quinton interrupts. His voice sounds furious. It's rare he lets so much emotion be heard in his voice and part of me is actually concerned that he has. What the hell was Professor Bennett about to say that could make Quinton react in such a way? It makes me wonder what they're talking about.

Besides, how is it shocking that he does so well? He's Mr. Perfect, after all. And considering what? Considering that he's an ass, because I am with you on that one, sir.

"Are we done?" Quinton asks.

I have a feeling that Professor Bennett was about to speak again before Quinton spoke. The professor has no time to answer because I'm suddenly pushed back onto the floor when the door is flung open to reveal Quinton, whose eyes are now on me. Said eyes narrow into one of his famous death glares, though this one is a bit different. It seems worse, angrier if that's possible.

"Eavesdropping, are we?" He hisses. He looks pissed. Actually, that isn't an uncommon emotion for him, but this time it isn't a mixture of annoyance but actual anger.

"No. I was told to come to the office," I reply, jumping to my feet quickly before he tramples me. "I was about to go in until you knocked me over, bastard."

Quinton probably didn't buy that, but he doesn't seem to want to talk anymore because he snorts and storms off. What crawled up his ass? Or is it that the stick has gone up a little farther than usual today?

I'm tempted to go after him and ask him those questions exactly until Professor Bennett appears behind me.

"Oh, hello Your Highness, you weren't busy, were you?" Bennett asks with a smile.

Well, I was about to be, but I don't want someone to see me go after Quinton. They might get the wrong idea and think I care or something, which I don't!

I shake my head and make my way into his office. I take a seat in front of his desk. Hopefully, this doesn't take too long. Maybe I could catch up to Quinton?

"We're gonna talk about my grades, right?" I ask. There isn't much to talk about. I'm average. I should do better. The usual.

And that is exactly how our meeting plays out. I know if it were anyone else Professor Bennett probably would have said some harsh things like 'what do you expect to do with your life with grades like this' or 'don't bother planning for college if your grades continue this way.' But since it's me, he simply asks that I do better next year, to which I nod and promise that I will.

Once I get out of Professor Bennett's grasp, I go running in the direction Quinton left. I don't know why. It's not like he'd be there. I was talking with Bennett for at least fifteen minutes. Quinton's probably already at his dorm or even in some dark corner, making voodoo dolls of his enemies.

As I thought, Quinton is nowhere to be seen. I ran for nothing. I doubt he would have answered any of my questions. He can't make anything easy for me. With a heavy sigh, I spin on my heels and head back to my dorm with even more unanswered questions about Quinton.

CHAPTER FOURTEEN

Year 2 of the war against Quinton and, sadly, no progress has been made.

Our sophomore year ended without too much trouble. Though our fights became more frequent, closer to the end, Quinton and I, along with everyone unfortunately caught in the crossfire, survived. I passed. Quinton, obviously, passed. Sophomore year ended, and the students were sent home, which Quinton seemed very reluctant to do. It seemed if it were allowed, he would even stay over summer break as well.

I saw the bastard a few hours before he left to remind him that our battle would continue next year. He did not look pleased with leaving. Not that he ever looks pleased at all, but he looked more asshole-like than usual. His brow kept furrowing in a way that reminded me of some fifty-year-old man. Most people tried to get on the first bus out of here for break, but he waited for the last bus to leave. If that doesn't say reluctant, I don't know what does.

I didn't even get to ask him questions or attempt to break into his room again to find myself some answers. Because breaking into someone's room is not wrong or creepy in any way.

Summer went by much slower than I had hoped. I spent most of my days going over political documents with my father. He was 'showing me the ropes,' I guess you could say. He took me on trips to meet political officials and learn how to speak and work with them, the usual. I couldn't wait for it to end, allowing me to return to school, where I could have a bit more of a normal life. No one can even begin to understand how boring it is working with politics. Everyone walks around acting as if they own the place and with egos the size of Jupiter, it's a pain in the ass. Now, put them all in a room, use your imagination to see what would happen. Trust me, it's never good.

When my junior year came around, I was excited and ready to go. I returned to campus to find that Langley and I were still sharing a room, but in the junior part of the dorm. I was happy about that. I didn't want to get a new roommate, which the school probably knew, so they kept me with Langley.

Langley and I once again shared most of our classes together. After a week of classes, I discovered Quinton was in none of them. I even looked for him during lunch, but we didn't even have the same lunch hour. I wonder if he's still at school.

Had he not made good enough grades and lost his scholarship? But there was no way. I had remembered hearing him and Professor Bennett speaking about how well he was doing. He couldn't have lost his scholarship, or rather Quinton would not allow himself to lose his scholarship.

It didn't take me long to discover that he was still in school. I asked Langley about him first, seeing as he always seems to know everything. It was funny, seeing his face drop in disappointment. I think his exact words after I asked were, "Man, I had thought you forgot about your man crush."

I hit him for that.

He informed me he actually shared an AP English course with him, the only subject Langley was good at. I asked if Quinton had said anything about me or spoke to Langley. The boy said that he never spoke with him or even acknowledged him.

His information didn't surprise me. Sounded exactly like something he would do. I was tempted to ask Langley to speak with him for me, but I did not know what I wanted him to say. What is there to say? I couldn't ask him to come argue with me. That would sound stupid.

Then I wondered if our teachers had done this on purpose. Were we separated because they didn't want a repeat of last year? Or was it simply because Quinton was placed in all the advanced courses while I was not, for obvious reasons.

Two months go by before I actually see Quinton on campus.

I am heading to my next class when I get this feeling, like my teeth are grinding. The hairs on the back of my neck stand at attention and a shiver runs down my spine.

I spin my head to the left and there he is. Quinton is on the other side of the courtyard, sitting in the shade of a tree with his nose in a book, figures.

For a moment, I wonder if I'm only seeing things, but realized it really is him. However, he got a haircut. The normally long black hair that once reached below his shoulders is now short. The back and sides are shorter than the front with the whole bangs sweeping into his face, which oddly suits him. Of course it does! Everything suits Mr. Perfect! Freaking hell spawn.

I nearly shout at the boy until I feel Langley pulling me down the hall, claiming that we'll be late for our next class. I look away for a moment to Langley to say I'm right behind, but when I turn back, still planning on yelling at Quinton, he's gone. A feeling of disappointment sets in that I do my best to ignore. Had he seen me and left? Or was he heading to another class, too?

Don't know because it's been a month since then and I haven't seen him so I never got the chance to ask.

Not that I want to see him or anything! I'm glad we don't have classes together. I don't have to see his sorry ass. Seeing him last month is proof that being near him is enough to grind my teeth. Obviously, we don't need to see each other. It drives us both nuts. It's better this way.

I definitely do not want to see him. Not even a little.

"What's wrong with your face?"

"Huh?" I rub my hand over my face while attempting to wake myself from the trance I had just been in. I don't feel anything weird about my face, though. "Nothing, why?"

"You look depressed or something." Langley scoots in for a closer look. I feel uncomfortable with us being so close. I can feel his breath on my cheeks. It reminds me of the time Quinton was this close. Oh shit, I'm blushing!

Why am I blushing thinking about Quinton? Shit, shit, shit!

Thankfully, Langley leans away soon enough not to notice the sudden heat under my cheeks. I do my best to hide myself behind my textbook in order to keep him from seeing them now. Don't need him questioning me about that, too. I don't even know why I am blushing! Stop it already.

"Depressed?" I ask, voice muffled from the book. I think about what he can mean by that. I'm not acting differently or anything. "I'm fine. You're seeing things."

Langley shrugs. "Maybe I am. My spidey senses must be off."

"Spidey senses? Sorry Langley, but you would never be a superhero. You're more the Robin type."

Langley glares. Come on, he knows he's a sidekick. He's more like my sidekick, which makes me Batman. Awesome, I love the Dark Knight. He's a total badass. Don't think I could pull off the voice, though. I've tried before and sounded like an idiot.

However, now Langley's comment has me thinking. Depressed, huh? Wonder what made him think that. I don't feel depressed. I'm not crying or eating tubs of ice cream. I'm not rolling around on the ground in tears, shouting to the world about my heartbreak or sucky life. I guess being depressed doesn't have to be like that, though. It could be a lot of things...

It could be wondering what someone is doing but not knowing why and being so confused that just thinking about it brings on a headache. It could be this inability to forget about someone, for good reasons or not. It could be the desire to see someone, even for a mere second, although their very presence makes your teeth grind. It could be thinking about the same person over and over, like, are they eating? Are they doing well in class? Are they thinking about me as much as I am them? It could be a longing sensation for someone that used to plague your days, but now is nothing but a ghost.

Not that I know the feeling or anything.

CHAPTER FIFTEEN

Who thought it would be a good idea to test kids on their knowledge of everything they've learned halfway through the year? Whoever it was needed to be tortured in the most brutal ways possible because midterms are by far the worst of any invention ever, along with finals of course. They are on equal terms. Some of my professors are kind enough to make our final only on the second half of the semester rather than the full term. I pray they have an eternity in heaven for that kindness.

I am not that great at studying. In fact, I suck. I will admit that. I do my best to take notes during class but there are times I fall behind, miss something the teacher said or consider it something not that important. Then when the test comes around, I ask myself what I should go over and what I shouldn't. Did I take down the right information? What is considered 'test worthy' and what isn't? How many questions will be on the test?

What about the textbook? Some professors tell us not to bother with them, while others want us to read over the chapters as we take our own notes in class. Are they going to include things from the book? If so, what? See, it's all very tough and I kind of got in trouble for making not so great grades last year. I passed, but my parents were not impressed. Being homeschooled, I made very good grades. I got special attention and didn't have the option of leaving if I didn't understand. I was forced to sit around and prove I knew what I was doing.

In school, all I had to do was smile and claim I understood. After my parents warned me that if I didn't bring my grades up, they'd pull me out of school. I tried my best to learn how to study. I asked Langley if he would help me, which he agreed to. His grades aren't perfect, but they're better than mine. I have even started making note cards! They're really helpful, actually.

I have made mostly B's with a few C's so far. My professors are now making sure that my parents see my grades, so I don't lie like last year. They said they would accept that as good enough progress, but they expect me to get better as I go along. It's tough. I'm nervous. I feel the pressure. I don't want to be taken out of school. I don't want to be home schooled again, so I have to do better.

Langley must be able to tell because the boy clears his throat to break my almost trance like attention on making note cards. I actually jump at the sound, which only proves how focused I was. My wrist hurts from writing so much. It's cramping. How did I not feel that? I end up twisting my wrist around beside me, hoping to make it feel better. Slowly, it does until the cramp is nothing but a dull throb.

"You were really going at it," he says, eyes looking over the work I have done. I've only gone over half the material I have and I've already got, like, fifty note cards. I know it's too much. Our professor told us there would only be about 40 questions, but I can't decide what isn't important and what is.

"You made too many," he states my fear.

"I know, but I have no idea what I should bother with and what I shouldn't," I groan, throwing my head against the table in hopes of knocking some sense into my brain. I don't think it worked, but it was worth a try! I'm so exhausted that I ignore the pain in my head. School, why are you so hard?

"Langley, gimme your notes." I hold out my hands for them.

"We don't have that class together," he counters.

"Read through mine and tell me what to do."

"I'm not your mother."

"You sound like Quinton."

"Ouch, that was unnecessary," Langley says with a scowl. I shoot him a lopsided grin that makes him roll his eyes.

Now I'm back to square one. I don't know what to study. I don't know what to make note cards about or what not to. I don't know anything. I'm about to yank out my eyeballs and offer them as a sacrifice to Satan in return for the ability to ace my midterm when a few sets of giggles catch my attention.

I feel eyes on me. I lift my head from the table to see Langley, who is looking to his right with a slight blush. I follow his gaze to see a group of about four girls looking our way and giggling. Why do they always travel in packs? It's nerve wracking. Seeing them all stare at me makes me wonder if there's something wrong with my face. Do I have crumbs on my jacket? Maybe someone threw gum in my hair?!

To make sure I have nothing on me, I look down and away to rub at my face. There's nothing, or at least, I think there's nothing. I turn back after I feel better about myself and watch as they continue to watch us. It's a little weird.

They seem to whisper something to each other. One girl pushes the other closer to us. The pushed girl has her back facing me, but I see her green eyes peering over her shoulder in our direction. Upon realizing that yes, I have noticed them; she jumps and turns back to facing the girls, who are still giggling.

"What are they doing?" I whisper to Langley, who is still blushing while looking at a pretty brunette. I make a mental note to remember her and tease him about it later.

Langley shrugs and replies, sounding as clueless as I am, "Giggling."

"I can hear that, but why?"

"How should I know?"

"You're useless," I growl.

"Like you're any better."

Twenty more giggles later, the green-eyed girl finally turns around. Her strawberry blonde hair is long enough to use as cover over her face. Even with her hair blocking most of her face from me, I can see she's blushing. With what appears to be a notebook against her chest, she walks over to Langley and me. Her blush darkens the closer she gets.

"Hello," she whispers. Good thing we are in the library or I wouldn't have heard her.

"Hey," Langley and I reply, waving or nodding to show that we heard her. It's awkward. Neither of us knows what she wants. It's not like it's Valentine's day or a dance is coming up. She can't be asking us to buy her a rose or accompany her... unless she's going to ask one of us out! Sweet! My parents have paired me up with girls before just to see if I could get along, but arranged meetings are always weird.

I'm broken from my thoughts of a possible girlfriend by her voice. She brushes her bangs from her face, finally showing that she actually is very cute. She's short with a heart-shaped face and naturally red cheeks. I recognize her, but I'm not sure where from.

"I overheard you talking with your friend, Your Highness," she says with a slight bow. My cheeks warm at the thought of her coming over to speak with me.

Langley rolls his eyes, putting his attention back on studying, seeing as she's not here for him. Jealous!

"And, uh, we share that class together and I, not to brag or anything, do very well in there. I have my notes here..." She holds out the notebook she carried over to me. "If you would like, I highlighted everything that I thought would be on the test. You could use it."

Cute, smart and caring! Jackpot! World, it seems you have finally gone easy on me. Not only did you fix my problem, but you fixed the problem by introducing me to a girl. A very cute girl, I might add. Please be single, please, please, please be single!

"Thanks," I reply, happily taking the notebook from her.

She smiles, her blush simmering down a bit but still dusting her cheeks a little. She seems like she wants to say something else, but she keeps looking at Langley. He's too busy studying to notice, so I kick him under the table.

"Ouch!" He shouts, glaring at me. I throw on a smile; tilt my head towards the girl to make him notice and hope that he gets my silent message. His eyes widen and he catches my drift. "Oh, uh, I've gotta be somewhere, so I'll be going. See you later, man."

He waves to me as he scurries off.

Once gone, the girl takes a seat beside me, a little closer than necessary, but I sure as hell don't mind. She can sit as close to me as she wants.

"I'm sorry, but I don't remember your name," I admit. Our professor had us introduce ourselves at the beginning of the year, so of course I don't remember her name. She has never talked to me before and, honestly, few people do, so I don't really remember my classmates. I pray it doesn't bother her.

She shakes her head with a soft laugh. "That's fine, Your Highness. My name's Gabriella, but Gabby is fine."

I spend the rest of my evening with Gabby. She helps me make my note cards and explains to me things I don't understand. I feel much more relieved about the midterms after speaking with her. I also feel much more excited as I return to my dorm, knowing that I will see her again tomorrow for another study session.

"Seeing you so happy about a girl kind of pisses me off," Langley says from his bed. He's on his stomach, head held up by his hand while he flips through a comic.

"Don't be jealous. One of these days, a girl will be desperate enough to ask you out."

"She asked you out?" Langley's sitting now, watching as my entire body stiffens. The movement makes him grin from ear to ear. "You didn't ask her out either, did you?"

"I'm getting to it," I grumble. Why did he have to ruin my perfect evening? We just hung out tonight for the first time so of course I didn't ask her out! "We're studying together tomorrow, too."

"Again? Lame. You should have asked her to the movies or something. Studying together is boring." Langley waves his hand dismissively at me, like he's disappointed in me.

I roll my eyes and huff in response. It's not my fault. I don't know what to do. I've never dated anyone before. I was stuck at my house until last year! I have never seen girls very often until now. The ones I saw were of other noble families, and it wasn't like we had privacy. There were always people around us, so it felt weird to even consider flirting or dating. How am I supposed to know what to do?

"Besides, how are you guys gonna make out if you're in the library?" Langley asks out of the blue.

I start coughing, having got something stuck in my throat after hearing Langley say that. The boy howls with uncontrollable laughter as he watches me desperately try to regain my lost breath. It takes a few moments to regain my composure, but now my cheeks are so hot, I'm sure they're literally on fire.

"The hell man?!" I throw a book at him, missing completely, which only makes him laugh harder. He's having a hard time breathing now too, though it's from his laughter and not choking. "We're not gonna make out. We aren't even together!"

"Who says you have to be?"

"Unlike you, I value a woman."

"Yeah, and I'm sure she'd value some tongue, so snap to it."

CHAPTER SIXTEEN

G abby is pretty, smart and kind. She is perfect in absolutely every way. She's fun to be around, laughs at my stupid jokes and does her best not to giggle at my stupidity but, occasionally, can't help herself. That's ok because even her laugh is perfect. Not only did I pass the midterms because of her, but also, I've been having a great time every day since spending time with her.

Langley is lonely since our time had been cut in half, but Gabby introduced him to that pretty brunette girl he eyed the other day. Her name's Ariel. She's pretty cool. As long as she treats Langley well, I like her.

I've been spending a lot of time with Gabby. We sit by each other in the classes we share. Sadly, we do not have the same lunch hour, so I'm with Langley, but that's fine. I love our friend time, even if most of it is spent teasing one another. After classes, I'm usually with Gabby as well. We haven't gone on any 'real dates,' because my father would send out an army with us.

Part of the reason I'm allowed at school is because I promised not to leave school grounds without an escort. By escort he means army. I thought it would be weird and uncomfortable for Gabby to have fifty or so men with guns tailing us watching our every move. She's not a royal. She's the daughter of a well-known and successful doctor, so, unlike me, she has never really lived with guards watching her regularly. Hell, I've had this kind of treatment since birth and I'm not entirely comfortable with it. And if they were around, we wouldn't have any privacy, so making out would be a definite no-no.

I want us to do something fun, though. Fun like a date, fun. I haven't asked her out though word around the school is that we are going out. Everyone may continue thinking that way! I'm fine with that and Gabby seems fine with that, but I would still like to ask her out officially.

I don't completely understand that things have to be 'romantic' because, honestly, isn't working up the courage to ask someone out already romantic? I guess it is different for everyone. I know that if I do something nice for her, she will appreciate that and, I mean, I'd like her to be happy, so I would like to do something romantic. I can't really do that on campus. It's a school campus. What could I do here?

Dating is complicated.

So another day goes by without me officially asking Gabby out. If I'm going to do it, I need to do it quickly. We've been hanging out for about two weeks and Christmas break is in a week. I guess, even if I don't ask her officially, we could still talk and call each other over break, but still I'd feel better if we were together.

With this thought in my mind, I walk around campus searching for either a spot or an idea. It's freezing out, seeing as it is winter. My hands are shoved so deep in my pockets that I think I've found space that was never there before. A scarf and hood shields my face, leaving only my eyes visible, which are stinging from the chilly breezes of winter air.

I'm not going anywhere in particular. I have no set place in mind because I feel having an open mind would be best. I'm simply looking. There is so much snow that students made forts from what plows have cleared from the pathway. Because of all that snow, a few locations that might have worked are no good. I could ask to have it moved, but I'm taking it as a sign this isn't the right place.

Damn, why couldn't we have met in the spring? Spring is a pretty romantic time, right? Girls like flowers, I think.

I'm so focused on looking for a good place that I don't notice in time the person coming around the corner. We run into each other with an 'umph'. Neither of us were moving very fast, so it didn't send us crashing to the ground, but I ended up stepping into a good bit of snow. My boots aren't high enough so now I have freezing snow running onto my toes.

"Shit!" I yelp, pushing past the person to take a seat on the bench a few inches away. I remove my boot, shaking the snow and water from it, not even paying attention to who stood before me.

"Idiot, watch where you're going." I know that voice.

"Quinton," I hiss, finally looking up to see black eyes boring into my own. He, too, is dressed in winter attire. The only difference between us is that I am colorful; probably not matching at all, while his clothes are pure black from head to toe. Figures.

"Aren't you a little old to still be in the emo phase?" I tease.

Quinton snorts. I only see his eyes beneath his black hood, but I sense that he's scowling. "Most labels are created by idiots who dislike things that differ from them."

He called me an idiot, didn't he? He called me an idiot twice within 20 seconds. I'm not as cold as I was before. My blood is boiling and we've only been in front of each other for a minute. I cannot understand how one person can make me feel so much in so little time. I'm half tempted to give him an award for being such an ass, but I rather not inflate his ego.

Quickly, I shove my boot back on in order to stand. My anger rises when I realize the bastard has gotten taller. I know that I've grown an inch or two since last year. I haven't hit my growth spurt yet, but it seems Quinton has or is about to. I remember us only having a two-inch difference last year. But now, I actually have to tilt my head up in order to see his face.

He's grinning beneath that scarf. I know he is. Whatever, our heights don't matter! We're only 16, so I have a chance to grow taller... but so does he. Forget it, forget it! Being taller means nothing!

"What a way to speak to your prince. Your parents haven't raised you very well, have they?" I wasn't thinking about it when I said that. Suddenly, the photograph I found in his room last year flashed through my head. My eyes widen a few seconds after his do.

I can't apologize, it may clue him in on the fact that I know about something I shouldn't, but I really want to because...

His eyes darken in a way I've never seen before. If I could see his face, I'm sure he'd be frowning. He has glared at me, been angry with me, but not to the extent that his body is actually shaking so that anyone can see. Quinton is the type to hide his emotions from others. He's an actor, you could say. One look at the boy and you can't tell if he's being sarcastic or serious, but right now an infant could see the anger pouring from his eyes. I feel the heat of his anger radiating off him and onto me.

I deserve to be hit. I'm waiting for it. We haven't fought all year. I should have known we would eventually, but I haven't seen him, so I haven't thought about it. This time, though, I doubt I will fight back. No one should talk about another person's family, especially when they know nothing about them. I said something I shouldn't have.

He surprises me by closing his eyes and, with a deep breath, says, "You know nothing of my parents. Do not speak of them again."

I nod stupidly, unsure of what to say. His eyes are still closed; fists still shaking and shoulders still tense. Maybe now he's going to hit me? He doesn't. I wonder if he wants me to apologize or does he want to say something more? We've been quiet for a while and he hasn't looked at me again.

I decide to speak first, seeing as he isn't moving.

"Sorry," I whisper, though I'm not sure why. There are a few people around. Most are inside on this freezing Saturday afternoon. A few people are scurrying by, probably going into town or something, but no one recognizes us since we're huddled up in winter gear. "I never should have said anything about your parents. That was low."

"Should have expected as much from someone like you," he grumbles, voice muffled from the fabric of his scarf.

That wasn't necessary. I bite my lip in order to keep back any insults. I figured I would give him that one, seeing as his eyes are no longer narrowed in a death glare on me. He must have calmed himself down. He deserves a low shot at me, considering I did the same to him. Just this once, though!

"Whatever," I huff, scuffing the tips of my boots against the sidewalk.

I'm not sure what else to say or if there is anything else to say. Suddenly, a strong breeze blows by; nearly sending me toppling over, but a hand on my arm stops me from hitting the pavement. Thank god for my scarf or Quinton would have noticed the sudden reddening of my cheeks. Why'd he have to keep me from falling, anyway?

I yank my arm away and cough out a thank you. It's been so long since we've even been close to each other and I use that as an excuse why my heart has suddenly raced. We're silent again, me staring at the ground and he, I'm assuming, at me. I'm biting my lip. My hands are shaking in my pockets. My legs feel like jello. I often feel that way with Quinton's eyes on me. Why? I don't get it.

"I need to tell you something," Quinton finally speaks. Looking up, I see that he now has his eyes focused on the building behind me. I look back to see nothing interesting there. Why is he staring at it?

The boy sighs and it actually sounds like he isn't sure what to say, which is odd for him, seeing as Quinton always knows what he wishes to get across. "I doubt you will believe me, but..."

"But what?" I ask, now curious, especially since it's Quinton.

He rarely has things to tell me other than that he thinks I'm the dumbest person on earth, but he seems to have something important to say. He won't make eye contact with me, though, and it's freaking me out a bit. Quinton always makes eye contact. He likes to hold you in place with his dark eyes, letting you know that he's got complete control of the situation. Seeing him actually look away like he may be embarrassed or unsure is so out of character that it worries me a bit.

"Break up with Gabriella," he says.

"Huh?"

Break up with Gabby? What? Why? How did he even know we were going out? Why does he care? And what the hell gives him the right to tell me to break up with her?! He knows nothing about her or me. Why would he say that unless he... shit... does he like her? No way. Quinton doesn't have a heart or feelings. He doesn't pay attention to girls. They flock to him, but he has never shown an interest in one.

The world cannot hate me enough to make my arch nemesis have a crush on my girl, right? I'm about to ask if the robot known as Quinton actually has romantic feelings for someone other than the reflection of himself in a mirror, only to be shut up by his voice.

"Never judge a book by its cover."

I don't have the time to ask him what the hell he meant and what a book cover has to do with me breaking up with Gabby before he's walking away, leaving me confused and curious.

What was that about?

CHAPTER SEVENTEEN

I did not inform Langley of my run in with Quinton. I didn't talk to anyone about it, actually. Not that I really have anyone other than Langley to talk to. I'm not even sure what the hell happened. I'm flipping over in my head what he said to me, but it makes no sense.

Don't judge a book by its cover? How...Quinton like. It's a famous quote. It could be used for a lot of things, but what does it have to do with Gabby? Was he trying to say Gabby isn't what she seems? Then what is she, some ninja assassin?

There is no way she is secretly evil, if that's what he's implying. She's cute and sweet and kind, the exact opposite of that asshole. I like her. She seems to like me. I enjoy spending time with her. There's no way she's any different from how I see her.

How would he know if she's not what she seems, anyway? He doesn't talk with anyone, especially girls. He keeps to himself, locks himself up in his room and pays attention to nothing other than his own life, so how could he know anything? He must have been trying to get under my skin, mess with my head for what I said about his parents.

But Quinton isn't the type to get involved with things he doesn't want to. So why did he tell me to break up with Gabby? That is getting involved. Not to mention, I doubt he is the type of guy to mess with someone's love life. He isn't that cruel, right?

So why did he say it?! Damn it, I'm so confused. I don't know what to do. I keep thinking that he wouldn't have said anything if he were lying. Quinton doesn't lie to me. He tells me when I'm being an idiot or I've done something stupid, so why would he lie about that?

Then again, we're enemies. Enemies mess with each other's minds. I should believe in the girl that I like over the guy that I hate, right? I'm overreacting. I need to forget about what Quinton said. He doesn't matter.

With that in mind I head to class, determined that today will be the day I ask Gabby out 'officially.' I ordered no one to use Dorm A's lounge this evening. The doors will be shut after classes today. Gabby and I will watch a few movies of her choice on the big screen TV. We're going to eat popcorn and chocolate while cuddling on the couch. It's basically the same as going to the movies, only we won't have to worry about phones going off or people talking.

It will be good. I hope.

Throughout the day, I try not to seem too obvious about it with Gabby. I think she knows already, but she has said nothing about it either. I thought it would be harder to keep a secret. I expected myself to shake or sweat or stutter, like I do when Quinton's around, but... nothing. My heart isn't racing at a pace that scares me. My stomach hasn't erupted with butterflies. My toes aren't curling. There's nothing that makes me nervous. I thought those were the feelings a person got at a time like this? Why aren't I getting them? I get them just from being around Quinton.

I pass it off as my nerves being so strong that I'm not noticing them. You know, like when you're in so much pain you can't feel it? That must be it.

"Got everything ready for tonight?" Langley asks, smiling upon seeing me nod my head happily.

I have everything prepared and ready to go. Things should go as planned. This will be my first 'date' and my first girlfriend. I actually never really thought about such a thing before as an option, since my own parents had an arranged marriage. I know they have never mentioned such a thing before about me, but I kind of always assumed it would happen, so dating it's definitely an experience.

"Hopefully, things go well." My mind flashes back to what Quinton said, and I wonder if I should postpone. No, no, it doesn't matter. He's being weird, that's all. I'm overthinking it.

Langley laughs, "They will. Everyone's already saying you two are seeing each other. If she didn't want people to think that, then she would have said something."

I nod. He's right. She does like me. I like her. People who like each other date. That's what normal people do and I need to be as normal as I can while I can. Once I graduate, I will be stuck in the life of politics till death. I must enjoy my youth and asking a girl out for the first time is part of that.

But what about what Quinton said?

I ask without meaning to, "Does Ariel talk about Gabby?"

Shit, why'd I ask that?

Langley doesn't seem to be suspicious about my asking, though. He shrugs and replies, "A little. They've known each other since middle school, she said. They're more like acquaintances than close friends, so she hasn't said much. Why?"

I shrug his question off. He doesn't pry, not seeming to think anything about it. Good. I don't know how I would have told him it sort of slipped out because of Quinton's mysterious words. I need to stop thinking about it. I'm being stupid.

It's time for our next class and I find myself without my textbook. I've been so busy thinking about the date and Gabby that I've been forgetting all kinds of things. I actually nearly left without brushing my teeth this morning!

I must have forgotten my book back at our dorm. I inform Langley that I'll be right back and to tell the teacher I am getting my book. He nods and heads to our next class while I run back to our room for my book. I find it quickly, lying on my bed where I had forgotten it. Quickly, I shove it into my bag and head back to class. It must have been fate...or the world missed messing with its favorite plaything because I hear a familiar voice.

No, it isn't Quinton.

It's Gabby.

I know eavesdropping is wrong, but when one hears their name, it's hard not to. I skid to the floor with my back pressed against the wall, leaving anyone within the classroom unable to see me. Some classrooms actually have windows on the hallway side as well, allowing people to see out into the halls. The room Gabby is currently in is one of those rooms. I hear Gabby's voice speaking to another girl. Their voices are hushed, nearly whispers. I hear them because they're up against the walls, but I doubt anyone around them does.

"I think he's going to ask me out tonight," Gabby says, but she doesn't sound excited at all.

I know I shouldn't judge someone by their voice. Some people express themselves better than others but, Gabby is usually the type of person who you can hear her emotions through her voice. She sounds kind of bored.

"Dating the prince, lucky you," a female voice says. She doesn't sound familiar, so I don't think I know her. Ok, let's be honest, I don't really know anyone. Of course I don't know her.

"I guess," Gabby sighs. The sound makes my stomach hurt. "He's nothing like I imagined him to be. He's lucky he's a prince. He doesn't have much else going for him."

Now my heart is racing, but not in a good way.

"He's kind of cute, but he isn't very smart. I felt like I was talking to a fifth grader when I was helping him study."

I can't breathe either.

"I definitely wouldn't bother with him if he weren't the prince."

My body shakes.

Quinton was right. I should have listened. Don't judge a book by its cover. Gabby appeared to like me and, honestly, it's not like she's the first. I thought we had the same feelings. I thought she enjoyed being around me. She seemed sweet and kind, but she's just another person wanting to use me.

I can't believe I fell for that. I should have known better. I am the prince. I am treated differently than other people. I can't be normal, because I'm not. I can't expect to go through the same experiences as normal people. I shouldn't even be in this school. I don't fit in. People don't speak to me unless they want something. They don't act kind to me out of respect. They don't smile at me because they're happy to see me. They don't laugh at my jokes because they're funny and they don't like me for who I am.

I forgot that for a moment.

I thought coming to school would change that. How could I be so stupid? How can school change anything? I haven't even made any other friends. None of them contact me outside of class or during break. None of them come to me first, asking to spend time together. I'm the one thinking we get along when, in reality, they don't even like me.

Heh, why would they? What is there about me to like? Security guards ready to tackle you if you make the wrong move surround me. I'm arrogant, annoying and stupid. I have no common sense. I even lack book smarts. There's nothing special about me; other than the title I was born with. Had I not been a prince, I definitely wouldn't be in a school like this.

I can't trust anyone. I wonder if Langley is even a true friend. I bet he even complains about me behind my back. I wouldn't blame him. I boss him around enough.

I hadn't realized how long I was sitting here until the bell rang, signaling class had ended. I skipped, by accident. Students pour out of their classrooms ready to attend their next class. Some stare at me, the boy sitting lifelessly on the floor while some walk by, not even noticing. Yeah... that would be me, the boy who was unnoticed if my father wasn't the king.

I wait for Gabby to appear, and when she does, she jumps at seeing me on the floor. She giggles, a giggle that I now know to be fake. Leaning over, she holds out her hand while asking, "Aron, what are you doing here?"

"I don't know," I answer, running my tongue over my teeth. I'm not looking at her. I can't afford to. I clench my hands into fists against my arms. "I guess I'm just thinking about how lucky I am to be a prince."

I turn to face her to see her eyes have widened a bit. She either thinks I heard or simply remembered what she said earlier. The girl seems nervous now, brushing her hair back while clearing her throat. "Yeah, that's a nice thing to be."

"To date one would be nice too," I hum, trying to see if she'll catch on. I think she is, by the way her mouth is opening, but no words are coming out. She must be trying to think of a way to apologize or lie about not saying what she had said.

Before she gets the chance to say anything, I jump to my feet. A few people have stopped to watch, listening in on the 'break up' of the prince and his cute lover. Good, maybe it will show people not to mess with me. I will not let them anymore.

"I was thinking I am a prince, so dating a girl like you isn't a great idea." I shove my hands into my pockets, pretending that what she had said didn't affect me when it really, really did. I mentally pat myself on the back for not falling apart right here and now. "I can get whatever and whoever I want, so why should I settle for someone like you?"

She gasps along with some people in the crowd. I hear a few whispers of 'asshole' and 'what a jerk.' If only they had heard what she said, but it's always the guy in the wrong. I don't care. People need to see me as a jerk in order to back off. It's safer when there is no one around to hurt you.

"Let's not speak to each other again. Breathing the same air as you will make me vomit." I brush past her quickly, leaving her, along with many onlookers, shocked and speechless. I would have stayed to relish in my victory, but my heart is racing so fast I think I might actually vomit.

I make it to the bathroom just in time to do exactly that. The contents of my lunch exit my stomach, tasting terrible coming back up. My head spins. My palms sweat. I feel sick, not in the flu kind of way, but betrayal. I feel betrayed. I was betrayed, and it's making me physically sick.

How many other times have I been tricked or lied to? I am sure it's more times than I could count... or will attempt to remember. Why was I born like this? Why couldn't I have been normal? At least that way I could see the difference between friend and foe. I hate it. I hate this. I knew I'd always get special treatment, but this, this is ridiculous.

Can't I even get a girlfriend? Am I going to be stuck in getting an arranged marriage with a girl that I may or may not come to love? My parents worked out but other kings and queens have not... a lot haven't, actually. I doubt I will be as lucky as my parents, especially with the way my life is going now.

Ah, my stomach hurts. I think I'm going to throw up again.

I'm leaning over the toilet, waiting for it to happen again when I feel a hand brush my back. I turn my head in order to tell Langley to go away, only to see that it isn't Langley kneeling behind me.

"What ar—" I can't. My stomach is churning. I don't throw up again because it's Quinton behind me, although I'm tempted to lie afterwards and claim his ugly ass face made me sick again. I decide not to because he actually stays during my upchuck.

One hand holds back my hair, keeping it from slipping into my face. His other hand hesitantly and softly rubs my back. He's new to this whole 'physical comfort' thing. At least I'm assuming he's trying to be comforting. Quinton is hesitant and soft, really soft, like he's scared if he rubs any harder I might break.

Truthfully, I just might.

I don't thank him afterwards. He doesn't ask me to. Neither of us says anything, even as I clean myself up or when he follows me all the way to my dorm. I don't ask him what he's doing, and he doesn't say it. When we arrive at my dorm he watches me go in and quietly leaves, saying nothing about what he saw or why he did what he did.

I'm glad. I think he knew I wanted to be alone.

I wonder why, during my time of need, it was my 'arch nemesis' that was right beside me.

CHAPTER EIGHTEEN

"What are you doing here? Weren't you and Gabby having your date tonight?" Langley asks upon entering our room, obviously unaware of what happened hours ago. I figured it'd get around the school in a flash. Apparently, it didn't spread fast enough.

When I don't answer, Langley asks another question, "Have you been here all day? I didn't see you in class. What'd you skip for, too nervous or something?"

He's laughing, but that laughter dies after realizing that I haven't budged or made a sound since he came in. I haven't moved since I came in actually, simply lying face down on my bed, hoping it would smother me.

Langley must be becoming concerned with my silence. A bed squeaks. It isn't mine, so he must be on his own. He clears his throat, probably trying to get me to look up, but I don't.

A few incredibly tense, incredibly awkward seconds pass before he says, "You're freaking me out, man. What's up?"

Now even Langley's voice puts me on edge. There's a stinging sensation in not only my chest, but my whole body. It hurts. I hurt.

I wonder if that concern in his voice is for real or another act. Many people act around me. After all, Gabby seemed to show through her voice that she was interested, but I learned the truth.

I know it's cruel to think about this. Langley and I have known each other since we were little. If he didn't like me, then he wouldn't still be with me, right? No way could a person who didn't even like someone put up with them for so many years. I can't help but wonder if that's truly the case. He could be like everyone else, using me to make himself look better.

Langley is a patient guy. I know because he puts up with me, but is that all he's doing? Putting up with me? Does he even care at all? Are we best friends or am I nothing more than an object to use for popularity and success? If I ask, will he tell me the truth or lie like all the others? I don't know if I can handle anyone else lying to me. I already feel like my head is going to burst.

If Langley lies to me too, I don't know what I'll do. His lie will be proof that my life has no meaning other than to rule over others. I won't be able to have friends or fall in love. I won't have any semblance of normalcy in my life, which is something everyone should have. That thought frightens me.

"Do you need to go to the nurse? I'll take you. Tell me what's wrong." Langley really sounds concerned. I like it, but I want to know if it's real or an act. I wish desperately for it to be true so that I can have some hope, some faith left. I have to ask, and if he tells me he doesn't and has never seen me as a genuine friend, then I will accept it.

Even if he doesn't count me as his friend, I count him as mine. He's always been there for me, always helped me and talked me down when I needed it. If that was all just an act then ok, fine, he's a great actor but I won't get mad. I understand people are naturally greedy and I have my moments as well. If it's Langley, it's ok.

Taking a deep breath, I admit, "She lied to me."

"What?" He sounds confused.

I push myself up, finally realizing how sluggish I am. My arms shake. They barely have the power to lift me. I make it into a sitting position, but I'm not facing Langley. I don't want to see his face when he tells me he doesn't give a damn about me.

"Gabby pretended to like me. She thinks I'm an idiot and that the only thing good about me is my title." My hands clench the sheets. I'm probably going to put holes in them. It's not only rage I feel though but also a mixture of sadness and fear.

"What the fuck?" Again with the sound of concern and anger but, is it real?

Finally, I feel a small enough amount of courage to ask. "What about you, Langley?"

Silence follows my question, a silence that puts me on edge, and I imagine Langley as well. My question isn't one someone hears regularly. In fact, Langley seems to be stumped by it for a few moments.

"What about me?" He asks, sounding confused and curious. His bed squeaks. When Langley is uncomfortable with a situation, he moves around a lot. I'm betting he's uncomfortable.

"Do you give a damn about me, or are you putting up with me? Tell me t—"

"What the fuck kind of question is that?"

I don't know what shocked me more, Langley, who is now grasping my shoulder with a strength I didn't know he had, or Langley's voice, which actually was pretty damn loud and interrupted me. Langley has never interrupted me. I always took it as a sign that he feared me because of who I am, but he just screamed at me. Hell, he's hurting me right now, but I'm too focused on the disbelief in his gaze to notice.

He's biting his lip and glaring at me. Langley doesn't glare.

"How could you ask that?" he asks in a hushed tone as his shoulders slowly relax to show that he really is hurt. He sounds offended, like he honestly cannot believe I asked such a question. He's looking at me now, waiting for an answer, but I don't speak. I want to hear what he says. "Listen to me well, Aron, and listen to all of it, got it?"

I nod, a bit too scared of how he's acting to say anything. He's so un-Langley-like. I've never seen him so mad. He's patient and keeps his anger in check, but right now I'm worried he's going to punch me.

"My mother told me to befriend you when we were little. To be honest, I didn't want to." Ouch.

"When we first met, you treated me like shit. You ordered me around, complained about everything I did, and never apologized for any of it. I thought you were annoying and a total asshole. I feared for the future of this country," he admits with his eyes locked onto me.

How can I stay quiet, though? He's dissing me like crazy. But his grip on my shoulder loosens, and he takes a seat beside me. The hand on my shoulder moves to wrap around my neck. I'm blushing, but only out of embarrassment. So is he.

"I won't lie and say that I was always your friend. In the beginning, I wasn't, but you've grown. You're not the way you used to be. You've treated me like a true friend. I trust you and I give a damn about you. You're my best friend and you would be, even if you weren't the prince. Don't forget that and don't doubt it, ok?" Langley bites his lip nervously. His eyes descend to the floor. He looks unsure of his own words, though I think he did a pretty good job.

A part of me is saying that he's lying. The paranoid part of me screams not to believe a word he said. A voice tells me he's the same as the others, that he's only pulling my leg. I don't know anymore. I don't know who to believe and who to trust.

But Langley looks to be hurting, honestly hurting. Another part of me claims no one could fake that kind of pain. Seeing the way he bites his lips and waits anxiously for a response makes me feel like shit. He looks like I physically harmed him, like I stabbed him in the back. I guess, in a way, I did.

I shouldn't have asked. He's my best friend and I'm his. I should have known that Langley was, is, and will always be there for me. He's a person I can trust. One person is good enough for me. After all, it's quality, not quantity, that matters, right?

"Sorry for making you say all that," I mumble, scratching nervously at the back of my arm. "I just..."

"It's fine," he huffs, finally pulling away from me. He runs his fingers through his hair, laughing nervously. We're not looking at each other, but I feel he's blushing with the same embarrassment I am. "That sounded pretty lame, huh?"

I nod, deciding that teasing is what we're best at and it will definitely make me feel better. "It was super lame."

"Yeah, well, you were acting like an idiot, so it's not my fault."

I smile, leave it to Langley to be the one to bring me back from my slump. What are best friends for?

"I was." I laugh. "Thanks, though, for telling me the truth."

I turn my head to see Langley looking at me as well with a smile. He shrugs and says, "I'll always be here to tell you when you've fucked up. I enjoy being one of the few people that can without the fear of beheading."

Laughing, Langley decides that the two of us are going to play video games for the rest of the evening. Video games have this way to make the two of us forget about everything and focus all our attention on the deaths of our opposing teams. Within an hour, I've forgotten about what happened earlier and am now immersed in a thrilling game. I don't know what I would have done without Langley to cheer me up. I'll never get a better friend.

CHAPTER NINETEEN

"You're doing this again?" Langley asks, seeing that my luggage is not packed and I am not moving to do so anytime soon. He already has all his things packed and waiting at the door for his driver to come up and help him with.

I nod. "Sure am. I enjoyed being here on my own last year. It was nice."

The boy rolls his eyes at me. "I don't see how you like being alone for two weeks. I mean, everyone likes their privacy, but isn't that too much?"

"Nope." Because I wasn't totally alone last year. Quinton and I ran into each other a few times. Not that I enjoy his company or anything.

There's a knock on the door that grabs Langley's attention. His driver has arrived. My best friend says goodbye to me and reminds me if I need anything to call, no matter what day or time. I assure him I'll be fine. I won't burn down the dorms or do anything stupid. He doesn't look totally convinced, but leaves anyway after making me promise not to go into another depression and lie on my bed all day like last week.

I definitely won't do that. There won't be anyone around to make me depressed; other than Quinton, of course. He causes more anger than depression and anger, I think, is easier to deal with, for me anyway. I don't mention that to Langley, though. It might be enough to make him stay behind, and I don't want to ruin his vacation.

The campus is nearly clear when I go out for a walk. There are a few stragglers saying their goodbyes for now or grabbing the last of their things. People are rushing, trying to get out of here before the blizzard that's been all over the news hits us tonight.

I don't know why they're rushing so much. The news is almost always wrong. They say we're going to get a snowstorm, but 80% of the time it hits north of us and we get a mere inch or two. I guess those mere one or two inches have piled up, though. The banks of snow next to the sidewalks are almost up to my waist. I could build tunnels in there!

I make a mental note to do so. I have two weeks, I could create a network of tunnels and one huge ass snowman. I wonder if Quinton would be up for a snowball fight? Pfft, yeah right. He's always got that stick up his ass, never wanting to do anything but read and insult me. I doubt he is the type to enjoy snow or anything other than reading, for that matter.

Why would I want to have a snowball fight with him? I hate him! Archenemies do not have snowball fights together unless those snowballs contain grenades. At least I thought that way until I felt the coldness of a snowball against the back of my head.

I yelp, the cool snow breaking through my barriers of clothing to run down my neck. It sends a shiver down my spine and I am left trembling while frantically trying to get the ice out. My arms reach back hoping to remove the snow to no avail. It's made it down my back now too, making my spine curl. Holy shit, holy shit! It's cold.

Ready to kill someone, I spin around to search for the perpetrator and realize that yes; I am definitely ready to kill them. Quinton stands a few feet away with another snowball in hand. I don't have time to react, seeing as he doesn't even hesitate. The snowball connects with my face, sending me straight to my ass with another yelp. This time the snow is going down my front. I get it out before it goes any further south than I am comfortable with, but that doesn't mean I am not freezing from it.

"The hell, Quinton!" I scream, pointing an accusing finger at the boy, who has started something I don't think he is ready to handle. He has another snowball ready. I scurry to the side, shielding myself behind a bank of snow before it hits me.

Ok, so I never pegged Quinton as the type of guy to enjoy a good snowball fight. I was obviously wrong. He seems more than happy to be throwing a pile of ice-cold slush at my face. It wouldn't be polite not to return the favor.

I return a snowball full force, hitting him in the shoulder. He sends a glare, ducking behind a tree, when he realizes I've got a second snowball ready. This is all out war. The campus yard has become our battlefield and I am not backing down!

The last of the students around have been avoiding this area for a while. Probably because a few kids dared to walk on by and ended up getting a face full of snow. Some shouted at us but after realizing who it was that was throwing the snowballs, they went running. A battle between Quinton and I is a battle no one wants a part of.

I don't know how long the two of us throw handful after handful of snow at each other. Long enough that my hair is now soaked even with a hat on and my gloves are no longer warm, but wet and cold. I can't feel my fingers, toes or face. My nose won't stop running and my cheeks feel like ice. My throat feels parched and I'm running out of steam.

Quinton must be the same. I can see how red his cheeks are from here. I don't want to stop though; it'll be like giving up. At the same time, I'm not sure my hands are functioning correctly enough to make another snowball. They're actually shaking as I sniffle and desperately try to scoop up another handful. All I do is shiver and drop half of it with a groan.

"Let's go inside!" Quinton shouts from his own fort. He leans on the snow, head resting on his arms. From here, I notice his back rising and falling as fast as mine. He's exhausted. He should be. We've been at this for hours. The sun is actually setting.

I nod, more than willing to take a break, as I can tell that I can't go on any longer.

"Yeah." My voice sounds hoarse. Shit, I hope I will not get sick. With my luck, I will.

The two of us drag ourselves to the cafeteria. There are a few students eating their late dinners or getting a snack. Quinton and I immediately go for the hot beverages. I grab myself a hot chocolate while he gets coffee. Figures. He has the taste of an old man. I can't stand coffee. It's too bitter for me even with sugar or milk. I've never liked it.

We take a seat across from each other. I feel eyes on us, students probably staring, thinking it to be really odd that Quinton and I are so close without fighting. Yeah, well, we were outside for a few hours throwing snowballs at each other. I think we're too worn out for any more fighting.

Quinton removes his jacket that's as dripping wet as mine. The black shirt underneath is mostly dry but damp enough that it clings to him, showing off muscles we all know he has to have. The boy takes off his hat, revealing the absolute mess of hair beneath. It's pointing in so many directions I can't keep myself from laughing.

"You look stupid," I cackle, wondering if it's gravitation-ally possible for someone's hair to point in so many directions.

Quinton snorts. "Like you're any better."

He reaches over, ripping my hat off to show that yeah, my hair is a total mess, too. I run my hands over it, attempting to tame it, but the damage has been done. He's seen it and he's smirking like the jerk that he is.

"Shut up," I huff, returning my attention to my hot chocolate. Can't he let me win an argument for once? Asshole.

I run my hands over my cheeks, hoping to help warm them up. They're so cold they hurt. I thought I had enough clothes on, but I guess during a snowball fight it's impossible not to freeze. Quinton is trying to do something similar, rubbing his hands together, blowing air into them and pressing his cold skin against his hot beverage. He notices my staring and asks, "What?"

"Nothing," I reply with a shrug. I wonder if I could get anywhere with him during the break. I really want to know why he doesn't go home. I guess it could be because he can't afford it. Maybe he lives far away and has to take a plane back or something? I could ask, but I doubt I'd get an answer. But it's driving me nuts!

"Sooo." I try to think of a way to ask him without making him feel the need to blow me off. I don't really think there is a way, but I'm going to attempt it. "You're not going home again for break?"

Quinton shakes his head. "Obviously not."

"Why not?" Way to beat around the bush, Aron.

Quinton rolls his eyes. Resting his elbow on the table and his head against his hand, he asks, "Why aren't you?"

He's trying to avoid the question by asking another. It's very Quinton-like, and it's such an easy way to evade a question. However, I think maybe I could tell him. Maybe that will make him feel like he has to tell me. Yeah, right, like I could guilt trip Quinton into something.

With a sigh, I ask, "Come on, what's so wrong about telling people about yourself a bit? The most I know about you is that you're an ass and you have a thing for crime novels."

"That's more than I want you to know."

Ouch. I'll admit that stung a bit.

Huffing, I place my elbows on the table as well and lean over. My mind is telling me we're closer than necessary. If there were anyone sitting near us to see how close we are they would probably whisper about us. Weird rumors would spread, but those thoughts didn't make me pull away.

"I'm pretty stubborn, you know."

"I'm aware." He doesn't keep any annoyance out of his voice. It makes me grin.

"You could just tell me or I could pull some strings and dig up some background information on you." My grin widens at his frown. Honestly, I wouldn't do that. If he is so hell bent on keeping me out, then I wouldn't dig into his personal life without permission. I think he knows that too, because he still seems reluctant to tell me.

But we both know I will continue asking for the rest of our school life together. I think he wants to avoid that because he finally gives in.

"There's no point in returning," he says, pulling away from me while his black eyes harden to reveal no emotion. His face is blank but his voice is dark, spine chilling. "She wouldn't notice."

"Who?" His mother? How could a mother not 'notice' her child returning home?

"That's why. You didn't ask to know anything else, so drop it." Quinton gets up after he speaks and begins heading for the cafeteria doors. I jump up to follow him with little thought. How can he tell me that but not say anymore? Who is she? Why wouldn't she notice? Why does it matter if she notices? Is it his mother? If it is, then what's wrong with her? Are they not on good terms or what?

See? He answered nothing. He only gave me more questions. The point of asking a question is to get an answer, not more questions.

I'm trying to get him to stick around, to explain it some more to me, but it seems the world found a way for me. Neither of us make it to the lobby or the exit. We both stop dead in our tracks, too busy staring out the window at the endless furious white to continue on.

The blizzard. We actually got it.

I can't see more than an inch in front of us. I can't see the other buildings or the trees, nothing but white swirling like a tornado outside. If either of us walked out in this, we wouldn't make it one step before getting lost.

I sneak a peek at Quinton, who seems to have realized that as well. He is no longer making his way to the exit but has turned around towards the library. I follow him again. There is no way I'm going out, anyway. We might actually end up having to sleep in the library tonight! This blizzard is crazy.

"Stop following me," Quinton hisses as he looks over his shoulder in my direction.

"You know, we might end up having to sleep in the library tonight," I say, smiling at how he immediately groans.

I doubt he wants to be alone with me right now, but it seems the world has other plans for us.

CHAPTER TWENTY

"Do you have siblings?"

No answer.

"What's your favorite color?"

The grip on his book tightens.

"Do you prefer beef or chicken?"

His eye is twitching in annoyance.

"Boxers or briefs?"

He chucks the book at me. I dodge; the book flies over the couch and hits a shelf. Both of us watch, slightly horrified, as the bookshelf squeaks and leans back, then forward, then back into place. Both of us exhale the breaths we held in fear.

"You shouldn't throw things indoors. Thought you were the smart one." I smile devilishly. It's nice not being the one to screw up this time, though technically the bookshelf didn't fall, so he didn't actually 'mess up', but it was close enough.

"Being around you kills brain cells," he huffs, getting up to retrieve his book.

"Do you have a question phobia?" I ask, watching him return to his previous seat. He gives me that 'are you an idiot' look, which is basically his answer. He doesn't believe in question phobia? I'm sure there's a scientific term for it, which he probably knows because he's friggin' weird, and I am sure he has it because he avoids them like they're his worst nightmare.

"What if I ask less personal questions? Will you answer?" I inquire.

Quinton, finally giving up, sighs and rests his book on the coffee table between us. His glare is set on me now. He looks less than happy about my game of '20 questions', though I am doing all the questioning.

"Cool! Let's begin, um, do you have any pets?"

"No." That's it. No explanation or anything?

"Why not?"

"Don't want any."

"Why not?" I ask again.

"Does it matter?" Quinton groans while rubbing his temple. I swear I see steam coming out of his ears. It's a simple question though, and it isn't personal! Is he going to make me be super specific and make him answer a question while also explaining it like it is some sort of essay?

"The point of asking a question is to get an answer. How is 'don't want any' an answer because it only brings up another question, which makes the first question basically useless. Really, I thought you were supposed to be smart." I thought my logic made perfect sense, but it seems Quinton does not think the same. He sends me another sharp glare before grabbing his book, signaling my game is over, lasting only one question. I think that's a new world record.

"Hey, come on! At least do something with me until we can get out of here."

"Watch TV," he says, flipping a page. He seems hell bent on keeping me from talking to him, asshole.

I'm about to do exactly as he told me to when the lights flicker off, sending us into darkness. Quinton groans because he knows the backup generators are about to kick on, but we were told to keep all 'unnecessary electronics' off during a blackout to save energy. TV is considered an 'unnecessary electronic.'

The lights kick back on and I grin. "Can't watch TV."

"Read a book."

Quinton doesn't realize what a dumb suggestion he has made until it's too late. The boy peeks over his book towards me like he's waiting for me to say something. He knows as well as I that I am the one who reads. It's my turn to give him the 'you're an idiot' look. He glares.

"We both know I'm not really the reading type." Hell, everyone knows that. I may study more than I used to, but that doesn't mean I've suddenly come to love books. I think I hate them more now, actually.

"Find some other way to entertain yourself. I'm not your mother," he hisses, returning his attention to the book. He hasn't got very far with me interrupting his concentration every few seconds. I see him from time to time preparing to turn a page, then he stops and has to re-read something because of me.

I grin, a devilishly good thought coming to mind.

Quinton seems relieved to have made it through two pages without my voice breaking his train of thought. His hopes are crushed by the sound of a 'click' coming from my lips. His eyebrow twitches at the sound of my tongue clicking to a made up beat.

"Stop that," he growls.

I do as he says, but hum instead. His grip on the book tightens. He's probably thinking of all the ways to get away with murder inside his head right now. To add to his annoyance, I slap my legs. The sound echoes through the empty library. Good thing the evil librarian isn't here to scold me for making a racket.

It's been about five minutes and he hasn't made it further than two pages. His patience is thinning. I see the veins throbbing in his skull until finally he slams the book against the table, hard. Dark eyes are glaring at me yet again. The glare doesn't even faze me anymore.

I smile and ask, "What's wrong, Quinton?"

"You're doing it on purpose," he hisses with narrowed eyes.

"You said to entertain myself. It's not my fault you can't read without silence."

"This is a library. It's supposed to be silent. If you're going to do that, then leave."

"Make me." I stick my nose in the air.

"Your maturity astounds me."

His anger only makes me happier. To piss him off more I stick my tongue out, proving that I really am immature, but it doesn't matter. The action sends him over the edge and he's jumping over the coffee table in an instant. I shout at the feeling of being tackled off the couch.

My shoulder hits the coffee table during the fall. That's going to leave a mark. We wrestle, rolling around on the ground, sending kicks and punches that, to be totally honest, aren't very rough. It is more like we are messing around, which is probably why the tussle only lasts a few seconds.

Quinton pushes himself off me, sitting next to the couch and resting his probably aching head on the cushion. "You're annoying."

I shrug, leaning my back against the coffee table I hit earlier. "I try."

"My dad never allowed me to have pets when I was little," Quinton says so suddenly that it leaves me shocked.

"Huh?" It takes me a second to realize he's answering the question from earlier. I open my mouth to speak but decide not to. I think if I stay quiet rather than ask more questions or pester him to answer quickly, he'll actually say more. Quinton doesn't seem to like to be forced into things, so it's better if I just allow him to go at his own pace.

The boy isn't looking at me. His eyes close when he speaks. "My father was never strict or had many rules. Most of the time I got things I asked for: toys, food, books and clothes, but the one thing I could not have, no matter how much I begged or asked, was a pet."

The topic seemed touchy. I feel there's a reason he was so reluctant earlier to answer but why? What's so weird about the rule of not having a pet? It could have been because they couldn't afford it or his father was allergic or something. Quinton, obviously, knows the real reason, but it doesn't look like he's willing to say.

"So why not have one now? It sounds like you wanted one." I'm trying not to sound pushy or like he has to answer the question. Quinton is actually speaking and answering me, so I want to make this last.

Quinton runs a hand through his hair. It looks like he's done with this question. He pushes himself to sit up fully, presses his back to the couch and turns his attention to me. "I don't want to answer that one. Ask something else," he says, arms crossed.

I feel a bit disappointed to not hear his reason but I won't pass up this chance. I worked so hard to get him to open up a bit. I've got to take it now while I can. For all I know, this may be a once in a lifetime opportunity! Grinning, I lean forward and ask, "Do you have siblings?"

"No." I'm about to comment on how I should have known that since he seems too snotty to have siblings to tease him, but Quinton shocks me by asking his own question, "Do you want siblings?"

"You're asking me questions?" I'm surprised. I never pegged Quinton as the type of guy to want to learn about others. He seems content not knowing anything about those around him. He shrugs, choosing not to explain why he's asking. I decide not to push my luck and just go with it. "Yeah, if I had a younger sibling, I'd want her to be a girl."

"Why?" With the way Quinton's looking at me, I can tell he has no desire to have a younger sister. Figures. Loner to the end.

"Because I'd like to have someone to tease but also love and protect. Oh! But if I had a brother, I'd want him to be older so he could give me advice and we could mess around but, it'd be him who'd get in trouble if one of us got hurt!" I laugh while Quinton rolls his eyes at my reasoning for wanting my brother to be older. I think it's a good reason. Everyone knows the youngest gets away with more!

"Have you ever had a girlfriend?" I squirm a bit after asking. The idea of Quinton being with a girl makes me uncomfortable. Maybe it's because he's such a bitter guy that I can't even imagine him having a girlfriend. Girls want attention. Quinton definitely can't give them that.

My cheeks feel really warm. I rub one of my hands against them, pretending to scratch it, when actually I'm testing the heat. They're actually warm; I'm not imagining it. Shit, I'm blushing. Ah, please don't notice. I don't even know how I would explain my blush.

Quinton either doesn't notice or doesn't care about my sudden blush. Instead, he answers; not sounding bothered, "Yes."

I'm surprised. Anyone would be. Quinton is someone I could never, ever dream of being in a relationship. Relationships involve feelings and caring for another human being, two things that Quinton is not capable of...or at least I believed he was not capable of. I'm half tempted to claim this 'girlfriend' doesn't count because if he had a girlfriend, they had to have dated in middle school.

Middle school girlfriends don't count, you're, like, 13. Dating at 13 is holding hands and cuddling and going on dates while your parents watch you like hawks.

"Middle school girlfriends don't count. When did you two break up?" I ask.

"A month ago."

My jaw drops.

"You were dating someone last month!?" My voice was loud enough to wake people in China, which makes Quinton send me a sharp glare. He doesn't seem pleased with how loud I'm being, or maybe he doesn't like the obvious disbelief in my tone. "Liar!" I point an accusing finger. "You're pulling my leg! You don't even go home during breaks, so how would you two even meet up?"

There was no way he had a girlfriend. There was no way! Why do I feel hurt?

Quinton rolls his eyes. "Believe what you want. Drop it, ask something else."

"No way! What's her name? Where's she from? How could she date a dick like you? You were blackmailing her, weren't you?" That has to be it. There is no way a girl would date Quinton, unless it was purely for his looks. I can't see him bringing a girl flowers or telling her she's beautiful or saying 'I love you,' so there is no way he was in a 'real' relationship.

How could he have even met a girl? You have to speak to one to date one and Quinton doesn't talk to girls. Well, I guess that could be why they broke up. Who would want to date an ass like him?

Quinton throws his head back with a groan. "I shouldn't have said anything."

"I want to meet her."

"No way in hell," he hisses, which only makes me not believe him more.

"Why not? Cause it's not true, right?" I don't know why Quinton would lie about that, though. If he was lying, he would have said they were still dating, right? What would be the reason for telling me he had a girlfriend if he didn't? Maybe I believe him and that's what bothers me most.

"Because divulging personal information about another person without their permission, whether it be your ex-girlfriend or not, is wrong."

Quinton has a point there. She isn't here to say whether she's ok with me knowing anything about her. If people don't know about her, then there must be a reason. Maybe she's shy? Or maybe she's embarrassed of Quinton? Heh, yeah right. What is there to be embarrassed about? He's smart, handsome, and obviously going to be incredibly successful. Or so all the girls say.

I huff, not liking that he has once again put me in my place. It bothers me to know he had a relationship with someone... that... that I know nothing about because I'm a curious person and I'm not jealous. Nope, not jealous at all! Heh... heh...

"At least tell me her name?" I bite my lip, hoping to get something out of him.

Quinton seems reluctant before replying, "Autumn."

Autumn? I never heard of her. There's a lot of girls here at school but Autumn is a pretty unusual name, so if I heard it I'm sure I'd remember it. Then again, she probably doesn't even go here.

Why am I so bothered about this?

"Why are you so shocked?" Quinton asks, cocking a brow.

"Because it's shocking," I answer, trying my best not to pout. "I didn't know you had feelings."

Quinton rolls his eyes at my answer. "If you can have a girlfriend, so can I. Oops, my bad. You didn't have a girlfriend officially, did you?"

I glare at the bastard for making me think about Gabby. Of course, he'd bring up something to piss me off. His smirk shows me he finds the greatest of amusements through humiliating me, not that I don't feel the same way, but what's that saying, it's fine so long as it doesn't happen to me?

"Why'd you have to bring her up?" I groan. "That's low."

Quinton shrugs, not seeming to care. "I warned you."

That's right, he did, or rather, he tried to. I didn't heed his warning and ended up getting hurt. How could he have expected me to listen, though? He's Quinton. The coldest, cruelest and most inhuman devil spawn that I'm sure has ever walked this Earth. I doubt if any person could ever reach his level of asshole-ness. Yes, there are levels. Since when did either of us listen to each other? Why did he bother trying to warn me? He hates me. I hate him, or I did hate him. He is making things complicated.

"Why?" I ask.

My curiosity always gets the best of me, but that's something to be curious about, right? Someone would want to know why a kid, who they thought hated them with an immense passion, would try to help them out. Enemies do not help enemies. If anything, one would expect Quinton to side up with Gabby and forge an evil plot against me. Quinton is the evil villain type. I could totally see him in a black cape.

Quinton shrugs, like he actually isn't sure why, which is weird. Quinton always has an answer to things, always has a way out, but right now it looks like he's actually not sure why. "I guess." He ponders over his thoughts. "I thought no one deserved something like that, not even you."

I should be insulted. It sounded like he was saying I'm the type of person who deserves to have some bad things happen to them, but instead, I feel kind of good. At least Quinton doesn't hate me to that point, to the point that he wants people to lie and deceive me. Strange how the one I call my enemy appears to be the one least likely to stab me in the back. I can believe that he doesn't hate me as much as he puts on...and the same goes for me. I don't know how to react with this new information or rather new feeling.

"Thanks," I grumble, avoiding all eye contact. I don't like feeling grateful, especially not towards Quinton. Knowing him, it'd go straight to his head, inflating his already colossal ego. "You know...for trying to warn me about her."

"You'd do the same for me," he replies, sounding so sure of himself, like he doesn't even have to question it.

And it's sad because it's true. I want to tell myself that I wouldn't, that I'd let the girl crush him into dust, break his heart, rip his very soul from his chest and spit on it, but just thinking about it pisses me off. I wouldn't want that to happen to Quinton. If I knew the girl he liked was messing with him, I feel that I'd definitely tell him. Sure, we may argue, insult one another and get in the occasional fistfight, but I don't want to hurt him.

Ok, that may be a lie. In the beginning, I'm pretty sure I did. If I broke one of his bones, I would be singing hallelujah, but it's different now. I still want to deflate that ego of his. I still want to beat him and prove him wrong. I still want to punch his smug face every time he disproves me; those feelings are still there and strong, but the hatred has simmered down. It's no longer what one could classify as hatred. Hatred is too strong a word. It's different. I don't know how to explain it. Don't know if I can quite put my finger on the feeling. The closest I can get to explain what I mean is this; I wish for us to be on equal terms. Is that understandable?

Times like this, when we're actually talking to each other, I hate to admit that I find them kind of enjoyable. Talking with Quinton is different. Quinton is different. I don't have to hide or pretend to be the perfect prince who could do no wrong. I can say whatever I want without the fear of him telling a newspaper about how 'incompetent' I am or how I'm a total idiot and this kingdom's future will be ruined thanks to me. I can tell Quinton anything. I honestly believe that. Shit, it's sad but true, and he'd never tell. Sure, he'd make fun of me, use it against me in our own arguments, but that's it, only between us...and I like that feeling. I like not being on edge. I like not fearing the consequences of my own words. It's nice...

Not that I would ever tell him that. Never, ever, ever!

"It's your turn." I mumble hoping to stop myself from thinking any further.

"Hmm?"

"To ask a question." I don't feel like talking about this anymore. It's uncomfortable. It makes me think about weird things...like the fact that I enjoy Quinton's company more than I let on. This is too mushy. I can't do mushy.

Our game of 20 questions goes on for a few more minutes. The lights flicker back onto full power, signaling that the backup generators are off and the power is back on. A few minutes later, security guards appear, claiming the blizzard ended a while ago and they have moved the snow from the sidewalks, allowing the students to return to their dorms. They request Quinton and I to do the same.

The two of us nod, get up and pull our layers of clothing back on. We look like penguins, bundled up so tightly and moving towards the doors at a wobbling type pace. I try to hold back my laughter, but it comes out, anyway.

"What?" Quinton asks, his voice muffled by his scarf.

"We look like penguins," I laugh, realizing my arms cannot lie straight at my sides because of the amount of clothing I have on. Quinton rolls his eyes at me, but doesn't disagree.

Pushing open the doors, I'm shocked at the amount of snow pushed away from the sidewalks. We have at least four feet of snow. It's like the walkways have their own walls. I'm half tempted to shove Quinton in it and cackle maniacally while I run but, to my credit, I resist such childish urges.

There's no way we can get into the courtyard with this amount of snow. We'll have to take the long way back to the dorms. We end up doing just that, but the long walk isn't at all a bad one. In fact, it's kind of nice, walking side by side in a comfortable silence. There's no fighting, no discomfort, nothing but silence and it actually feels ok.

When we come to a fork in the path, Quinton turns one way and I the other. I blink rapidly, watching Quinton's back for a moment before asking, "Where are you going?"

Quinton faces me. "To my dorm," he replies.

I realize then that our dorms are in opposite directions. Shock runs through me when a feeling of disappointment consumes me at his words. I'm disappointed that we're parting ways so soon. Our conversation was going so smoothly, smoother than any conversation we had before. I know we weren't talking during the walk and now I want to slap myself for not doing so. I wanted it to last for as long as it could, considering it'll likely never happen again. I'm sure Quinton went along with it knowing that if he didn't, I'd bug him until we could return to our dorms.

"Ah...right." I actually have to stop myself from requesting him to follow me back to my dorm. Langley isn't there. He could sleep in his bed, but sleeping with the enemy in the room is weird. Rather, that's what I tell myself. Not to mention if Langley finds out I'd get an earful. Who would sleep with the enemy? That's madness.

Nodding to myself more, I say goodbye and head to my dorm. Is it sad that I peer back a few times just to see him walk away?

As I lie in bed, I replay today's events; the snowball fight with Quinton, hot chocolate and 20 questions. It was definitely different from our other encounters. It seems like only when there is no one else around can we have a 'civil' conversation.

It's also only when we're alone that I learn anything about him. I learned a lot more about Quinton today than I have over the past year. How pathetic. That thought alone is enough to put a smile as wide as a mile on my face. End me now, I've gone mad.

Some of it could be insignificant, but to me, if Quinton divulges anything, from his middle name to the length of his pinky toe, it's important. He's not an open book for anyone to read. Getting Quinton to speak is hard enough, so getting him to speak about himself is a miracle. I should get a freaking award! Seriously, give me one. I have worked hard to get to this point. Some things are sticking out more in my mind than others, though.

The girlfriend. Now that stands out the most. Thinking about it makes my chest hurt. I actually have to bring up my hand to rub against the area, hoping to lessen the slight pinching sensation. It must be because it's so shocking that I feel so odd. Quinton never seemed to show any interest in anyone, but maybe even the demon Quinton is interested in things like sex, right?

A blush forms on my face at the idea of Quinton and sex. Wait! No! I mean, the idea of Quinton being interested in sex. It's definitely not the idea of sex with Quinton that is making me blush. Nope, it isn't. It isn't. It isn't.

What kind of girl could date Quinton? They're broken up, but it was only a month ago. They could get back together, but the guy is an asshole without a single romantic bone in his body, I'm sure of it! People usually want romance. They want to be woo-ed and Quinton cannot woo.

I laugh aloud. Quinton, woo someone? Yeah, right! I can't even imagine him buying her flowers or apologizing for something he did. The bastard would probably assume it's her fault, and they'd get into an argument, so how? How!?

What's she like to put up with him? Is she nice? Understanding? Or is she possibly exactly like him? Shit, the world does not need a female Quinton. There is no way the universe could be that cruel. The world wouldn't make two people who could be described as the biggest assholes on earth get together. If they ever reproduce, they'd have an army of glaring evil children that would probably conquer the universe.

She'd have to be like him though, to put up with him unless he acts differently around her. That wouldn't be surprising. Perhaps Quinton cares about her. He hates me so, of course, he'd treat me the way he does. That doesn't mean he'd treat her the same way. So how would he act around her? Is he nice? Does he take her on dates? Pay for her to see a movie? Does he say things like 'I love you' or tell her she's beautiful? Does he laugh and smile around her? What would that look like? What does his laugh sound like? Do they hold hands and kiss? What's that like? Have they... slept together? How long were they dating? Were they serious?

Why do I care so much? Gah, it doesn't matter. I don't need to know every little detail about him or his relationships. It doesn't matter. I don't care. I don't care at all.

CHAPTER TWENTY-ONE

Maybe I do care because I find myself on the verge of doing something that could get me into a hell of a lot of trouble. Here I am, shielding myself behind a tree like a total stalker, watching Quinton make his way to the front gates, exit pass in hand.

He's leaving campus grounds. To where? His ex-girlfriend or possibly soon to be girlfriend again? I really want to know, really, really, really want to know. How can I get out, though? You have to show your pass to the guards and they open the gates, allowing you to get out, but they know me. The guards know I am not allowed to leave campus grounds without an army to watch after me so, how?

Ideas like climbing the wall come to mind, but there's no actual way to climb them. Feet of snow still cover the ground. I probably can't make it to the wall without freezing to death first. Not to mention there are cameras everywhere. Sure, security is lax during break, but there's still someone watching security footage. So how do I get out?

It's too late. Quinton has already gone through the gates and is on his way towards town. If I made it out now, I'd probably catch up, but seeing as I still have no plan of escape, it's too late. He'll be long gone before I make it out.

Grumbling, I make my way back to the dorms. This sucks. Can't dad be a little less protective and allow me access to the outside world? It's kind of hard to have fun when there are a hundred bodyguards watching my every move. I can't even go to a fair! If someone approaches me, they get tackled. What a pain.

I wonder if I asked if he'd change his mind. What if I went in disguise? It's winter, so I'd be bundled up under layers of clothing. No one will recognize me! There are a few movies out that I'd like to see. If I asked dad he'd just say I could watch whatever I want when I get home on our own TV since if he wants it, he gets it, but I have never been to a movie theater before! I really want to go and if I asked Quinton to go, then maybe he'd be ok with it.

"No."

"Come on, please dad! I swear this will be the only time I ask!" I'm begging on my knees here. Not that he knows that since we're speaking over the phone, but still. "How am I supposed to hang out with friends if all we can do is watch TV on campus?"

"I said you could leave but you need an escort," Dad answers, referring to the army of men he would send with me.

"An escort is one or two guys, not an entire army!"

"I do not send an army."

"Fifty is an army, Dad." To me it is. They're on all sides of me. I can't even see past them! It's like a wall of penguins surrounding me. I don't know what my thing with penguins is about lately, but they seem to fit well into my life. "My friends are weirded out with so many people. We can't talk normally or feel comfortable with so many eyes on us."

"I don't see why—"

Of course you don't! You're used to it!

"They should only feel that way if they have something to hide. Do they have something to hide?"

"No, you're too suspicious of everyone!" I shout, banging my head against the mattress. He treats me like a five-year-old. "I swear we will go straight to the movies and come straight back and—and I'll take that kid I was telling you about!"

"The one that pisses you off? Why would you take him?" Dad laughs. Ah, I have not told him about how recently we've kind of been getting along. A little.

"Ah, well, we've kind of been on good terms lately and he's top of our class in everything! He's like a superhero or something, I swear. He's better than any guard you will send with me, I know it!" Trust me, I have felt enough of his hits to know that he'd knock out any attacker if he was going 100%. Not that I need to tell my dad that, because then he'd definitely say no. And probably kick Quinton out of school.

"I don't know, Aron. You realize you aren't like everyone else, right? If something were to happen to you…"

He's right. I know he's right. As much as I try to be normal, try to be like everyone else, I'm still not. I receive death threats daily, some more real than others. There are people who would hurt me whenever they get the chance. There are also people who would run towards me the moment they see me and they could or could not harm me as well but, that doesn't change the fact that I'd like to do things like everyone else.

I want to go to the movies with friends. I want to go to the park or to a fair and play games or get cotton candy. I want to get a license and a car. I want to walk out the front door without worrying about being recognized. I want a lot of things that I'll never get, but right now I have a chance to get something I probably won't get again. Is it wrong for me to take the only chance I could get?

"I know that." Maybe my disappointment came across more than I thought because I can practically hear the hurt in my father's sigh. I'm sure he doesn't want to say no. I'm sure he wants to let me go but I understand his reasoning. "It's fine Dad, forget I asked. I'll watch it at home. Thanks for listening."

"Aron, hold on," Dad groans. "Listen, you can go- "

"Really?!" I don't think I've ever been so excited before! Holy shit, I think I'm going to cry.

"Listen, I have conditions."

"Ok, sure, I don't care what they are!"

"You may go with this friend of yours, but you have to take two guards with you. I will tell them to keep at a distance and to dress like civilians. You are not to leave their sights, do you understand?"

I nod until I realize he can't see me nodding. "Yeah, I understand."

"And when you're outside, I want you bundled up. People cannot see your face; keep it hidden even when you're in the theater. You may go out for the day and do as you wish, but if the guards sense any danger or say you cannot do something, then you must listen. This will not be a normal thing either, so don't continuously ask for it. Ok?"

I didn't even expect for this to be a onetime thing, so I don't care. I nod so quickly my neck hurts. "I understand, thanks, Daddy!"

"Don't Daddy me, you little shit," he laughs. "I want you to understand that I'm allowing this because I believe you are old enough to know that you have to listen and be careful. You understand you aren't like everyone else, Aron. I want you to have these experiences of hanging out with you friends, I really do, but..."

"It's fine, Dad. I'm glad you're allowing this at least once. If it never happens again, I'd be fine with that." I think he feels bad for hearing me say that, seeing as I'm sure he wishes for me to have fun like everyone else, but I want him to know that I'm grateful for his decision today. "I'm going to go ask my friend when he wants to go. Thanks again Dad, I'll call you with the date we're going out, love you."

"Love you too, son."

After hanging up, I scream. I scream so loud I'm surprised my window didn't break. I'm sure someone will be on their way up, asking why I screamed my head off, but I don't care. My heart's racing. I can't keep still. I can't believe my dad just agreed to let me go off campus for a whole day without an entire army in toe!

Sure, I will go with two bodyguards, but they'll be dressed as civilians. He said he'd tell them to keep their distance so it'll be like they weren't there at all! Not to mention I've never been to a movie theater. We have one of our own at home so that I would stop asking to go, but this is different. There will be other people there. I'll have to buy a ticket and get movie popcorn and candy and soda!

Ah, now I have to talk Quinton into it. For all I know, he may not even want to go or even consider it. I could ask someone else, but there isn't anyone else on campus I'd like to go with. Wait a second. Why do I want to go with Quinton? He'd be lousy to spend a whole day with! He'll probably say no just to be an ass. I'm being stupid. I should ask someone else to go.

How has it come to this? This is practically like a...a...date. I shiver at the thought. I'm definitely asking someone else.

And yet here I am, standing before Quinton's door with jello legs. I can't seem to stop shaking. Why am I so nervous? Stop it, legs. If you keep this up, I'm going to topple over.

It's getting dark out. I'm only assuming Quinton has returned from town. Hell, he could still be out enjoying his single life, doing things I rather not think about because thinking of Quinton like that is disgusting. Yep...

While raising my fist, I realize that it's not only my legs that are shaking but also my whole body. I see my fist moving from side to side. Crap, what's wrong with me? I shake my head and grasp my wrist with my other hand. I don't know why I think that will stop my shaking.

I knock a little louder than I mean to, but when am I ever quiet? I'm biting my lips nervously and I think I'm actually shaking more thanks to the obvious sounds of movement within. A few seconds pass before Quinton opens the door. He looks surprised to see me.

"What do you want?" He asks, keeping the door only halfway open, probably to keep me from coming in, asshole.

"I was wondering if you had plans this Thursday." I wasn't sure if he'd want to go tomorrow since he was out today. He may have been gone only an hour or he may have been gone all day, I'm not sure. So I thought that two days from now would be a good option.

"Why?" Quinton is reluctant to answer. I'm reluctant to answer. I have to though or he won't come along, not that it matters. I can just go ask someone else.

"Uh, it's just that I got permission to leave campus," I mumble. I can barely hear myself speaking. When Quinton doesn't ask me to repeat myself, I take that as he heard me. He still doesn't answer if he's busy on Thursday though, so I take that as his way of saying to continue. "I...I have to have two guards come along, but they'll be dressed as civilians and they'll keep their distance, so it's not like they'd bother us or anything. I wanted to go see a movie and w-was wondering if y'know...you'd come along...or something..."

Stupid, stupid, stupid! I sound stupid. Why did I ask him? I could have asked someone else or even gone on my own. It's not like Quinton would be any fun to hang out with for the day. He'll probably insult me all day or he won't even agree to go. What will I do if he says no? That would be...

"Ok."

"Huh?" What did he just say?

"What time do you want to leave?" He asks, finally letting his hold go on his door. He leans against the doorway, waiting for my answer, but my mouth has gone dry. Honestly, I don't think I expected him to agree, so to see him waiting patiently for our time of departure finally makes my legs give out.

"What's wrong with you?" Quinton asks, having jumped down to the floor after I had fallen over. My legs continue shaking.

"Uh..." How am I supposed to answer that? "It's just...my dad never lets me do anything like see a movie in town, so when you said yes...I think I realized this is actually happening." Yeah, let's go with that.

Quinton rolls his eyes.

I inform Quinton of the time we'll be leaving and what I planned for the day. He didn't seem to have any complaints because he did not comment on much of anything other than nodding at what I suggested. After I made sure he knew what we were doing, I headed back to my dorm, where I am now lying in my bed, staring up at my ceiling in disbelief.

I can't believe I'm actually going out into town this Thursday...

I can't stop shaking.

CHAPTER TWENTY-TWO

I'm up three hours early on Thursday morning. My clock flashes 5:00 am at me, proving that I have officially lost it. I can't even sleep. That's how excited I am for today. Why I'm excited about hanging out with Quinton for a whole day, I'll never know, but I am.

I guess because this will be the first time I've gone into town on my own, or rather as 'on my own' as it's going to get, seeing as I'll always have guards around me. I push myself out of bed and get ready, occasionally sitting around and watching whatever crap is on TV this early in the morning.

After informing Quinton of my plans for today, he recommended going to a café around 8 for coffee or whatever I felt like getting. I, of course, agreed. Having never been to a café, I was more than excited at the idea of going to one. I've had coffee from cafes before, which is how I learned I don't like coffee, but I've never been inside. I always asked a maid or butler to go fetch me a French vanilla cappuccino, seeing as those are the only 'coffee like' things I will drink.

I feel like a kindergartner on a field trip.

I swear the world hates me because when I look at the clock; it says only 57 minutes have passed. Damn, it isn't even 6 yet. Quinton seems like the early bird type, but I doubt even he's up this early. Ugh, can the time go any slower?

It can, because it did. By 7:30, I'm ready to gouge my eyes out. Said eyes feel heavy, but they won't close. My legs won't stop shaking, my hands won't stop sweating, and my heart's ready to burst out of my chest. I groan as I rub my hands against my face. This is crazy. I need to calm down.

I repeat this to myself for a good twenty minutes before deciding to get up and head to Quinton's. It's nearly 8 so I'm sure he's ready to go. My assumption is proven correct when I make it to his dorm to see him exiting it, dressed and ready for our day.

"Good morning!" I shout louder than necessary. Quinton doesn't comment, seeming to understand the reasoning behind why I'm so excited.

"Morning," he says in a gruff voice. He must not have gotten up too long ago. Maybe he isn't the early bird type after all?

"The guards will be at the gates, but once we get into town, they'll back off enough to appear as a separate group," I say, my voice still sounding overly excited. I have every reason to be. This is actually happening. My conversation with my dad wasn't a dream but real! I'm going into town. Holy shit!

Quinton nods. The two of us silently make our way to the gates. My hands shake even as I show the security guards my pass. We exit the gates, guards in toe, and I swear my legs are about to give out again until I feel a hand on my arm.

"Don't fall, idiot," Quinton mumbles, his hot breath fanning over my cheeks.

Thanks to the scarf wrapped tightly around me, he doesn't notice my sudden blush. "Uh, thanks."

Quinton removes his hand, and my arm suddenly feels cold. I blame it on the weather.

We make our way into town and, just as father promised; the guards back off enough to appear as a separate group. I feel myself grinning so widely my cheeks might split open. Thanks to the enormous amount of layering I'm wearing, no one notices me. All they can see are basically my eyes, and it's not like many people are paying attention. Everyone is doing their own thing, completely ignoring the two teenage boys going into a café.

The café is warm. Even the colors give off a warm feeling, dark browns and creams that go well with the color of coffee and doughnuts. I find myself, like a child, pressing my hands and face against the glass, examining the enormous amount of doughnuts laid out before me. There's so many I don't know what to get.

"They smell good," I mumble, my breath fogging the glass. "I don't know what to get."

"Get what you like," Quinton says, pulling out his wallet.

"Ah, I can buy it," I offer, pulling out mine as well. He's already handing his cash to the girl behind the counter, who is giggling at him, might I add. Even outside of school, he's a chick magnet. I hate him.

"Why?" He asks, giving me an odd look. "This isn't a date."

"What? I d-didn't say it was. It was my idea, so I thought." What am I even saying? I'm making myself look more stupid than the other day.

Quinton smirks. "Are you going to get something or continue bumbling over your words all day?"

"Shut up," I hiss, deciding to get a French Vanilla Cappuccino along with a doughnut. It doesn't take long to have it brought to me, and the two of us find a booth situated so that people can't easily see us. I have my back facing everyone so I can remove my scarf and jacket, allowing me to breathe.

"Do you come here often?" I ask, blowing on my steaming drink. Normally I'm not much of a cappuccino drinker either, but they're fantastic on days like this where I feel like my fingers are going to freeze and fall off.

Quinton nods. "More so during breaks than during school."

"I knew you'd be the type of guy to like coffee. You probably sit around sipping on it while reading the newspaper," I tease.

"It's good to be aware of what's happening in the world."

"It's, like, you're fifty or something."

"Or rather wiser than most."

How very Quinton, turning my insult into a strange form of a compliment. I hate him. I knew I should have picked someone else to hang out with for the day. Ten minutes in and I'm ready to punch his smug little face. He knows it too because the bastard's still smirking in that 'I'm so superior' kind of way.

"I hate you," I grunt, sipping from my drink.

"The feeling's mutual."

Yet he agreed to come spend the day with me. Would two people who really hate each other go out for coffee together? We both know the answer to that, but are too stubborn to admit it to ourselves. Maybe Quinton has already accepted that and is simply playing along with me, knowing that I'm too stubborn to admit it. That's probably how it is, seeing that he's always a step ahead of me.

"The movie doesn't start until three. What should we do now?" I ask, seeing as it's around 10 now. Quinton mentioned earlier that there's a good place around here to have lunch, which we'll go to around noon or one, but that means we've got time to kill.

"We can hit the main street. They have some shops you might like," he answers, weaving through the streets with ease. Perhaps it was a good thing I brought Quinton because I would have gotten lost had I come on my own, or with someone who didn't know the streets.

As we walk down the main street, I hold my scarf closer to my face. There are a good bit of people out, though they aren't paying any mind to Quinton and I. Still, I press my scarf closer, shielding everything but my eyes. Quinton stops at my side, gesturing to a few stores he thinks may catch my interest.

For the next two hours, Quinton basically watches me pull everything from the racks or shelves to examine them. I drag him from store to store, and by drag I mean literally, because there were more times than not when he insisted that he simply stand outside and wait for me.

"You're spending quite a lot of taxpayers' money," Quinton says as he gazes at my growing pile of purchases.

I send him a glare that he rolls his eyes at. Hey, he's the one who agreed to come along when he's aware that I don't exactly get out much...or at all. I choose to ignore him, not wanting to ruin my day by having yet another argument. I continue to pull out shirts, holding them against my chest in order to see if I like them or not.

Quinton sits on the floor, watching as I grab one object after the other. Every now and again I hear him chuckle when I find yet another shirt I like and toss it into the 'I'm getting this' pile at his side.

"Aren't you getting anything?" I ask, peeking at the boy out of the corner of my eye.

Quinton leans back on his hands and shakes his head. "No, unlike you, I'm not made of money."

"I can get you something," I offer, feeling bad because I'm the only one getting things. It was my idea to come out today anyway, so it's only right that I get him something, right?

Quinton snorts. "I don't need anything."

"But is there something you want?" I doubt he means to, but his eyes dart to the side. He's looking at something, but quickly he catches himself and gives me a sharp no. I laugh. "Yes, you do, you were just looking at it. What is it?"

I dig through the wrack that I believe he was looking at. Behind me, I hear Quinton getting up. He grabs my arm, pulling on it as he says, "Seriously, there's nothing I need."

"I didn't ask if you needed something. I asked if you wanted it," I huff. I thought he was supposed to be smart? Doesn't he know the difference between want and need? Even I know that!

"What does it matter? I don't want you buying me anything," he grunts, sounding annoyed.

"You could just tell me what it is or I can grab something at random and buy it for you," I suggest, sending him a grin over my shoulder. His glare tells me he doesn't like my idea.

Grumbling to himself, he reaches to the rack of clothes slowly. I watch, as he seems to have an inner battle with himself over whether he should actually pick out what he wants or grab at random. I don't see what his problem is. It's not like this store is crazy expensive. Then again, nothing to me is expensive.

"Come on, just get it!" I shout, slapping my hand against his back.

He grunts before grabbing a black leather jacket, tossing it into the 'getting this' pile. I grin. "Now, was that so hard?"

"Shut up," he hisses, throwing himself to the floor again to wait for me to finish. "Hurry up, the movie's starting soon."

"Hurry up, the movie's staring soon," I mock in a high-pitched tone. "You sound like my mother."

"If you didn't act like a child, then I wouldn't have to."

Ohoho, I am not buying him that jacket. Here I am, trying to be nice, and he's being an ass. Typical Quinton. Why did I bring him again? I must have been nutty for even considering dragging his ass along for the day!

After paying for the mountain of clothes I got, the two of us make our way to the theater, after I dropped off my bags to one of the guards since lugging them around the rest of the day would be a pain. I'm shaking once again in the theater. Quinton keeps giving me that 'quit it' look, but I can't help it. I've never been to a movie theater.

"It's nothing to be so excited about," Quinton says as we wait in line to retrieve our popcorn and drinks.

It isn't for him; someone who I'm sure has been to the theater many times before. I, however, am completely different. It's the experience that excites me. I have my home theater, but most of the time it's just me sitting there and that—I don't know—it goes to show how alone I really am and that bothers me.

"You don't get it," I say to him. Even my voice shakes with excitement.

By the time we're seated, I feel like my heart is going to explode. It isn't only the idea of seeing a movie that makes me this way, though; it's the whole day. Thinking back on it, I realize I am doing things today that normal teenagers do. I went to a café, ran around in a few stores, got lunch at a restaurant where a meal costs less than $50 and now here I am, with a "friend," at the movies.

"You need to get out more," Quinton says beside me, his eyes on my hand that's shaking against our shared armrest.

I chuckle. "Yeah, well, that will not happen but, thanks for, you know, hanging out with me today."

Quinton shrugs like it's no big deal when, in fact, it is. "Whatever."

"You could have said no," I mumble. The lights are dimming, signaling the movie is about to start. The people who were previously talking fall silent.

"I could have," He hums.

I want to ask why he didn't, but I keep thinking if I do, it'll lead into an argument that will ruin this day, so I simply nod and turn my attention to the big screen.

CHAPTER TWENTY-THREE

My day of-partial-freedom is over before I know it. I wish I could have stopped time, even if it were for another thirty seconds. The thought of not having such an opportunity looms over my head like a cloud of despair. I know not to ask my father for such a day again. I pushed him this time, but that does not mean he will be pushed again.

He already informed me that this would not be an everyday occurrence. I'm lucky I got today. I won't ask for another, though deep down, I really want to. I'd really love to come out more often, even if it's with Quinton.

He may be an asshole, but he's not totally intolerable. There are moments where he seems a little human, where he smiles or chuckles at something I said or did or he changes the subject, aware that it may lead to an argument that would ruin this day for me. There were a few of those moments today where we could have argued. I did nothing to stop it, but Quinton would navigate our conversation in another direction. He could have allowed himself to wreck this day for me, but he didn't, which makes me think he does. Though they're buried deep, have some feelings for those around him.

Or right now, his actions prove to me he doesn't completely hate me. Our movie ended. We got dinner at a different restaurant, joked around a bit and were now on our way back to campus; much slower than necessary.

It's colder now than it was this morning. The sun set a while ago, seeing as it sets so early during the winter. The wind has picked up, causing the both of us to bury our faces nose deep in our scarves that are wrapped tightly around our necks. Our hands are shoved into our jacket pockets, even with gloves my fingers are chilled and I'm sure his are too.

Most people are rushing to get home in order to get out of this cold weather. Quinton does not ask why I'm dragging my feet, nor does he insist I move faster. He could. He should. It's freezing out here. I'm sure he wants to be in his dorm right now, in the heat, wrapped up in a blanket or taking a hot shower. Instead, he's walking slowly beside me, eyes red from the cold, dry air.

I wonder if maybe, somewhere very, very deep in his chest, if there's a heart. He should tap into it more often. He's a lot better company with his mouth shut.

Sounds like something he would say to me.

I smile at my own thoughts. The movement beneath my scarf catches Quinton's attention, causing him to ask, "What?"

I shake my head. "Nothing, was just thinking you might have a heart after all."

"Of course I do," he scoffs. "You can't live without one."

I roll my eyes at him. "You know what I really mean."

"Hmm." His shoulders shiver at a sudden powerful gust of wind that nearly sends the both of us toppling over. The wind should be enough of a hint for me to move faster, get home now before we both freeze, but my feet do not pick up their pace. I want to enjoy being off campus a little longer.

"Did you have fun today?" Quinton asks. I can't see what kind of expression he's making with his face covered, but I doubt he'd have any expression at all. Quinton rarely shows anything.

Smiling sadly, I nod. "Yeah, it was great while it lasted."

We make it to the gates much sooner than I wanted. I inform the guards that there's no need to help carry my things to my room. I can do that much, and they look like they're about ready to turn into human popsicles.

Beside me Quinton grabs a few bags while saying, "I'll help."

"It's fine," I mumble, knowing that even if I said that, he'll still help. He's as stubborn as I am. Maybe that's why we fight so much? It's hard to talk with someone who is as bullheaded as you are.

Quinton eyes my dorm, seeming not to like the obvious difference. While his dorm is nice, mine is extravagant. It's to be expected. The students who live here are from noble families. They're people of importance, not to say that Quinton and the students in Dorm D aren't important! That's just the way the world works, I guess.

While parents of the students or Dorm D may complain about the obvious difference, they cannot do much about it. The parents of the students in Dorm A, however, hold money and power. They will pay the school as much as it needs to give their students an excellent education and to live in an environment similar to the one they live at home.

"Talk about favoritism," he whispers, probably not meaning for me to hear.

I chuckle. "Jealous?"

"Annoyed." Shocker.

"You're always annoyed." I kick open my door, seeing as my hands are mostly full.

Quinton doesn't walk in until I actually say he's allowed in. I don't see why he needs my permission. What is he, a freaking vampire? I burst into his room without his permission. Perhaps he's trying to show me he's better than me. That pisses me off.

"Don't forget your jacket," I say, grabbing said jacket and tossing it at him. He catches it, surprised I remembered, or that he had forgotten. The boy nods to me one last time before exiting, leaving me alone.

I wonder what Langley would say if he knew I spent the day with Quinton. I bet he, along with everyone else, would be shocked. We don't seem to get along, but like I said earlier, that's hard to do when we are so stubborn. He's stuck up and always tries to show how I'm beneath him while I'm too stubborn to admit defeat.

I know I can say whatever I want to Quinton and he won't back down either. It's fun having someone to battle with, you could say. It's fun having someone who doesn't cower at the sight of me but stands stronger and taller. I will only admit to myself that I respect that part of Quinton. He definitely doesn't let others think themselves better than him...because I would imagine a few people are better than him. He's Mr. Perfect after all. Pisses me off.

Today, he wasn't so bad. Actually, it was fun. I had a great time. Quinton wasn't as much of an ass as he usually is. He even agreed to go along with me, which I am still shocked about. It makes me wonder if maybe...just maybe...are we...possibly...

Friends?

Ugh, the word doesn't sound right. Quinton and I? Friends? That's hilarious. How could we be friends? Do friends punch and kick each other? Do friends argue every time they meet? Do friends break into their friends dorm room and look through their belongings? Do friends glare at one another and hiss and shout at one another because their anger is so out of control they can think of nothing else to do?

No. They do not. So we are not friends...

But do enemies feel guilty for hurting each other? Do enemies watch over or even carry you to the nurse's office after hurting one another? Do enemies warn each other about fake girlfriends? Do enemies have snowball fights and drink hot chocolate together? Do enemies play 20 questions during a blizzard? Do enemies go together to hang out for the day?

No. They do not. So we are not enemies...

Then, what are we? Friends? Enemies? I flip through my mind for a word to describe the relationship between us, but to be honest, I can't think of one. Knowing Langley, he'd call us 'frenemies.' I roll my eyes.

My time on campus ends without my running into Quinton again, whether or not he did that on purpose, I do not know. I return home as I promised to my loving parents, who ask all kinds of questions. My mom insisted I tell her every detail of my trip into town. I told her as much as I thought Quinton would feel comfortable with. Although he's not here, I still feel like he can somehow hear me, knowing him he probably can. Freak. I bet he has some super machine in his dorm that can detect when others speak of him. Seriously, I wouldn't be surprised if he did.

"Your grades have improved, that's good," Dad says, eyeing the report card I actually brought home with me this time. Though the grades are still not perfect, they are better than before. "Maybe sending you to school was the right thing to do."

"Maybe? You mean definitely," I laugh.

I bet, had I started in school, I wouldn't like it. I think people naturally take things for granted, like school. I never got to go, so now that I am going, I love it. However, no one seems to understand why. All the students who have been in school since kindergarten laugh and say I'm crazy, claiming that school sucks. I wonder if they would think that way had they started out being home schooled. It also depends on the person, I suppose.

"And what about friends? Have you made many more?" Mom asks from across the table. She's always the one to ask about my personal life, wondering about girls and stuff. "You seem to be in a better mood of late. Is there someone new in your life?"

Mom wiggles her eyebrows and I don't mean to do it, but my cheeks heat up. She squeals, thinking that I have met a girl. She even starts tugging on my father's sleeve while saying, "We might get grand kids after all."

"Mom!" I shout, slamming my hands against the table. She's fucking embarrassing! "I don't have a girlfriend, if that's what you're thinking."

"What?" she pouts, looking disappointed. "But you're blushing."

"It's because you made that w-weird face while asking!" Or rather because I immediately thought of Quinton.

Dad laughs while Mom continues to pout. I'm hoping they bought it. I don't even know what to say.

"I did make, I guess, you could say a friend," I mumble. I have told them about Quinton before, but I only described him as 'this annoying kid in class.' I thought if I told my dad too much about him, he might try to kick him out, which I don't want. If he's going to get beaten, it will be by me! "He and I went on my day out together."

"So you really took him? That kid that pisses you off?" Dad asks, forgetting his manners and speaking with a mouth full of food. Mom slaps his arm for that. He completely ignores her, continuing to chew with his mouth open. On purpose I bet.

I nod. "Yeah. We don't have any classes together this term, but we've hung out a little outside of class. He's not that bad, I guess. He's gutsy; I like it. But he still pisses me off; he's always so smug and acts all cool! He never messes up, Mr. Perfect know it all, bastard!"

"Aron!" Mom gasps.

"Well, he is!" Ugh, just thinking about his smug face makes my blood race. I want to punch him even when he isn't here. He doesn't have to say anything to piss me off. His existence bothers me, but at the same time, it doesn't. I don't get it! What's wrong with me? "I don't really know if we're friends, per say. If anyone were to ask me, I'd definitely say no!"

Mom is giving me an 'of course you would son, boys are so silly' look. Yes, that's a look.

"And if someone were to ask him, he'd probably say no, but I mean, if we weren't friends, we wouldn't have hung out together over break, right? Do enemies hang out? I keep thinking about whether we're friends or enemies because we don't act like friends, but we don't act like enemies," I add.

I keep telling myself that we're enemies and I hang out with him so I can discover his weakness but, lately; I haven't been trying to do that at all. When was the last time I've thought up a scheme to expel Quinton or to knock him down a notch? Now that I think about it, I don't want him expelled. I told myself before that I wanted him gone, but now the thought of not seeing him hurts.

"You're definitely friends," Mom says, not seeming to put much thought into it, which baffles me. How can she be so sure? I haven't even told her anything we've done or said to each other. "Boys are stubborn and never want to admit when they're wrong—"

"Hey!" Dad shouts. It's Mom's turn to ignore him.

"It sounds like you two just don't want to admit that you get along better than you let on. Stubborn boys."

Which is completely true. Wasn't I saying that to myself earlier? I didn't even tell mom anything, nothing important at least, and she found that out. If I think about it, then...then we're definitely, ugh, we are friends.

Shit, Quinton and I are friends? It sounds wrong, so very wrong. I want us to stay enemies, but we haven't been doing very 'enemy' like things to each other lately. I even bought him a jacket. Enemies don't buy their enemies things, that's weird. Friends buy friends things, though, that's normal.

Whatever, it doesn't matter if I think we're friends or not, because Quinton would definitely not think the same. He puts up with me, that's it. We aren't friends. Definitely not.

CHAPTER TWENTY-FOUR

With Christmas vacation over, a new holiday arises; Valentine's Day. The word sends a shiver down my spine. Had everything gone well with Gabby, this would be a good day for her and me, but since I have yet to find myself a girl who likes me for me rather than my title, I am alone. Langley and Ariel, the girl he met at the library too, are still on good terms, so I have a feeling they're doing something together this holiday.

I could ask some guys, but I don't want to ruin any of their plans. I get a feeling that if I ask, they'll go along with me purely out of fear rather than because they don't have plans. For a moment, I think about asking Quinton to hang out until I realize how weird that would be. But because my heart races at the thought of it, no, no, nothing like that, because that would signal that I may like him, which I don't! So, no, Quinton is out of the question.

I sigh, resting my head on my desk. I stare at the abundance of reds, whites and pinks decorating the walls. Beside me, Langley is on his phone flipping through different flower shop sites trying to decide on the best thing to get Ariel. Langley is so concentrated I'm half expecting his eyes to pop out of his skull. He doesn't notice how hard I'm staring at him until he has found what he was looking for or given up on his search.

The boy jumps upon seeing my eyes on him. "W-What?" he stutters, cheeks becoming a light pink.

"How romantic of you," I say with a teasing grin. "Getting Ariel flowers, aren't you original?"

"Shut up, at least I have a girl to give flowers to," Langley replies with an equally teasing grin. Said grin makes me scowl and turn my attention away from him. Sure, bring that up. I'm already depressed about being single...

I wonder if Quinton got back with his ex. If he did, poor girl, I bet he doesn't even celebrate Valentine's Day. Seeing so much color probably makes his eyes bleed. What could possess a woman to date that thing? He's the biggest stick in the mud to ever walk this earth. Except he hung out with me for a day and was as nice as he could which makes him kind of an ok guy.

Class ends with everyone bolting out of the room. The hall is filled with nothing but talk about this weekend, plans for the special day. Hell, there's even a dance being held Saturday night, the night before Valentine's Day. I have been asked to go by a good many people but declined all of them. I don't really want another Gabby in my life.

Langley tried to talk me into going stag for fun, but bei,ng in a room full of lovebirds makes me even more depressed. I'm not exactly desperate for a relationship, but when I see two people happy together, I get ,a lle envious. Once Valentine's Day is over, I'll fee,l better. For now, I'm in my own personal hell.

"At least you got chocolates," Langley says, arms full of gifts that were presented to me. I too, have an, armful of gifts; some are still in my locker while others were sent to our dorm. I can't imagine what awaits us in our room.

I nod, throwing a chocolate into the air and catching it. Delicious. "I guess. I'd prefer a girlfriend."

"You can't get a girlfriend if you don't hang out with girls," Langley says, shoving a handful of my chocolate into his mouth. He smiles sheepishly at my glare. I don't really care, but it,'s fun to mess with him.

Shrugging, I open my locker only for an avalanche to come piling out. How did they even open my locker? Langley chuckles at the mass amount of gifts lying on the ground. I'm going to have to get someone to help carry these back.

"I can't get a girlfriend if none of them like me," I whisper, thinking back to Gabby. How am I supposed to date someone if I can't trust her?

In my eyes, if you cannot trust them, you cannot be with them. It does not matter how much you claim to love them, there has to be trust or the relationship is over. It's too painful and annoying to constantly be lly look ur shoulder, wondering if your significant other is cheating or even in love with you. I can't trust many people. One of the many perks of being me! Yes, that was said with complete sarcasm.

Langley, deciding to end this conversation quickly, frowns but forces a smile while saying, "The guys are planning on pulling a prank on Quinton."

My eyes widen as his words sink in. "W-What? When? What for?"

"What do you mean what for?" Langley laughs, leaning against the row of lockers. "Because he's Quinton. I guess they heard he's coming to the dance Saturday night—"

With Autumn?

"I bet he's got himself a date since he's a chick magnet, for some reason, but we plan on knocking the two of them into the fountain outside the dance hall. Almost everyone knows about it so it may not sound like much, but i,f everyone sees it'll be some good public humiliation. Maybe that j—"

I slam my locker shut, causing Langley to jump out of shock. He looks from my recently slammed locker to me. I have my head hanging low, allowing my blonde locks to shield the anger in my eyes.

I'm angry? Why? For reasons unknown, my fists clench. I want to punch something so I ,settle with my locker. The action causes people around us to stop and stare. Some begin to point and whisper as they walk by.

I've been arguing with myself a lot lately over whether Quinton and I are enemies or friends. If I had a 100% answer, this predicament I find myself in would be solved much quicker. A friend would never allow such a thing to happen, an enemy would.

"What's wrong, Aron?" Langley asks. I'm glaring at the ground but i,n my mind I'm glaring at him. I shouldn't be thoug,h; it's not his fault. I've been telling everyone how Quinton and I are enemies so, o,f course, Langley would tell me about their plan but...

But...

"Nothing," I lie, turning away from Langley and heading to my dorm, completely ignoring the mess of gifts on the floor. "Nothing's wrong."

I hear Langley shouting after me. I ignore him. I'm mad. I'm confused. Part of me is saying to tell Quinton about this plan, at least for Autumn's sake. I'm assuming that's who he's taking. They've probably gotten back together. She's a girl I've never met, so I cannot judge her. I feel like I should tell him since I doubt he'd want something that embarrassing to happen to her, but we're enemies. I've wanted to publicly humiliate him since I first met him. We fought and argued over everything. He's beyond annoying. We don't get along and I want him knocked off his pedestal, but why do I feel so bad?

Guilty. I feel guilty.

Didn't Quinton warn me about Gabby? Shouldn't I warn him about the dance? I'm torn. The feeling of being torn is only making me feel worse. My brain says to let them do it, let them point their fingers and laugh at the outcast. Something else tells me there is no way in hell I should let that happen.

At the same time, I doubt such a small prank would bother the spawn of Satan. Everyone will be shocked to see his expression never changes. I bet someone could catch him masturbating in public and he'd probably still show no emotion and strut about the campus with a god-like ego. Besides, there's no guarantee that he's going to the dance or if he'll even be near the fountain. What are they going to do if their plan doesn't work? Force him over?

I snort at the thought. Quinton isn't forced into things he doesn't want to do. He'd kill over before someone had the upper hand.

Although I'm thinking all this, I keep thinking what if—what if it happens and what if it bothers him? I could save him from the humiliation and it's not like anyone would know. I could see him after class, talk to him in private and tell him I'm only doing this because I feel sorry for the poor girl who will also be humiliated.

Yeah...I...I could do that...Am I trying to talk myself into it?

My head hurts. I don't want to think about this anymore.

I kick open my dorm door to see that yes, security has brought up the many gifts I knew I would get. They're all piled in the room, but I'm too lazy to move or look through them. I head for my bed, falling onto it with an 'umph.'

I pray to fall asleep quickly in order to escape reality. My head is pounding, begging me to forget about Quinton and the dance. Please, bless me with the ability to sleep. I am not ready to face the real world and the difficulties that come with it. Allow me some peace. Sleep is the only way I figure I can escape, but, honestly, when has that ever worked for anyone?

Trying to sleep off your problem is possibly the worst thing someone could do. It doesn't work. I awake with a headache that has only gotten worse and my problem has not gotten solved. In fact, I feel even worse for sleeping rather than contemplating how to go through with this.

I sit up with a groan. It seems even the world itself wants me to stop this from happening. Why? Why do I have to do it? Can't I be the asshole who lets something bad happen to his may or may not be friend? I don't want to be the better man here!

It's gotten late. I peer at my clock that tells me I have slept through dinner. I didn't even hear Langley come in or go to bed. I see him across the room, lying in his bed, fast asleep. My clock tells me it's 1am, meaning I slept for almost 10 hours. Somehow, though I slept longer than usual, I fall back into a not-so-blissful sleep while thinking of ways to tell Quinton not to go to the dance tomorrow.

CHAPTER TWENTY-FIVE

I, yet again, stand awkwardly outside Quinton's dorm room. My heart's speeding up and my palms are perspiring. Students pass by, eyeing me, the suspicious boy in all black with his hood hiding his face. Of course I'm hiding my face! I don't want people to know I'm helping Quinton out. It's better to let everyone continue believing we're enemies. I feel more comfortable that way.

Taking a deep breath, I finally force myself to knock. There's movement inside. It could be his roommate, but I'm proved wrong when the door opens to show Quinton shirtless. It's still early, so he hasn't begun getting ready for the dance. His sweats hang low on his hips, showing more than I'm comfortable with. I can't take my eyes off him. Please put some clothes on...

"What do you want?" He asks, not even bothering to keep me out. Ha! Finally, he has learned to roll with it. I'll come in if I want.

"I, uh, is Taylor here?" I ask, peeking around his room. If he were here, I would have seen him already. Their room doesn't actually leave any place for him to hide.

Quinton rolls his eyes, probably thinking something along the lines that I was before replying, "Obviously not. Why?"

"I need to tell you something...about the dance." I take a seat on his bed, bringing my legs up to cross them. I wrap my fingers around my ankles, forcing myself to play with the hem of my jeans to keep me from staring at Quinton, who still hasn't put a shirt on, damn it.

"How did you know I'm going to the dance?" Quinton asks, narrowing his eyes on me.

"I didn't snoop around to find out about it or anything, so stop giving me the death glare, man," I hiss at him. How come he always assumes I'm the one digging up dirt about him? Technically, him going to the dance isn't dirt, but whatever, you get the point!

I guess I do snoop around him a lot, though, so it's understandable. We've been on decent terms lately though! He should at least pretend not to think of me as the prime suspect.

Quinton, looking at me suspiciously, eventually hums to show he's listening to whatever I have to say. He sits in his desk chair, spinning it to face me. It's even harder to keep my eyes from straying to his chest. Why am I even staring at his chest? Who cares if he has an amazing body? Eh, I mean, his body isn't amazing. It's average, very, very average.

"You're drooling."

Shit, was I? I bring my hand up to brush against my lips, realizing that, no, I was not. My lips are dry and closed, that asshat. I glare at the smirking demon. Damn him for making me look like an idiot. I should leave and let them shove him into a fountain or a wall or off a cliff! Preferably a cliff. That way he'd be dead.

"You shouldn't be making me look a fool when I'm about to tell you something important," I say to him, sitting straighter than before because damn it, he's sitting like a prince, a half naked prince. I'm the prince here, not him! Trying to look better than me...

"You don't need me to make you look a fool," Quinton replies, his smirk only growing. Seriously, I hate him.

I remind myself that I am doing this for the poor girl who doesn't deserve what's coming to her because if I don't, I will get up and leave. Forcing myself to speak, I tell him, "The guys are planning to shove you and your date into the fountain at the dance."

Quinton, for probably the first time in his life, is speechless. His head tilts to the side, like he's trying to decipher what I'm saying. He actually looks lost for a moment before his eyes darken. His glare is set on me and he asks, "How do you know that?"

"Langley told me," I answer, not realizing until his hands clench into fists that he probably thinks I planned it. I didn't! For once. But with the way he's glaring, I know that's exactly what he's thinking. I don't blame him, but he should know I wouldn't mess with someone I've never met! "It wasn't my idea. If it was, I wouldn't have told you!"

"Or you actually felt guilty for once in your life," Quinton says through clenched teeth. His anger always causes me to be angry.

I'm offended that he'd think I'd come up with something so immature. I have done nothing that stupid since the time I broke into his room and I don't plan on doing anything like that again. I'm also offended because...because, I guess, maybe part of me thinks we are friends. Maybe I also believed he felt the same, thinking of me as a friend rather than an annoyance, but I see now that he doesn't trust me and that pisses me off.

Am I the only one that thought we were getting along recently? Am I the only one acting like an idiot trying to decide whether or not we're friends? Apparently so. Quinton doesn't concern himself with me as much as I do him.

"Think what you want," I growl, pushing myself off his bed.

I'm disappointed when he doesn't try stopping me, doesn't try asking me to prove that I didn't do anything. I'm even more disappointed with myself for even bothering to go over. I should have known that, to Quinton, I'm just an annoying brat.

With a huff, I leave to return to my dorm, where there is no devil from the depths of hell to annoy me further.

"What's wrong with you?" Langley asks upon seeing me return to our dorm room. I bet there's steam coming out my ears right about now. I'm so pissed.

"Nothing." Yes, hissing definitely shows that nothing is wrong, Aron, way to go.

Langley, obviously aware that something's up, steers clear of me while getting ready for the dance. He's as silent as possible, occasionally bumping into things and whispering a quiet 'ouch.' He really can't sneak worth shit. How'd we even break into Quinton's room that one time?

Don't. Don't even say Quinton's name. Don't think about him at all. He's the biggest asshole to ever walk this earth. I don't give a damn about him or his daddy issues. Screw him. I try helping him out because he did the same for me, but this is what I get? Friends, my ass.

"I'm going now," Langley says, making me realize that somehow I've complained about Quinton in my mind for hours, which pisses me off more. I go from telling myself not to even think his name to complaining for hours in my head. Something's wrong with me.

"If you change your mind," Langley says, inching towards the door. "There's another suit that your mom sent in your closet. I'm sure it'll be fun."

Langley's trying his best to get me to come along in hopes to better my mood, but he fails. Sighing sadly, he tells me goodbye and leaves the room, all dressed up for Ariel. The dance won't start for another hour, but everyone is running to hair salons and flower shops or whatever they need for the final touches.

It's so quiet I can hear the people outside my door. It's his fault if he doesn't listen. I don't need to go to talk to him about it. It's his own damn fault for pissing me off.

Deciding that the silence isn't helping my conscience, I turn on the TV. There's nothing but love stories on. This weekend is going to be pure hell. As I'm thinking this, there's a sudden knock at my door.

Assuming that it's someone trying to talk me into going to the dance or the guards bringing up more gifts, I open the door. It is neither of the two options I thought of. Standing there is someone that I rather pretend does not exist and a girl, a very beautiful girl, actually.

Her silky black hair is pulled back into a ponytail, a few curly strands left to frame her thin, russet brown face. Her hazel eyes are brought out even more from the black eyeliner and red eyeshadow. She's a bit on the shorter side, but her red sleeveless dress drapes down her legs and onto the floor making her appear taller. She's freaking hot! And to think this is Quinton's date.

"What? Why are you here?" I ask, doing my best not to look at the boy beside her. Being near him is making my blood boil. My head is about to pop off. "And who are you?" I glance at the girl out of the corner of my eye.

I'm pretty sure I know who she is, but you never know. Quinton could be a player. The inner me rolls its eyes. Yeah right.

"I'm Autumn," the girl says sweetly. His ex, which means they're back together. Somehow, that pisses me off.

"And he's here to apologize." She jabs a sharp, manicured nail into the spawn's chest. My lips twitch into a smirk at the thought of someone getting Quinton to listen. I bite my lip to keep myself from laughing. Who knew he'd be whipped?

"I'm not doing anything," Quinton hisses, hands shoved into his suit's pockets. Scowling, he attempts to back away, only to have Autumn wrap her arm around his with the grip of a python. But for some reason, I don't like her touching him.

"I'm sorry about him," she says to me, keeping her hold on the boy, who is struggling to set himself free without physically harming her. "This little boy is still learning his manners. He has a lot of issues."

This little boy? Holy shit, I'm in love. Why doesn't she go to our school? Please transfer!

"Autumn," Quinton growls. I can't believe it, but he actually looks a bit embarrassed right now. He isn't even looking at me. I've finally found someone who can make Quinton embarrassed. I like her. I'd like her more if she'd get her paws off him, though. Wait, no...

"You can say that again," I say with a grin. Quinton attempts to glare at me, but it's not nearly as scary as he wants it to be. "But, uh, why are you apologizing for him?"

Did he tell her about what had happened earlier? I didn't think he'd care enough to talk about it. The idea of Quinton actually discussing this matter with someone else, like he actually cares, makes my heart skip.

Autumn nods. "About the fountain thing? Yeah. I told him he was a dumb ass for not speaking with you about it. He's supposed to be smart, but when it comes to people, he's a total airhead."

She's bad-mouthing him, and he isn't even doing anything about it. She's wonderful! Where did he find this perfect person?!

"I like her," I say to Quinton, who does not seem pleased at all with the two of us getting along. Maybe that's why he didn't want us to meet? She seems a bit like me, gutsy enough to stand up to the oh so perfect Quinton. Having two of us in his life would be too much. "How'd you get such a great girl? Are you blackmailing her?"

Quinton finally pulls his arm from hers. Autumn doesn't seem hurt at all to see him storm off. In fact, I think she was expecting it. She doesn't even look shocked. Smiling, she says, "We're childhood friends, actually."

Childhood friends? No way is she dating him out of pity? That has to be it. Why else would she date that hell spawn?

"Quinton has friends?" I chuckle.

"Yes, I know, very shocking," she says with a grin. "Our mothers knew each other, so we hung out a lot when we were younger—" Before she has time to say anything else I hear Quinton shouting for her down the hall. She huffs, pouting. She turns to see the boy at the end of the hall and shouts back, "Calm your shit, Quinny!"

Quinny? Holy sweet mother of—did she just call him Quinny? Give me a minute here. I am going to die! It sounded like a damn pet name. His face scrunches up at the sound of the adorable name, or maybe it's because he sees the enormous grin on my face. Oh, I am calling him that from now on. It's perfect. Seeing the way his shoulders tense at the sound makes me grin.

I laugh because she is nothing like I expected. Quinton is so...Quinton-like. To think he dated, or rather is dating, someone like her is crazy. Turning back to me, Autumn sighs and says, "We told security we were coming up to talk a friend into going to the dance, so we can't be up here long. Anyway, I just wanted to tell you he didn't mean to be an ass. He's too stubborn to admit when he's wrong, so please don't let that affect your friendship."

"Friendship?" Who said we were friends? Is what I wanted to ask but Autumn beats me to it.

"Yeah," she nods with a questioning expression. She gestures with her head over her shoulder to the brooding boy down the hall, then looks back to me. "He said you're friends. He talks about you all the time."

"W-What? You're joking," is all I can say, my voice hardly above a whisper out of fear of Quinton hearing and coming to stop Autumn from speaking the truth. My chest feels heavy, a good heavy that I'm not too sure I want to focus on. Autumn quirks a curious brow, seeming to be confused by my confusion.

"Are you two not? Quinny said you were," she says innocently before waiting for a response, but I have none. I don't even know if I am breathing right now. After a moment of silence, she hands me her cell number, telling me to text her if I have any problems with Quinny before running off, waving goodbye to me as she does.

Had I not been so shocked, I would have waved back.

He said you're friends. He talks about you all the time.

Was she serious? Are we even talking about the same person here? There's no way he would...

My cheeks are really hot. I press the back of my palms to check if it's my imagination. Sadly, it is not. There's an inferno behind my cheeks. I'm blushing and, without my permission, my lips twitch back into a painfully wide smile. I end up having to shield my face behind my hands out of embarrassment.

Why did she have to tell me that? My heart won't stop racing.

CHAPTER TWENTY-SIX

I couldn't go to the dance, not with what Autumn told me. Knowing me, I would do something stupid, like follow Quinton around, give him all my attention and desperately ask him if what Autumn said was true or not. It's sad that I know that's what would happen. How can I not though? Quinton doesn't exactly treat me like a friend, so hearing that he feels we are friends is baffling to me.

I can't stop blushing. My cheeks are on fire. My heart's racing. I'm shaking. Shit, something's wrong with me. Hurry, give me a computer in order to look up my symptoms on google. It'll probably say I'm on the verge of death, that's what I feel like.

I shouldn't be acting like this. Who cares if he said we're friends? Who cares if he talks about me? I—I—gah, of course I care! I've been wondering this whole time if we're friends or if he even gives a damn about me. So it makes sense that I would be interested, or rather curious, about hearing that perhaps Quinton feels the same.

I went from wanting him to hate me to wanting him to be friends with me. I still hate his guts and want to punch his face in, but I want to hang out with him. I want to talk to him. I want to learn more about him, ask him questions, learn his likes and dislikes. I want to know that he gets as worked up about me as I am about him. No, that's not the right wording—that makes it sound like I like him or something haha...

Heh...heh...

Which I don't! I definitely do not. No way in hell do I like Quinton. He's a guy, and he's Quinton. I like girls, girls, girls, girls! Like Autumn, she was gorgeous, and she seemed funny too, which is always a plus. Women with a sense of humor are sexy. She seems nice too. I bet we'd get along. Quinton being with her pisses me off a bit—I mean her being with Quinton pisses me off, not that him being in a relationship pisses me off because that would sound like I like him, which I don't!

I don't. Nope. I'm only jealous he has such a beautiful girlfriend, not that he is in a relationship or anything. It's because of her.

I am so full of shit it's sickening.

I groan as I throw my head into my pillow. I pray that it'll somehow smother me to keep these weird thoughts at bay. I hope the mattress swallows me whole, much like it did to Johnny Depp on Nightmare on Elm Street. Sure, I'd prefer living, but if living means being so messed up in the head that I can't even think straight, then maybe it'd be better to be dead. Something tells me that, even in death, Quinton would plague me. After all, hell is where he spawned from. I bet he visits there frequently.

I can't believe I'm even thinking about any of this. I'm stupid, so stupid. It's not a big deal, none of it is. I'm overreacting. I really need to get a girlfriend or something. My mind is messed up. I fear my conscience.

With this thought in mind, I approach Ariel on Monday morning. Langley is behind me, shrugging at the girl's questioning gaze. Although she's dating Langley, I don't talk with her much. We don't share a lot of classes and I have no desire to be the third wheel. Langley gets all lovey-dovey with her and it can get super awkward. They're still in that 'puppy love' phase, so I rather not be involved in all that disgusting shit.

"Um, do you need something, Your Highness?" She asks. The title she uses makes me a bit embarrassed. She's dating my best friend. She doesn't have to call me that. Actually, even if they weren't dating, I'd rather not be called that.

"Aron is fine," I say with a smile, trying to make her feel less pressured. She looks to Langley again, who shrugs and shakes his head. "Actually, I have a request."

"What is it?" She asks.

My cheeks heat up before I even ask; "Could you...possibly introduce me to some of your girlfriends that are single and will not stab me in the back?"

Langley howls with laughter. I would have elbowed him had he not fallen to the floor from laughing. Ariel is doing her best to hold back her giggles, but I see her eyes sparkling with the greatest of desires to laugh. She places a hand over her lips and tries to ask without gigging, "I'm sorry, what did you say?"

"Don't make me ask again. I'm already dying of embarrassment here! Look at Langley, stop laughing, asshole!" I kick said asshole, who only laughs harder. Why is it so funny?

Excuse me for having no social skills with women whatsoever! I haven't really had the time to date, let alone had women around me to date until recently!

Ariel taps Langley with her foot, trying to give him a 'stop that' look, but her attempts to hold in her laughter fail. She ends up giggling as she says, "I could introduce you to someone. I didn't know you were having such trouble in the romance department, Your Majesty."

"Apparently, money really isn't everything," Langley laughs, earning himself another kick from me.

"Shut it," I hiss and narrow my eyes on the boy who is not at all threatened. "I am tired of being a third wheel, ok? I need some lovin'!"

"Obviously, since you're desperate enough to ask my girlfriend to find you a girlfriend," Langley says, grinning like the Cheshire Cat. His laughter has finally died down enough for him to stand. But when he sees how red my face has gotten, his laughter returns full force. He clutches at his stomach, that shakes with every breath. His eyes look about ready to pop out of his skull.

"You look like a tomato!" He exclaims, pointing an accusing finger at my flushing cheeks and even pokes at them teasingly. I slap his hand away.

"Screw you all," I growl, turning to leave them and to, hopefully, go play a sport or something in order to bandage my damaged masculinity.

Ariel stops me by grasping the sleeve of my shirt. She tugs and says, "It's ok, A-Aron." Wow, she said my name this time. Someone give her an award! "I'll ask some of the girls, so don't be embarrassed about it. People need help every now and again. Even Quinton has a girlfriend!"

Oh, right, I forgot about that. Quinton didn't tell me how it went. Not that I expected him to. So I guess he and Autumn are dating again. My chest feels tight suddenly.

Pretending not to know anything, I ask, "How did that go?"

"It didn't work," Langley replies, and starts laughing again. He is no longer laughing over me, which piques my interest. "You should see Ronny's face! My god, she decked him so hard!"

"Decked? Who did?" I'm confused because Ariel's not bothering to control her laughter now either. I obviously missed something. Maybe I should have gone because these two are enjoying themselves. Don't leave me out of the loop guys!

"His girlfriend," Ariel replies, trying to control herself enough to speak to me. "Ronny attempted to dump the punch on them when everyone realized they were avoiding the terrace."

Langley nods, grinning from the memory. "But his girlfriend saw him coming and punched him! His face is all black and blue. She didn't even get in trouble because the guards figured Ronny was being a pervert and trying to see girls wet. It was great!"

The more I hear about Autumn, the more I like her. Childhood friends? Maybe Quinton learned how to fight from her. She is feisty. To think she'd have the guts to punch someone with political connections. She's brave; I'll give her that. I'd like her more if she weren't with Quinton. Gah, weird thoughts. See? This is why I need a girlfriend. My mind needs something to occupy it or I get lost in thoughts that leave me shivering.

"So, nothing happened to them?" I ask.

Langley shakes his head in the negative. "Nah, they never went outside. I think someone told them but don't know who. It was still fun, though. You should have come."

I shrug and bite the inside of my cheek. "Maybe next year."

I do my best to keep myself from smiling. Knowing that the two of them had a good time is a relief. I feel good about getting over myself and telling Quinton rather than allowing the guys to humiliate him. Once again, I am left feeling pathetic for thinking such thoughts. There was a time I would have given anything to see Quinton a total mess, and yet, now I rather not.

I can't let Langley know, though. He'd go nuts if he knew Quinton and I were 'friends.' Ok, nuts isn't the correct term, but he'd be questioning me on what's changed. I don't have a clue what I would say to him either, and that makes me wish to keep it a secret even more. If I'm left there stuttering out an excuse that makes little sense, the boy may discover something I'm not sure I am willing to hear yet. I need more time to go over my thoughts, to discover exactly what it is between Quinton and me.

Whoa, saying between makes it seem like there's something between us. Wow Aron, you've got such a way with words.

"Still, I can't believe Quinton has a girlfriend," Langley says at my side. I'm not as shocked because I knew before him, not that I could tell him that. "She's hot too! It's crazy."

"Sure is," I mumble to myself. I didn't believe it at first either, but now I know. I've actually met her, spoken a bit with her. He is actually dating someone. It bothers me more than I want to admit. Because Autumn is hot, not because Quinton is in a relationship. Obviously that's what is bothering me.

I guess I don't know. Autumn never said they were dating. She might simply be a friend. Who knows, Quinton could be friend zoned! Yeah, right. That's so stupid even, I roll my eyes at the thought.

Langley, though shocked, is not as affected by the news of a girl in Quinton's life because he easily switches to another subject. I'm sorry for him because I'm not paying much attention. My mind is elsewhere, on Quinton, again. Damn it, what's wrong with me?

The one I wish to never plague my mind seems to be the only object that does.

I think about him too much to be considered normal. He must have put some fan girl drug into my drink. I can't think of another reason I can't seem to get that asshole off my mind. It irks me. To make matters worse, I'm trying my best to find anything to think about, yet my brain seems to thoroughly enjoy focusing on the dark-eyed beast.

I keep wondering what he's doing, where he's at, why I haven't seen him, although I know exactly why I haven't seen him. We don't have any classes together. The only time we see one another is by chance in the hall, which is very rare. We went almost half a year without seeing each other once, so why am I expecting to see him when I turn a corner and disappointed when realizing that I didn't?

I have this strange urge to go see him, an urge that leaves me questioning myself. Why? Every time we speak, we argue in one form or another. I have more fun speaking with Langley, but I can't focus on what he's saying. Instead, I'm wondering what Quinton and I could be talking about right now, or rather arguing over. I don't care so long as it's with Quinton. Sad, I'm sad and pathetic.

Langley and Ariel stare at me oddly when I suddenly whack myself in the face with my textbook. I do it again and again until Langley asks with a quizzical expression, "Are you possessed?"

Sighing, I answer with the utmost seriousness, "Yeah, I think I am."

Possessed by the Quinton fan girl syndrome, it must be contagious!

Ariel clears her throat, insisting that the three of us get ready to leave, seeing as study hall is nearly over. I nod in agreement and slowly get my things together. Just as I finish packing up, the bell rings, signaling the end of study hall. Ariel waves goodbye to the two of us. I grimace when she leans up to press a kiss to Langley's lips, who grins like an idiot then looks at me with that same expression remaining on his face. I gag at their mushy shit.

Langley is speaking beside me about something that completely escapes me. Yet again, I am lost within my consciousness, pondering over something, or rather, someone, that I shouldn't. Just as I think of how bad this day has been, the appearance of the demon that plagues me worsens my day. How is it we go nearly half the school year without bumping into each other, yet there he is now, sitting beneath a tree in the courtyard?

My legs stop without my permission. Langley doesn't even notice, continuing to walk and talk as if I'm next to him. I tell myself to look away before Quinton notices my obvious staring, but it's too late. He looks away from his book to see me creepily staring.

My cheeks burn at the feeling of his dark eyes watching me curiously. Without my consent, my body reacts on its own. Shyly, I raise my hand to wave at him. Why am I waving at him? I haven't a clue, but even as I think about this, I don't stop. Instead, part of me is hoping that he shows his own sign of hello or acknowledgement.

Holy shit, I'm a total idiot! Hoping he acknowledges me? What's wrong with me? If people see they're going to think we're fr—

Quinton raises his hand to wave just as awkwardly back, his face clearly showing that he does not know why I'm waving or why he's waving back. The action shoots through me like a beam of light that warms me from the core. For some reason, I smile, something that seems to confuse him more because he gives me that 'you're an idiot' look I know too well, but he doesn't stop waving until I do.

"Aron, what are you doing?" Langley asks, finally realizing I am no longer following him. His question breaks me from my trance or whatever the hell I was just in.

"N-Nothing!" I answer, rushing after him before he notices Quinton and I looking right at each other. My cheeks are still warm. My heart runs a marathon. Langley has to notice but says nothing.

There's something incredibly wrong with me. Heart, can you take a break there? I need a breather.

CHAPTER TWENTY-SEVEN

After three failed attempts, I accept my fate that I am really never going to get a girlfriend. You'd think being a prince would make it easy to pick up girls. Well, okay, it is, but that's not the point! The point is that I don't have a clue which of those girls are into me because I'm me and not because I'm 'The Prince.'

Even with Ariel's help, it's hopeless. Though the girls were kind, most appeared to be trustworthy, but none of them—none of them felt right. They weren't comfortable around me, I could tell. Their eyes always watched me, waiting to see if what they said had upset me, hurt me, or bothered me. They were frightened. They were nervous and not in the '*I like this guy, so he makes me nervous*' kind of way. No, it was the '*this is the future king of our country and I must respect and obey him*' kind of way. I don't want that.

My mother does not fear my father. She speaks her mind, tells him when he's being an idiot or when he's making a wrong decision. Mom doesn't tiptoe around him like he's a bomb waiting to explode. She treats him as a normal human being, as a normal husband who often forgets their anniversary and sheepishly tries to apologize with some flowers. My parents are lucky to have each other. I want a relationship like that. I don't want my lover to fear me. I think it's safe to say no one does.

I need a partner, not a subordinate.

Sighing, I inform Ariel of the failed 'date' with another one of her friends. She frowns, says she will try looking harder, but I insist she not bother. I'm only in high school. I've got time. But I hoped that I'd find someone, anyone, because my mind is straying to places it shouldn't.

Class ends and I have no desire to be the third wheel, so I leave Ariel and Langley, who are so lost in each other they hardly notice me leaving. I'll let them off the hook this time, only because they look genuinely happy around each other. Just because I'm a miserable guy without a girl doesn't mean I should take it out on them. Oh, but I want to though. The temptation is strong in this one.

Not sure of what I want to do, I head to the library without my knowledge. Again, I am reminded of the obvious lack of connection between my mind and body. My feet seem to enjoy doing whatever they please without the consent of my head. Perhaps Quinton is right. I am an idiot, so much so that my brain doesn't even care what my body does and simply allows it to do as it pleases.

I don't even realize I'm in the library until I'm already standing in the reading area, peering at the kids studying or drowning themselves in books. I immediately feel out-of-place seeing as me and books do not get along so well. Why did I come here again? I don't read or study so the library should be the last place on my mind, yet it is the first place I come to.

I don't have time to answer my question before I hear a voice that sets my veins aflame. Whether that is a good or bad thing, I do not know.

"Idiot."

"Quinny." I turn to face the scowling beast, who seems more than unhappy with my remembrance of his pet name. The boy rolls his eyes at my triumphant grin and heads to a section of the library. I follow him like a puppy.

"What are you doing here?" Quinton asks, pulling a book from the shelf to inspect the back. Even as he speaks, he doesn't look at me. That pisses me off. I hate when people don't look at me when they talk. I bet he knows that and does it on purpose, freaking bastard.

I shrug and reply, "To study."

He snorts, the sound being enough to inform me he isn't buying the shit I'm selling.

"What? Don't believe me?" I don't know why I'm being defensive when it's not true. I don't even know why I'm here. I came without thinking, which doesn't bother me as much as I thought it would.

Quinton replies with a confident, "No."

I roll my eyes. "I study."

"I've never seen you here."

"Are you saying that you look for me?" I ask around a teasing smile and cocked brow, feeling momentarily victorious. Why does the idea of Quinton looking for me make my heart skip? Stop doing that. You aren't meant to skip because of him! Stupid heart, get yourself together.

"As if I'd waste my time." Quinton huffs.

"You wasted enough of your time to call me an idiot."

His eyes stop in their reading of the book. He stills for a moment at the mention of earlier. Quinton could have walked away; completely ignored me and I probably never would have found him. He was the one who spoke to me. He and I share a common problem; the inability to ignore one another. That thought brings a smile to my face that I try to push away by biting nervously at my lips.

He scoffs, quickly dispersing whatever he was thinking to say, "Seeing you takes away one's ability to make rational decisions."

Whatever, be stubborn. I grin at my 'victory', because everything between us is a competition, and continue to follow the boy through the bookshelves. I don't know what he's looking for, a book to read or something to study, but I don't really care. I enjoy seeing the way his dark eyes keep looking back at me in annoyance, yet he says nothing nor insists that I leave him be, instead he allows me to trace over his steps.

"I heard the dance went well," I say after about the third aisle, my fingers dancing across the spines of books that we pass. The different textures make my fingers tingle.

Quinton grunts to show he heard me but says nothing. I roll my eyes; can't he reply like a normal human being rather than rely on grunts and moans? Why am I always the one doing most of the talking? He needs to work on his antisocial behavior.

"Autumn punched someone." I say, remembering what Langley had told me earlier.

My comment makes Quinton smirk, a smirk that tells me he is quite proud of his girlfriend for doing such a thing. "She did."

"Never knew you liked the violent type."

Quinton places the book in his grasp beneath his arm. He finally faces me and asks, "Is there a point to this conversation or are you just trying to bug me?"

Point? Maybe. Bug? Definitely.

Shrugging, I grin and ask, "How'd you two even get together? I bet she had to ask, huh? You don't have a single romantic bone in your body."

The idea of Quinton being romantic sends a shiver down my spine. The idea of him asking someone out makes my stomach churn, and I mentally slap myself for such reactions.

Why am I poking my nose in any way? His relationship with Autumn is none of my concern, yet I can't stop myself from asking.

"Coming from Romeo without his Juliet, that means nothing." Quinton brushes past me towards the clerk. I growl and chase him, ignoring the few stares of the surrounding people. They're probably waiting for a fight. After all, Quinton and I haven't fought in...i n...whoa, a long time. How long has it been? I can't even remember.

"Stop acting so smug about having a girlfriend. I bet you two won't last another month!" Or rather, I hope you don't.

The evil librarian sends me a warning glance, but seeing as I'm following Quinton, who is checking out a book, she says nothing since I'm leaving. Why I'm following him, I'm not sure. Yet again, I find my body reacting without my consent. Whenever I think *stop, don't follow him,'* my body replies with 'sorry, what did you say? Follow him? Ok!' He annoys me but I can't stop myself from speaking to him. My mouth and brain coordination appear to be pretty shit. I think I have a mental problem. My brain is messed up. It needs to be checked. I better make an appointment before I go insane, if I'm not already.

"What are you talking about?" Quinton asks with a cocked brow. "I don't have a girlfriend."

Wait, what? Sorry, I was lost in my head and may have misheard, but when Quinton doesn't reiterate what he says, I speak. "Did you two break up again?"

My heart is racing at the thought of Quinton being single—I mean, of Autumn being single, yeah! Not him, Autumn, since she gave me her number and I can ask her out, not because Quinton is single and I can ask him out. I'm not interested in guys, especially not him. If I ever had an interest in men, it wouldn't be Quinton. Definitely not.

Quinton gives me that 'get away from me, idiot' look before saying, "Again? I told you we broke up."

"But you two went to the dance together..."

"You don't need to date a girl to take her to a dance," Quinton replies like it's an obvious answer. How is that obvious? I'm so confused.

"So you still like her and she went with you out of pity?" I laugh as I playfully punch his arm, begging for details. He shoves me away, hard enough to make me stumble. It takes me a mere second to catch back up to him. People are staring at us funny again, now probably because it looks like we're fighting with the way he's shoving me away and I'm hitting his arm.

"Why are you so curious about us?" His eyes narrow on me. Dark orbs glisten over with an emotion I cannot read, not that I'm good at reading his emotions normally. He's as easy to read as hieroglyphics to me.

"Why wouldn't I be? The ever so great Quinton is in a one sided romance!" The inner evil me laughs manically at the thought.

His face shows no sadness or discomfort. The conversation doesn't even seem to bother him. Wouldn't most people be embarrassed or sad? Why is he acting like its nothing? Makes me wonder if perhaps he broke up with her? No way. She was a babe. They didn't look unhappy together, so what went wrong? Then again, if Quinton is involved, then everything is wrong. Quinton is the piece that's wrong.

As I said before, I bet this boy hasn't got a single romantic bone in his body. Girls like romance and Quinton clearly does not. Though, I suppose, he could, seeing as Quinton is always going above and beyond. For all I know, he could be the most romantic guy in the world—has anyone else started laughing at the thought because, holy crap, it's tough for me to keep it in! Ok, no way, I'm going to die laughing thinking about this. I need to stop before I do laugh out loud and my sanity is questioned by people other than myself.

"Comforting to know our future king finds joy in other people's misfortunes," Quinton says, voice as normal as ever. By the sounds of it he isn't bothered by being single. Did he even like her? He's acting as if it's nothing.

I laugh. "Only your misfortune brings me joy."

"I'm honored." His voice oozes sarcasm.

"You should be, but seriously, what happened? You two seemed close." I attempt to pry, wishing to know the entire story for whatever strange reason.

Quinton stops in his tracks, making me do the same. I hadn't realized how long we were walking together until I see his dorm. We're standing a few feet from the doorway. There aren't many people passing by, so I don't feel too embarrassed or worried about speaking with Quinton like this.

He gives me a curious look as he asks, "Why do you care? We aren't friends."

I don't think he realizes it, but he just sucker punched me in the gut. The air is knocked out of me the moment those words leave his lips. I feel my mind go blank. My heart stops. My hands feel clammy. I can't breathe properly and my mouth won't stop gaping like a fish. Quinton continues to look at me in confusion like, he honest to god does not think we are friends, like he doesn't know why I'm asking and...

Ouch. Whoa, ouch. I may have never voiced my thoughts of us being 'friends' to him, so I suppose he has the right to be confused but... but Autumn said...

"I just...thought..." What? That we're friends? How am I supposed to say that after what he just said? Sure, Autumn said he confessed to us being friends, but she could have said that to mess with me. She could have said that to make me forgive the bastard for angering me. What she said didn't have to be true and now I'm believing it wasn't.

As if Quinton would have feelings for another human being. You would need a heart to feel. Quinton obviously lacks said organ.

"You thought what?" He asks, taking a step closer to me. I feel the heat radiating from his body, warming my cool skin. The cool February air has suddenly become hot to me. I feel as if he's challenging me to continue, as if he already knows what I'm about to say but believes I won't actually have the courage to speak it.

Black eyes watch me like an ant under a magnifying glass. They watch my every movement, from the licking of my suddenly dry lips to the twitching of my fingertips at my side. He's analyzing everything I do for a reason I do not know. If he had a tail, I imagine it'd be swinging with predatory intent.

My heart's racing from his gaze. Although I'm nervous and incredibly uncomfortable, I somehow work up the courage to say, "I thought we were friends."

Ok, I more like shouted it. Luckily, no one is around to hear any of this, which I find odd. Classes are over. You'd think there would be a crowd around the dorms, but luck must be on our side because, some way, somehow, no one is here to hear my true feelings. If they did, I'm sure I would have died of embarrassment by now but, hey, I may die anyway because for once in Quinton's demonic life the boy actually appears shocked.

At least I think he's shocked. The emotion comes and goes so quickly I hardly have time to notice the widening of his eyes or slack jaw. His apathetic expression returns quickly though he says nothing, another once in a lifetime thing. Man, give me an award for getting some type of reaction from this hell spawn. I'm a bloody magician!

Quinton always has something smart to say, but now he seems at a loss for words, so I speak for him.

"I thought we were friends," I repeat, much softer than before, and though I know my gaze is shaking, I do not remove it from the lock I have with his own. I'm not sure why I need to repeat the one thing I have been telling myself over and over isn't true.

I wish at this moment I could read minds... or at least Quinton's, because I don't have a clue what he's thinking.

With eyes as dark as ever and a face as expressionless as ever, the boy sighs like our conversation has actually taken a physical toll on him. Rolling his eyes, he says, "Being close doesn't mean anything."

"Huh?" Where did that come from?

Quinton must see my confusion because he groans, "Autumn."

"Ah!" Oh yeah, I said I thought they were close, but hey, he has said nothing about what I said earlier! And now he's turning to walk away from me, which means he probably doesn't plan to, but he didn't disagree, which means he could, maybe, in some way feel the same?

That thought alone makes me short of breath.

CHAPTER TWENTY-EIGHT

Once we're in Quinton's room, I ask with obvious disgust, "So you two are childhood friends and you dated her out of pity because you're a total asshole?"

"How does that make me an asshole?" Quinton inquires with squinted eyes that show the wheels turning in his head. He sits in the chair by his desk while I'm seated on the bed.

"No one wants to be dated out of pity! It's wrong!" Right? I'm not the only one who thinks this. Because Quinton is looking at me like I'm an idiot-oh wait, he always does that!

For the thousandth time since we ran into each other, Quinton rolls his eyes. "The point of dating is to discover possible romantic feelings for one another that may not be there originally."

"So you wanted to like her?" I ask.

He doesn't answer.

"But you didn't because you're crazy." Obviously he is. She's hot. She can actually speak to him without having the greatest of desires to rip out her hair. Well, maybe she did. I, for one, have not ripped out my hair yet, though sometimes I've wanted to. No, scratch that, I rather felt the urge to rip out his. Either way, he's lucky he had her!

Again with rolling his eyes. If he keeps that up, they're going to roll out of his skull, or rather, one can hope.

"Taking dating advice from you is idiotic." Quinton swings one leg over the other as he says that. Why does he have to look so superior all the time? One of these days, I'm going to punch that smirk right off his face or kick or tear. Doesn't matter. One way or the other, I will get him to stop looking so smug all the time.

Grumbling, I grab one of the boy's pillows from his bed to toss it at his head, which he easily dodges. Now he's giving me that *'you're so mature'* look. Is it sad that I can read his looks now? They are as clear as day to me. It means I have spent more time with him than I should have, but, seriously, assholes need to stop expressing themselves through smirks and looks. It's irritating.

"Whatever. Anyone would say you're an idiot. She was hot and one of the few people who seemed capable of putting up with someone like you," I huff while pointing at the boy.

Quinton must find our conversation more boring than homework because he's burying himself in a textbook now. I feel my eyebrow twitch at the fact that he enjoys reading a shitty textbook more than speaking with me. I like to think I'm a fun guy. Wait, Quinton doesn't like fun, so that may explain it. Whatever, I'm better than a book, aren't I? Pay attention to me, damn it! Wait—I mean—no, something is seriously wrong with me.

Regardless of my insane thoughts that can't seem to decipher whether or not I want his attention, I'm about to beat the shit out of the arrogant bastard anyway for ignoring me until he speaks.

"Looks aren't everything," he says. How very Quinton. "If that were the case, you'd never get a girlfriend."

What. Did. He. Just. Say? I'm going to kill him!

My face must reveal my thoughts more than I mean for them to, because I barely make out a smirk on Lucifer's face. He's the devil, I'm telling you! He turns his head enough to show me his dark eyes and Quinton may not smile, but his eyes sure as hell tell me he enjoys teasing me. They are practically sparkling with delight. I'm serious. I'm going to kill him. The jail time will be worth it.

"I'm going to kill you," I state my thoughts to the demon who does not seem at all shocked nor bothered to hear them.

"You'll try," He states his own.

"I'm a prince." I slam my hands against my chest as if to emphasize my point. "I can do it and get away with it."

"Abusing your power already, Princess?"

I pounce him on instinct. Not expecting my sudden attack, Quinton has no time to brace himself. The two of us topple to the floor as a mess of limbs. Rather than throwing punches or kicks, we simply roll across the floor to get the other to let go. It doesn't hurt and I swear I see the smallest of smiles on his face during the tussle. However, I know better. Quinton does not smile.

We're rolling around the floor, causing ourselves to knock into things like the desk and beds. Somehow, I end up ramming Quinton a little too roughly into his bed, causing his pillow, which was already hanging a bit off the edge, to fall. Remembering what I found in there a year ago, I look down to see the same picture fluttering out and onto the floor. Quinton hasn't realized it yet and I wonder if I should take this opportunity to question him about it.

I grab the photo before the boy has time to realize it has revealed itself. Holding up the photo before his eyes, I ask, "What's this?"

Shock fills Quinton's face. For a moment, I wonder if a bad replica has replaced the boy because the amount of emotions he's showing on his face is abnormal. Abnormal enough to make something within my mind click and realize that there is certainly a story to this picture.

There's shock, fear, nervousness, anger and more swimming in his eyes that, for once, seem at a loss for what to do. Quickly realizing his strange behavior, Quinton shakes his head furiously, dispersing the normally concealed emotions and replacing them with apathy yet again. I have to give the guy credit for keeping his emotions in check. If I were him, I imagine I'd go ape shit crazy. He reaches for the photograph, but I pull away.

Now I'm even more curious. How could a single picture change him so much? Who is this man? What happened? Why does he keep this photo? He can't honestly expect me to see such a reaction from him and not question it. I've had such questions running through my mind before, but now I feel there may be a chance, even a slim one, to learn the truth.

"Hand it over." Quinton demands, urgently reaching once again for the picture.

I pull myself farther away, now on the other side of the room near Taylor's bed. Quinton still has his back pressed against his bed, eyes narrowed on me. I have a feeling he's about to jump me and take the picture by force. That's fine because I have been attacked by him before. It may have been a while since we last had a physical confrontation, but that doesn't mean I can't handle him.

"No." I shake my head stubbornly. "I'm curious. Who is this?" I point to the burned out man. "It's a little weird to keep a partially burned photo."

"My mother is in it. Why would I throw it out?" He's trying to use that gigantic head of his to get himself out of this.

"I'm sure you have other photos with her in them." I argue. I may not be as smart as he is, but I will do my best to get an answer.

Growling, Quinton gets to his knees, leaning over and holding out his hand. "I like that picture. Give it back."

"You don't burn pictures you like." I am tempted to say 'but you don't like anything,' however, I felt in this situation it would be a little too immature, even for me.

"It's none of your damn business, Aron." He spits my name out like garbage. It makes me flinch. For so long we've been "getting along," so hearing him speak down to me much like he used to actually makes my chest tighten. I don't like the feeling and part of me is scared of that.

"Of course it is! We're friends!" My shout startles him enough to make him back away, but only for a second. He crawls over to me, placing one hand on Taylor's bed that is behind me and, while on his knees, leans over me. I am so taken by how close he is that my mind goes blank. All thoughts seem to shatter and disperse to opposite ends of the galaxy as my eyes remain fixated on his that grows closer with every passing second.

We're too close. I can feel his breath on my cheeks. I can feel his body heating up my own. I can smell his cologne mixed with a scent that is uniquely Quinton. I can see how truly dark his eyes are, barely revealing the black pupils. I can count every eyelash, every blemish, every scar...

We're too close.

"Everyone is allowed their secrets," he says darkly. The huskiness of his voice only worsens my blush. Part of me wonders if he realizes what he's doing to me. I pray he doesn't. Such power is not meant for anyone.

Shouldn't I be bothered by the proximity? But somehow I find myself aroused. I have found myself with a dry throat yet again, something that happens mostly with Quinton. I'm shaking. I'm sweating. I don't know where to look. I think during a time like this, my eyes stay locked with his, but I can't keep myself from looking at his lips.

Pink and plump and wet and...

I panic. I don't even know what I'm thinking about right now. His eyes, lips, heat? My mind is going straight to the gutter and I am hell bent on keeping it out. I need to focus on the picture. Yes, the picture, not Quinton and the way his collarbones are clearly visible at this angle or how I could easily reach out to feel the muscles I know are lying beneath his shirt...

The picture, Aron! Damn it!

"I would never burn my father out of a picture," I somehow manage to say, though my voice is way too breathy. Breathy? Seriously, Aron? Can you dig yourself a deeper hole because right now you're already six feet under?

Too enraged to notice my awkward behavior, Quinton growls, "Who said it's my father?"

"By your angry tone, I am guessing I was right." I clutch the paper even closer when Quinton reaches for it. His hand wraps around mine and I curse myself for actually enjoying the touch. Feeling the warmth of his hand around mine is driving my brain into a wall over and over and over and over—

"If you don't let go—"

"What?" I ask, challenging the boy. "You'll hit me? Come on, Quinny, we've tussled before. That doesn't scare me."

"Why are you so damn stubborn?" Quinton hisses, finally pulling away. I realized after he had moved that I was actually leaning into him. He was not the one coming closer, but I was. Had he noticed? Why didn't he say anything? Why was I leaning on him?

I need to see my doctor. I think I've gone insane. No, I know I have.

"Why are you?" I ask, doing my best to disperse the thoughts of how I miss his heat, how I miss how close he was. Those are not the kinds of thoughts I should have right now. "Just answer. It's not like I'm going to tell anyone."

Which is true. Quinton and I have realized that our hatred for each other has lessened over the past year. I will take whatever secret this is to my grave.

Quinton seems more annoyed than ever. I say that because I can actually see his annoyance, which he rarely allows. Running his hands over his face, he groans, "I don't expect you to tell."

I pout. If that's the case, then what's his problem? I ask, "Then why not tell me?"

"Because you'll—" Quinton stops himself before he finishes. I can't imagine what he is going to say. I'll, what? I won't understand. I will think it's stupid. I find myself unable to read his expression yet again. He is doing his best to keep me out and he's doing a damn good job of it.

"Whatever, I don't care. Keep the damn thing," Quinton spits out, getting up from the floor and heading to the bathroom. I never expected he would be the kind of guy to lock himself in a bathroom to get away from a conversation, but that's what he does. The water is running, signaling he has gotten into the shower. I know he will not be in there long, but I do not wait.

I could see on his face that he had no intention of telling me, no matter how much I bugged him. It appears the boy has reached his emotional limit for the day and had no intention of allowing me to bug him further.

I take my leave, without the photograph, of course. I go over what happened all the way back to my dorm. I don't even say hello to Langley when I enter. Instead, I lie on my bed, thinking of the burnt photograph while wondering what someone could do to their child to have them burned out of a picture, yet they still keep it?

CHAPTER TWENTY-NINE

Standing outside Professor Bennett's office, I can't help but feel guilty. I have gone back to my old ways, snooping around to find information about Quinton rather than asking him. If the jerk would tell me rather than ignore me for, like, 3 days, then I wouldn't have to resort to such things. It's his fault—I tell myself to make myself feel better about what I'm about to do. I had remembered coming to the office to speak about grades a while back. I overheard a bit of the conversation between Professor Bennett and Quinton.

"It is especially shocking for you. Who would have thought you'd do such a great job considering who your—"

"That has nothing to do with one's abilities."

I believe I now know what Professor Bennett was about to say; considering who your father is. It makes sense but at the same time, doesn't. As someone who desperately wished to not be compared to my father, yet I always am. I understand the questions, possibly running through Quinton's mind. How does my father's action define me in any way? Yet, everyone continues to compare me as if the answer is clear.

Quinton sounded angered after hearing such a thing. He sounds angered when the photograph is brought up. I doubt he'd want to be compared to someone he hates, so it makes sense.

I thank the gods today for making me who I am. If I were anyone else, I doubt I could get away with this. Not anyone can walk up to a professor and ask about another student's family and get an answer. I suppose he could say no, refuse to tell me anything and send me on my way, but I don't believe that will happen.

With a deep breath, I knock on Professor Bennett's door. After I hear him say 'come in,' I enter and the professor smiles upon seeing me, a smile that I see many people fake in my presence. It would be nice if I could enter a room without everyone forcing themselves to act in a way they believe would make me happy.

"Your Highness, it's nice to see you," he says, gesturing at an empty seat in front of his desk. He puts away whatever he is working on to focus on me. "What can I help you with today?"

I wonder how to word this. Should I straight up ask who Quinton's father is or beat around the bush? The teachers know that Quinton and I are not fighting like we used to, but that does not mean they think we are friends. That development in our relationship was recently discovered between ourselves, so I doubt—

Whoa, wait, relationship? That makes it sound weird...like we're involved or something. Which we aren't! And I don't want to be! Of course I don't. Like I'd want to be in a relationship with Quinton heh...heh...

Professor Bennett clears his throat, making me realize I had been silent for a little longer than necessary. Quickly, I shake my head, erasing those ridiculous thoughts and focusing on what's important right now. I take the seat offered to me, clearing my throat as well, either because I needed to or to stall time. Perhaps a bit of both.

"Professor, I was wondering about Quinton's parents." I say with as much confidence as I can muster. His face tells me he is confused. I don't blame him. I try to think up some bullshit excuse to get something out of him. "You see, the other day I insulted his upbringing and his parents. He seemed to get angrier than usual and I want to apologize, but I don't know what to apologize for."

They will believe such a lie, right? We argue all the time and I bet a teacher would rather I apologize than continue fighting. At least, that's what I think they would want. Who knows, they all may be secretly praying we kill each other so they don't have to put up with us anymore. I know I would be if I were them.

Professor Bennett appears very uncomfortable. His shoulders tense and lips tighten into a thin line that reveals he is neither happy nor mad, but somewhere in between. It's strange to see him so unwilling to answer when he normally jumps at the opportunity to help a student. What could make him so jittery? He bites his lip and asks, "Are you still fighting with that boy? It'd be best if you two didn't get too close. Quinton is an exceptional student but..."

"But what?" I ask. At a time like this, I wish to be skilled at things such as psychology or the movement of the human body. I may be able to decipher that Professor Bennett is uncomfortable, but I can't seem to discover why. Why is this a touchy subject? Why is he making it sound like the idea of Quinton and I spending more time than necessary together is a bad thing?

I feel angry that Professor Bennett doesn't want me around Quinton. Sure, he probably thinks we're physically fighting like we used to, but it doesn't seem like that's the reason he doesn't want us associating. Is there something wrong with him? Mr. Perfect is perfect, so what makes him so worried? What could make a teacher want me to avoid a student? I recall earlier on he wanted me to ask the boy for help, yet the idea of us being closer than necessary bothers him. Again, why? I never thought it possible to ask why so much.

"You say you want us not to be close, and yet, when I first came here, you suggested Quinton as someone to speak with should I need help. So using him to achieve my goals is fine, but befriending him is bad?" I ask, slightly shocked at my tone that speaks more than my words. Professor Bennett's eyes widen, seeming to hear the undertone of my voice as well and being just as shocked at hearing it. His mouth gapes like a fish and I take his silence as an opportunity to continue.

"What is it that makes Quinton a bad influence? He's intelligent, far more intelligent than half the population, dare I say that. He is obviously going places, so shouldn't you feel the opposite? Shouldn't I want such a person around me?" Asking such things brings back memories of Quinton and I, all the fights, the desire to crush him, the wish to have him expelled, yet here I sit defending the boy I once despised. Isn't it crazy how time changes you? How you can go from absolutely despising them to...

Professor Bennett clears his throat, clearly uncomfortable with this conversation. The man coughs, holding his hands over his lips as he speaks. "Some people are above others."

"Above?" The word comes out like rotten food. I can taste the obvious disgust on my tongue and the vile that it has made within my stomach is enough to make me shiver. I let out a laugh, a laugh that sounds repulsed at hearing it.

"Above?" I repeat the question and nod to myself. "Yes, I suppose that is true."

Professor Bennett smiles and looks ready to say how he's glad I feel that way, but his smile falls when I abruptly stand. The chair scrapes against the floor, whether or not it left marks I honestly don't care. Actually, I hope it did.

"I agree with you," I say, looking down at the man that seems at a loss. "Some people are above others. Just like I am above you right now. Forget what I asked. I wouldn't want your biased opinion. If you'll excuse me, Professor."

I exit Professor Bennett's office with haughty steps mixed with frustration. The squeaking of my sneakers against the floor are the only sounds that reach my ears, seeing as my mind is roaring like an inferno within me. What the hell made him think he could speak about one of his students like that? Oh god, and to think...

I stop in my tracks to aggressively rip at my hair as I groan to myself. I used to think like that! I used to think I was above Quinton but hearing someone speak of him like that now makes me want to...makes me want to...I don't freaking know, but it's bad! I want to punch him, push him off a fucking cliff, push him into oncoming traffic. I don't know, but I want it to be painful.

My question wasn't answered either! Now I have even more. I can't think of a thing that could explain it. I shouldn't be shocked. I'm not the brightest crayon in the box, trying to decipher the puzzle that is Quinton's life is far too difficult for me. I desperately wish to know, especially now. I got so pissed that now I want to take my mind off it, preferably by learning about the dark demon's past.

I stop in the path towards my dorm. Looking behind my shoulder, back at the school building, I bite my lip. I could try the library. The internet knows all!

With a heavy sigh, I turn and begin heading to the library. I could have used my own laptop, but if Langley were at our dorm and were to ask why I was looking up Quinton, I feel I'd stutter myself into a stupid trap. So I find myself minutes later sitting here before a computer with a heavy heart that is continuously battling it out with my brain. Look him up? Don't look him up?

Perhaps the question should be; betray him or not? Because that's what it feels like I'm about to do. We're friends now, or at least I think we are. Friends don't look up each other's past. Then again, not everyone is friends with Quinton Underwood, one of the most unsocial, unreadable and mysterious bastards to ever grace this earth! But...

I can't.

Even after I decided earlier to find out more about the mystery that is Quinton, I can't get myself to do it. I feel like I'm betraying his trust. I shouldn't have to snoop on the Internet in order to find out something about my friend. That's wrong, isn't it?

There's no question about it. It is wrong. I shouldn't do this, but I really want to know. I feel like my head and heart are having a full out battle. My mind is saying look it up, look it up while my heart is screaming, it's wrong, it's wrong. Damn it, couldn't I have become friends with Quinton after I've found out about his dad? If we weren't friends, I wouldn't feel bad about snooping.

"What are you doing?" An all too familiar voice asks from behind me. I nearly fell out of my seat from shock. I was so lost in my head I didn't notice Quinton behind me.

Cursing, I look back to see him watching me. I should have gone to my dorm. What made me think I wouldn't run into him at the library? He basically lives here! Shit, I even have his name typed into the browser but I haven't pressed enter so there's nothing up!

"Uh…" How do I say I was thinking about looking you up but decided against it because I feel guilty? I smile sheepishly. "Nothing…nothing at all."

"You've been staring at the screen for ten minutes." Which means he's been watching me for ten minutes. What a creeper! Says the boy who was about to google search someone because he is too curious for his own good.

"So you have been staring at me for that long?" I ask in hopes of changing the focus from me to him.

My question makes him realize his mistake. He doesn't need to answer since we both know that the only way he would know that is if he was watching me. My cheeks heat up at the thought. Stop that, cheeks!

Shaking his head, he says, "That doesn't matter. Why are you trying to google me?"

'I want to know about your dad, but you won't tell me because you're a stubborn ass and Professor Bennett is a piece of shit,' is what I want to say.

I scratch my head nervously. "I just… was curious."

"About my father." That certainly wasn't a question. Then again, Quinton never questions. He states things.

I nod dumbly while avoiding all eye contact. "Yeah."

"Why?" He asks.

"Why wouldn't I be?" Ok, now I'm looking at him because I'm thinking he may actually not be so smart. Isn't it obvious?

"You're so weird," Quinton sighs, running his hand through his hair. His face should appear to be annoyed, but it's not. Rather, he looks, dare I say it, slightly amused. I want to say he's on the verge of smiling, but Quinton doesn't smile. I must be hallucinating. "You've always told me you've hated me and yet you seem to be the person most concerned about me. Why is that?"

His question stumps me. I find myself backed into a corner that, honestly; I lead myself into.

Yes, why is that Aron? Since I have met Quinton, my life has been a roller coaster of emotions. I've gone from loathing him, to accepting him a bit, to being friends without even meaning to. Sure, realizing we are friends was more of a recent development, but we realized it; as in he hasn't said we aren't, so, he must think we are. I never thought we would ever get along, but we do, weirdly.

I think about him all the time. I worry about him. I want to know about him. I want to see him, speak with him, be around him because we're friends, just because we're friends! Ah, I sound so weird. I don't mean it like that. It's just because we're friends, no other reason. Just that!

"Because we're friends..." but it feels wrong saying we're only friends. Deep down, I know there's more of a reason than that. "Because I care, because I want to know more about you."

My admission shocks Quinton enough to show it. Seeing his stunned expression is something that I shouldn't be capable of making him do. The thought that my words dazed him enough to show it makes me panic. Don't look like that. It's getting my hopes up because now my heart is racing at knowing that it's me, me who made him make such a face. I'm the one who made the normally stoic boy show something other than apathy. It both scares and excites me.

Quickly, I jump from the computer chair to shout with a blush on my face red enough that anyone could see. Hell, put me on a runway and use me as a freaking beacon. I'm so red. "I take that back! I don't...I don't want to know more about you. What I mean is I...I..."

What? Shit, what do I say? He's still shocked. Stop acting shocked, you're making it worse! Quinton, you're supposed to say something like 'you're an idiot' and make this weird heart fluttering disappear. But he doesn't. He says nothing and instead stares at me with those dark eyes that seem to entrap me.

The room suddenly feels small, as if the walls are closing in on me and my unknown feelings. It's suffocating. I can't be around him. Dear god, I need to get out of here.

Before Quinton can question my sanity, not that I'm not already questioning it, I rush back to my dorm. Fuck finding out about his dad. I need to find out what's wrong with me. Why is my heart racing? Why can't I stop blushing? Why are my hands shaking? Why can't I stop thinking about him? I know why, but I don't want to admit it.

Heart, please, stop racing. I can't do this. I'm not ready for it.

CHAPTER THIRTY

"What the hell are you doing?" Langley peers down at me.

"I dropped my pencil."

"And you take five minutes to pick up your pencil?" Langley asks, watching as I duck behind a trash can. Peeking over said trash can, I scan the area to see the one I am hiding from is now gone. Sighing, I jump up and pretend that I've found my pencil, announcing to Langley that we may continue on our way to class.

"You're acting really weird," Langley says, watching to see if I duck behind some other object or begin ripping my hair out, shouting about aliens and the likes since I'm sure he's officially put me down as crazy. That's fine. I've put myself down as crazy a long time ago.

Rolling my eyes, I reply, "No, I'm not. I told you, I dropped my pencil."

"You've been—" Langley makes air quotes, "'Dropping your pencil' for nearly a week. I'm thinking there's something wrong with you. Are you sick dude? If you are, stay away from me." Langley throws a hand over his mouth to keep my 'sick' away from him.

Shoving him, I say, "I'm not sick."

Not in the way he's thinking. If Langley knew what's actually going on in my mind, he would probably be disgusted. I don't know what's wrong with me, but there is definitely something wrong. After I spouted that 'I care about you' crap to Quinton, my heart can't stop racing. Seeing him makes me nervous. Somehow, we have continuously run into each other and each time Quinton, the asshole, silent Quinton, attempted to speak to me about what happened, but I ran.

Seriously, the world does shit like this on purpose. We went nearly half a year without seeing one another. Now that I am trying to avoid the boy, he's around every corner, in every hall and, basically, everywhere I wish him not to be. What's up with that?

Let's not forget that Quinton, who would probably remain mute his entire life if he felt he could get away with it, suddenly decides that now he wishes to speak. Didn't he ignore me before? Wasn't I always the one who had to start the conversation? Now it seems he'd love to have a chat with me because every time I see him, he gets this look in his eyes. A look that has my toes curling and I can't handle having him in my vision, so I bolt in the opposite direction. Why does he want to talk now? Can't he be the normal Quinton that never starts a conversation? Please. I cannot deal with this. My heart is trying to tell me something I'm not ready to admit to.

I can't hear him. I can't see him. Just the thought of him makes my heart race. See! It's doing it right now! Stop that, you little shit!

I place my hand over my chest like that will help. Taking a deep breath, I try to think of anything but that black-hearted asshole... oh great, now I'm thinking about his hair and his eyes and how he isn't always so black-hearted. Sometimes he can be gentle and really cool and it makes my legs feel like jello, damn it! Snap out of it, Aron! Quinton is just...just a friend. Please heart; tell me he's just a friend.

Because of these reactions, I have been hiding every time I have seen him, which is way more than I'm comfortable with. If he tries to talk to me about it, I don't know what to say. I could easily say I didn't mean it, but thinking about it, that's not true even though I really want it to be.

"You know besides the constant dropping of your things there's been other weird things about you lately," Langley says, breaking me from my thoughts. I force a smile. What is he talking about? He couldn't possibly know about Quinton..."You've been lost a lot in the empty place between your ears. It's weird."

"Empty place! Hey, are you saying I don't have a brain?" And here I thought Langley was on my side. I see how it is.

Smirking, Langley completely ignores my question in favor of asking his own, "What's up? Do we need to have another therapy session?"

Honestly, yes, but I can't imagine how Langley would react upon hearing what I have to say. I don't even know how to react! I'm not even sure what I have to say. What am I feeling? Ok, so I know what it is, but the question is why am I feeling it and towards Quinton of all people! If I'm going to have such feelings, can't I have better taste? Anyone is better than Quinton!

I'm more bothered about my feelings being towards Quinton than I am the fact that I have feelings towards another guy. Liking a guy? Whatever, but liking Quinton? That's a whole other story!

I know there's a spark in me every time I see Quinton, but my brain is screaming at me not to admit it, to continue ignoring and go on believing that I am a high school boy with interests towards girls and girls only. My heart doesn't skip when Quinton's near. I don't blush at those stupid, annoying and cocky smirks of his. I don't get excited upon hearing his voice. Nope. Nothing like that happens, not now, not ever. Who am I trying to kid?

What's worse is even if I want to talk to someone about this, I can't risk doing so. I am my father's son. I am an idol of sorts. Should the wrong people discover I may or may not be carrying feelings for another man, the results could be disastrous. Not only will I be buried beneath tons of articles and shows talking about my newfound interest, so will my father. People are much more open-minded nowadays but that doesn't mean they would be ok with such a thing. There are still those who wouldn't be ok with it and not to mention I'm kind of expected to have children. I need an heir.

If I think about this anymore, I'm going to spiral into a dark void and never return. Not that I'm saying I'm not there already, seeing as my depressing thoughts are already taking a toll on me. My head is aching from the amount of thinking I've been doing the last few days. I am not used to such brain activity, and it's wearing me out. I am at such a loss that I'm wondering if I have entered another dimension, and this all is a figment of my imagination.

Classes end for the day, thank god, seeing as I had paid no mind to any of the lessons. I couldn't even try, which is sad. Sad to think that a man has held such power over my mind that nothing and no one could possibly overthrow him. Power like that should belong to no one, yet it seems Quinton is surprising in more ways than one.

Langley leaves to hang out with Ariel for the evening while I head back to the dorms. I'm somewhat glad for that. As great as it is to have such a caring friend, it is also troublesome. Troublesome because I don't have a clue how to answer his concerned questions, I'm still having trouble answering myself, so answering another is impossible.

My heart has sunk to the darkest pits of depression as I think about my current predicament. There are too many thoughts, too many emotions running through me right now that I don't understand how I'm functioning at all. Shouldn't my brain be too busy worrying to have the capability to inform my legs to keep moving? I'm mentally exhausted.

I'm too busy thinking of Quinton to notice that the one haunting my thoughts grows near. It isn't until I see a pair of sneakers in my path that I follow the legs up to their owner to realize the bastard is standing right in front of me with an annoyed glare. No shocker there. If there were anything but a glare I'd send him to the nurse for a checkup.

"H-Hey Quinton. H-Hi Q-Quinton. Quinton, how-how-hello."

End me. Please. What did I even say?

Now he's raising his brow at me in that questioning manner that is only making things worse. I feel sick and not in the 'I'm going to vomit' way more like 'I'm such a fool, so I desperately wish to get away from this situation or I may die' type of way. Yes... that's a specific feeling.

I am about to do as my thoughts wish and bolt to the other end of the Earth. However, it seems Quinton has grown tired of my constant will to run. His hand shoots out so fast I haven't time to react. He has a hold on my wrist so tight that it'd take a body lifter with a crowbar to pull us apart. Does anyone have one around? If so, I need both.

"You're avoiding me," he states more than questions because Quinton never questions.

"Uh..." Well yes, yes I am, but apparently not well enough because we can't stop running into each other, damn it! And where is Langley when I need him? I could so easily use him as an excuse to not speak with Quinton.

How did we go from hardly seeing each other to running into one another daily? The world hates me. It really does.

Swallowing the lump in my throat, I say, "N-No I'm not. Stop flattering yourself. The world doesn't revolve around you."

Apparently my world does, but that's beside the point!

"Is this about before?" Quinton asks, letting go of my wrist once he has realized that I'm not attempting to run, though now it is an option. I move around him to continue my path to my dorm. Part of me thought he wouldn't follow, but alas, the world continues to enjoy my misery because, of course, he follows me.

Before could mean a lot of things, like the picture or the time I spat out that 'I want to know more about you,' crap, or perhaps he noticed my insane blushing and wants an answer. If he wants to focus on only one of those moments, though, he can go ahead and do that! I'll put the others into a category for later.

"I don't know what you're talking about." Because playing dumb is always the answer.

I don't need to see Quinton to know he rolled his eyes at that. I can hear it in his voice as he says, "Wanting to know mo—"

I spin around fast enough to shove my hand over his mouth in order to shut him up. Again, I don't need to see it in order to know he's smirking. Actually, I can feel it against my palm. Still blushing like the idiot that I am, I grumble, "D-Don't say it. Pretend you never heard it."

"I would have had someone not started avoiding me like the plague," he says beneath my palm. Feeling his lips move against my skin sends a shock down my spine. I'm forced to pull it away or else I might do something crazy.

"Like we saw each other often to begin with," I mumble, more to myself than him. He heard and releases an annoyed sigh. He sounds as if our conversation is taking a physical toll.

Quinton speeds up in order to walk beside me. The action causes me to bite the inside of my cheek in an attempt to make pain lessen my blush. Now I'm blushing just from him being a little closer than normal? Great! Seriously...please, world, if I'm going to like men at least give me good taste in them. Quinton? Of all people? Do you hate me that much?

"Will you continue this childish nonsense or are we going to talk?" Quinton inquires. We've arrived at the dorms and I am unbelievably tempted to have the guard escort Quinton out. I feel that would be too much of a dick move. Oh, but the temptation...

I don't do it. Damn me for being such a great guy.

"Why do you sound annoyed? You should know I am the definition of childish behavior." I send the boy a grin that only seems to piss him off more. Someone woke up on the wrong side of the bed this morning. Then again, he always does. "What exactly are we supposed to talk about?"

Quinton doesn't answer but opts for awkward silence all the way to my room. Once at my door, I look at him to check if he is planning to answer. He simply stares back at me with a blank expression and no words. Now who's being childish with the silent treatment?

"Do you plan on following me into my room as well?" I ask, silently praying he doesn't notice how worried I sound.

He wants to talk in private? But it's so much harder to control myself in private. Can't we sit on a bench in public somewhere in order to keep myself from doing something stupid? Not that it's ever helped before, but one can hope.

Quinton opens the door and allows himself in. I once again feel the temptation to have security remove him. What the hell?

"Who said you could come in?!" Because I don't remember giving him permission! Stop acting like the prince here! We both know the real prince is me!

Completely ignoring my obvious annoyance with him letting himself in, Quinton makes himself comfortable on my bed. Quinton stares up at the ceiling and asks the next question as if the idea of talking about it doesn't even bother him, "Don't you want to know about my father?"

He really knows how to pique my interest, doesn't he? Damn it. Suddenly, I don't care about him letting himself in. I'll yell at him about that later. For now, I wish to unravel the mystery that is Quinton Underwood.

CHAPTER THIRTY-ONE

"Your father." The man in the picture, the man I've had questions about for over a year. Not that he knows that, but some things are better left unsaid. I take a seat at the end of my bed. With my eyes locked on the floor, I ask, "You're...going to tell me?"

"You'll only google me if I don't." He states matter-of-factly.

"No, I wouldn't!"

I mean, I tried, but I didn't do it. I can't bring myself to do such a thing. After gaining his trust, or rather a small amount of it, I wish not to lose it. Besides, the internet can only give me one half of the story. I wish to hear the truth from Quinton's own mouth.

"I'm not that much of a dick." I tack on with a reassuring grin.

I look back at Quinton in time to see him smirk and say, "Yes, you are."

I roll my eyes. I think if he had said that last year it would have resulted in a full out fistfight but, somehow; it doesn't bother me now. It's like we've finally come to realize that we're only messing with each other, even if sometimes I do still feel like punching him in the face. That's probably a feeling I'll always have. It's just how we are. He has a very punchable face. What can I say?!

"Whatever, I didn't do it, so shut up." I stick my tongue out, proving Quinton's beliefs about how childish I am. I don't care. I can be childish if I want to.

Quinton snorts at my behavior and falls silent. I don't push him to talk because honestly; I don't want to press my luck today. If he's going to willingly tell me about his father, then go for it! I don't want to do anything to change his mind. For once, I'm going to keep my mouth shut and wait for him to speak, which I should get an award for, by the way. Do you know how hard it is to keep my mouth shut? It's exhausting.

"My father was my role model." I jump at the sudden sound of Quinton's voice.

He has been silent for almost fifteen minutes. I was thinking he would not speak but, now that he is, I am making sure that he has my complete attention. "He was intelligent, kind and was always there for both my mother and I. He never missed any event I was in and bragged about me to any person who would listen. He took me camping, taught me how to play basketball, even helped some of the neighbor kids. I was like every other child who thought that their dad was the best. He was my hero."

Quinton nods at his own memory as if to affirm it. "He rarely raised his voice. He rarely got into arguments with my mother. When people looked at him, they saw a good man and an even better father."

He still isn't looking at me, but keeping his dark eyes on the ceiling. I squirm uncomfortably because so far it doesn't sound like there is any reason for Quinton to hate his dad. I don't want to imagine how he went from being 'the best dad', 'my hero', to getting himself burned from a picture. What could one possibly do to change their child's opinion of them so drastically? I have my ideas, but I imagine the authentic story is far worse than whatever I can come up with.

In the blink of an eye, Quinton's gaze turns cold, colder than I've ever seen it. It's as if the both of us were suddenly thrown onto an icy tundra. The very air in the room chills me and I know it's my imagination, yet it baffles me how a simple memory can cause such a reaction in him.

Fond recollections of his father disappear in a flash. Whatever memory has resurfaced to replace the once fond ones makes his entire body stiff. The normally stoic Quinton has rage, confusion, fear and sadness etched across his face. Even from here, I can feel his muscles tense and hands clench to fists as he spits out the truth. "One day, my mother and I were ripped from our lives when the police raided our home. I was dragged away from my father as we were told that he had been charged with the rape and murder of nearly a dozen women. My father, the kind, caring father who could do no wrong, was revealed to be a bloodthirsty monster. Paparazzi were outside our door, family and friends gawking at not only him but us, the family of a monster. We couldn't believe it. How could we have not known what he was? Was it we never saw the signs, or we didn't want to see them?"

Is he asking me or himself?

I can see the wheels turning in Quinton's head at his own thoughts. Even now, years later, he doesn't fully understand how he hadn't seen what his father really was. For once, his thoughts are written on his face, right for me to see, and now, part of me wishes not to see it. Seeing the normally composed Quinton look lost puts everything into perspective that even the smartest of people can be left clueless. He looks confused and that scares me because Quinton always has an answer, always has a plan. Yet, his father leaves him stumped even now.

I recall the times I've seen crime novels and shows on his laptops. Something tells me that, perhaps, his interest in them started because of his father. Was he attempting to learn more, hoping to understand how he never noticed or why his father was the way he was? Was he trying to see if it was just his family who couldn't see the monster hiding in their own home?

Quinton refuses to remove his stare from the ceiling. I am glad for that because if he were to look my way I get the feeling I wouldn't be able to handle it, seeing directly into eyes that are normally so sure of themselves but are now swimming with confusion.

"They even discovered he had killed and buried one girl beneath our garage. *Our garage.*" He spat those words out. His eyes show how disgusted he is at the memory. "He only renovated the damn thing so he could bury one of his corpses under there." His voice is shaking with a hint of rage and disgust. "How many times have I played there? I was right there; over top of her and I didn't even realize it!"

I've never heard him shout before and the sound shakes me. Quinton doesn't lose his composure, but he is breaking his own rule now. He is anything but composed.

The boy takes a deep breath. "He was found guilty and sent to jail for life, leaving my mother and I to suffer the wrath of the families who lost their daughters, wives, sisters and the news companies hungry for a good story."

Quinton suddenly sits up, causing me to jump. He has now turned his gaze from the ceiling to the floor. I can see the flames in his eyes at the memories that I'm sure are overtaking him. My breath has long since been held. My chest is hurting and I'm at a loss for words while Quinton seems to be full of them, for once. The secretive Quinton is spilling his guts to me, the kid he has always found to be annoying and, maybe if I weren't so shocked, I'd be having a fangirl attack.

"It didn't matter that we had no clue. My friends weren't allowed over out of fear. My mother was seen as some naïve woman who simply refused to realize the truth rather than the victim who had her whole life torn to shreds. I was just a kid, yet I couldn't even escape the wrath of the world. People don't care about the truth. They make up their own minds, regardless of how that will affect others," he babbles on, his feelings seeming to explode after years of being closed up.

He finally stops with a heavy sigh that reveals to me how desperately he has actually wanted to say that. I can't imagine what it has been like keeping that a secret, holding everything in out of fear of being judged. He must be relieved to be rid of it.

Speechless can't describe how I feel afterwards. My mind is reeling as it attempts to think of something, anything to say in response to such a shock. What does one even say? Sorry? Sorry doesn't exactly cut it. It isn't exactly something one hears every day. In fact, I never even considered that as an option. Who would?!

I know there are many who have dark people in their lives. There's probably more than I can imagine who has experienced having a killer or a rapist in their lives. No one really wants to admit to it, though, seeing as one may judge them for it. Quinton, especially, must feel that way.

"How could I not have heard of that? It had to have been on the news?" I ask. I don't even recall Quinton's name. Then again, I didn't watch much news, but one does not need to watch the news in order to hear such a story.

"I was 7." Which meant I was too and most people at school would have been young as well, so obviously most of us had no interest in the news. "My mother took back her maiden name. I obviously didn't keep my father's name either. I was kept out of school and quickly sent to live with my grandparents in another state after my mother began drinking a lot. I never appeared in court and most teachers kept such a thing to themselves, seeing as it caused such an uproar before."

Like Professor Bennett, who dared to be shocked that Quinton has gotten as far as he has just because his dad was a psycho. What does that have to do with his own abilities? I see now why he never wanted to tell me. I see why he has trust issues. I don't blame him. I would too, everyone would.

And why go after the family because of something the father did? If they had no clue what happened, then attacking them is just wrong. I can only imagine what was thrown at them, what people said or thought of them. He couldn't even go to school because of it. The boy was only 7 for fuck's sake. How could he realize what his father was? Blaming a child, it's sickening.

A pair of snapping fingers in front of my face breaks me from my angry thoughts. I shake my head to see Quinton holding his hand before me. His anger no longer shows on his face, but his eyes remain dim, devoid of emotion, or perhaps filled with so many that I don't have a clue where to start.

"You were daydreaming," he mumbles. Mumbles. Quinton doesn't mumble, and the sound is enough to stir me. Suddenly, I realize I have said nothing, which may have bothered him. How many people have discovered the truth and then turned their back on him? Does he think I will do the same?

But honestly, I don't know what to say. I can think of a lot of things, but none of them sound right. I bite my lip, unsure of how to deal with what I've been told. Honestly, my view of Quinton has only gotten better rather than worse. He's gone through a hell of a lot more than most people and has only done well for himself. Dare I say it, I respect him.

He is probably the coolest guy I've ever met. Not that I'd ever tell him that! His ego does not need to be enlarged anymore than it already is! But I imagine the people who know the truth about Quinton's past do not feel the same as I do. A lot of people would be turned off from the thought of being around the child of a serial killer. They probably can't get past the fact that his father killed someone to see that he's a smart and talented guy who is nothing like his father.

Realization hits me. I, of all people, understand Quinton's dilemma the most. As strange as it sounds, but I do. He isn't like his father because relation does not mean you are the same. I know this because I'm the same way.

My father didn't kill anyone, but he's a good man. When people look at me, they expect greatness because I am my father's son. They don't see me as Aron, the teenager, Aron, the boy who only wishes to be like everyone else. They see Aron, our king's son, our future king. They want to see greatness and I only feel as if I'm disappointing them.

Quinton is the same. When people look at him they don't see Quinton, the talented, smart and strong teenager, but Quinton, the son of a serial killer. They won't look past that and instead judge him based on things that he should not be judged on.

I don't blame him for not telling me. I can't imagine having the guts to tell anyone that.

I should at least let him know that knowing this changes nothing. He's still the same as me. I won't turn my back on him for something he has no control over.

Taking a deep breath, I look away from him because I know if I'm looking at him as I say this, I'm going to blush, not that I'm not blushing already. "This changes nothing. You aren't getting a pity party from me if that was what you were trying to do." I cross my arms, pretending to not notice how he has moved closer to me. I feel his breath against my cheek, which grows in heat with every passing second. "But thanks for telling me. I... I of all people, understand the feeling of being judged based on their father. I'm not going to, you know, change my view on you or whatever."

What am I saying? This is not a very good pep talk. Shouldn't I be saying something nicer? Like, I don't know. I don't have a clue, ok! Who even can come up with a pep talk in the middle of a time like this? I'm not a freaking presenter. This shit is too hard!

My heart does back flips when the boy rests his forehead against my shoulder. My eyes widen to the size of saucers as my toes curl. Shit, shit, he's so close. The heat seeping through my shoulder is scorching. My mind is screaming move while my heart is spilling nonsense that I rather not think about. I feel his lips moving against my shoulder as he whispers nearly inaudibly, "Most people push me away after learning the truth."

A lump has formed in my throat that just won't go away. If he keeps being this close, my heart won't be able to take it. Thankfully, the boy pulls away before I listen to my urges and do something stupid.

Snorting, I act as if him being so close isn't driving my nerves insane. "As if I could do that. I've been trying to get rid of you since we met, yet somehow you're in my room without my permission—" a crumpling sound piques my interest. Finally tearing my eyes from the floor, I find Quinton has dug through my schoolbag to find a bag of Doritos, which he is now—"and eating my chips, goddamn it! Put those back, you jerk!"

Ignoring me yet again, Quinton pulls away from me to shove a handful in his mouth. I shout more and when he only replies with another handful of my chips, all hell breaks loose. In the end, Quinton eats all my chips while I moan into the carpet about how he only seems to get closer and closer to me, though on the inside I couldn't be happier about that fact.

Looking at Quinton, who appears to be both mentally and emotionally exhausted, I can't bring myself to stop from asking, "Why do you keep it then?"

The boy looks at me quizzically.

"The picture," I elaborate.

Hearing of it makes him scowl. He turns his gaze away yet again to say, more to himself than me, "You wouldn't understand."

"Try me." I push myself a little closer to the boy that is trying to close in on himself again. I won't allow it, not when I'm finally getting a glimpse.

"It's stupid," he says, and again, it sounds like he's trying to convince himself of that fact more than he is me. I am reminded that Quinton is a confused teenage boy who went through a traumatic experience that has left him scarred.

"I'm sure it isn't," I hum, tapping him playfully on the leg in hopes to be a bit assuring. When he lets out a sigh, I know that I have won. I must restrain myself to let out a shout of victory.

Quinton adjusts himself where he's sitting in order to place his back against the wall. Moments ago I could clearly see what he was thinking, but now he has put a layer between us in order to hide what I am assuming to be a hurricane of emotions within. He doesn't remove his gaze from me as he says hardly above a whisper, "I love my father, but I hate what he is. Does that make sense?"

I'm taken aback by his question. Once again, the always so confident of himself Quinton seems at a loss and he's asking me, me, the so-called biggest idiot he has ever met. However, he appears to be honestly interested in what I have to say in response to his admission. An admission that leaves me a bit confused until I think about it.

"Yes, it makes sense," I answer with a nod that grows stronger and stronger until I force myself to stop from getting dizzy. I attempt to put myself in his shoes. I imagine what it must have been like, seeing your idol dragged away in cuffs. He was so young and confused that he didn't understand what was going on. His loving father turned out to be some crazy killer, but Quinton didn't know him as that. He knew him as the man who cared for him since birth. What was and is still going through his mind?

"You said it yourself. He was a great father. He took you camping, taught you basketball, probably put you to bed every night and made you feel better when you were sick, much like my dad. You knew him as your father first and a killer second. People..." I try to think of how to phrase this without sounding stupid. I want to relieve him if I can. "People can't expect you to forget the loving memories of your father. You can be disappointed, shocked, and disgusted by him and what he has done, but asking a child to stop loving their parent, who was their hero for so long, is the harshest punishment I can think of."

He keeps the picture that, I imagine, he burned the day he found out the truth. Guilt must have overtaken him after because he didn't understand. He couldn't possibly comprehend at that age what was going on. He was lost and confused. He still is. He keeps it as a reminder that his father is a monster, but Quinton didn't always know him as that.

"Those memories you have of him, the good ones. They're worth cherishing." I nod at my own words, keeping my gaze on the apathetic boy before me. Perhaps my eyes are dysfunctional because I swear I see the corner of his lips tilt upwards into a smile that disappears in a blink of an eye. I shake my head, now growing a bit worried by his prolonged silence. Clearing my throat, I say with a cough, "But what the hell do I know? I'm just some dumb prince who can't understand basic English."

"True," Quinton agrees with a teasing grin that puts me at ease. Seeing the expression that he usually wears, I realize I prefer it over his troubled one.

After Quinton dropped the biggest bombshell known to mankind, I decide that talking further will only put the boy in a more panicked state. Instead of probing or talking about our feelings, which we basically already did, but hey, let's pretend it didn't happen, I put a video game in, allowing Quinton to watch and to speak only to insult me. I suspect my plan to calm him works when I see the way he's laying beside me.

Rather than having his back stiff against the wall, he has his head propped on my pillow with one arm behind it. His other hand rests calmly on his chest while his legs stretch out on my bed as if he owns it. His shoulders slowly relax, as does his whole body, until it looks as if he is in his own room rather than mine.

I smile to myself. I don't want to say much more about what Quinton has just told me. I imagine it's not something he wants to talk about more than he already has. It must have been hard, hard for him to decide to tell me something so personal. In fact, he probably would like to forget it all together, to push as much of it as possible to the back of his mind and lock it away in a vault.

I do my best to remain focused on my video game rather than staring at the still recovering boy beside me. Silence falls between us, save for the noise from my game, but it is not awkward or tense. In fact, it's rather soothing, and I relax with each passing moment. However, I should know better than to relax around Quinton. I'm too busy focusing on said game and my own thoughts to realize what Quinton is doing before it's too late.

Now, here I sit, in the most panicked state I've ever been. Thoughts of how I can escape run through my mind, but to no avail. When I think I've finally gotten control over myself, Quinton exhales, his breath sending my mind into a haze. My hands clench the controller with terrifying strength. I hear the poor object cracking within my grasp, but I don't know what else to do in an attempt not to just touch him.

Shit, what's wrong with me? I'm getting worse. Touch him? You've got to be kidding me. Why am I thinking about Quinton like that?! Fuck, think about girls, girls, boobs, nice soft skin and—

Quinton moves in his sleep, and it only worsens this already terrible situation. My eyes, which I have kept off him for a short while, eventually go back to his sleeping form to take in the rare sight of a defenseless Quinton.

While I was playing, the boy fell asleep. He no longer lies on his back, but has turned to his side. Before I thought it was bad, but now, it's worse! During his turn, his hand that was resting on his chest has gone to rest on my thigh. My freaking thigh. His fingers twitch in his sleep, sending a jolt of excitement up my thigh to my friend that is deciding that now would be a great time to wake up.

I squirm to pull myself away from him, but surprisingly, the boy is a cuddler. The idea of losing his heat source must have bothered the sleeping beast because his hand spreads out over my thigh. The action causes me to bite my lip to keep back a groan. Quinton pulls himself closer so that he's cuddling against my side.

What do I do? What do I do? What do I do! If I wake him up, he'll...he'll see.

My body is definitely wide awake now. My blood is running south, growing warmer with each breath that brushes against my thigh.

I can't let him stay there, though. What if Langley comes back? I doubt he wouldn't notice the obvious problem in my pants or the fact that it is caused by a guy. If I wake Quinton, though, he'll see. I mean, he's already down there; it's kind of hard to miss.

No matter how I look at it, this will not end well.

Every twitch of Quinton's fingers and every passing breath are sending my entire body into overdrive. Before I thought I was crazy, but now, I know I am because my mind keeps thinking of how easy it'd be to reach down and touch him. How easy it'd be to...kiss him. Pillow...pillow...I need a pillow or something to hide the obvious tent forming in my pants.

I do my best not to squirm too much while reaching for a pillow. Every time I move, I look at Quinton in case I've somehow woken him. So far, he seems to be in a deep enough sleep not to notice my body moving to pull the pillow out from behind me and place it over my lap.

I keep telling myself it's easy to wake him and this will be over, but I can't force myself to do it. I torture myself by staring at his sleeping form, the way his lips seem to be curved upwards in a slight smile unlike his normal scowling self, how he breathes through his mouth in his sleep causing a slight noise, almost resembling the sound of a child's breath, to be heard. Holy shit, what am I doing?

I press the pillow over my lap and finally work up the nerve to kick the boy's leg. The action causes him to stir and let out an annoyed groan. He doesn't wake but instead moves his hand further up my thigh and beneath the pillow. My breath catches as he's unbelievably close to...

I can't do this.

"Quinton!" I shout. My face burns with a blush, but there are worse things to worry about than my embarrassing blushing. Thankfully, I was born with a powerful set of lungs. The shout wakes the beast as he takes a sharp intake of breath and opens his eyes to find himself in what I'm assuming to him is an embarrassing position. I try to tease him in order to put the focus on him rather than my blush or the pillow over my lap. "You're a cuddler."

Quinton glares at the accusation, saying nothing as he pushes himself up on his elbows. His eyes narrow more from sleep than his glare and he leans his neck back, causing it to crack.

"You let me," he replies, causing me to give him a questioning glance.

"Pardon me?" What the hell is that supposed to mean?

Quinton looks at me, tired, but still looks smug. "I wouldn't have if you hadn't let me."

"You didn't do it slowly!" That's a lie. He turned towards me first and when I didn't push him from his heat source, he got closer by cuddling, but he doesn't need to know that, smug bastard. "You just started groping me in your sleep!"

"Groping?" He cocks a curious brow and looks down. For a moment, I panic. I think somehow he has seen my erection beneath the pillow. Come on, he isn't that great. He doesn't fucking have X-Ray vision but still a part of me freaks out.

When he simply scoffs and turns away, I sigh with relief. That sigh is short-lived as suddenly I find the jackass but centimeters from my face. The sudden intrusion of my personal space causes me to curse and narrow my gaze on the asshole who dare to get so close. Hell, I can feel his breath on my lips.

"You're blushing," he says before I can comment about his bad breath or how being so close makes me want to vomit. Instead, all the insults I thought I could throw at him became lodged in my throat at his statement.

"N-No I'm not!" I answer far too quickly. The both of us know I'm lying through my teeth. Quinton gives me a 'cut the crap' look that I only glare at. I doubt my glare is covering my blush, but I can try, damn it!

Quinton rolls his eyes at my antics, which he should be used to, really. Why does he act like it's so new for me to deny everything he says or glare at him? It happens all the time. He should expect it.

"What a bullshit lie," he sighs. The action only strengthens my blush, seeing as I feel the sigh against my lips. Somehow it makes my legs squirm, an action that does not go unnoticed. Quinton's eyes roam to my legs that have shivered just seconds before. I bite my lip and curse every god of every religion I can think of for putting myself in such a shit situation. Someone up there must really hate me.

Quinton, instead of calling me an idiot or saying I'm disgusting, says nothing, which I find shocking. I expect him to say something, anything, like he normally does. He needs to make a smart remark about my stupidity, but… he isn't saying anything. In fact, he's staring. Just staring. At me.

Black eyes bore into me with an intensity I didn't know anyone could have. He searches for something. What that something is, I don't know. I know nothing right now as he leans closer, so close that our breath is mingling. Our lips are but seconds from touching and I'm not doing anything to stop it.

Hell, I'm sitting here waiting for it. My hands are shaking, toes are curling, and heart is about to jump out of my chest. I'm expecting it and I'm not trying to stop it!

Our eyes are closing and I swear I feel his lip brush against mine… when the door opens.

Quinton is off the bed before Langley has time to process a thing.

Knowing that my face resembles a fire hydrant, I throw myself back onto the pillows to bury my shame. Quinton mumbles something like 'see you later' or he could have threatened my life. I don't even know.

"Dude, Quinton was here," Langley states the obvious. My bed shakes upon the impact of his body. He's somewhere behind me, but I don't look. My face will make him suspicious. "Why was Quinton here?"

I can't answer. I'm too busy running over the last couple of minutes.

Quinton and I almost kissed.

What the hell?

What. The. Hell. Just happened!

I can't believe it. I won't believe it. Quinton was this close. He was so close to kissing me and I wasn't trying to stop him! No, no, no, I was just sitting there like a love struck fool with sweaty palms and a beating heart. I was waiting for him to. I was expecting it. I was excited.

I'm messed up. There's something seriously wrong with me. I died. I died in my sleep and went to hell because there is no way that just happened.

"You alive in there, Aron?" Langley asks at my side.

I nod, but give no verbal reply. If I speak, I fear my voice will shake and give the truth away. Langley attempts to get the truth out of me, but after about fifteen minutes of questions and no verbal answer, he sighs and gives up on his endeavor. He leaves me to wallow in my thoughts that are everywhere and nowhere.

There's so many questions my brain doesn't even know where to start. How can one person feel so much at once without exploding? It shouldn't be physically or mentally possible to have so many thoughts running through your mind at once. I'm confused. I'm scared. I'm happy. I'm sad. I'm angry. I'm everything all at once and it's swirling within me like a typhoon. What do I do? Is there anything to even do other than lie here and mope? I don't think so.

Even now, at least an hour later, my body is still shaking. Langley has long lost interest in my mental breakdown. Every so often he looks at me to confirm I'm still alive, but once he sees my chest rise from a powerful inhale, he turns back to his game.

Honestly. What's happening to me? And what's happening to Quinton! I mean, he was the one leaning in. Ok, so maybe I was too, but he started it! He wouldn't have...have attempted to initiate a possible k-k-k—god I can't even think of it. So I'm not the only one feeling this way?

Ha! As if. I roll my eyes at the thought of Quinton's heart wavering as mine is. He was obviously just messing with me. He noticed my blush and took it as an opportunity to get back at me for all the times I messed with him in the past. That's the only explanation.

But I hope it isn't true.

CHAPTER THIRTY-TWO

"You're still doing this?" Langley groans upon my sudden drop. The boy looks down at me, neither concerned nor confused. It's somewhat sad that he expects this behavior from me. I'll yell at him about it later.

"Shut up," I hiss, peeking my eyes ever so slightly over the trash to scan the surrounding area.

Up ahead is the one boy who has been plaguing my mind for far too long. I never knew it was possible for someone to think of another so much. Shouldn't I be bored thinking about him? Nope. Apparently not, because he even haunts me in my dreams.

Langley looks about the yard. He does not know who I'm avoiding or maybe he does, but hasn't said it. Sighing, he announces he is going to leave me if I don't pick up my pace. Snorting, I stand, but only after realizing Quinton has left my sights.

"Why aren't you even asking about it?" Not that I want him to, seeing as I'd do not know how to reply, but I'm still curious why he hasn't said anything.

"I don't want to know why you're avoiding Quinton."

My eyes widen. How did he know? My face must have voiced my question because Langley chuckles and asks, "When is it not about Quinton?"

Sadly, he makes a point. I groan at the fact that it is always about Quinton. Langley chuckles at my groan but thankfully says nothing more on the matter. Good. I haven't had the time to think of an explanation for my constant ducking and hiding.

The day goes by in a flash with no signs of Quinton. A part of me is saddened by not seeing the dark-haired and even darker hearted boy. Those thoughts I quickly disperse since I'm doing my best to stay in denial about my obsession.

As the day turns into night, I can't keep myself from falling into yet another dark abyss. My thoughts are nowhere near good. To keep myself from moping, I flip on a game, only to regret it. It's the same game I was playing last night before Quinton nearly...

I slam my head against the wall. Langley gives me a questioning look but doesn't ask. Instead, he announces he is leaving to spend more time with Ariel. No surprise there. I lazily wave him off, leaving me in silence, seeing as I had to turn the sound off on the TV because it was only bringing back more memories.

"What am I doing?" I sigh.

I wish the world would be kind to me and I don't know, give me a sign. Literally. Put a giant board in front of me explaining what's happening to me, to Quinton. I want it to explain everything that happened last night and what I'm supposed to do now. How can I expect to solve this—this whatever it is! Can't life be simple, for once? We all need a break every now and again.

The sudden sound of my phone interrupts my thoughts. I got a text message. I raise a questioning brow, wondering who it could be, seeing as the only person who really texts me is Langley. If he needed something, he'd come back in. The only other person I text is Autumn, though she rarely texts me during the school week. She's active in a lot of school related things so she's usually busy.

I reach for my phone and stare at the message that makes a shiver run down my spine.

Autumn: Are you and Quinny fighting?

I don't know how to reply. Sort of. Maybe. Not really, since to be in a fight, one has to be fighting and we aren't fighting. I'm simply avoiding him, which could make someone conclude that we're fighting, but avoiding does not always mean there was a fight. Wait a second, why is she asking?

My curiosity gets the better of me. Quinton must have told her something to make her think that. Did he talk to her about our almost kiss? Shit, he wouldn't, right! Hell, he probably wouldn't even admit to himself about the almost—kind of—sort of kiss. Maybe it wasn't even an almost kiss to him. For all I know, his crazy ass could have come up with some other reason why he was so close to my face, like he was searching for any sign of my intelligence or something equally ridiculous.

Aron: No. Why?

I hold my phone a few inches from my face, waiting impatiently for an answer. I don't get a text. I get a call instead. I nearly drop my phone, not expecting it to suddenly start ringing.

"Hello?" I answer.

"Quinny keeps asking me if you've said anything to me," she says, getting directly to the point. Normally I would enjoy someone who doesn't beat around a bush, but at the moment I wish her to not be so blunt.

"Uh, like what?" If she doesn't know what happened, then I sure as hell am not telling her. I don't want to admit to myself, let alone out loud, to another person.

"He didn't ask anything specific, just if you and I talked about him. Should we have talked about him? What'd he do this time?"

Almost kiss me, though it's still questionable whether or not it was an almost kiss for him, but again, rather keep that to myself. However, a part of me enjoys knowing that Quinton is feeling something about whatever the hell this is that's going on. So... I'm not the only one knowing that something is going on, which means the almost kiss was an almost kiss to him too!

I curse at my own thoughts, making Autumn ask what's up. I shake my head as if she can see me. "It's nothing special. We're just being our normal selves."

"Bull shit." She sounded like Quinton right there. Before I get the chance to voice my thoughts, the girl continues, "If you were being your normal selves, he wouldn't text me about you. Quinton never texts me about other people! Probably because he doesn't have other people in his life, but still. Something is up. My spidey senses are tingling."

"Spidey senses? Really?" I scoff.

"You are so lucky we don't go to the same school or I'd be barging into your dorm to beat the answer out of you," she says. I easily envision her doing exactly that, making me shiver.

"Violence is never an attractive trait." I tease.

"Take your own advice, Princess." I pout at her words, but before I get the chance to reply with my own witty banter, she asks, "So if you two aren't fighting, then what's up? I know something has to be going on if Quinny is asking me about you."

Right?! I thought he was supposed to be the smart one. He should know that Autumn would suspect something if he asked about me or anyone for that matter, so why did he ask? Is he that bothered by it?

I bite my lip as if somehow the action would force my brain to provide an answer. Sadly, it doesn't and Autumn only sees that as an even bigger sign of something being wrong. She huffs from the other line and continues to pester me, "The fact that you can't even answer me only proves it more. Spit it out. You know I'm only here to help. I know how Quinny is—"

Yeah, since you dated the bastard, or maybe you're the crazy bastard since you dated him. Whatever, both of them are crazy!

"He's hard for even me to read and I've known him forever! I can only imagine what it's like for you, so if I can help, I'd like to."

I would like for her to help too, but it's not that simple. It's not like homosexuality is as looked down upon as it once was, but I'm not like everyone else. I don't have the choice to live my life as I want to. I have to play by the rules, so even if...if a part of me accepts the fact that I do like Quinton, it doesn't matter because...it'd never work. We'd never work. He'd be miserable with me, I know it.

"It doesn't matter," I finally reply, which obviously isn't what she wants to hear. "Forget that he asked anything. It's better to just... forget about everything."

Autumn sighs and replies, sounding slightly annoyed. "Whatever is going on, the two of you need to work it out. Pretending the problem doesn't exist will not fix it. I'm going to call your prince charming."

"Say what!" I shout, nearly toppling out of my bed. "Don't you fucking dare! I will end you—"

But it's too late. She hung up, leaving me frozen to the bed. Well shit, she wouldn't actually call him, would she? Yes. Yes, she would. But that doesn't mean he'll do anything! Knowing Quinton, he'll brush off whatever she has to say and completely ignore what has been happening between us. At least I hope so, for my sake.

Unfortunately, the world has once again found happiness from my discomfort. I don't see why that shocks me, seeing as it always had enjoyed shoving my life into a plastic bag and shaking it until it's become a crumbling mess that I desperately attempt to scrape back into said bag with raw hands.

Sadly, my hypothesis of Quinton not acting upon Autumn calling him is incorrect because here I am, hiding beneath my blanket as I hear a knock at my door followed by a familiar, "Idiot, I know you're in there."

As if. He can't see through doors! I shouldn't say that because he probably can that stupid Mr. Perfect-Asshole. Huffing, I decide against deceiving him, seeing as he will most likely get in one-way or another, so I rather not antagonize him further. "Go away!"

Great, like that won't antagonize him, Aron. You're a bloody genius.

For a moment I think he does as he's told, but this is Quinton we're talking about, so why I even thought that is beyond me. A few seconds pass before the door opens, which reminds me I didn't lock it earlier after Langley left.

Quinton steps in with a look that says more than words. His face is screaming at me at how stupid he thinks I am. The look is unnecessary. I know I'm stupid Quinton, no need to rub it in!

I puff out my cheeks and grumble, "I forgot the door was unlocked."

"Obviously." He says with a shake of his head.

"Obviously," I mock him and he, being his typical self, rolls his eyes at my 'childish behavior'.

Quinton, not even bothering to ask, heads over to me and takes a seat near the edge of my bed. Silence follows for what feels like an eternity. My digital clock says otherwise, showing that it has been about 5 minutes. I hate time.

"Autumn called me," Quinton finally says. To keep myself from revealing too much, since my face has now decided that red is its new favorite color, I continue admiring my absolutely stunning alarm clock. It's such a pretty color of black. "She insisted we talk this out."

My eye twitches upon hearing him. She insisted? The only reason he came over was because she insisted. The thought of Quinton only wishing to talk this out is because his ex-girlfriend insisted on it makes my teeth grind. My blood boils. Deep, deep, and I mean super deep down, I like Quinton because part of me thinks this might be jealousy I'm feeling.

"She insisted?" I ask, continuing to examine my alarm because if I am to look at Quinton now, I know I will punch his pretty boy face. "Do you always do what your ex tells you to?"

My jaw clenches as I feel myself becoming more and more irritated. Quinton doesn't do things he doesn't want to. He doesn't listen to others willingly. He's stubborn and full of pride so for him to so easily come over simply because Autumn insisted on it bothers me to no end. I'm wondering if they should have broken up because it seems to me like little Quinny still has a thing for her.

Oh wow, I am getting sassy now.

I run a hand through my hair, continuing to keep my eyes away from Quinton. I bite my lip to keep myself from shouting. Instead, I practically spit my words out, which honestly is probably worse, "Who knew you could be so obedient, Quinny. I can now see who wears the pants in that relationship."

Quinton snorts, which further pisses me off. Everything he does pisses me off, but right now I'm just extra pissed off. Know what I mean? It's as if I have been set aflame. My entire body is desirable with boiling rage that is on the verge of boiling over a very tall glass.

"What is your problem, Aron?" He asks.

Without looking at him, I can tell he's scowling. Quinton is sounding annoyed as well, though his annoyance is understandable. I'd be annoyed too if someone was acting like a little shit, which is currently how I'm acting.

I know how irritating I must be at this moment, yet I can't stop myself. It just came out! I want to grab him and shake him or punch his know-it-all face in. Ugh! He's so aggravating. Why couldn't he have said he was worried or didn't want to ruin our friendship? Hell, it didn't have to be something cheesy like that! He could have come over and said nothing, but simply talked to me about what happened. Why'd he have to say Autumn insisted on it, making it seem like he couldn't give a shit less what happened but only wanted Autumn happy. Damn, he's so stupid!

I'm pissing myself off more by thinking about it. I need to stop. He needs to leave. This conversation needs to end and I need to take a freezing shower to cool me off or I may burst into flames, taking the entire campus with me.

"Nothing," I groan and get up. I feel too close to him. I walk to my desk where I pretend to clean it up by moving things around. "I don't have a problem and we don't need to work anything out so you can leave."

Because that sounded so convincing. Great job, Aron! Your voice wasn't oozing with obvious annoyance. Nope. Sounded perfectly fine to me! Wow, I'm very sarcastic when annoyed. I'm a sassy little bitch.

"You're a terrible liar," he breathes against my neck. When did he even get that close to me?

I spin around; ready to tell the jerk to fuck off, only to regret it. The boy quickly places both hands on either side of me, locking me between him and the desk. It's like he somehow knew that my knee jerk reaction would be to escape from this trap. My eyes narrow upon realizing that he purposely got this close.

I feel his breath hitting my already red cheeks, though I'm no longer sure if it's from anger or embarrassment. With each breath our chests brush and I wonder if he really needs to be this close in order to trap me here. I wonder whether he can feel the erratic beating of my heart that seems to believe being love stricken is more important than boiling rage. My mind is angry while my heart is in googly-eyed mode. The two things need to get in line because it's hard being angry when your heart keeps screaming about how plump his lips are while pondering over whether they are soft, unlike his personality.

"Move," I order, because being this close makes it hard to be angry. Stop leaning over all attractive-like or I will be forced to take drastic measures!

"No," is his oh-so-elegant reply. Why I thought that would work, I'm not sure.

I take a deep breath. "I swear to fucking god if you don't move—"

"You'll hit me? Come on, Aron, I thought we grew out of that," he scoffs with yet another roll of his eyes because even in an argument, he has to be the 'cool' one. The action angers me further and I go to push him out of the way, only to have him grip my wrist to keep me from doing so. The touch is electrifying. I shouldn't be, because he's only holding my wrist. What's wrong with me?

"You're acting weird," he says before I growl about the hold on my wrist. Black eyes narrow on me like a hawk eying its prey. I squirm in his grasp and quickly cast my eyes downward.

I shake my head in denial. "No, I'm not. You're hallucinating."

"Wow, impressive argument."

"Shut up! God, you're so infuriating! And don't even comment about how you're—" I use my best Quinton voice for the next part, "—shocked that my brain can even process such a word!"

My Quinton impression gets me a raised brow and curled lip. "That didn't sound like me at all."

"That's not the point, goddamn it!" I shout and finally pull myself from his hold. My attempt to flee is blocked by him placing his hand back on the desk. This causes my eye to twitch for what feels like the hundredth time today. "Let me try this again," I sigh. "Please leave."

Quinton actually looks to be considering it this time, but after a quick second, he shakes his head. "No." Again, my eye twitches. "Not until you tell me what your problem is."

Perhaps I have reached my emotional limit for the day because without meaning to I spit out 'my problem,' "Why'd you fucking say that?!"

Quinton cocks a brow at my sudden outburst. He must not have expected me to answer so easily and, hell, neither did I. My head hurts. I'm shaking. I'm mad, irritated, confused and, dare I say it, aroused all at once so I don't know if I can remember my left from my right at the moment. Quinton is causing me to go insane, so excuse me for bursting without meaning to I'm having a crisis! Anyone would be, don't judge me!

"You couldn't have just said you were concerned about me or you wanted to actually work out whatever the fuck is wrong between us!" I crazily throw my hand between the two of us, adding a few good punches to his chest. He does not keep me from doing so, but allows it without comment. "Instead, you said Autumn, who is your ex-girlfriend and who has known you since forever, insisted you do so! That makes it seem like I'm the only one who fucking cares and that you're just...just..."

"An ass?" He supplies.

"Yes! A totally fucking huge ass who only cares about himself and is infuriating me on purpose because he's a fucking ass! How come I'm the only one who is confused about what happened the other day? Did it not even occur to you it didn't bother me we almost kissed?! And for a moment I actually believed you might have been feeling just as confused because Autumn said you asked about me, which clearly means you care, but then you come over and fucking say that shi—"

And I would like to take this moment to remind myself and the world that Quinton is supposed to be the smart one. It is his job to be calm and logical. He thinks about his actions before doing them. He keeps his cool in serious situations, to know what to do and when to do it. Out of the two of us, it is clear who uses his brain more than the other, but I guess even a genius can be stupid sometimes because Quinton makes the biggest mistake of his life.

He kisses me.

An arm around my waist keeps me from pulling away. Apparently, breaking apart from this kiss is a huge no-no in Quinton's mind. His other hand entangles itself into my hair with a grip that shows just how confused and frustrated he is as well. I am shown through touch that I am not the only one lost what is happening between us.

The warmth radiating off his chest onto mine is enough to sear my bones. Part of me hopes it does, hopes that the inferno between us scars so I'll never forget the moment Quinton lost his cool and dove in for something that neither of us is quite sure we are ready for.

He feels too close yet too far at the same time. Because of my inner turmoil, I wish to shove him away, but the feeling of his lips on mine that sends a bolt through me only makes me want more. Not sure of what to do, I grip his shoulders with a force that I'm not sure if it's meant to push away or pull him closer. He seems as unsure as well, seeing as the grip he has around my waist is almost pleading. The kiss, at first, is a simple touch of our lips, though probably more vigorous than it needs to be seeing as neither of us really planned it, but soon I feel a curious tongue pressing against the seam of said lips.

I'm not in my right mind or I easily would have denied such a thing, but my body wants something that my mind is unsure of. I think we all know which won out of those two. Making yet another poor decision for the evening, I part my lips to allow Quinton to completely shatter any thoughts or regret of letting him take control of the kiss.

He smirks against my lips while wreaking havoc within my mouth, running his tongue across anything he can in order to see what kind of reaction I'll make. I should have known the bastard would take some type of sick pleasure out of making me moan because he enjoys the way his tongue can evoke these noises from me that, later, I will punch myself for making. However, I'm a little busy tasting the forbidden fruit that I've been aching for, so my self-hatred will be saved for another time.

My lungs ache from lack of oxygen, but I have no desire to pull away. The thought of this ending and the possibility of Quinton realizing his mistake and never allowing such a thing to happen again almost makes me wish to suffocate and die with this bliss coursing through my veins. However, Quinton also needs oxygen to live, so he pulls away from the kiss, leaving the both of us gasping.

Somehow, I keep an eye lock with Quinton after possibly the most embarrassing event of my life. I'm unsure of what he's thinking. His eyes are as dark as ever, revealing nothing that is currently going through his mind. I, on the other hand, must be an open book. I know I'm blushing redder than a tomato right now. My palms are sweaty and my legs are continuing to shiver, which I know he feels seeing as his leg is currently resting comfortably between mine. He must also feel the obvious reaction in my pants, although he's no better.

A part of me almost feels proud to know that I have evoked something within Quinton that he actually may understand as little as I do. The boy's lips are bruising from the force that was used earlier. Mine tingle too. Although the both of us are gasping and more aroused than I ever thought we could be, it doesn't feel wrong. No feelings of disgust are rising within me. I wait, thinking that in a second or so my mind and body will finally realize how wrong it is to have enjoyed such a thing with Quinton, but there's nothing; nothing but the desire to lean in for another.

Uncertainty and actually some acceptance are what I'm feeling right now. I can no longer deny to myself, or Quinton, that I don't like him. I just let the bastard shove his tongue down my throat. I moaned like some love struck fool and I'm still clinging onto him for dear life. It's pretty obvious how I feel, but that doesn't make it any less irritating!

I'm frustrated because it's Quinton. I'm confused because it's Quinton. Why him? He's annoying and a total bastard. He's everything that I hate put into a single person, yet somehow I want to speak with him. I want to be around him. It drives me nuts! Though something tells me that perhaps Quinton feels the same way. That thought makes it a little better. The idea of annoying Quinton in any way brings me great joy.

Quinton, having found whatever it is he wants to say, finally relinquishes the death grip he has on me, though he does not pull away. Instead, he keeps a gentle hold on me and says, more to him than me, "I didn't come over because Autumn wanted me to."

I am going to pretend my lips don't curl into a smile upon hearing that. Biting the inside of my cheek to keep my grin at bay, I do my best to sound like I am not ecstatic, "Oh, then why did you come over?"

His eyes narrow angrily at me and I can no longer keep myself from smirking. The action only causes a low growl to erupt from his throat that I cannot deny, only makes me happier. His face practically says 'you know damn well why,' but you see, I don't. Quinton can easily say he wanted to shut me up, or he wanted to tease me. He could be the douche in this situation and crush me completely, so I want to hear him say it. I want him to admit that maybe, deep down in the black abyss of his heart; there may be some feelings towards me.

"Why did you come over, Quinny?" The nickname only causes him more irritation. I see his eye twitching as mine did earlier, but oh boy, it's fun to piss him off!

The boy releases his hold on me and grumbles something to himself. I now use the hold I still have on him to keep him close. He can easily brush my arms off, but he doesn't. Instead, he glares at me with dark eyes that state how much he hates me right now.

"Come on, say it. Tell me," I say in a singsong voice that he groans at.

Finally, Quinton musters up enough guts to grumble out angrily, "Because I wanted to."

My face breaks into a smile without my permission. It may not be exactly what I wanted to hear but, for Quinton, it's one hell of an improvement!

This sickening sweet feeling erupts in my chest that makes my toes curl. I can't believe he said that, yet somehow I feel so much better. Any anger I have towards him is gone with what most people would call simple words, but for Quinton to say such a thing is a miracle.

I know he's at his emotional limit for the day when he finally brushes my hands away. For a moment, I think he's angry with me and is instead going to beat me to death before disposing of my carcass.

"It's late. I should go," he says, looking at my clock.

I check the time to see that it's about time for the dorms to lock up. Langley will be returning soon and Quinton will have to check back into his dorm if he doesn't want to get into trouble. Seeing as something rather important just happened, I find myself rather annoyed with time again this evening. What the hell? You go slow when nothing important happens, but when Quinton kisses me, you pick up and force him to leave with little explanation!

Too busy cussing time out in my head, I don't notice Quinton moving to my door before it's too late. I hear it open and have enough time to look in his direction to see him giving me his famous smirk. He orders more than asks, "See you at my dorm after classes tomorrow."

He leaves without hearing an answer, which bugs the hell out of me. Does he think I'm going to go along so easily? Why should I?!

"What the hell?!" I holler and run to the door. Throwing it open, I look down the hall to see he's nearly gone. I don't care if anyone hears me. That bastard is far too cocky. Why his dorm? What makes him think I want to see his ass after class? How dare he order me? I'll go if I want to go! "Who said I'd come over?!"

Quinton doesn't bother turning back or answering. He simply throws his hand up in a lazy wave goodbye. He's far too cocky. No way in hell am I going to his dorm tomorrow!

Sure, I'll keep telling myself that.

CHAPTER THIRTY-THREE

Wow.

Uh, there is no word in English nor any language that could describe how I am feeling. Here I am, sitting stunned on my bed as I try to piece together what just happened.

Quinton, the most closed off and bitter man to ever grace this earth... kissed me. And I, the most awesome and sexiest being to ever live... let him. Not only did I let him, but I enjoyed it.

I slap my hands to my cheeks in utter humiliation. Damn it, what is wrong with me? How could I have been so dramatic?! Toes curling? Legs shaking? Lips tingling? The fuck is wrong with me?! The fuck is wrong with Quinton? He kissed me. We're both messed up.

I never imagined a day would come when I would find myself attracted to another guy and why Quinton, of all people? Couldn't my heart yearn for someone less annoying? Couldn't I have liked a guy who wasn't some prick with a stick up his ass? Honestly. This is ridiculous. I don't even—what the hell am I doing?

Pressing my face into my hands, I inhale deeply to calm my panicking heart. Perhaps my parents were right. I should have continued being home schooled. Everything is so messed up. I'm messed up. I don't know what to do about...whatever the hell this is. What is this, anyway?

Quinton and I, what does it mean now?

I bite my lip to keep back a smile at the memory of our kiss earlier. My lips are still tingling from it. My heart is still racing. It feels really hot in here. Damn it, why'd he have to leave before I could even ask what that was?

Knowing him, he'd say a kiss. Thanks Mr. Obvious, but that's not what I want to know! I mean, he hasn't even admitted aloud that we are friends, so kissing is something that neither of us should have done.

I press the back of my hand to my lips to cool them, but my whole body is on fire. I need a shower… a freezing shower. I get up to do just that. It's a good thing I do too, seeing as moments after I enter the shower, I hear Langley return. It would have been awkward to see him when I'm so messed up.

He definitely would have noticed my odd behavior.

I feel better after the shower. My body has cooled down, but my mind is still attempting to process what happened earlier. As I step out of the bathroom, I say hello to Langley, who lies on his stomach as he plays one of our games.

"What's up?" He says, concerned.

"Nothing," I reply, unaware of what he's talking about. Am I still blushing or something? I feel my cheeks, but they aren't that warm.

Langley pushes himself up into a sitting position. He looks me up and down as if checking for something. It makes me nervous, so I do it too. I see nothing off. What the hell is up with him? He's freaking me out.

"You have this lost look," he says, waving his hand in my direction. Even he seems a bit confused what it is he's talking about. "Like you are totally confused. I guess that's the usual for you."

"Hey!" I pout. "I'm not dumb!"

"I never said that," he grins. "But seriously, you ok?"

Ok? Technically, yes. I am physically ok. Mentally, I am more fucked up than I'm willing to admit. I believe that I've officially gone off the deep end. I kissed the boy who was once my arch nemesis that went to being a friend and is now something that I cannot put into words. I feel funny when I see him. My heart races when he's near.

I don't have the courage to speak to Langley about this. I hate keeping it a secret from him. I would love to talk to my best friend about the most frustrating and confusing ordeal of my life, but I'm not ready. Hell, part of me still denies my true feelings, so I cannot even fathom admitting it to someone out loud.

I try to reassure him by putting on a smile. "I'm fine, really."

He doesn't seem totally convinced. His eyes are full of questions, but he doesn't ask any of them. Instead, he sighs and returns to his game but does not forget to say, "You can talk to me if you need to."

"I know." This time I don't need to smile. It comes naturally, and that seems to ease him. He returns my smile, then offers me a controller, which I gladly take. I rather be playing games right now in order to keep my mind off things I am not ready to think about yet.

I keep myself preoccupied in class the next day as well. I pay attention. I take notes. I do my homework and, hell, I even read my textbook during the study period, which never happens. Langley even asked me if I needed to go to the nurse. Ha, funny Langley. You should be proud of me, doing work all by myself!

I had to do it, though. If I didn't, my mind would get lost in an abyss that I may never come out of. Last night's events would have plagued me the whole day if I didn't keep myself preoccupied with other things. I had to keep my mind busy to keep myself sane.

Not to mention tonight. Quinton said to go to his dorms after classes. Should I go? That asshole didn't even ask if I was busy. Not that I ever am, but he doesn't know that! Besides, a miracle could have happened, and I may have actually had plans tonight. That jerk needs to learn to ask rather than demand things! But I really want to go.

He has some explaining to do. I do too. I let him kiss me. I could have shoved him away. I could have punched him, shouted at him for doing such a thing. I could have not allowed him to shove his tongue down my throat! Instead, I let him. I enjoyed it and, damn it, wasn't I just talking about preoccupying myself with other things to keep myself from thinking about this?

Damn! See, this is what happens when I'm not busy. I keep thinking about him and the kiss and his stupid face. Damn it, Quinton, you're so annoying! Why do you have to be so unreadable? Why can't you actually be a normal human being and not an emotionless robot? Can't you just...tell me what's on your mind? Shit. This sucks.

I really need to go to his dorm, though. Even if I don't want to listen to him, I need to go. If I don't get answers soon, my head will explode. He should know my brain can only handle so much and after what happened last night, isn't it obvious my mind would become lost? Unless...he did it on purpose. That bastard!

He left on purpose to drive me mad. I am so kicking his ass later.

"Where are you going?" Langley asks at the end of the day. He turns to head for our dorms while I am clearly heading in the opposite direction. Oops, forgot to come up with an excuse about where I'm going.

"Uh..." Well, this was an unforeseen situation. I could be honest and say I'm going to Quinton's, but that would be weird, right?

Langley, as if he can read minds, chuckles and asks, "Are you going to Quinton's dorm?"

"N-No!" I answered too quickly. Now I'm blushing and Langley does not look convinced. I turn away from him and attempt to stutter my way out of this one. "I'm going to the library."

"But the library isn't over there."

"The gym."

"You don't work out."

"So what if I'm going to Quinton's?!" My mouth seriously needs to learn to keep itself shut. It's going to get me into serious trouble one of these days.. Oh wait, it just did! Good job me.

Langley's grin is so big it's sick. He didn't even have to pressure me. It took ten seconds to get me to admit to it. He knows me too well. He has to go.

Langley throws an arm around my neck to force me to look at him. I scowl and pull away, only for him to pull me closer. Chuckling, he asks, "What are you going over there for? I thought he was your enemy. Come to think of it, he was in our room the other night. What's up between you two?" He wiggles his eyebrows, which only pisses me off more.

"Get away, you son of a bitch," I hiss, pushing the boy off me. He continues to laugh.

"You two are suspicious."

"We are not!" I holler. Sighing, I walk away from him. I have no plan to talk about it so he needs to drop it. I don't even know what to say or how I would explain it.

"Try not to have a lovers' quarrel!" Langley shouts after me, which only makes me speed up faster. It isn't until I make it to Quinton's dorm that I realize I didn't even deny the 'lover' part. I smack myself for that. Something tells me Langley knows what is happening.

Shaking my head, I try to forget about that. I'll talk to him later once I find out what's going on. How am I expected to tell him if I don't even know myself?

I awkwardly stand outside the door with my fist raised, ready to knock, but I don't do it. I am once again battling with myself. Go in? Leave? Forget this ever happened? I roll my eyes at my own thoughts. As if I could forget.

Taking a deep breath, I force myself to knock. Seconds feel like hours before the door finally opens to reveal...Taylor. He looks at me, slightly confused, before asking, "Your Highness, what are you doing here?"

That bastard should have told me if he wouldn't be here immediately. Damn it, that son of a bitch! I am going to break his neck. I hate him, truly I do.

"Is Quinton here?" I ask, trying not to sound nervous. I suspect it worked when Taylor asks nothing about it.

He shakes his head. "Not yet. He should be back soon, though." The boy turns his head to look at the clock. Smiling, he welcomes me in and says, "I have a study group tonight, so I'll be leaving. You're welcome to stay and wait for him."

Ah, so that's why he wanted me to come to his dorm. Taylor will not be here. My room would be no good since Langley comes and goes as he pleases. I mean, it is our room, so of course he would, but unlike Taylor, Langley doesn't go to study groups. He doesn't have a set time for being gone.

Taylor smiles before leaving shortly after I arrive. I feel weird being alone in Quinton's room. Wait a second! I turn my head to examine the room as if to make sure I'm actually alone. When no one jumps out to scare me, it finally hits me.

Quinton and I are going to be alone in his room. His roommate is gone for the next couple of hours, which means there will be no interruptions. It will just be the two of us. The two of us, who had shared a rather long kiss the night before. Did he invite me over because he knew we'd be alone?

My cheeks go from their normal paleness to an unbelievably dark shade of red in seconds. I slap my hands against them in order to use it as an excuse for why they have become so red. If Quinton sees me like this, he'll know something's up for sure. It's his fault! How else could I take this situation? We're alone, with no possibility of an interruption. Not that I'm expecting anything to happen that would need to be interrupted. My mind is totally not in the gutter. I'm not thinking of kissing him. Nope, not at all!

It's sad I can't even convince myself.

The one plaguing my thoughts has finally made their appearance. The door opens to reveal Quinton, who does not seem at all shocked to see me. That kind of pisses me off. He shouldn't be so confident in himself, the bastard.

The boy doesn't even say hello! He just walks in and sets his stuff down before undoing the tie on his uniform and tossing his jacket into the closet. I continue to glare at him as he does this, waiting for him to give me some form of acknowledgement. Why I do this, I don't know, seeing as I know, he's doing it on purpose to annoy me.

"Isn't it common courtesy to say hello to your guests?" I ask around a scowl. He doesn't even look back at me.

The boy shrugs. "Like you know anything about common courtesy."

My jaw drops at the audacity of this asshole. He was the one who told me to come over! At least act like you're somewhat pleased to see me.

"You invite me over to just insult me? If that's the case, I'm leaving," I huff, pushing myself off his bed to head to the door, only to have the boy walk over to me and push me back down. I shoot up a glare that only sharpens upon seeing his smirk.

"You walked into that insult," he says and takes a seat beside me. My childish urges surface and I have the biggest desire to push him off, but somehow resist seeing as I know he'll tease me more if I do that. Jerk.

"Whatever," I huff. Looking down at my feet, I do my best to hide my blush as I ask, "So why'd you want me to come over?"

"You're really asking me that?" His voice tells me how stupid he finds my question. Well, he didn't say why! I have my assumptions but assuming is bad! It's better to say why.

I grumble. "You're not the most readable person."

I feel him shrug beside me, neither denying nor confirming. Oh, come on, we both know that's true. He's difficult to read, he knows that.

The air in the room becomes heavy with silence. Neither of us speak. I can't keep myself still. I swing my legs to distract myself from how near Quinton is. His arm is against mine. There's enough space on the bed for us to be apart, yet he's right there. I could move. He could move. Neither of us do.

One of us needs to speak, but I have no idea where to start. 'So how about that kiss last night, huh?' Is not something to ask in this situation. Neither of us can deny it happened. I mean...we made out in my room. It wasn't even a peck. It was a full on lips to lips, tongue-to-tongue action!

"Give me your phone," Quinton orders, holding out his hand. His voice shocks me, seeing as it had been so quiet. I jump and, without really thinking about it, remove my phone from my pocket. He snatches it before I have time to say whether he can see it.

"Hey!" I shout as I see him open my contacts list. What the hell is he doing? I try to peek, but he moves so that his shoulder is in my face. I don't bother leaning over to look, because being that close to him will only worsen my already blushing face. He'll point it out. I know it.

Moments later, his phone vibrates. After it does, he tosses my phone back at me. I barely catch it, earning him another glare from me. If I had dropped my phone, my dad would kill me! Just because he has money doesn't mean he wants me spending it on new phones. Grumbling about his lack of manners, I look down to see...

"You gave me your number?" I ask, seeing that he had sent a text from my phone to his. He knows me too well because he didn't even put his name. Instead, he put 'The Asshole,' which makes me chuckle. My chuckle turns into full on laughter when he shows me his phone, revealing that he put me down as 'Princess.' I should be insulted, but I find it funny.

Quinton puts his phone back in his pocket. If my cheeks had cooled down from earlier, they heat up easily now. I have Quinton's phone number. The idea makes my toes curl.

"Don't text me for stupid reasons," he says, grabbing my attention yet again. "I will block you if you do."

"I feel like you're challenging me."

He rolls his eyes. Seriously, it's a challenge, right?

CHAPTER THIRTY-FOUR

I skim my fingers over the vast collection of Quinton's books. He must have recently got a bookshelf for them, seeing as I don't remember this being in here before. It's filled with books from top to bottom. I expect all of them to be crime novels, however, Quinton never ceases to amaze. There's a wide range of categories going from, and this shocks me beyond belief, romance to horror to comedy. He really seems to love books. All books. He truly is the definition of a bookworm. Find him a good piece of literature and he'll read it regardless of genre.

Seeing so many titles brings on a headache. I probably haven't read this many books in my life, yet these appear to be new, meaning he has read these recently. Not to mention our textbooks. This kid is a machine!

"Have you read all these?" I ask, pulling out a book that appears far too difficult for me to read, some type of psychology book. The back says something about reading 'unconscious body movements,' which makes me immediately put it back. Like I could understand any of that shit. Explains how Quinton always seems to know everything. I bet he uses this shit to read people, weirdo.

"Yes," the boy replies.

I glance back at him to see he's focused on his homework. After exchanging numbers Quinton decided that his homework was more important than talking about what happened yesterday. I didn't argue since I had and still do not know where to begin.

"Recently?" I ask.

"I read multiple books a week."

My jaw drops because multiple books clearly means more than one. I've probably read two full books in my life! Why is he such an overachiever? How does his brain even function? Tell me he donated his body to science because I would love to find out how the hell his brain works, seriously.

"So you're a total bookworm?" I tease.

Quinton snorts. "I appreciate good literature."

I roll my eyes at his response. It's something he would say, all cocky and shit. I move from the books that I could never dream of reading to his bed. Falling onto it, I groan then push myself to the top in order to see what Quinton is working on. It's math. I stick my tongue out at the sight. He's in advanced math so I have no clue what he's going over. Hell, I have no clue what we're going over in my math class! He seems at ease with it though, flying through the problems confidently.

I roll onto my back before pushing myself up into a sitting position. I have no desire to watch the nerd do his math homework so I attempt to find myself some form of entertainment. Somewhere in the back of my mind I hear a voice telling me I could leave but I ignore it completely. There's a TV but I doubt he would appreciate me watching TV while he tries to study. Wait, why do I care? Screw him! He's the one who invited me over.

I hop off the bed and head for the TV. There seems to be a gaming console as well. I grin because finally there's something I can do. However, as I go to turn it on, I realize one minor detail. Quinton doesn't play video games. Before I turn either of them on, I look back to Quinton and ask, "Is the gaming console yours?"

"What do you think?" He replies.

It's Taylor's, isn't it? Quinton doesn't play video games because he's a fucking weirdo. I don't want to play it without his permission. That's just rude. Plus, I may mess up one of his games and that'd make me feel worse. Damn it, why can't Quinton be a normal teenager and actually enjoy video games? Or at least enjoy doing something that I can do too.

Quinton huffs behind me, catching my attention. I turn my head back to see that he's finally leaving his homework to join me on the floor. I watch, slightly confused as he turns the gaming console on to put in a first-person shooter game. I pull one of his moves and cock a brow when he grabs a controller and hands me the second one. Quinton sees my confusion and says, "This is the only two player game he has."

"You're playing?" I ask, continuing to stare at the boy. "Do you even know how to play?"

He doesn't answer, which makes me grin.

He doesn't, does he? Oh, this is going to be great! Finally, I have found something that I will probably be better at. It's a miracle! Quick, someone record this experience.

"I swear if you knife me one more—" Quinton shoves my arm seeing as I came up behind him and knifed him. I've been doing it the whole game seeing as Quinton is seriously the worst at this. He is so bad. It is sad how bad he is!

I roll on the ground in laughter. "I cannot believe you are this bad! You suck!"

His aim is terrible. I even got him an automatic weapon, so he didn't have to aim, just hold the trigger and eventually you'll get them. He just seems to flail around the screen and he still hasn't found out how to throw a grenade. I sure as hell am not telling him because, holy shit, this is the best thing I've seen in my entire life.

"How do you do that?" He asks, examining the controller after I tomahawked him. I've been doing that a lot too, seeing as he has made it so easy. I haven't used a gun on him yet, he's that bad.

Chuckling, I ask, "Why would I tell you that? Not like you could use it anyway."

He shoots me a glare that only makes my grin grow. However, I must be getting on his nerves because the next time I knife him, he tackles me to the ground. I wasn't expecting it, so I let out some strange form of a curse word.

"What the hell?!" I cackle, as he attempts to wrestle the controller from my grasp.

Seeing as he's obviously no longer interested in the game, I toss the controller to the side and focus on getting him off me. We roll across the floor, throwing pathetic punches and kicks. I even bite his finger when it gets too close, which he got me back for by tugging on my hair, and he calls me immature!

During our tussle, we maneuver ourselves towards the corner of the room. I let out a startled yelp when I'm pressed into the corner, preventing me from moving anymore. Quinton rests himself between my legs, and to make his position more obvious, he holds my wrists on either side of my head. I feel my cheeks flush. I blame it on our scuffle rather than the proximity of our faces. Seriously, does he need to be this close? I can feel his breath on my face.

"You're annoying," Quinton says.

I'm somewhat annoyed by how calm he looks. Does he even remember our kiss, or did it really mean so little to him? He looks the same as always with a blank expression that only breaks to show his annoyance towards me.

I shrug. "So are you, but you don't see me bitching about it."

I wait for some type of witty reply, but nothing comes. Instead, Quinton seems more interested in keeping me in an eye lock that makes my insides churn.

Why isn't he speaking? Is there something on my face or what? He's staring at me like an ant under a magnifying glass. It's hell-a uncomfortable.

I squirm in his grasp, only to realize it to be a terrible idea. My movement causes me to slide closer to him, practically making our bodies press together. Each breath brings us closer. I force my eyes to the side to keep my brain from exploding. My heart bashes itself against my chest. I pray to whoever is listening to keep my obvious nervousness from showing on my face. Seeing as so much time has passed, and he has yet to move, I become impatient.

Keeping my eyes glued on anything but him, I ask with my best voice of annoyance, "Are you going to move anytime soon? This position is really weird."

"Not if you compare it to last night."

I practically choke on my saliva upon hearing him mention the kiss. I mean, he didn't say kiss, but it's obvious what he's talking about. After my coughing fit, I finally look to him to see he's waiting for some type of response from me. What does he want me to even say?

"You have a strange way of bringing up what happened yesterday. Why couldn't you just talk about it or something earlier and not shove me up against a wall while we are entirely too close?! Why do you make everything so weird?" He glares at how high I raised my voice, but screw him. I will announce whatever I want to the world. He's the one who caused me to raise my voice anyway by being such a weirdo. Wouldn't a normal person have brought that up earlier rather than wait?

Quinton must be fine speaking this way because he still doesn't appear to have any desire to move. I don't know how he can remain so calm when my legs are practically cradling him.

"You're the one making it weird," Quinton states, earning him a curious look. "You've been blushing since you got here."

"What?! I have not!" Which is a total lie, but fuck him, it wasn't that obvious! I know my cheeks have been a little hot since I got here, but it's his fault. We're alone in his room and, after what happened yesterday, of course, I'd be nervous. I didn't know if he'd jump me again! "A-And blushing isn't weird! Just because you're a heartless robot doesn't mean everyone else is!"

"You wouldn't stop staring at me."

"Because you went to do your homework and left me alone! I was looking at everything in your room, not just you. Get over yourself!"

"You haven't tried to move."

My brain shuts down upon hearing that. Blinking rapidly, I inspect myself to see that he's right. I have been saying that I'm uncomfortable, and this is weird, yet I'm not trying to get away. Looking at my wrists, I see he isn't even holding them. I could easily shake his hold. My legs aren't tense or trying to press my body closer to the wall in order to get away, but simply allowing me to sit close to him. If I hate this as much as I said, wouldn't I be trying to get away?

My heart practically stops all together as my entire body heats up. I can officially say that I am flushing from head to toe. Quinton's apathetic face turns into a taunting smirk. My blushing doesn't keep me from glaring daggers at the douche that dare find my embarrassment funny. Whatever, he's no better! He could have been the one to move.

Huffing, I purse my lips and ask through clenched teeth, "Then why haven't you moved either?"

Quinton's smirk doesn't lessen as he states, "I'm not the one complaining they were uncomfortable."

"Oh, whatever!" I shout and begin kicking my legs childishly. "Stop trying to mess with me, you ass, and let me go before I knock out your front teeth!"

Quinton, who I am now sure is losing his mind, leans in close enough to shut me up. If you're wondering how close that may be, let me just say that if I move only a little, our lips will be touching. A lump forms in my throat, one that I have to use the utmost effort to swallow. Sensing my lack of brain activity with him being this close, Quinton's smirk turns into one with obvious devious intentions.

"Your threats are hardly worth hearing," he says moments before doing exactly what I am hoping for—I mean fearing, yeah, yeah, that.

Any thoughts of escaping his grasp disappear when he brushes his lips against mine. Unlike last night's kiss, that was pretty rough from the start. This one is much softer, gentler, without the possibility of bruising later, yet somehow it makes my body shiver just as much. His hold on my wrists is not rough, nor is the pressure between our lips. Though we pull away for a moment for breath, we, and yes I mean we because I've officially gone crazy, lean back in for another and another and another until the feel of his lips is permanently engraved into my mind.

I think, with how hazy my mind is, I would have happily gone the rest of the evening kissing, but Quinton pulls away enough to allow some semblance of sanity to return. His smirk has vanished, but he doesn't look disgusted or annoyed. He doesn't look apathetic either. I can't quite put my finger on it. If I had to pick one, though, I'd say he looks content. However, the bliss of the moment is ruined when he opens his mouth.

"You like me."

That wasn't even a damn question. He simply stated it like it was a goddamn fact! That cocky little shit. What the hell makes him think that?! Maybe because I let him kiss me. Twice. And why the hell does he have to ruin the mood? I would have preferred he got up and started ignoring me again. At least then I wouldn't be annoyed with every arrogant word that comes out of that stupid fucking face of his!

I scowl, completely forgetting about the feelings of the prior kiss. "Like hell I do."

"So you kiss guys, for what, entertainment?" He asks teasingly.

I easily remove my wrists from his grasp now in order to shove him away. He falls back, allowing me time to remove myself from being trapped in the corner. I get up and angrily glare down at the boy, who doesn't seem at all bothered with this situation.

Shit like that is why he pisses me off. This is such a drastically distinct moment for me. One I never expected, and I thought Quinton would feel the same. He doesn't look phased though, like this is normal and that bothers me beyond belief. I have been taught to like girls my whole life and I have liked them, but not to kiss a guy I hated for over a year is unexpected and weird and scary. How is he so calm? Why isn't he bothered?

"Why aren't you at all bothered?" I ask. I don't really give a damn if he thinks I like him, or should I say know because let's face facts here.

He raises a brow and gives me a once over before asking, "Why does it bother you?"

"Are you serious?" Did I call this demon a genius before? I take it back. He's a dumbass. "We are arch enemies!"

"People don't have arch enemies," he sighs, sounding like an adult scolding a three-year-old. Screw you!

"Close enough!" I holler and point an accusing finger at said arch nemesis. By now Quinton has gotten off the floor as well and is now giving me his signature 'you're an idiot' look. "You dated girls before, right?"

He nods.

"So you like girls, yet you kissed me." I slam my hands against my chest as if to prove that, yes, I am a boy. No boobs here, none! "I'm a guy. You're a guy. We kissed, twice!"

I hold up two fingers like somehow that will put it into his thick skull.

Quinton lets out an exhausted sigh and scratches at the back of his neck as he states, "You know bisexual people exist, right? And, like, way more sexualities."

"Uh, well, yeah." I never thought I'd fall into any of that and to suddenly be here is, it's a lot!

"Besides, denying the truth is pretty stupid at this point, don't you think?" he adds.

My mouth opens to retort, but nothing seems to want to come out. I continue to gape like a fish out of water, which allows Quinton time to continue, "If you like someone, you like them. What does gender have to do with it?"

I seriously need to learn not to give him time to think. He comes up with such good responses. I can't think of anything to say. I don't want to say he's right because that will only inflate his already colossal ego, but I can't deny that what he says is true. I've known, though denied it, that I have liked him for some time. It isn't disgusting. It doesn't feel wrong. Like he said, if you like someone, then you like them, you can't help it.

Hey, wait.

"So you like me too, then?" My question catches him off guard. My eyes widen at the way his face breaks for a moment to show shock. I grin at myself for somehow noticing his split second of sudden nervousness. It's gone in a second, but I know I saw it!

"I never said that," he says, but it's too late. I totally saw his nervous face a second ago.

I laugh and poke childishly at his cheek. "Liar, I totally saw your face break there for a second! You practically admitted it a second ago! You totally have a crush on me."

Quinton swats my hand away before brushing past me to return to his desk. I follow him and lean over his shoulder to watch as he pulls out studying materials.

Ha, he's trying to avoid me. Why does he even try? He knows I don't give up so easily.

"Come on, say it!" I shout as I shake his chair. For at least five minutes, I do this before the boy finally turns to face me with a look that could kill. I simply smile at it, seeing as I have survived that look many times. "You like me too, Quinny. Admit it."

"I find you..." His dark eyes give me a once over before saying around a smirk, "Tolerable."

"Tolerable! The fuck do you mean tolerable?"

And for the rest of the evening, I insist on Quinton giving me something other than tolerable. Sadly, he grows annoyed with me and kicks me out an hour later. Whatever, I'll take tolerable for now, but one day he'll say he likes me!

CHAPTER THIRTY-FIVE

I never thought the day would come when I would become too nervous to send a text message. It's a text. How can that make one so nervous? It's not as if it's such a serious thing. People text each other all the time!

My hands can't stop shaking though, and every time I think I've worked up the nerve to send a message, I drop my phone on my mattress and walk away. Langley is looking at me with concern, seeing as this is the tenth time in the last fifteen minutes that I have walked to my phone before throwing it on my bed.

"Something wrong dude?" Langley asks while running his toothbrush across his teeth.

Acting as if I haven't been pacing back and forth between my bed and the bathroom, I reply with a nonchalant shrug, "Not really."

Langley rolls his eyes at my obvious lie. I use brushing my teeth as an excuse to stall, but Langley isn't having it. He finishes up brushing his teeth and leans against the doorway, blocking me from leaving. I shoot him a glare, which isn't at all scary, with a toothbrush hanging from my mouth.

"You've been staring at your phone since you got up. Waiting for a call or something?"

"No." And it isn't a lie! I want to send a text, but should I? I shouldn't, right? Because Quinton doesn't seem like the type who would enjoy texting. I bet he doesn't want me messaging him first thing in the morning. He even said not to send him useless shit, or he'd block my number. A 'good morning' or 'what's up' text would probably be considered useless, right? I'm not even sure why I want to text the bastard in the first place.

Just because I have his number doesn't mean we need to message each other. It's not like either of us promised to message the other anyway. What would I even say? Good morning?

What's up? How are you? Knowing Quinton, he'd either ignore or insult me, and I don't know if I can handle his sass first thing in the morning.

Langley allows me to pass him in order not to be late for class. I toss on my uniform and grab the needed things for class. I take another look at my phone. It seems so innocent, yet it brings heat to my cheeks from one look. Sighing, I push it into my pocket and walk out the door with Langley behind.

I'm on my way to class when my phone vibrates in my pocket. It's sad my heart skips a beat. I can't even lie to myself that it didn't. Langley stares at me oddly from the corner of his eye as I fumble to pull my phone out. Sadly, all I see is a spam message from my phone company.

Growling, I slam it back in my pocket. Langley now has to jog in order to keep up with my annoyed steps. He asks me something, but it goes in one ear and out the other.

Damn Quinton. I thought for a moment having his number would be nice, but now it's only pissing me off! Should I text him or not? What should I even send him? Anything I say could be entitled as 'useless shit,' because to Quinton 99% of the world is 'useless shit.' He should have given me a list of acceptable things to discuss! And I know there is no way in hell he'd message me first. Quinton never initiates conversation. I'm sure if, given the chance, he would remain mute his whole life!

During class I zone out, not that I don't do that normally, but now I am actually thinking of something else rather than zoning out because of being bored. Sighing, I avert my gaze to where my innocent phone lies, yet it still gets a glare from me. It's not my phone's fault, but I feel the need to blame my anger on it either way.

Langley, probably feeling bad for the inanimate object receiving my wrath, nudges me with his elbow to grab my attention. I drift my glare from my phone to Langley, who gives a sheepish grin and holds up a piece of paper.

Langley: What did your phone do to deserve the death glare?

I roll my eyes and brush my lips to hold back a chuckle. Snatching the paper from his hand, I scribble back a response.

Aron: Nothing and it wasn't a death glare.

Langley: Your eyes were shooting laser beams, dude.

Aron: They were not!

"Boys, is this something that you'd like to share with the class?" Professor Kent asks, appearing out of freaking nowhere and snatching the paper from Langley's grasp. The both of us stare up at him, not really worried seeing as there isn't anything on there that could be embarrassing.

"I just wanted Aron to stop glaring death at his phone. I think he's waiting for a call from his girlfriend," Langley responds, causing the class to erupt with laughter. I whack him over the back of the head. Now he's the one receiving the death glare that he only smiles at.

Professor Kent rolls his eyes and requests we pay attention before returning to his lecture. As soon as he walks away, I kick Langley in the shin. He covers his mouth to hold back a yelp, but I see his shoulders shaking to hold back his laughter. Asshole.

"So, you going to tell me why you've been obsessing over your phone, or should I start making assumptions?" Langley asks at my side while the two of us head for our next class. I pretend not to notice the way he glances at said phone that is in my hand when it usually is in my pocket.

I pucker my lips into a pout. I don't want to say why it'll be wei-

"Does it have anything to do with Quinton?"

How the heck?!

"I'll take that as a yes," Langley laughs, somehow seeing the shock on my face as an answer to his question. I quickly stutter out some bullshit excuse like 'I haven't been obsessing over my phone,' or 'I met some cute girl,' but Langley is having none of that. He actually pulls a-and he'd kill me if I said this-Quinton and gives me that 'cut your shit,' look. "That's a whole load of shit, Aron and we both know it."

"Doesn't matter cause it has nothing to do with that bastard!" My flushing cheeks totally help with my denial.

Langley actually runs his hand over his face slowly and with a low groan. "You should be better at lying by now, but whatever, I'm grateful since it's so easy to read you—"

"Hey!"

"You two have each other's numbers now or something? I can't believe he'd give you his number. How'd you manage that? Did you blackmail him?"

"Wha-what! Why am I the one doing the blackmailing? He could have finally realized my superiority and begged me on his knees to pretty, pretty please exchange numbers with me!" Hell, I can't even keep myself from silently laughing at myself for that.

Langley, on the other hand, openly laughs aloud, like it's the best thing he's heard. My hands form fists in anger at the audacity he has to laugh so openly.

"Right, your superiority, that's great, man!" Langley slaps my shoulder in his laughter. The action annoys me. Why does he have to be such an ass? Why is everyone in my life an ass? I need a new friend. "You two are getting pretty chummy—"

"Like hell!"

"Am I being replaced?" Langley's eyes grow wide as he fakes an offended gasp. He throws a hand over his heart dramatically and goes on, ignoring my shouts of denial. Seriously, stop ignoring me! "I can't believe you'd choose him over me. I am truly hurt, but I guess that saying is true."

"Huh? What saying?" Is it sad how easily distracted I am? I was so ready to shout at him more about ignoring me so much, but now I want to know what he means. Damn my curiosity.

"Opposites attract," Langley says with a wink.

My entire body stiffens in both embarrassment and shock. My lips pathetically open and close, words failing to escape each time. This only brings more laughter to Langley, who seems far too pleased with what he has caused.

"You should text him though," Langley suddenly says through his snorts of laughter. He gestures to my phone, which still rests in my hand. "If you have each other's numbers now, it's because you want to message each other, right?"

Right. That's what most people would think, but..."He said he'd block me if I send stupid text messages."

"Sounds very Quinton-like."

"Right!" I throw my arms wildly in the air. "What is stupid stuff, then? Is a 'what's up' or 'good morning,' stupid? Can I small talk with him or is he saying only to message him when I'm in the mood to have a serious conversation? You know how I am. I don't have serious conversations, at least not like the ones Quinton probably enjoys, so what the fuck do I do!" I stomp my feet childishly against the ground, earning me a few curious looks from passersby. I don't even care and continue to pout at my dilemma.

"Won't know the answer until you try," Langley answers with a shrug. "He'll give you a second shot. Maybe."

"I felt better until the maybe part."

Langley shrugs and walks into the classroom, leaving me outside the door. I bite my lip and bring my phone up to stare at the screen, my thumb resting just above "The Asshole." I smirk at the name. The fact Quinton named himself that goes to show he knows me better than I thought. With a deep breath, I finally send a text.

Aron: What does one define as 'useless shit'?

Smirking to myself, I place the device back in my pocket, only to jump in bewilderment a moment later. Arching a brow, I glance down at my pocket to see my phone lighting up within. Langley is smiling far too broadly beside me. Not trusting the sly bastard, I push away from him. He fakes hurt as I pull up the text far away enough so that he can't attempt to see without me noticing. There's no way he replied that fast...

I nearly laugh at seeing that he actually answered me quickly. Opening the message, I'm nervous until I read it over.

Quinton: I am shocked you bothered to ask. I figured you'd find out after I blocked you.

Aron: It must be tiring being such an asshole even when you're texting.

I press the back of my hand to my lips to keep back a grin. How obvious would I be if Langley saw how much I'm smiling from a text? Though, honestly, part of me thinks he's put enough hints together to know what's up. Whatever, he doesn't need more fuel to add to the fire.

Class begins and I am utterly amazed that I receive a reply from Quinton. Langley appears shocked too, seeing as his eyes mirror my own. Who would even think the great Quinton would risk missing anything during a lecture in order to text? Is it sad my cheeks heat up at the thought? Shit, it is, isn't it?

I have to bite my lip to keep back a shit-eating grin. I continue to press the back of my hand against my lips as I read over the text.

Quinton: It's easy. Speaking with you causes most people enough inconvenience to unleash their inner asshole.

Ah, why the hell am I so excited about a text? I'm seriously messed up if I can't keep myself from smiling just from some stupid messages! And the rest of class goes no better because the bastard actually continues to text me throughout it. I am forced to turn my head from Langley and rest it against my arm on the table. I wait impatiently for every reply and each one, though all of them reflect how much of an utter bastard he is, brings a smile to my lips.

Damn. I'm messed up.

Langley may have said nothing, but I can see the curious glances he gives me throughout the next classes. He has definitely noticed how unusually happy I get upon receiving a text. I try not to pay mind to him though, seeing as I do not know what bullshit lies I'd give him to explain why the message brings me joy. Thankfully though, he doesn't ask and maybe that's because he knows I would lie.

During lunch, I am shoving my sandwich into my mouth when I ask Quinton what class he's in. His messages weren't coming in as quickly the last few classes, so I assumed he was in a class that required more attention. However, right now he's replying with lightning speed.

Quinton: I have a study hall now.

Without thinking much of it, I type out a reply and only realize after I've sent it how stupid I am.

"Shit!" I holler, jumping to my feet. The action catches the eyes of those around me, but Langley is not at all surprised by my outburst. He is far too used to me. "Shit! Shit! No, no, wait, how do I—" I look at Langley and Ariel in horror. "Can I delete a message that I've already sent?"

"How the hell should I know?" Langley replies, not seeming to care about my mental panic. Beside him, Ariel is looking at me in slight distress. She isn't as used to me as Langley, so she is shocked by my ability to go from calm to freaking out in under a second. "Why?"

"No, no reason." I sink into my seat, slamming my head against the table with a groan. I curse my stupidity. Ariel is whispering to Langley, probably about how she never expected me to be this insane. I am even more sure that's what she said when Langley cackles and replies with something like 'you'll get used to it.'

Doomed. I'm doomed! How dumb could I be? I hold up my phone to glare at the message I dared to type without thinking it over.

Aron: I'm on lunch. Can I come see you?

Who asks that? And how the hell is he to respond? If he says no, that will crush me, but if he says yes...my cheeks flare at the thought. Oh god, what if he says yes? Should I...go? Should I play it off as a joke? I shake my head hard enough to leave me dizzy.

Why am I acting like this? Grinning over text messages, sending dumb texts, wanting to hang out when we get the chance. It's too much like a hopeless romantic. Why would he want to, anyway? This shit makes it seem like we're dating or something, which we aren't! At least... I don't... think we are. We kissed and shit, but that doesn't mean we're dating or anything...right? Ah, I'm getting such a headache.

My headache only continues to grow as the moments pass with no reply. Though I do my best to keep my attention on the conversation between my friends, I can't keep myself from looking at my phone every few seconds. The pace of my heart escalates with each passing moment. Said heart nearly jumps out of my chest at the sudden buzzing of my phone. I grab it with a speed I didn't know I possessed, yet I can't bring myself to open the text.

Langley and Ariel are probably pretending not to notice my odd behavior. Neither of them asks anything, but I feel their eyes on me the longer I sit still. My hands shake and I have to use every ounce of will I have to force myself to open the message.

Quinton: I'm in the library.

Somehow I am up and grabbing my things before I even realize it. Langley asks where I'm going, but I'm already moving out the door with my lunch. My cheeks flare in embarrassment as I stride towards the library at a speed probably faster than necessary, but I can't keep the excitement out of my step. I open the doors and, with more enthusiasm than I'm willing to admit, search for Quinton.

I find the boy, as expected, in a far corner of the library, away from everyone. He has papers strewn about him with a rather confusing Advanced Chemistry book before him. He's leaning over to see the words. His lips move as he mouths the word. Occasionally, he presses the end of his pen between his teeth to nip at it before scribbling down something he has deemed as important.

My conscience can't help but think back to what else has been on his lips and what I would prefer on his lips, but that's not important.

Flushing, I shake my head. I'm staring, aren't I? I slap my cheeks, the sound echoing enough to grab Quinton's attention. He sits straight and turns to see me a few feet away with wide eyes and my hands against my cheeks. Dark eyes roll at the sight, yet he holds up his hand and beckons me closer with his finger.

I move over to Quinton without a complaint and sit across from him.

"H-Hey," I mutter, more to myself than him.

"Hello." Black eyes bore into me with enough intensity to send a shiver down my spine. He clearly caught the action because a brow rises to hide beneath his hair. I bite my lip, hoping the pain will fight off my blush. It doesn't.

I place my lunch on the table with a clearing of my throat. He glances at it then back at me. I pull out my half-eaten sandwich and ask, "Want some?"

"I have lunch next," he says with a shake of his head.

Still his eyes are on me as I take a rather large bite. I'm hoping having food in my mouth will keep me from saying something stupid. Knowing me though, I'd be able to be an idiot regardless of how much food is shoved down my throat but let's not talk about that!

With a very hard swallow, I push down my sandwich and go in for another bite. It's hard to eat, though, when Quinton is staring so intently at me. Why is he even staring? Is there something on my face? Curious, I run the back of my arm across my face. I peer at my sleeve, seeing nothing on it. Puckering my lips in confusion, I glance back at Quinton to see a smirk on his face. The smirk is devious enough to make my toes curl.

"W-Why are you staring at me like that?" His eyes are screaming evil intent.

"No reason," he shrugs and returns to his studying. With that evil smirk remaining on his face, he says, with more confidence than I like, "Just thinking you must really like me."

My blush spreads from the tip of my toes to my ears. I can feel the heat in my veins growing at an accelerated rate. The fact that my voice shakes as I speak goes to show how full of shit I am, "Shut up, you make it sound embarrassing."

Wait, that shouldn't be what I'm mad about. I should be mad that he said I liked him. I should have said I don't! Damn it Aron, think before you speak!

Quinton shrugs, his eyes never leaving his work as he speaks, "You are the definition of embarrassing."

"The hell I am!" I shout, slamming my hand against the table. I hear an annoyed 'shh' probably from the evil librarian. I flinch at the sound, then return my glare to Quinton, who is totally ignoring it. "You're an asshole, you know that, right?"

"Is your vocabulary so limited, Your Highness? I'm beginning to think cursing is the only form of communication you have," Quinton teases around a coy grin, one that, though it makes my blood boil, also makes my heart skip a beat.

Damn it; stop skipping beats because of Quinton! I know I can't deny I like him now but, please, this is too much for me.

My nose scrunches in annoyance. Growling, I lean forward to spit back at him. "I'm beginning to think you don't have a single kind bone in your body."

"You shouldn't think that. It should be obvious."

Why was my heart fluttering earlier again? This guy is so not worthy of my affection.

My thoughts must show on my face because Quinton rolls his eyes and, to my shock, raises his chemistry book in order to shield us from view. My body stiffens when he moves in for a quick and chaste kiss. Innocent as the action may have been, I feel my mind swirling into a gutter where I am ashamed to say not so innocent thoughts lie.

"I never thought I'd find a way to shut you up," Quinton says as if he hadn't kissed me for any reason other than to just kiss. I can't seem to stop myself from blushing. I have to rub my chest to make sure my heart isn't actually bursting from it because it sure as hell feels like it is.

"S-Shut up," I sputter, shoving my sandwich into my mouth yet again. I can't come up with anything to say. What is there to say? I would never imagine in a million years that

Quinton would do that. It's decided. He's pure evil. He did that to mess with me, and it worked.

The end of his study hall and my lunch comes to an end. I actually have a class after this. Not that I was considering staying with him during his lunch if I could. That would be ridiculous! Haha...ha...

"See you later," I mumble to the boy, who nods to show he heard me before heading to the cafeteria. I slowly make my way to my next class. It's hard to focus on anything around me when my lips are tingling.

I press my fingers to my bottom lips, rubbing the skin that feels warm to the touch. It was such a simple touch, yet it made my lips tingle as if we had kissed for an eternity. Even now my heart is racing, my mind reeling and tongue sweeping over my lips in an attempt to taste the brief kiss. My body shivers at my own thoughts that are nowhere near innocent. Damn, I run my hand through my hair as a shaky sigh leaves my chest.

I really do like the bastard, huh? To think I'd get so messed over such a simple kiss. Does it feel this way to everyone? Or am I being oversensitive? It's probably me.

Somehow I make it to class late, but at least I make it. Langley watches me with concern, seeing as I am so dazed that I am pretty sure I'm walking with unstable steps. The professor shouts something at me about being late that I pay no mind to. I sink into my chair, still biting and licking at my lips. Beside me, Langley is taking in my obviously unstable self.

A pair of fingers snap themselves before my eyes. I blink rapidly, thinking I might have only seen it in my head, but when I hear Langley whisper my name, I realize he had done it. Turning my head, I face the boy, who is leaning over to whisper to me. "Are you ok?"

Ok? Technically, yes, I am. I have no injuries, nor am I frustrated or annoyed. At the same time, one could say I'm not ok at all. I have fallen hard for the biggest asshole on campus and I'm incapable of escaping his icy grasp, yet oddly, I am ok with that. Fuck, he is driving me nuts.

I slam my hands over my face in hopes of keeping my obviously strange behavior from being noticed. Langley already knows, but I don't need more people asking or starting rumors. I inform Langley that we can talk later since there's no way we could have a serious conversation during class. We'd get caught. Neither of us are able to keep our voices down. Our whispers are others 'inside voices.'

The day ends and Langley is more than curious about my behavior. The moment class lets out, he's asking if Quinton had slipped me some drugs or something. I laugh. I bet Quinton won't even drink until he's 21, so drugs are out of the question.

"Actually, I have a question." That will definitely give me away the moment I ask it but Langley is the only person I can think of asking. The boy nods, showing he is listening intently. He waits for us to get closer to our dorms where there are fewer people capable of listening in. "Uh, when you and Ariel are together, what does it feel like?"

"Huh?" Langley scrunches his nose in confusion. He eyes me suspiciously.

"Like do you get all bubbly for no reason? Is every kiss just as nerve-wracking as the others? Does a simple peck of the lips leave you as breathless as, y'know, other stuff?"

Seeing the shock on Langley's face makes me groan. I spin on my heel, ready to leave out of pure embarrassment, but Langley grabs my arm to keep me from doing so. I lower my head to glare at the ground.

"Sorry, sorry, forget what I said!" I wave my hands between the two of us, hoping to physically wipe the questions away. "I'm being weird is all!"

"Hell yeah you are," Langley agrees with a nod. "But I'm not bothered that you asked or anything." Langley scratches at the back of his head, seeming to be as embarrassed as I am about this conversation. I put on a sheepish, apologetic grin in hopes of making him a little less embarrassed. The boy chuckles and opens our dorm door. After tossing his things onto his bed, he finally answers my questions. "I'm always nervous with Ariel."

I take a seat at the edge of Langley's bed. The boy crosses his arms as he thinks over how to answer my questions; "Although it's been a few months since we got together, I still get nervous and giddy. Her actions both frighten and excite me. I fear how she'll react, but also excited to see how she reacts. Every kiss makes me happy, whether it's a quick peck or..." He glances at me, a blush forming on his cheeks. "Or...more than that..." I grin at his blush, which earns me a whack across the head. I yelp but do my best to hold back my chuckles as he continues. "I think it's totally normal to feel that way about someone you like. It takes some getting used to, but it's not like the feelings die down, it's more like...you accept them? Or rather expect them? I don't know, but it's normal to feel giddy or nervous around the one you like."

Langley looks at me to see if I am pleased with his answer. Seeing as I have nothing more to ask, he lets out a relieved sigh and asks with a still very obvious blush, "Are we done? I can't handle these serious talks. It gives me the shivers."

He physically shivers and rubs at his arm as if to wipe the conversation away.

I laugh. "Sorry, but you're the only one I have to talk to, really."

"Ugh, you're making it worse!"

I roll my eyes but thank him for the advice. He waves me off, claiming that he's done with my shit and rather hang out with his girlfriend. I am shocked to see him leave without asking why I bothered asking. He must be curious about who I like... unless he already knows. He hasn't mentioned it though so, maybe not? I shake those thoughts from my head.

I move to remove my uniform, changing into a pair of sweats. I fall back onto my bed with an 'umph'. I put my arms behind my head and allow my legs to swing off the end. So it's normal, huh? I'm not sure if I like that. The idea of sputtering like an idiot everyday around Quinton annoys me. I hate him seeing me so worked up, especially since the bastard seems to thoroughly enjoy it.

I click my tongue at the thought of Quinton's smug expression. Maybe it's a bad idea to think of Quinton, though when my eyes feel this heavy...

Warm lips that I easily recognize as Quinton's run over my own roughly, because nothing with Quinton is ever soft. Except maybe the moist cavern behind his lips. My tongue eagerly explores the newfound territory, running over every crevice with curious fascination. Quinton lets the occasional shiver run down his spine, refusing to moan. The action encourages me enough to suck on his tongue, pulling it to my mouth. His low groan makes my entire body tingle. He eagerly pushes through, doing the same to me as I did to him. I can't keep myself from moaning and normally the sound would piss me off, but I'm too busy enjoying the way his hands spread my thighs, allowing his hips to rest against mine.

I hiss into the kiss at the friction between us. His hips continue to brush against mine in a teasing way that forces me to thrust upwards in hopes of keeping up the dizzying action. He presses forward quickly after my sudden willingness to grind against him.

I have to pull away from the kiss in order to take in a shaky breath. Said breath is once again lost when Quinton begins to nip and suck at my neck. My back arches shamelessly, forcing our bodies together. Even the friction between our chests is driving me wild. Everywhere he touches is on fire, yet I don't want to pull away, but get closer and closer to that ever-growing heat.

The hand that isn't holding Quinton up tangles itself into my hair. His fingers grip my hair, tugging at it as if to order me to elongate my neck for him to mark. I oblige, more than happy to feel his lips trail over the newly exposed skin. Noises I don't know I am capable of escape my lips. I feel him smirking against my skin. "Too easy."

I grunt and somehow knee him in the side. The action makes him stumble, and I use this moment to gain control. I reverse us; I am now the one resting between his legs. He glares at me, obviously not liking this newfound situation until I'm kissing down his chest, growing closer and closer to my destination.

His hand entangles itself in my hair as I suck at his hip. He grunts and his hips twist and shake beneath me. The action sends a shock of pleasure straight through me, one that encourages me to continue. My hands are shaking as they undo his pants, pushing them along with his boxers down...

I wake up with a start. My phone rings loudly beside me, thankfully waking me from that...that...

If my cheeks weren't blushing earlier, they certainly are now. I push myself onto my elbows to stare shamefully at the obvious bulge beneath my sweats. It's embarrassing how heavily my chest is rising and falling. Each breath I take is shaky, and it takes every amount of effort I have in order to push myself off the bed. My legs nearly give out as I move myself to the bathroom, completely ignoring the ringing of my phone.

Shit. Right now I need a freezing shower.

CHAPTER THIRTY-SIX

L ying face first on my bed is about the only thing I can do right now. I'm too ashamed to move. Even after a very long cold shower that did absolutely nothing and resulted in me only imagining even more shameful things in order to get off, my legs continue to feel useless. My stomach is flipping and churning at the memory of what I had just dreamed, what I had just used to get off.

It's not like I haven't had wet dreams before. I am a healthy teenage boy with enough time on his hands to enjoy himself. I've jerked off plenty of times, but not once have I ever got hot at the thought of some pompous, smug, bastard such as Quinton.

Sure, he's a good-looking guy, not that I would ever say that to his face because it'd inflate his already massive ego, but still. I guess I shouldn't be that shocked. We made out. I enjoyed it more than I will admit. I... I like him, so it isn't an unexpected event. When you like someone, they are the ones in your fantasies.

I wrap my arms beneath the pillow, only to press it harder against my face. My breath warms the surface and, in doing so, does the same to my face, which is already hot thanks to my blushing. I inhale deeply against the fabric. I have realized that I have been lost in my mind a lot lately. Ever since I met Quinton, I seem to be stuck in my head, constantly thinking about my actions.

My phone suddenly beeps loudly, reminding me it had been ringing before I took a shower. I slowly grope about the end table in search of the device. Eventually, my hand grasps it. I turn my face just enough to peek an eye out to see I have a missed call from my mother along with a voicemail. I open it to listen to what she had to say, "Hey sweetie, it's mom! I just wanted to check up on your plans for spring break. I'd really like for you to come home. Call me once you hear this. Love you!"

Oh, right, spring break is almost here. I shouldn't be surprised. Valentine's day wasn't that long ago. I haven't really thought of my plans. For Christmas, I spent half of it on campus with Quinton and the other half at home. Spring break is only two weeks long, so last year I went home to please mom. I wonder what Quinton plans to do for spring break. He's never gone home for breaks. We spent time together over Christmas break. Maybe he'd like to come to my place over spring break.

I shoot up with wide eyes. What the hell am I thinking? No way, I can't ask him that. I slam my hands against my cheeks to physically knock sense into me. After that dream I had, who knows what stupid thing I'll do over break? When Langley visited, we always shared a bed since my bed's so big. Although we have many guests' rooms, we could put Quinton in one—no, that's not the point! No way I can't. I can't. But I really want to.

Wait a second. When did my phone get in my hand? Hang on, is it ringing? Who the hell am I even calling? Before I have time to pull my phone away in order to look, a voice that makes my eyebrow twitch answers, "What do you want?"

"Is that any way to answer your phone?" I scoff, feeling the urge to roll my eyes at him even when he isn't here. Quinton pisses me off without being near me.

"It's my phone. I answer it as I see fit."

I think I roll my eyes more when I'm speaking with Quinton than in the rest of my life combined. He has that effect on people, y'know, making them have the desire to pop his inflated head off his stupid shoulders.

"I regret calling you." I hiss.

"I regret answering."

Seriously, I will not ask. Fuck it, I am not inviting him to my place over spring break. I knew it was a bad idea, yet my body moved without my knowledge, or permission, for that matter. He's probably going to say no, anyway. He doesn't even go home for break, so why come to mine? This was stupid. I need to hang up.

"Did you have a reason for calling?" Quinton suddenly asks after my moment of silence.

"I did, but I'm changing my mind."

"Must not have been important, then. I'm hanging up."

"Hey, wait a second, asshole!" Wait, no, that's not what I wanted to say. I mean hang up, go ahead and hang up. I totally don't want you to come! "I wanted to know if you'd like to come home with me for spring break!"

I need to staple my mouth shut one of these days...

Silence follows my request, which only makes me even more nervous. If I wasn't shaking before, I am now.

"Uh...I mean you don't have to come." I'm scratching at the back of my neck. "I haven't even asked my folks yet, though I doubt they'd mind. I just thought you're always here over break by yourself and y'know... maybe you'd... want to leave campus for once... or something. Whatever, forget I as—"

"I'll go." He interrupts. Normally, that would irk me beyond belief, but I actually calm down at hearing his voice.

"Huh?" Did I hear right? Is the world ending? I spin around my room in search of zombies or aliens that have invaded the earth because, seriously, the world must be ending. Quinton said he'd go.

"I said I'd go, idiot. I knew you were dumb, but this is ridiculous." He teases, bringing a scowl to my face, and a slight blush, but who cares about that? The scowl is what's most important!

"I just... didn't think you'd agree to go so easily. I figured it'd be a battle to get you to come along."

"Implying you'd be willing to battle in order to get what you wanted? Hm, didn't know you would miss me so badly over break, Princess." I can hear his smirk through his voice. Damn freaking piece of crap, mother fudger, ugh!

"Screw you. I changed my mind. I don't want you to come, you fucking asshole!" And I hang up. Only to call my mom moments later in order to ask if it'd be all right to bring a friend home over break. I do not have a problem, I swear.

It takes a little convincing, but mom eventually caves. Part of me thinks she recognized Quinton's name, and perhaps she wasn't too sure about allowing him over. She also may be worried simply because she's never met the boy, but I've talked about him before, so they know a bit. She insisted he be searched before his arrival, which I didn't find unusual since she and dad always insisted on it. She said she'd tell dad about it and he would call later if he came up with anything, like possibly making Quinton take a psych evaluation or something. I don't know, he can get a little crazy sometimes.

I send Quinton a text afterwards asking if he's alright with being groped by men. Shortly after I get a reply,

Quinton: I don't know if I want to know why you asked that.

Aron: My mom said you may come home with me over break as long as you're ok with being searched.

Surprisingly, I receive a quick reply yet again. Not that I'd ever say it aloud, but his quick replies make me feel proud. The great and ever busy Quinton will give up enough of his own time to text me. Come on, most people would feel like they've accomplished something in life! I should tease him about it, but then he might stop.

Quinton: That's fine. I expected there would be more, for example, signing a paper claiming my family can't sue if I'm killed during an attempt to assassinate you.

Aron: Did you just make a joke? I didn't know you could do that. You're improving, Quinny.

Quinton: It wasn't a joke. I was being serious.

I laugh, wondering if that is another joke. That makes it funnier.

The evening continues on with a few texts back and forth with Quinton, mostly me telling him plans for break. It's in two weeks, so I remind him to make sure he's ready early. My mom always sends an earlier car, ever excited to see her baby boy.

"Hey man," Langley says when entering since he probably would have scared me shitless if he didn't announce himself. I'm too busy staring at my phone to notice much else.

I glance over my shoulder back at him. "Have fun with Ariel?"

Langley's bashful grin is answer enough.

I roll my eyes and say, "You're gross, dude."

"Says the one who blushes just from hearing the name Quinton."

"Like hell I do!" I shout and press my hands to my cheek to make sure it isn't true. The action only makes Langley laugh harder than he already was. "Fuck off!"

"Have you decided if you're going to head home for spring break yet?" Langley asks. I already know he's going home. He always does. Actually, I recall him saying that Ariel may come for a visit. They have been dating for a while now, so it's about time they meet each other's parents. Good for them. Ariel's a good girl. Langley's lucky to have her. Look at my best bud, growing up so fast!

I nod and further bury myself into my comforter. "Mom already insisted I come home. She's going through withdrawal, apparently."

Langley laughs and with a sigh, says as if he's annoyed, but his face shows otherwise, "Don't worry, Aron. My mom says shit like that, too."

I nod, mimicking his annoyed tone but, truthfully, we both love our mother's so it's fine when they go a little bonkers. "I feel most moms do. It's in their DNA."

"I'm nervous that my parents are going to meet Ariel—" Ah, I knew he told me that. "You know how my mom is. She's going to interrogate her. I don't want her to be uncomfortable."

"True," I shrug. "But it'll be fine. I'm sure Ariel will know she doesn't mean harm. I can't even imagine how Quinton's going to act around my folks."

"What?" Langley stares at me with an arched brow before his face breaks into a shit-eating grin.

Oh no, I didn't mean to say that. I wasn't going to tell him about Quinton coming home with me during break! But it's too late. Langley has heard me and now he's giving me this look, like he just fell on a gold mine.

"Quinton's going with you during break?" Langley bites his lip to calm down his far too pleased grin.

I glare at him before my face heats up, then I bury my face into my pillow again. "No, you heard wrong."

"No, I didn't. You said Quinton is meeting your parents. He agreed to that?" Langley laughs. I feel my bed dip, signaling he has made his way over to me. He slaps my back as he speaks. "What's up with you two? I thought you were 'arch enemies'?" Langley tries to mimic my voice near the end, which he fails horribly.

"We are!" Because denial is always the best option.

"Uh huh. You're suspicious," he teases.

"I am not! You're just being weird!" I pull myself from my pillow to glare at the boy, who is still smiling. He gives me a 'cut the crap' look. It really is useless to hide things from Langley. He knows me too well. I need to get rid of him! He knows too much.

"It's not weird or anything." I mumble. "We've been getting along better recently..."

"I know. I didn't say it was weird." He hums, trying to make himself seem like he isn't attacking me when we all know he so is. He is just waiting for me to blurt something else stupid out. Like I said, he knows me too well, and this friendship needs to end!

"You're thinking it." I point out, even pointing an accusing finger in his direction.

"Well, yeah," he says bluntly, then waves his hand dismissively through the hair. "But whatever floats your boat, dude. I don't care if you two are making friends. That's good actually." Langley nods approvingly, which makes me stare at him quizzically.

"How so?" I ask hesitantly because, honestly, he gives me the feeling that I won't like his answer.

Langley pats me ever so lovingly on the back. "When you annoy me, I can pass you off to Quinton."

I kick him off my bed for that. Langley hops back up easily, full of laughter, and changes the subject by claiming that he's going to take a shower, allowing me to return to burying my embarrassment into my bed sheets. I shouldn't be surprised he's ok with it. Langley has made it obvious that he has basically known that Quinton and I aren't enemies anymore. However, I prefer he continues to think we're only friends. I don't think I can handle telling him the truth yet. He's the only true friend I've really got. The fear of losing him is strong enough to keep the truth in.

CHAPTER THIRTY-SEVEN

"I need break to get here faster," Langley groans from his desk. A loud 'thunk' follows his words making me chuckle. I glance in his direction to see he has face planted onto the desk. His arms dangle at his sides showing he has given up on whatever he's working on.

"We have a week left, Langley. You'll live," I laugh, returning my attention to my homework.

It's been a week since I've made plans with Quinton to come with me over break. He has called his mother, who apparently is fine with it. I wished to ask more, why she's ok with not seeing her boy so often, but he looked exhausted after speaking with her so I remained silent. I'll get him to tell me some other time.

For once, I'm actually doing my schoolwork because Professor Kent said if I turn this in on time he won't give me extra work over break. I can't have work over break. It's called a break for a reason! Besides, I probably wouldn't work on it even if he gave it to me. I would forget or half ass it, but honestly, who puts actual effort into work given over break?

Quinton. Quinton would.

Langley slams his arms onto the desk, nearly toppling over his lamp. The both of us stare at the shaking object and let out a relieved sigh when it safely stops, remaining on the desk. I send him an annoyed glare that clearly says I would not help clean up anything he breaks from his thrashing. He sheepishly grins before sighing while running his hands over his face, "Why is school so long? My brain is going to explode. Who even understands chemistry? Why does everything sound like a different language? None of these words make sense."

I shrug; scribbling answers I'm not completely sure are right on my paper. "Why are you asking me? I'm worse off in Chem than you are."

"True. A rock knows more chemistry than you."

"I'm not even insulted, seeing as that is a hundred percent accurate."

"Speaking of break, though." Langley glances at me from the corner of his eye. By the way he trailed off towards the end, I sense his question will bother me in some shape or form. "Quinton still going home with you?"

My toes curl beneath my comforter at the mention of Quinton spending break with me. I have to bite my lip to keep myself from smiling. Trying to act cool about it, I shrug and mumble, "Yeah, he is."

Langley, seeing through my bullshit, grins and pushes himself from the desk. His chair slides across the floor to land next to my bed. I jump a bit from the sudden action. "And how, exactly, is that going to play out?"

"What do you mean?" I ask, keeping my eyes on my homework rather than the grin on his stupid face.

"Your arch enemy is staying at your place for two weeks. What are you guys even going to do? Play checkers?" He teases.

I turn in order to kick Langley away. He cackles as his chair spins across the floor, landing him somewhere near his own bed. I bury myself once again beneath my comforter, attempting to continue on with my homework while replying, "Hell if I know. We'll do something a-and stop asking about it!"

"I'm only a concerned friend. I mean, having my best friend's enemy staying at his home, how could I not be worried about his wellbeing?" Langley gasps, faking innocence. I don't even bother to look at him, seeing as the obvious grin that is on his face will only annoy me more.

Thankfully, the world decides that Langley's teasing needs to end. My phone rings. I toss my homework aside and reach for said phone to see that it's my dad calling. Smiling, I answer it, "Hey dad. What's up?"

"Hey bud, what are you up to?" He asks with a voice that sounds a bit off.

"Uh, doing some homework that needs done before break. What are you doing?" Dad usually isn't much for small talk. Normally, when he calls, he talks about whatever is on his mind. This means he's either calling with bad news or simply because he's bored and thinks I have nothing better to do than talk with him. Not that I'm complaining or anything! I enjoy talking to my dad, but seriously, he calls for weird reasons sometimes.

"Not much, just doing some paperwork," he sighs, sounding tired, not that it's unusual for him to sound that way. I'm about to ask if he's been sleeping enough, seeing as sometimes he overworks himself, but he speaks before I have time to ask.

"I wanted to talk about your friend coming over for break," he says.

"Oh yeah, sure. I already told him he'd have to go through searching and such. I told him to be prepared for more than that just in case," I laugh, trying to ignore the way he said that. It sounded bad, like I'm not going to enjoy what he has to say.

My laughter disappears the moment he asks, "What all do you know about this boy? I remember you telling us about him and I'm very glad that you're making friends at school, but have you ever met his parents or spoke with them?"

I feel my grip tighten against the phone. I don't think I like where this is heading. "No, I haven't met them."

But I know about his dad, which I am sure that's what he is trying to get at. I clench my eyes as if that will somehow help what I feel is about to come.

My jaw hurts from the sudden grinding of my teeth. Perhaps, if this wasn't about Quinton, I wouldn't be so bothered, but my blood is boiling. Swallowing the lump in my throat, I do my best not to sound as annoyed as I know I am when asking, "Why do you ask? Is there something I should know?"

"It's complicated. After some research on the boy, I've found out some things that I do not have the right to speak to you about if you don't already know. To put it simply," he takes a deep breath that makes me anxious. "I don't think you should continue your relationship with this boy."

Excuse me?

"I was more than happy to allow a friend to accompany you over break, Aron, but after learning more about him, I found out a few things. It's about his father. Did you know what he did? Probably not, and I won't tell without your friend's permission, but I simply cannot have you around such a boy—"

"His dad was a crazy asshole, so what?" I grunt, interrupting my dad, which I think shocks him, seeing as he remains silent afterwards. He probably should speak though, seeing as the longer we sit here in silence, the angrier I become. "How the hell does that matter?"

"Aron—"

"That is such bullshit!" I turn my neck, hearing it crack as I do so. My head pounds with a headache. My hand is clenched so tight I know there are marks on my palms. I am doing my best not to cuss out my father since I know most parents would react in the same manner but, fuck, am I pissed. What the hell is everyone's problem?

"How is that in any way his fault?" I scream into the phone, somehow forgetting Langley is still in the room. I don't know if he's watching me or not, and I don't care. I'm too pissed. "That isn't his fault! Why do his dad's choices have to affect him, too? He's a good guy! Sure, he's anti-social, has a monumental ego, and he pisses me off all the time but—but he's the first person who has ever had the guts to stand up to me! He tells me when I'm being dumb or when I'm acting like a spoiled brat. What his dad did doesn't define who he is! You and I should know how that feels, to have people assume things about us because of who we know or who we are related to! He treats me like a human being and—and if you have a problem with us being friends then get over it because I won't stop hanging out with him even if you have to drag my ass out of school!"

Some time during my screaming, I have stood up. Now I see Langley staring at me with wide eyes. I'm sure mine are as wide now, seeing as I have finally realized that I have screamed at my dad, who is still silent. However, the anger within me hasn't subsided.

Huffing, I grumble one last thing; "Don't bother sending a car this weekend. I'm not coming home for break."

I toss my phone onto the bed, opting to leave it there, seeing as Mom will probably attempt to call after hearing what Dad has to tell her. I'm out the door before Langley has time to recover from the shock of my shouting. I don't realize where I'm going until I'm already there, standing in front of Quinton's door with my fist raised. I should feel bothered that this is the first place I go to when this angry, but I'm not. In fact, I feel myself calming down just being here.

I knock on the door rougher than I meant to. I hear movement inside, causing my fingers to flex at my side. Seconds later, the door opens to show Taylor, who looks me up and down before asking, "Um Your Highness... are you looking for Quinton?"

I nod, fearing that if I speak, my anger will frighten the boy further. He nods and shyly moves out of the way to allow me in. I step past him, my eyes immediately searching the room for the asshole. I find said asshole lying on his back, his nose buried in an advanced chemistry book. Figures. Langley and I are desperately suffering through chemistry while this asshole is easily making it through advanced. Smart and good looking should be illegal. He needs to stop being so freaking perfect.

Quinton lowers the book just enough to see his dark eyes. "To what do we owe the pleasure, Princess?" He asks, voice a bit muffled from the book.

Taylor, probably sensing the tense atmosphere, stutters some excuse to leave. He rushes to his desk, quickly pushes whatever he was doing into his bag, and runs out the door. The door shuts behind him, leaving Quinton and I alone. Quinton moves his book back up to continue studying when he sees I am making no move to speak.

I'm not sure where to start or what to say. Would it bother him to find out my dad wants us to stop speaking because of his father? Even if he doesn't say it, I feel it would bother him. It'll be a reminder that his father's choices will haunt him forever. He'll never be able to tell anyone the truth without facing the consequences.

But, I can't keep it in. I have to tell him because, if I don't, I may just blow a top.

Ha! I already did that.

"My dad doesn't want us to associate," I finally get out through clenched teeth. "He found out about...about your dad. He asked if I knew about it and then he was all. I can't have you around such a boy!"

I wave my hands crazily in the air along with my ranting, "Can you believe that? I mean, he doesn't even know you! He didn't even give you a chance, and he goes and fucking says that!"

I swing my arm through the air because I need to speak with my hands now. "What does he know about you? What gives him the right to judge you based on your father's actions? You were so young, and it wasn't your fault he was a crazy bastard! I hate people like that, people who judge others based on who their mother, father, brother, sister, whatever it's not fair! You're not your dad, so why does it—"

A hand entangling itself into my hair breaks me from my violent rant. Said hand in my hair soothes my scalp before bringing my face upward to peer into a pair of black eyes. Quinton grabs my hand with his other and brings it up to inspect. I watch as he uses his thumb to open my fingers that were clenched the entire time through my shouting. I blink at the blood that has come from my nails breaking the skin.

"Idiot," Quinton huffs, releasing my hair. He grasps my wrist in order to drag me towards the bathroom. I quietly follow, watching curiously as he dampens a rag that he uses to wipe the blood from my palm and nails. "Only you would get so bothered by something so simple."

"The hell do you mean simple?" I bark, pulling my hand from his. I hold up my hand to inspect it while speaking. "It's not simple. You should be pissed too!"

"It doesn't matter," he states, swatting my hand away to grab my attention. "Most parents would feel that way. You can't blame him. He's trying to protect his kid."

"By treating another kid like dirt? As a parent, he should know better."

"It doesn't matter either way," Quinton insists, now rubbing at his temple, probably to fight off a headache. He always claims that I give him one. I can't help it he can't handle my awesomeness.

"I don't get how it doesn't matter. Please, enlighten me, o' wise one," I grumble, crossing my arms with an annoyed huff.

Quinton gives me a look that says how much he cannot stand me right now. Whatever, like there ever is a time where he can stand me. Sighing, he shakes his head and asks, "Do you judge me because of my father?"

"No, of course not!" He knows I don't. We talked about this. I, of all people, understand where he's coming from. There is no way in hell I am putting any blame on him for the actions of his father.

"Then that's all that matters." He whacks me over the back of the head afterwards and returns to his book, leaving me confused. Honestly, he should be clearer. He knows I'm an idiot and I don't fully understand his words.

Spinning on my heel to face him, I ask with annoyance, "What do you mean by that?"

"I'm not explaining. Drop it," Quinton grunts, flipping a page and highlighting whatever he deems important.

I stomp over to his bed. Before he has time to see what I'm up to, I yank the book from his grasp. He stares at the space where his book once was. Sighing like the weight of the world is on his shoulders, Quinton turns to me with a glare. "Give that back, dumbass."

"Not until you tell me what the hell that was supposed to mean!" I holler. "I'm already angry enough with my dad, but now you're only pissing me off more!"

"Need I explain everything to you?" Quinton groans. He holds his hand out for his book but answers my question as he does. "Why should I care what anyone else thinks of me if you know the truth?"

Oh.

My jaw drops. Did he really just say that?

I drop his book into his lap without meaning to. I couldn't help it. My entire body feels on fire. I actually take a few steps back out of embarrassment as my cheeks flush. Shit, my heart is beating really fast. So fast that I have to rub my chest in order to make sure it hasn't burst. Quinton, seeming to thoroughly enjoy my embarrassment, smirks but says no more as he continues reading over his homework.

I flop onto the bottom of Quinton's bed, burying my face in his sheets in order to hide my face. I don't want him to see it anymore. Feeling his gaze on me makes my stomach squirm.

I can't think of anything to say, nor do I want to, out of fear that my voice may reveal more than I wish. He doesn't care what others think as long as I know the truth? God, that's so cheesy. He basically admitted that only my opinion matters. Shit, hearing that shouldn't make me feel so happy.

Quinton, who I would like to remind everyone is the biggest asshole ever, seems to miss seeing my flushing face because I feel the bed move. It's too late to react. The boy is at my side in no time, pushing me from my stomach to my side in order to peer at my flushing face. I am about to hide it with my hands when he leans in to catch my lips with his own.

Losing all ability to think, I don't put up a fight when he pushes me onto my back in order to rest himself comfortably between my thighs. The anger within me diminishes with each stroke of his tongue against the seam of my lips and it completely shatters when I part said lips, allowing Quinton to remind me how he really is perfect at everything, including kissing. Not that I will ever tell him how much I thoroughly enjoy tasting him because... well, no one deserves that kind of power.

I suppose I can be angry later, after I have thoroughly enjoyed myself with Quinton. Yeah, yeah, that sounds like a good idea.

CHAPTER THIRTY-EIGHT

"Whatever happened between you and your dad is driving me nuts!" Langley hollers at the end of class on Friday. Nearly everyone is leaving for spring break tonight, which should make the boy beyond thrilled and yet he is glaring at me as if I have just kicked his cat.

"How so?" I ask. My phone has been on silent since the argument. I didn't want to listen to either of my parents. I may not be angry at Mom, but she would be capable of convincing me into coming home. I am not doing that! Not without Quinton.

"Because!" Langley screams, pulling out his phone. He shoves it in my face. I go cross-eyed for a moment before focusing in on the amount of missed calls on his phone from my parents. "Your parents have been calling me constantly trying to get a hold of you! And I, being such a great friend, have covered for you as much as I can but you can't avoid them forever. You haven't seen them in months. You need to head ho—"

"No," I growl, sending Langley a glare of my own. He frowns. "Dad has to apologize on his knees in order to get me to come home."

"That's overdoing it."

"Like hell it is. He deserves it."

"Because of Quinton?" Langley asks.

The question sends a shiver down my spine. He heard me yelling, but he doesn't know the whole picture and I don't plan on telling him. I wouldn't tell him about Quinton without his permission. I'm not that much of a jerk. Ok, so at one point I was, but I'm past that!

I nod, keeping my mouth shut, for once.

"What'd he say about him?" Langley inquires. "You guys rarely fight. It's weird."

It is weird. Honestly, it's been so long since we last fought. We had a pretty big fight a few years ago when I was trying to convince him to let me go to public school. It was the first time Dad ever screamed at me. I had been lectured before, spanked when I was younger and told no. Rarely, but it happened. However, he had never screamed at me. It shocked me so much that I didn't talk to him for nearly a week before Mom insisted we get over ourselves and apologize. We did, obviously, seeing as we both fear my mom more when she's angry than anyone else.

"He told me he didn't want us to associate," I answer, deciding to reveal some of the problem. "He didn't even give him a chance."

Langley remains silent but nods. Neither of us say more on our ways to the dorms. Langley probably wants to ask more, but he has to leave soon. His things are already packed when we get back to our room. He says his goodbyes after I help carry his belongings to his car. With a wave, he jumps into his vehicle but, before leaving, shouts towards me, "Make up with your dad, Aron! If you two talk, I'm sure everything will work itself out!"

I roll my eyes at him. "Thanks Mom, I'll brush my teeth three times a day too!"

"You better, cupcake. No one likes a man with yellow teeth!" Langley cackles, waving as he drives away.

I shake my head at the idiot known as my best friend. He is right, though. Taking my phone from my pocket, I see I have even more missed calls and texts, most of them being from Mom asking me to reconsider. I want to see her, but Dad needs to apologize first.

Suddenly, my phone buzzes. Talk about timing! I nearly drop the phone out of shock. Thankfully, my reflexes work for the day, and I catch it. If I broke it, my parents would kill me.

Sighing in relief, I glance at the caller I.D. to see that it's my dad. I clench the phone tightly, debating on answering or completely ignoring the call. Oh, the temptation to prolong his pain is great.

"If you aren't calling to apologize, I'm hanging up," I say, though my voice shakes.

I don't normally speak to my dad like this, and it bothers me. He is going to end up grounding me for a month! He'll make me sit around in more of those boring meetings with Mr. Coralline. I can only handle so much. Give me some time to prepare myself for a future like that. Let me enjoy life now! Anyway, getting off topic a bit here.

"This conversation is already off to a poor start," Dad mutters into the phone. Somewhere behind him, I hear Mom shouting at him. I have to hold back a chuckle. Figures Mom would be the one to get him to call me.

"But it can end nicely depending on what you have to say," I reply. I'm heading towards Quinton's dorm now, seeing as I know he isn't busy. He has no plans to leave campus and, well, why the hell not? I'm bored and I'm in the mood to piss him off.

"From our last conversation, I assume that you are aware of Quinton's father."

"I am," I hum. "He told me a while ago."

"And that does not bother you?" He asks, sounding confused.

If he's trying to apologize, that's a poor way of starting.

Grumbling, I answer, "No. Why would it? His father's actions do not define him." My shoulders tense. I roll them in order to stop myself from shuddering. "I don't feel like talking about this anymore. I'm hang—"

"Wait, wait, wait!" I can actually view Dad waving his arms wildly as I do when in a panic. Guess we all know who I got it from. "Your mother and I discussed it and we're sending a car for you. It's on its way now. You may bring your friend with you, ok?"

I stop in my tracks and look at the phone from the corner of my eye. Though my dad can't see me, I continue to make a suspicious face. "What's the catch? There's always a catch."

"I wish to speak to him."

Say what now? My jaw drops before I scrunch my nose and ask, "What? Like a marriage interview or something?"

"You know what I mean," Dad sighs and again I can visualize him running a hand down his face. "Make sure the two of you are ready. Your ride should be there shortly."

"I haven't heard it though."

"Heard what?" He's trying to play dumb.

"Two words." I hold up my hand as if he can see me. I even wiggle my two fingers because part of me thinks Dad can actually visualize me performing such an action.

"You're a real ball buster," Dad grunts, making me laugh. "I'm sorry."

"Ah, beautiful," I laugh before hanging up. I can't say I'm very comfortable with my dad saying he wants to "speak" with Quinton, but at least he's going to give him a chance. Hopefully Quinton will agree. Actually, scratch that. I don't care if he agrees. He's stuck with me during spring break, whether or not he likes it. He has already signed over his freedom to me!

I make it to Quinton's dorm shortly after hanging up with my father. I knock, since I'm not sure if Taylor is still there or not. When no one answers quickly, I push open the door to peer within. My eyes focus on the packed luggage at the edge of Quinton's bed that was once for our spring break. I guess I shouldn't say "once," seeing as I am going to inform him we are still going to my place, but he doesn't know that! Taylor is obviously gone. His game consoles and knick knacks are missing.

"Are you going to stand in the doorway all day?" A voice asks that makes my teeth grind. Knowing exactly who that voice belongs to, I do not hesitate to reply with obvious annoyance.

"I was trying to be polite and not barge in, in case Taylor was still here." I make my way into the room, slamming the door behind me. The action makes Quinton roll his eyes. He moves from the bathroom to his desk, where he takes a seat and appears to study. Before I lose him to his geeky nonsense, I rush over to his side, slamming my hands against his desk to catch him.

Though he doesn't jump, he seems a bit confused by my actions. He drifts his eyes from his book to me, arching a brow that asks what the hell I'm doing without him having to say it.

"I talked to my dad a little bit ago. I guess he'd like to—" I hold up my hands to make quotation marks in the air. "—speak with you." I glance at him from the corner of my eye to see how he reacts. I am not at all surprised to see him remaining expressionless. "So if y'know...you still would like to...come over, then the car should be here soon. I mean, your luggage is still packed—" why am I trying so hard to talk him into it? "And you have been on campus since forever, so it'd probably be nice to leave y'know..."

Quinton, who has remained apathetic throughout my entire whatever the hell that was, shrugs and says, "Not like I have better plans."

I bite my lip to keep back a smile. I will never say it out loud, but I was worried he wouldn't come along. I do not know

what I would have done if he rejected me. The idea sends a shiver down my spine.

"Cool. Cool, then that's cool." I mumble, hoping that the excitement does not show through my voice.

"Your vocabulary astounds me."

"Shut up!" I kick the boy's chair, which moves slightly because of the force. Pain shoots up my toe and I have to hop on one foot as I rub at my throbbing feet within my shoe. Quinton says nothing, but his face shows how pleased he is with my discomfort. I send him a glare. "Stop looking at me like that."

"I'm not looking at you like anything."

"You are!" I point an accusing finger and allow my foot to fall back to the floor. "Your eyes are practically screaming 'way to go, idiot.'"

Quinton shrugs, but neither confirms nor denies my accusation. He doesn't need to. I know he is thinking that I'm an idiot. In fact, I am positive that's what he always thinks when I'm around. Asshole.

"Are you going to stand around shouting at me all day, or are you going to get back to your dorm to finish packing? I am not standing around waiting for you because you're slow," Quinton huffs, standing from his desk in order to put a few of his schoolbooks into a bag.

I bite my lip. Damn, I probably should go make sure I have everything. Knowing me, I forgot to pack something important, like my phone charger. Oops, I don't think I packed that.

"I'll call you when the car's here!" I shout, sprinting out the door to return to my dorm.

I can't believe I forgot to pack so much. I mean my deodorant, toothbrush, phone charger, my laptop and its charger. I didn't even have much to pack seeing as it's only a 2 week long break and I have clothes at home! How could I forget so much? How did Quinton know I'd forget to pack stuff?

I send the bastard a glare, though honestly he saved me, but still it pisses me off. He doesn't even notice my glare as he sets his belongings in the back of the car. The driver tries to do it for him, but Quinton simply looks over at me and says smugly, "I can take care of myself."

The hell does he mean by that? Grumbling, I do the same, insisting that I can put my own things in the trunk. The driver gives me a strange look before returning to the front of the car. Quinton and I jump into the back. I vaguely hear our driver commenting on how long it will take to make it to the airport. Quinton's interest is piqued at that. He looks at me, and I swear there's excitement in his voice. "We're taking a plane?"

"Yeah," I nod, removing my jacket as I do. It's too warm in the car to wear it. "It is a private jet. We will be on it for about two hours. Why?"

He shakes his head, choosing to watch the scenery pass by his window rather than speak with me. I huff. Obviously, he asked for a reason. Is he scared of heights or something? My face breaks into a grin at the thought. The idea of a quivering Quinton, hands forming fists as his knuckles turn white because of the force, lips in a thin line, sweat rolling down his face as he desperately tries to keep the fear off his face...ah, finally, he will appear to be a bit human! It would be great.

Wow, I really have problems.

From the corner of my eye, I see Quinton eying me suspiciously. He doesn't ask but continues glancing at me until we make it to the airport. Quinton's face scrunches in annoyance throughout the search of not only his belongings but himself, too. I can't keep in my laughter when the officers pat down his legs. His eyes are practically burning with the desire to toss these guys into the nearest dumpster, but I give him credit for neither complaining nor acting violently.

"Why did I agree to come?" he sighs after his belongings have been rummaged through. The obsessed freak's hands twitch when he sees the guards putting his things back into his bags differently than he had originally packed them.

I shrug, continuing to laugh despite his glare. "I warned you!"

He says nothing, and causing no harm to others, survives the searches. It isn't until we are walking into the jet that I see Quinton's eyes brighten. Whatever anger was once there is now gone and replaced with what seems to be excitement. He moves up the stairs behind me onto the jet. I continue peeking over my shoulder to see his reactions.

Inside, his eyes are ever moving. He is so busy looking into the cockpit that one of my guards nearly runs into him. Quinton quickly moves away from the cockpit upon realizing he is blocking the entrance. He follows me to the seats and, rather than look towards me, he raises one of the blinds to look outside.

To prove how much of a trance he is in, I raise my hand to snap my fingers. He doesn't even flinch. I snap a second time. No reaction. I don't even think he hears the pilot announce that we're to be taking off and to buckle our seat belts.

"Quinton!" I am finally forced to shout. He blinks and slowly looks at me. "We're taking off. Put your seatbelt on."

Quinton nods and does as I tell him. The boy bites his lip when the jet moves. I am, for a moment, tempted to tease him about his strange behavior. However, any thoughts of teasing leave my mind when the jet speeds up. For the first time since I've met Quinton, there seems to be nothing but pure excitement on his face.

I should have known that Quinton's "excitement" differs from the average person. He doesn't smile from ear to ear or exclaim wildly about how "cool" or "amazing" it is, but it's still clear he's excited.

His normally dark eyes sparkle like a kid in a candy store. His body, that is usually always upright and proper, is relaxed to where I wonder if the boy in front of me is really Quinton or an imposter. I am now sure that we have spent too much time together because, somehow, I clearly see his enjoyment. Yes, enjoy. Who knew Quinton could enjoy anything?

Again, I'm tempted to point out his behavior but we rise into the air and he leans so close to the glass that his breath fogs it and I can't bring myself to say a word. It's not every day I see Quinton so...cute. Shit, it should be wrong to think that, but he is really cute right now.

The silence between us is not at all awkward. Watching Quinton's reactions is entertaining enough to me. I examine every minor change in his features. The way he scrunches his nose when the jet jolts or moves oddly, the upward twitch of his lips when he glimpses the land beneath us, his widened eyes at the way the clouds seem to change color from the sun. I don't even realize my staring until Quinton finally looks at me from the corner of his eye. When he sees that, yes, I am obviously staring, he faces me to ask, "What are you staring at?"

I shake my head, feeling my cheeks heat up with embarrassment. "Nothing. I should be asking you that. You've been staring out the window for like an hour."

Quinton says nothing, but his eyes return to the window. He leans back, allowing his body to relax while he rests his head back on the seat.

"Hey." I look between Quinton and the outside world. "Have you ever flown before?"

Quinton doesn't look at me as he shakes his head. "No. Never."

"Oh." So that's why he's so excited. I guess I was like that the first time I flew. It was so cool feeling us take off and land. Seeing the land beneath us was scary, yet amazing to think that, somehow, someone came up with a way to make a giant piece of metal fly. "How did you usually get home during summer break?"

"Either my mom got me or I took a bus. Not all of us are made of money." Quinton stares out the window, but that doesn't keep me from glaring at him.

"We've been gone an hour, and I'm already regretting bringing you along."

Quinton shrugs and it is only now that I realize his eyes are falling half-mast. His legs are stretched out before him. Actually, I feel his leg brushing mine. When had it even gotten there? I can't bring myself to mention it though because he looks so comfortable, like he doesn't have a care in the world. Quinton never looks so content yet somehow being on a plane; on his way to spend 2 weeks with a boy that he has claimed to be both annoying and an idiot. He looks more relaxed than ever.

Pride surges within my stomach that brings a smile to my face. I have to bite my lip in order to not appear creepy. My cheeks actually kind of hurt with how hard I'm smiling. Hey, you'd be too if Mr. Proper was acting like this in front of you, so shut up!

The remaining flight is quiet between us. Quinton never takes his eyes off the sky while I can't seem to take mine off him. I internally curse the boy for keeping my attention on him without even trying. I make a mental note to annoy the hell out of him because of it later. For now, I'll leave him be because he's way too cute.

CHAPTER THIRTY-NINE

When we descend, Quinton leans towards the window, watching curiously as we grow closer and closer to land. The jet jolts upon touchdown. We remove our seat belts and get up to begin our journey from the airport to my home, which is only about a half hour drive.

"Dad is probably going to want to speak with you as soon as we arrive," I inform Quinton, who nods like the idea doesn't bother him. I'd be bothered if I were him. "Doesn't that bother you?"

"What? That your dad, the king, wants to speak with me, a lowly commoner?" Quinton asks with a soft snort. "Not really. Should it?"

"It bothers me," I grumble, more to myself than him. "He's making it seem like he has to approve of you before allowing us to be friends."

"It's a little late for that."

My jaw drops, though Quinton does not seem to have realized what he just said. I jab the boy's side with my finger to bring his attention to me. He sends me a glare that only intensifies when he sees my goofy grin.

"What?" He asks hesitantly, making me laugh. Seriously, he either reads minds or knows me too well because it was so clear in his voice that he senses what I have to say next will be something he does not like.

"You just admitted that we're friends."

He denies it immediately. "I did no such thing."

"But you did!" I point an accusing finger at the boy. "You said it was too late for my dad to approve of us being friends, which means you already think of us as friends."

Because us kissing clearly isn't proof that we are at least friends. Right, way to go, Aron.

Quinton sighs, neither confirming nor denying what I say. It shouldn't be such a big deal. But come on, this is Quinton. Getting anything out of him is a hassle, so even when his admissions are evasive, I am going to relish in the victory!

I'm not shocked to see Quinton looking at me with a raised brow when we reach the gates to my home. I smile sheepishly while shrugging my shoulders. My house has always had walls around it. Security has an easier time that way. There are cameras all around the border, watching every person, every movement. One can barely see the tip of our home over the towering granite walls.

The guards at the gates let us pass. Within the walls is an extensive yard with, courtesy of my mother and the gardening crew, beautiful rows of flowers and trees to give it a little, as mother put it, pizzazz. I will not comment on how many times I have gotten lost in my garden, nor will I ever allow Quinton to know of it because he'd never let me forget it.

Straight ahead is my home made of beautiful white marble with intricate pillars holding up the dome entrance. The windows on the first floor are all large and long, while the others above are simpler, with a few balconies here and there in the more prominent guest bedrooms. All the windows are tinted; allowing us our privacy, seeing as there are the occasional paparazzi that sneak inside to snap a picture or two... before being chased by the guard dogs. You'd think they'd learn to stay away after getting their butts chewed on, but apparently they enjoy that kind of treatment.

Quinton continues to stare at me with this 'you are totally ridiculous' expression. Is it sad I can tell what he's thinking by his looks? It's bad isn't it...?

"Stop giving me that look! We're at my home. You may have forgotten, but I am the prince. Obviously, we have crazy security!" I don't know why I'm trying to defend myself, but I am.

Quinton sighs just as the car comes to a stop before the entrance. Quinton leans towards me in order to see out my window. I try to ignore how close he is, but it's hard when I can feel his breath against my cheek. I bite said cheek, hoping the pain will lessen my blush.

"This is no home," Quinton says, annoyed. "It's a castle."

"That happens to be my home! I live here so it's a home and stop giving me that annoyed look already!" I order around a scowl. It's not a pout, it's a scowl because I am a man and men do not pout.

"How many times have you gotten lost in your own home?" Quinton asks around a teasing grin.

"None!"

Quinton's eyes say he doesn't believe me. And he shouldn't because I still get lost occasionally. I stick my tongue out at him before jumping out of the car. Quinton is getting out on his side. The doors open to show my mother, who smiles upon seeing me. I smile back and open my arms as she does the same while running towards me.

"Welcome home, sweetie!" She squeals, enveloping me in a hug. She runs her fingers through my hair when I rest my head on her shoulder. Her hand rubs my back as she speaks. "I missed you. I was worried you wouldn't be coming to see me over break. You know I can only go so long without seeing my baby boy!"

I can feel, taste, and smell Quinton's smirk. I don't need to look back to know that the bastard finds amusement in my mother treating me like a child. Screw him! She's my mom, she's allowed! Damn it, stop looking at me! I know he's looking at me!

"It would have been Dad's fault," I say after pulling away from her. "Yell at him about it."

Mom rubs my cheek for a moment before turning her gaze to the boy behind me. I follow her gaze to see Quinton removing his and my luggage from the trunk. I'm about to yell at him for doing it but my mother is already speaking, "There's no need to do that, sweetie. We can't allow our guests to do all the work."

Quinton has already removed our luggage, though.

"It's fine. It's my luggage after all," he says, walking towards us. My eyes nearly pop out of their skull when he bows before my mother, who nods her head back.

The hell is with that? He didn't bow when he met me! That little prick...

"It's a pleasure to meet you, Your Majesty"

My jaw is probably scraping against the ground. Who the hell is this guy, and where did Quinton go? He only ever calls me Your Highness as a taunt! Yet he is bowing to my mother and acting all proper and shit. That asshole! How come I never got royal treatment yet my mother gets it instantly?!

Mom smiles and holds out her hand to take his. Quinton shakes her hand while she speaks, "No need for such formalities, Quinton. You can just call me Mom!"

"Mom!" I holler, my cheeks burning with embarrassment. I slam my hand against my face to shield myself from Quinton's dark gaze. I doubt he'll call her that. If he ever did, I wouldn't know whether to cry or laugh.

"Sorry, sorry, Cora is fine," she giggles. "Anyway, we heard so much about you!"

I can't look even if I want to. I keep my hand over my eyes so I don't have to see how Quinton is looking at me. I know he is. I can feel it and it's making me blush from head to toe. I shouldn't have brought him!

"Really?" Quinton asks. His smirk is obvious in his voice. It is beyond sad, I know that. We need to stop spending so much time together. I need more friends or something.

"Oh yes! At first Aron made it sound like you two were enemies, but I saw right through that!" Sure you did, Mom. "It was obvious you two would get along eventually. He told us all about that 'annoying jerk' from class—"

"Mom, please," I call pathetically, still shielding myself with my hand. My whimper is ignored.

"Then can you believe he asked us if you two were friends? If he has to ask, isn't the answer already there? He can be so oblivious sometimes."

"No argument there." I'm going to fucking kill him. And I would have if my blush would simmer down. However, it only grows the more Mom speaks.

"Thank you for putting up with him," Mom says.

"He is a hassle." He is enjoying this too much.

"I know. He's such a problematic child." She agrees, making me sigh.

Please Mom, I'm going to die.

Thankfully, she takes pity on me and insists Quinton and I come in at once. Dinner is apparently almost done. Dad is supposedly finishing up some paperwork in his office and will be down shortly to join us for dinner. I'm kind of dreading that.

"I do hope dinner is to your liking Quinton," Mom says, leading us to the dining room. I am still hiding behind my hand as I walk to Quinton's side.

I feel Quinton's arm brush against mine when he says, "I'm sure it will be."

And even if it isn't, he would never say. Mr. Perfect-Bastard. Once my mom is gone, I am kicking his ass. He is enjoying my embarrassment far too much! And why the hell is he acting all nice with my mom? Not that I'm complaining. He should act kind to her, but he treated me like shit when we first met! I never got a bow. He's probably doing it on purpose!

My thoughts must be showing on my face, because Quinton smirks beside me. I stick my tongue out at him to show that I am not amused. We reach the dining room, where Quinton and I sit beside one another. My mother sits across from me. We leave the seat at the head of the table for my dad. The table is set and the butlers come out with our food.

"So, Quinton, I'm sure my husband will interrogate you later when he arrives," Mom says while cutting into her dinner. I roll my eyes. Even mom knows of the interrogation to come. "I will try to ask my own questions that he hopefully will not ask you."

Quinton nods, not seeming at all bothered by my mom admitting to prying. Most parents pry, though, so it isn't all that weird. Besides, Mom means nothing by it, unlike Dad. My mother is simply curious about my school life, who my friends are, or rather, if I am making any. Langley was the only friend I really had, but now my list seems to grow with Autumn, Ariel, and the demon beside me. I bite my lip to keep back a frown at the thought of father coming down to interrogate Quinton. It bothers me more than I could put into words.

However, my irritation is put on a momentary hold when Mom asks, "Tell me, is my son seeing anyone?"

I spit my drink across the table. Mom laughs, then scolds me about getting soda on the table. The butlers rush over to clean it; one even pats my back to make sure it's all out. Quinton doesn't do a thing though! He simply stares at me with a 'what a dumb ass' expression that turns positively evil as he answers my mother without tearing his eyes from me. "I believe he has his eyes on someone."

That bastard!

With wide eyes, I stare at the boy who couldn't possibly be planning on telling my parents, right? We haven't even really admitted to each other that we're in a...relationship. Unless he still doesn't think we are? Does he? I've never asked. Tell me I don't have to ask. Knowing the bastard, he'd deny it only to piss me off, then I'd deny it to piss him off. It'd be a never-ending cycle. I'm not in the mood for a headache like that!

After my coughing fit dies down, I stutter out, "M-Mom, why are y-you asking something like that?" I send a glare to Quinton, who is not fooling me by pretending to be innocent while eating his dinner. "And you!" I point a finger at the boy. "D-Don't be spewing shit to my mom."

"What did I tell you about that language of yours?" Mom scowls and kicks me beneath the table. I yelp. What the hell? Why is she abusing me, her son? Ignoring my hurt expression, she continues speaking to Quinton. "So he has his eyes on someone? Who is she? What's her name? Do you know her?"

"I know them." Quinton is enjoying this too much. He's actually answering her with full sentences, unlike me. All I got is a 'hn' or a glare. "Good looking, intelligent, and could teach him a lesson any day of the week. They're out of his league."

I slam my foot into his for that. He doesn't even flinch, continuing to glance at me from the corner of his eye. Does he have no shame? He's talking about himself! He just admitted that he's good looking, intelligent, and like hell, he could kick my ass! Sure, we haven't tussled for a while, but I'd totally end him.

My cheeks are on fire as my mother continues to pry the "girls" name from Quinton when, in reality, she's speaking to the person I have my eye on. Quinton is enjoying it too much, but he refuses to reveal "her" name. Eventually, Mom gives up but thanks Quinton for willingly telling her about it.

"This is harassment," I huff angrily, stabbing at my food. "You're double teaming me."

"I have to! You never tell me anything," Mom says, wiggling her finger at me. "I knew Quinton would be a nice boy. He'd never let his friend's mother worry!"

"I would never dream of doing such a thing, Cora." I'm going to fucking kill him. Wait, didn't I say that already?

Mom squeals. "He called me Cora!"

I attempt to kick him again. He avoids my kick. Instead, he traps my leg between his. I growl and try to pull away, but his hold is tight, and he doesn't even seem bothered by it. It must be hard to continue to eat while holding my leg hostage, but he makes it look easy. I groan and throw my head back on the chair. I should have never brought this asshole!

Just when I think this couldn't get any worse, the dining room doors open. All eyes turn to see Dad coming through the doorway. Immediately, Quinton stands and politely bows to my dad, who seems taken aback by his manners. I hiss in embarrassment and shield my face in my hands as Mom insists Quinton doesn't have to do that and to sit back down. Quinton does as she requests only after he introduces himself. "It's a pleasure to meet you, Your Majesty. My name is Quinton Underwood and I will be in your care for the following two weeks."

My jaw drops at how proper he's being. Mom continues to giggle at how 'cute' and 'well-mannered' he is. I want to smack him silly. How come he was never this proper to me?

"The hell man?" I finally ask, catching his attention. He turns from my dad to see an annoyed expression on my face. "You were never proper with me! How come my parents are getting special treatment?"

Quinton arches a brow and answers as if my question is the stupidest thing he had ever heard, "What have you done to get special treatment?"

I puff my cheeks out in anger. He is so getting his ass kicked!

Now both my parents are laughing, which relieves me a bit. Dad had a pretty blank expression when he walked in earlier, but he is smiling now. I hope that means he is in a decent enough mood.

"It's nice to finally meet the famous Quinton," Dad says, causing my blush to only worsen.

Don't mention that I spoke about him, Dad! He already heard from mom.

Dad sticks out his hand, which Quinton takes to shake while saying, "I hope we can learn much about each other."

And by learn, he means to force out information because that was the terms to our agreement. Again, I have to bite my lip to keep back a frown. Can't he trust me a little? I can pick out my friends. Not to mention judging someone based on their parents' actions is wrong. Quinton had nothing to do with what his father did, so why make it seem like he did something wrong? It's freaking dumb.

My aggravation must be showing on my face because I feel a nudge against my shoulder. I blink; realizing that I have been glaring daggers at my food, and look over to see Quinton has sat back down. He nudges my thigh now with his hand as if to say 'stop looking like that.' I roll my eyes at him and look at my dad, who has taken his place at the head of the table.

"So, Quinton, why don't you tell us about yourself?"

Quinton and my father go back and forth a bit with questions. Most are seemingly innocent, questions that most parents ask their children's friends at their first meeting, but that doesn't make me any less bothered. I know he's being nice now and will eventually lead up to asking about Quinton's dad. Each question seems to get more and more personal.

"How long have you been attending Thorton's?" Dad asks. He peers at me for a moment, as if to gauge my reaction to his question. I don't bother hiding my annoyance even with Quinton, who finds it in his right to pinch my thigh and he calls me childish!

"Since my freshman year, sir," Quinton replies. Although I am staring at my plate angrily, I can feel Quinton's gaze on me. He isn't even bothering to look at my dad, I can tell.

"Really? How did you achieve that?" Might as well ask how a poor person got in, Dad. Wow.

"I got in on a scholarship."

"That's pretty impressive," Dad hums and sips from his glass. I hear rustling, which means he's probably eating, but I don't bother looking his way. If I do, I might flip out. "You must get good grades."

Without meaning to, I reply to Quinton. "He has the best grades in our year."

Finally, I tear my glare from my food to shoot it at my dad. He stares back but says nothing as I continue on with little thought. "Quinton is in every advanced course they offer. He has the best grades in all of them too, the best grades in the entire school, in fact!"

Quinton kicks my shin beneath the table to tell me to shut up, but I don't. The words are coming out defensively that I don't even mean to do.

"He doesn't need money to get into the school because he's smart. He's the best in our self-defense classes too and he's already got offers from colleges. He isn't even a senior yet!" I recall our professors discussing the offers with Quinton between classes. "Plus, he may seem like a total ass all the time, but he's always there for me when I need him, like with Gabby..." Why am I defending him so hard? "And he doesn't suck up to people because of their titles!"

Quinton has his hand on my shoulder now. He squeezes it hard and attempts to call out my name to stop, but everything keeps spilling out of my mouth without meaning to. I know he doesn't need me to defend him or anything, but it won't stop.

"Stop beating around the bush, Dad. Just ask him about his father! Do it, I know you want to!" I point an accusing finger at him. "You judge based on what you hear or what you are told rather than on the person and who they are as a human being! You're just like everyone else!"

I stand up quickly, knocking into the table as I do. Mom tries to calm me down but I'm already grabbing Quinton by the wrist and dragging him out of the dining room and towards my room.

"Aron." Quinton tugs gently on his wrist but continues to follow me. "Aron."

I shake my head, stubbornly dragging him to my room.

"Aron!" He finally stops following me. I stumble back, not expecting it.

I don't release the hold I have on his wrist as I sigh and ask, "What?"

"Your dad just wants to know about me," Quinton sighs, taking a step forward. I feel his chest pressing against my back. The warmth sends a shiver down my spine. "It's normal."

"It isn't. He's judging you because of your dad. I can see it in his eyes. I can hear it in his voice. It pisses me off," I snap, turning my body to face Quinton. We're far too close, but I don't bother pulling away. "Why doesn't it piss you off?"

"Wasn't the point of me coming over for spring break to prove to your father that I am not what he thinks me to be? By the end of the week, I'll have changed his mind." Quinton smirks confidently. His words relieve the tension that I hadn't even realized was in my shoulders. I smile but grumble about cocky bastards. I tug on his wrist once more in order to lead him the rest of the way to my room. He doesn't stop me or pull away. In fact, I feel his fingers move in order to intertwine with my own.

I'll never tell him how he so easily calms me down with something as simple as a touch. Too much power for his already inflated ego.

CHAPTER FORTY

"Tell me we aren't sharing a room. Putting up with you for 2 weeks is already tough enough," Quinton says.

"Hey! The hell is that supposed to mean?"

"That you're exhausting enough without us having to share a bed." My cheeks heat up a bit at the thought of sharing a bed. Not that I want to share a bed or anything! Heh… heh…

Quinton, being the dirty bastard that he is, catches onto my change in appearance and smirks that annoying smirk of his. With his arms crossed, he leans forward. Our noses brush lightly when he speaks, "Unless you want us to share a bed."

Now my blush is painful. I push the bastard away while he chuckles. "No way! That's fucking disgusting!" Because making out with the bastard is obviously not as bad as sharing a bed. God, I need to see a therapist or something. I'm going insane! "Your room is across the hall."

He rolls his eyes at me. "And you brought me here instead of my room. Why?"

"Because I was pissed off. Why do you need to go to your room now, anyway?"

"To unpack." He states.

I wave my hand at the boy. "You can do that later."

"Oh?" He cocks a brow. "Did you have something else in mind for us to do?"

Is it just me or did he try implying something with that question?

I bite the inside of my cheeks, hoping the pain will help my slightly muddled brain. The way he's looking at me is making my toes curl. Seriously, does he want to do something? Here? Like what? Kissing or…

"Try not to think so much," the boy sighs and brushes my forehead with his knuckles. "Your brain will overheat."

"It will not!" I slap the fist away, desperately attempting to recover some of my pride and failing miserably. "I'm not as dumb as you believe."

"I've heard that before, yet you haven't proven me wrong." He snorts.

"You know I hate you, right? Like, with a passion."

"Does one normally kiss someone they hate?" He is evil incarnate.

I slam a hand over his lips. "What the hell are you saying right now?"

"You're being abnormally shy," he says beneath my hand. He reaches up afterwards to swat my said hand away.

"I'm not shy!"

"Hn. I'm going to unpack my things."

"Hey! Don't just go!" I watch the boy completely ignore me and head across the hall to his own room.

He is so aggravating. I hate him. Seriously. Why Quinton of all people? World, do you hate me so much? Give me better taste. I don't care anymore if it's a guy as long as it's not him! He is infuriating.

I swing my arms childishly in anger.

Shortly after Quinton left, my mom arrived. Shyly, she peeks her head into my room with a cordial smile, one that I return. Taking that as permission to enter, she makes her way to my bed where she sits, then pats the space next to her. I sigh, but do as I'm told.

"You know your father loves you very much, dear. He cares about you and only wishes to know about your friend," she coos and runs her fingers gently through my unruly blonde locks.

I shrug. "He never interrogated Langley. Why? Because his parents are diplomats. Quinton is a good guy, Mom." I purse my lips and glare at my door as if, somehow, I could see through it and into the room across the hall. "Even if he's a total ass."

Mom laughs heartily, guiding my head to her shoulder. "I'm sure he is. I'm sure he is. You two seem close."

"Huh?" My heart skips a beat. "No. Not really, I guess. I don't know. Why do you say that?"

"You defended him like an overprotective boyfriend."

"Hah?!" I jump out of her hold in embarrassment. "N-No I didn't!"

"Don't be shy—" Why is everyone calling me shy? I'm not shy, damn it! "I'm glad that you've found someone to be close with. You've only ever had Langley and even then the two of you became friends because of his mother and me." She gestures for me to sit back down. Hesitantly, I do, but keep my eyes glued to the floor out of embarrassment. Mom reaches for my hands and cups them in her own. "Quinton is different, though. You grew close to him on your own. I always worried about you, but it seems my baby boy is growing up so fast. He can take care of himself."

"Mom!"

"Listen, I know you are angry with your father, but I swear his intentions are good. Besides, he is going to love Quinton either way."

Finally, I look at my mom with curiosity. "What makes you think that?"

"Because you want him to, and honestly, when has your dad not given you something you've wanted? You're spoiled rotten."

"Well, when you put it like that," I chuckle with a shrug. "I suppose that's true."

It so is. I guess I was annoyed because Quinton and I are so similar in that department. We're both judged with no one having tried to get to know us, but dad wouldn't purposely try to isolate me. He'll see what a good guy Quinton is in no time.

"Now, why don't you give Quinton a tour of the place before it gets too late?" Mom pats my back, pushing me off the bed.

I nod and eagerly saunter over to Quinton's room, where I don't knock. Kicking the door open, I waltz in to find Quinton pulling some books out of his luggage to sit on the bedside table. When he sees me, he frowns. That bastard.

"Don't look so happy to see me," I huff.

"I would never."

I purse my lips in annoyance. Why was I eager to come over here again?

"Do you want a tour of the place before it gets late?" I ask hesitantly. He might be too tired from the flight, so maybe he doesn't want to... not that I care if he wants to!

"Sure." Ah, but I feel a smile on my face after hearing that.

"Ok! Let's go!" I run over to grab his arm, easily pulling him towards the door. The fact that he isn't struggling to get away should tell me something, but I'm too focused on showing Quinton around. "These areas are mostly bedrooms! Mom and Dad are down the hall—" I point towards the end where two large oak doors lead to my parents' room. "We don't really use them unless Dad has his boring meetings."

I pull Quinton to another part of the house. "These are the game rooms!"

"You have game rooms?" He sounds annoyed. I grin at the scowl on his face, showing that he is totally jealous that I basically have an arcade in my home.

"Jealous?" I wiggle my eyebrows.

"Shocked that your father would waste his money on such a thing."

"Waste his money? Dad probably uses it more than me!"

"Seriously?" His face shows slight disgust. "How old are the two of you? Five?"

"And a half."

Quinton rolls his eyes, allowing me to continue steering him through the game rooms.

"We have board games too if you don't like arcade games. We have, like, every console ever invented!" I gesture to said consoles that are sitting beneath a huge TV that Quinton glares at. I'm tempted to tease him about it but resist seeing as there's more.

"We have an indoor pool and hot tub along with an outdoor one—"

"Why have two pools?"

"Don't interrupt, Quinny. It's rude." I tap his nose that crinkles in distaste.

He groans. I think he's regretting this tour. He allows me to continue showing off, but I saved the best for last! The place I know he will like most.

"And here." I push open a pair of large oak doors to reveal a large round room full of Quinton's favorite things. "Is our library!"

Quinton may be hard to read, but it's clear in his dark eyes that his interest has been piqued. They almost seem to twinkle upon seeing the vast collection.

"Why have such a substantial library when you clearly have no interest in books?" He sends me a sly smirk as he heads towards a row of books.

"I may not like to read, but my mom reads a good bit. Plus, I used to be homeschooled, so they wanted me to have access to a library like an ordinary student." I am in a private high school now and still hardly use the library. Quinton is just weird, enjoying books as much as he does. Who likes to read? Yuck!

Quinton continues scanning over the books. I silently follow the boy as he pulls out book after book, examining the backs of them before putting them back. Why isn't he taking any? I brought him here so he could grab some if he wanted. I know he wants to, as if Quinton could pass up the opportunity to read a good book.

"You can take them, you know," I finally speak, eyes glancing at the book that he now has in his hand. "If you don't finish them, you can take them to school. I will bring them back the next time I come home."

For a moment, it looks as if he's going to decline my offer. However, his eyes look about the massive library full of books that he probably would have trouble getting his hands on. He bites his lip then hesitantly puts the book under his arm, along with a second, a third, a fourth. Holy crap, how many does he want?

Laughing, I take two books that he grabbed and ask, "Are we going to have to get you another suitcase?"

"More like two or three." He seems so eager to get his hands on them. I can't help but laugh. Eventually we make it back to his room with arms full of books. Yeah, he'll definitely have to get another suitcase to fit these in. Unless he reads them all before he leaves. Knowing this bookworm, that's a possibility.

"It's getting late. Wanna watch some TV?" I ask around a yawn and a short stretch. Quinton shrugs, so I grab his remote to flip on his TV. "What do you want to watch?" Wait, why am I asking? I don't care. I'll watch whatever I want.

"Anything is fine," he replies. I feel his bed dip, signaling he has taken a seat beside me. I peek at him from the corner of my eye and regret it immediately, because now I'm blushing again.

He's so close. I look beside me to see open space where I can easily move to in order to put some distance between us, but I glance at his side again. He has space too, so why the hell is he so close? Our arms brush. I should move, but I don't.

I opt for some good old Bruce Willis in the Die Hard series. Quinton doesn't complain but makes a comfortable back support out of pillows and leans against them. I can't help but stare. It's so weird to see Quinton in an environment outside of school. He's only in a pair of sweats and a tee, which he wouldn't be caught dead in at school. His eyes are half lidded, showing that he is perfectly comfortable here beside me with our bodies touching.

I don't even bother moving my leg when his own rests against it. In fact, I have to bite my lip to stave off a smile. If he sees it, I'll surely be teased. I can tease him too because he is making no move to pull away either! But he isn't blushing like an idiot.

During the movie, I must have fallen asleep. I don't know when or how long I have been asleep. When I wake up, I am in a difficult situation. Should I call it comfortable or uncomfortable? The warmth spreading throughout my entire body tells me I am very comfortable.

Swallowing the lump in my throat, I look at the boy, who has his head resting comfortably atop my own. Quinton is definitely a cuddler in his sleep and I have become his personal teddy. One of his arms has thrown itself over my waist while his legs have tangled with my own, making it impossible to leave. Not that I have bothered trying. I should push him away, tease him about how I knew he wasn't all evil, and the kindness had to come out sometime.

Instead, I roll onto my side, allowing Quinton to hold me even more tightly. Our chests are flush together and now there is no way he is allowing me to leave. I would probably need an iron bar to pry us apart. I sigh and easily fall back asleep, hoping that when I wake, I am still in a position that will leave me blushing.

Sadly, I wake up within a cocoon of blankets.

I slowly squirm my way out of bed while grumbling about cold-hearted bastards and make my way to my room where I change, then head downstairs for breakfast. I'll find Quinton later. Right now, my stomach is growling angrily for food. However, it seems I am not the only one whose stomach growls awakened them because when I make it to the dining room I find not only my dad, but Quinton as well.

I slam my back against the wall outside the room before either of them can realize I'm there because... well, nothing wrong with eavesdropping on my boyfriend and my dad, right? Totally normal.

"I do hope my questioning hasn't bothered you too much," Dad says through bites of his own breakfast.

"Not at all. I understand." Hearing Quinton say that makes my teeth grind. What bothers me is that he shouldn't understand and shouldn't be ok with it. Why does he have to go his whole life pretending not to be bothered by it? It's bullshit.

My father's words silence my inner ranting. "It wasn't just because of your father that I wanted to learn about you."

Huh?

There's a squeaking sound, most likely from my father moving his seat. I can envision him leaning closer to speak with Quinton, much like how he does with me when speaking of serious matters. "I'm sure you know well that Aron, well, all of us are often approached by people with not the best of intentions."

"I am very much aware of that," Quinton replies, my mind giving me a flashback of Gabby that I shake away.

"I have always been concerned that sending Aron to a public school would cause him having to learn the hard way that the world is full of greedy people. There will be those who try to unsettle him, try to catch him while he's off his guard and my Aron is... very softhearted."

"Soft hearted might be an understatement," Quinton adds, making me put in a mental note to punch him later for it. The hell does he mean softhearted? Wait, is that an insult or a compliment?

Dad chuckles before continuing, "Hearing about your father, part of me was afraid that you may have been attempting to use Aron in some way to make yourself look better. I see now that it isn't the case and I apologize for being overly protective, but he is my son and I love him very much."

I rub at my warming cheeks that are flushing from the embarrassment. Ah, Dad, stop being so cheesy. Now I'm going to have to hug you later and apologize.

I'm ready to waltz my ass in there and eat me some breakfast when Quinton darkens my blush by speaking. "I know you do, but if I could make a request."

My father hums.

"For the longest time, I forced myself to become accustomed to being dragged down by my father. Others' words often bothered me, what they thought of me, but I accepted and expected it. I had the best poker face more times than not. However, Aron has this nasty habit of seeing through that, knowing when something is off with me, even when I believe that I'm hiding it well. Sometimes," he snorts. "Actually, most of the time, he's more bothered by it than I am, as if he's being angry with me because, as he's said to me, I should be irritated by it. In a way, I'm thankful for his overreactions, but to be frank, I do not at all like seeing him like that, so my request is that you do not bring my father up in front of him again. I think it's safe to say that neither of us like seeing him like that."

The energy in my legs is zapped away. I'm left sliding down against the wall until my ass hits the floor. Shocked beyond belief, I sit there, stunned and so utterly...infatuated with that no good asshole who is somehow entirely good and, fuck, my heart feels like it just took a shot of adrenaline. It feels as if it's about to fly up out of my throat. My entire body trembles as I try to shake away the overwhelming amount of emotion coursing through me.

Did he really just say all that? Shit, I didn't... I don't know what I mean.

"It appears Aron has got himself quite a friend," Dad says around what I can easily call a relieved sigh. "I'd have to say you care for him a lot."

"I'm afraid so," Quinton replies, and though I want to be mad at him for making it sound like it's a bad thing, I can't. Not after everything he said. I wish I could have recorded all that. I could live the rest of my life happily with those words alone.

Too excited to move, I sit in place until my heart finally returns to its normal pace. The conversation between my dad and Quinton escapes me. With my heart thumping inside my ears, I can't hear anything. I desperately try to calm myself. Eventually, my legs work once again. I push myself up, take a deep breath and chant to myself to act normal as I push open the doors to the dining room.

The asshole munches on a piece of toast while still talking to my father. Neither of them even notices me walk in until I'm pulling a chair out across from Quinton. Both finally look at me, one with a blank expression and the other with a smile. I'm sure you all know who did what.

"Good morning, sleeping beauty," Dad says to me with a smile before affectionately ruffling my already messy hair. I push his hand away, grumbling nonsense that even I don't understand. My eyes keep themselves on anything but Quinton. If I look at him right now, I may do something I regret—like kiss him.

"Quinton and I were thinking you'd never wake," Dad adds.

"More like hoping." Can Quinton not be so annoying first thing in the morning? I just woke up! I can't even glare. I'm so tired. Ok so that's not the reason, mainly because of what he said, but still let's say it's because I'm tired.

"Quinton and I were having a nice little chat about how the two of you met." Oh hell no! "That you fought over a chair."

Ok, now I can glare and, who even cares about what he said earlier, I do just that because he fucking told my dad that?

"I hate you," I hiss at the boy smirking behind toast slathered in jelly.

"You tried to order him out of a chair?" Dad chuckles.

"Like a princess," Quinton snickers, earning himself a swift kick to the shin from me. He doesn't even flinch. In fact, I think he actually enjoyed my reaction because his grin only grows more devious.

"I did not! I asked—"

"Ordered."

"Asked!" I huff.

"You ordered him, I know you did," Dad laughs, earning himself a glare from me as well. "It sounds like something you would have done then. You used to be such a cheeky little thing."

"Cheeky? I wasn't cheeky! What the hell does cheeky even mean?" I shove some scrambled eggs that Ms. Donovan, our cook, had so kindly put before me. She is giggling to herself as she walks away; clearly she heard part of our conversation.

"And you—" I point my fork at the dark-haired boy across from me. With a mouth full of egg, I ask, "Why are you telling my dad that?" Quinton grimaces at my table manners but, fuck him, he's an asshole! "Are you trying to tattle on me? And you call me childish!"

"No," Quinton snorts, and throws a napkin at my face. I clutch said napkin in my fist as he speaks. "He asked how we met, so I told him the truth. It isn't my fault you acted like a spoiled child."

"You acted like a total ass!"

"Of course I did. You were trying to use your title to get a freaking chair in class." Now that he says it like that, it really sounds stupid. His response stumps me, so I opt to shove my mouth full of food. The bastard smirks as my dad laughs at the two of us.

"I like this boy," Dad laughs, and in doing so, causes me to choke on my egg.

I slam my fists against the table while Dad pats my back to get the remnants of my chewed egg from my throat. After regaining my composure, but none of my pride, I look at my dad with wide eyes and ask, "Uh... say again?"

"I like him. He's funny."

"Funny!" I screech. I am tempted to take my dad to the hospital to be inspected for brain damage. "How is he, in any way, funny?"

Quinton seems to enjoy the compliment, though. He's leaned back in his chair, arms crossed and a smirk permanently set on his smug pretty boy face. His eyes are locked on me, watching my response with amusement.

"The way the two of you speak to each other. It's as if you've been best friends for ages. Not everyone has a friend like that. You should consider yourself lucky."

Ok, hold the phone. Wasn't he trying to interrogate Quinton the other day, yet here he sits talking about how he likes him? Well, I guess after Quinton's little speech, it'd be hard not to like him. Damn it, now I kind of wish he didn't like him.

I switch my gaze between the two of them who have fallen back into conversation. Mom soon joins breakfast, and it goes by quickly. Quinton is, surprisingly, quite talkative around my parents. I mean, compared to how he usually is. My dad, Mom, and I obviously speak more, but he always answers when spoken to and never appears rude. He is still incredibly snarky with me, though, which my parents thoroughly enjoy. I think Mom and Dad tear up a bit in their laughter after all the, as mom put it, couple bickering we had during breakfast.

"Couple," I hiss, walking to my mom. "What couple? Crazy parents and crazy ideas, the lot of them are nuts."

"Are you talking to yourself?"

I shake my head to break myself from my rambling trance. I didn't even notice Quinton walking next to me until he spoke. I rub at my eyes, that are still a little crusted over from sleep. With a yawn, I reply, "No. You're hearing things."

"Sure," he sighs.

We fall into an uncomfortable silence. Normally, or rather recently, our silences have been pretty comfortable. I have become accustomed to Quinton's silent nature. It's calming. However, it feels as if right now he has something to tell me. Should I ask or tell him I already heard his conversation with my dad?

"I talked to your dad before you woke up this morning," he finally says, breaking the silence between us.

I sigh in relief and annoyance. Relieved that it's not silent anymore, but annoyed that he spoke with my dad without me around, even if it went well. What if it hadn't? I would have preferred being there in case that happened, though I was outside the door but only by accident!

"Yeah? About what?" Because playing dumb is always the answer.

"I told him I am not my father..." Which must have been before I eavesdropped. However, I feel there needs to be an and at the end to that sentence. There's something else he wants to tell me, that I technically already know, but he doesn't know that!

"And?" I nudge his side with my elbow. He still won't look at me.

"And..." he sighs. "I asked that he not bring up my father in front of you, seeing as it upsets you so."

The dumb smile on my face is not necessary, but I can't get rid of it. My cheeks actually kind of hurt from how big I'm smiling, and Quinton still isn't looking at me. Good. I don't want him to see this stupid smile that practically reveals my feelings. I'm probably blushing again, scratch that, I know I am. First I overheard him and now he's admitting it to me, even if he left out his big speech. Holy crap, I'm feeling it all over again!

"So, you didn't want me to be upset?" I ask, my voice giving away how happy I feel. The boy snorts. "Which could be attributed to you caring about me?"

It's fun being the one to do the teasing. For once, Quinton is on the receiving end! I prefer it this way.

Quinton ducks into his room. I swiftly follow. I am not passing up such an opportunity to tease him! He messes with me all the time, so it's time to return the favor.

"That's a stretch," he replies, making his way over to his stack of books. I hop in front of him before he gets there. He immediately sharpens his gaze, obviously trying his hardest to look annoyed. Most people would fall for it, but I'm not most people.

"Aw, you're being abnormally shy," I mock and, oh, now the glare is so real. The bastard actually reaches up to grip my cheeks, squishing them together to force me to make that stupid fishy face, but I can't stop laughing.

"Shut it. My ears bleed every time you bellow."

I can't stop laughing even with knowing how stupid I probably look with my face squished together. I reach up to push his hand away. The grip he has is surprisingly weak. I barely put any effort into moving his hand from my face. It drops to his side. I go for something that I've wanted to do, even if I don't wish to admit it. I'm not sure why, but I felt like I wanted to. Maybe because of what he said earlier, or maybe because I'm down bad. Probably a bit of both.

I push myself up to brush my lips against his. They part open in shock, seeing as I've never started a kiss before. I don't give him enough time to respond and pull away, flushing while Quinton blinks down at me apathetically. Silence follows until he opens that annoying hole on his face.

"That was pathetic."

"Shut up! Like you could have done better!" I know you have, but let's not think about that, shall we?

I don't exactly have much experience in the romance department, so people can't expect me to suddenly know when the right time is to shove your tongue down someone else's throat! Not that I'm thinking of doing that or anything, but seriously, I don't know what to do here! What kind of experience do I have? Exactly, none!

I shove his chest, pushing him out of the way so I can stomp out the door before dying of embarrassment in my bed. However, a hand grabbing my wrist and pulling me back to press me against a wall stops me. A shocked squeak escapes me, that I'll never admit I made, when Quinton presses himself against me, keeping me trapped between him and the wall.

"I do believe I have, but you dare say I couldn't?" I swear to god he purred that and no, it did not send heat straight to my groin. I have some sort of disease that is making my entire body burst into flames. It clearly has nothing to do with how our hips are becoming fast friends or the way his eyes fall half-mast as he leans in close enough to breathe his next words against my lips. "Are you challenging me, Princess?"

"Ah... uh... uhm..." Sorry, my brain is a pile of mush because of the fingers brushing against my throat. Please tell me he can't feel how fast my heart is beating. It will only add to his already massive ego.

"N-No?" Am I? Did I? Shit, I don't even know. "It wasn't a challenge. More of a statement."

"Hn."

"That you're a bad... kisser... or something." I'm practically telling him to prove me wrong! Stop, Aron, you're digging your own grave!

And dig it I did, seeing as the moment those words leave my lips, his lips are against them, completely shattering everything I said. My legs would have given out if he weren't so flush against me. I grip his hips to push or pull him, I haven't the foggiest because I'm too focused on the lips moving against mine, soft and sweet, nothing like his wicked personality.

Icy fingers push past the warm barrier of my shirt to brush over my stomach. The sudden intrusion causes me to hiss. The dirty bastard presses his tongue past my lips to wreak havoc on poor little me. His tongue dances with mine before pressing it back where it belongs as he continues to explore the expanse of my mouth. When his tongue retreats, I eagerly return the favor, thoroughly enjoying the dominance I'm finally getting in the battle.

My lungs feel tight, but the idea of retreating from this warmth is almost enough to make me believe suffocating is a perfectly fine way to die. But then I won't be able to feel this again, so I pull away, gasping pathetically. For once, Quinton is not so refined. His lips are slightly plump from the kissing. His chest heaves as fast as mine. Though his cheeks aren't aflame, it's clear the kiss affected him too.

"Really..." I breathe; my hands shake as they grip tighter to his hips. "Really bad."

Ok, did I seriously say that? I might as well have put a sign on my forehead saying 'kiss me asshole!' Quinton, obviously knowing I only said that in order to continue, plays along with my wishes and moves back in for another kiss that sends me soaring.

Hold it! Are we moving?

I feel my body being guided away from the wall, but I'm not fighting it at all. During the move, I turned the two of us. Quinton runs into the bed and falls back onto it with me in his lap. Our lips fall apart during the fall, but he makes no move to flip us. He seems more than content with having me in his lap, though I'd prefer if he were in my lap. Why do I have to be in his—ah, sorry, my brain is no longer working with the way Quinton is kissing and nipping my neck hard enough to leave marks.

"Shit," I groan when he runs his tongue over the tender flesh. "D-Don't leave marks, bastard!"

He grunts and continues to explore my neck, finding new places to elicit a groan from me. No fair! Why do I have to be the one pathetically moaning here while he remains silent?

Not enjoying being so obedient, I work up enough courage to push Quinton onto his back. Before he has time to protest, I bring my hips down hard against his. His back arches, pressing our chests together as our hips rock after realizing how amazing it feels. Shit, still no noise, though.

I do my own exploration of his neck, nipping and sucking at the tempting nape that continues to reveal more and more to me as he bends it back. Damn, now I understand why he was sucking hard enough to leave marks earlier. It's hard to pull away from the pulse beneath my lips. Feeling it only encourages me more, seeing as there's no denying that his heart is beating as erratically as my own as we rock into each other.

Neither of us can deny how our bodies are reacting. Our play is sending jolts of electricity through me. I don't think I can stop even if I wanted to. I don't think I've ever been so turned on in my life, and to think it's because of the biggest asshole to have ever existed! End my world...

Quinton's cool hands run up my chest, peeling my shirt from my body. Without my permission, a moan slips past my lips, one that has him smirking up at me. I bite a little harder than necessary into his collarbone. Quinton tugs at my shirt and somehow speaks with no sign of embarrassment, "Off."

What the hell? I was panting pathetically earlier, and he sounds normal! It's because he only said one thing. Quinton grows impatient, so he tugs more roughly at my shirt, signaling that he will happily rip it off.

Chuckling, I do not move and ask, "What's the rush?"

Quinton moves a hand to my ass where he pushes down and brings his hips up to resume our grinding. I hiss at the shocking friction between us. Our shared trembling speaks for itself.

Nodding, I sit back up, as does he, in order to remove my shirt. He follows suit, tossing both of them to an unknown location. My eyes linger on the heaving chest, glistening with sweat. I watch as a bead of sweat rolls down his neck to dance across his collarbone before disappearing down his chest, over a tone stomach, then into a happy trail that rests over a bulge that excites me more than I want to admit.

I have to force myself to swallow the lump in my throat. Looking at his body and the tone arms that wrap themselves around my waist, I can't help but ask myself why I ever fought with this guy. Not that I'm a twig or anything. I do excellent in our self-defense classes, but for some reason, seeing Quinton makes me shiver in a way that almost frightens me.

"See something you like, Princess?"

Damn it, why did he have to notice? I roll my eyes and squirm in his lap. Shit, I'm still in his lap.

"No," I attempt to reply without sounding breathy... and fail horribly. "Just wondering how something so ugly could exist."

Nice. Don't let it go to his head, Aron, good job.

"Oh?" His smirk tells me I won't like what he's about to say. "Perhaps I should leave then? You can finish on your own, right?"

Is it sad that I actually whimpered when he said that?

My whimper amuses him because he chuckles before diving back in for another kiss.

I'll let him do as he wishes, but only because I want to get off and doing it by myself is not ok with me right now. I'll insult him later or something whenever my dick isn't acting up.

It isn't until I feel the path my hands take I realize what we're doing. I'm already undoing his jeans with shaking hands. He must have felt them because before I get the damn zipper undone—fucking zippers—he has his hands around my own, stopping me.

Quinton pulls away. Dark eyes narrow on me as if to ask if I really want to continue. We are kind of moving fast. Hell, we haven't even verbally admitted that we're—you know—together or something. But, come on, we both know neither of us will admit to it.

Neither of us can really deny the truth, either. I nod with a little more force than I mean to. It must have made me look really eager, because the asshole smirks. I have to wipe it off or I am going to punch him, so I lean in to capture those smug lips.

Now his hands are working on my jeans. Unlike me, he easily opens the button and unzips the zipper. There's a moment before he presses a cool hand beneath my pants to grasp my arousal. I moan into the kiss. My pleasure throbs in appreciation at the first touch it's gotten from him. Not wanting to be won up by the bastard, I push my hand past his boxers. Feeling him somehow excites me more.

I can't keep myself from moaning when Quinton runs his hand across my shaft. I do my best to do the same to him. I've touched myself but never another, so I wonder if I'm doing ok. When Quinton's hips thrust into my hand, it encourages me enough to continue. Not that I am any better than him, seeing as my hips are thrusting as roughly into his hand as he is.

Quinton isn't nearly as vocal as me, but every now and again, like when I caress his tip with my thumb while nipping his neck, he grunts. It's pathetic how the sound actually makes me shiver. I, on the other hand, can't keep myself from cursing when something feels too good or groaning against his throat whenever he tries to tease me by slowing his pace. It's a lot. It's like nothing I've ever experienced. It's amazing and terrifying and somehow perfect.

My orgasm hits me hard. I have to bite down onto his shoulder to keep myself from shouting. Quinton follows shortly after me. Damn, my heart skips a beat when I hear him quietly whisper my name against my ear. Hearing that makes the embarrassment that comes afterwards kind of worth it.

Hold on. I only complained about the kissing, so why exactly did we do that? The day has come when Quinton has turned me on. Hell has frozen over. Heaven's gates have crumbled. I'm doomed!

"My hand is sticky," I grumble, feigning annoyance to conceal my obvious embarrassment. I can't even pull away from his shoulder. If he sees how badly I'm blushing, he'll never let me live it down, and I don't know what to do now. Cuddle? Tease? Act like it never happened?

"Sounds like a personal problem."

Being the immature brat that I am, I slam my hand against his chest, leaving said stickiness there. Not that there wasn't already seeing as he made as much of a mess between his legs and chest as I had. He grips my hair with his other hand to remove my face from his shoulder to glare at me.

"Did you really just do that?" He pushes me off him.

I shakily catch myself and send my glare back at him.

"I'm getting a shower. You should do the same," he says, walking to his bathroom, seeming perfectly ok with the obvious mess on his stomach and thighs while I can't stop blushing.

"Y-yeah, I will too then," I mumble, seeing as he's no longer in the room.

The shower turns on. I scurry to my room, grabbing my shirt to cover the obvious mess on my body. If anyone saw me like this, I would die. Not that the embarrassment isn't killing me already.

CHAPTER FORTY-ONE

After a long, blistering cold shower full of embarrassing thoughts and memories of what happened earlier, I emerge clean and no more ready to face reality. For about thirty minutes, I pace my room, mumbling nonsense to myself. By nonsense, I mean attempting to decide whether to waltz over to Quinton's room and act as if nothing happened or remain in my room. There are probably more options, but those are the two I'm focusing on.

I can't stay here, though. I invited Quinton over for spring break so I can't ignore him, leaving him in his room for 2 weeks while I wallow here in misery, embarrassment, or happiness? I don't even know what I'm supposed to be wallowing in. But what does one say after that?

Gah! I've never been in a situation like this before. The closest I ever got was with Gabby and we may have kissed, like, twice. Not that strange, right? Quinton and I have kissed before. People who kiss usually do more than kiss. We are also kinda... sort of... dating. I say sort of because neither of us have officially said we were.

Damn it. I'm overthinking this, aren't I? I'm overreacting. I need to take a deep breath, go over there and... ask about the weather or some shit. I don't know.

It takes around fifteen minutes to work up enough courage to make it out my door and another ten to force myself to knock. I actually considered running back to my room, but it's too late. Quinton opens the door revealing his hair to be already dry, so he, like myself, finished his shower a while ago.

"I'd say something about your long ass shower, but seeing as your hair is already dry," he flicks said hair with his finger. "You must have finished a while ago." Now he's leaning against the door frame with a smug expression. "What's wrong? Feeling shy again?"

Is this going to be an ongoing joke between us because it's seriously pissing me off? I'm not being shy. I am thinking about serious matters, damn it! Growling, I do my best not to sound as annoyed as I feel. "I wasn't being shy."

"Uh huh." He doesn't sound or look convinced.

"Maybe I wanted some time to myself. I don't need to be up your ass all the time."

"Could have fooled me."

"Would it kill you not to be an ass?" I huff. It's not a rhetorical question. I am being dead serious, yet he doesn't answer me. How rude!

The heartless bastard shrugs before moving into the hall beside me. I watch him curiously, wondering what he's doing until he sticks out his thumb, gesturing behind him while saying, "Let's swim."

"Swim?" I didn't even notice he put on swim trunks. I look down to see that I am in sweats. "I didn't know you liked to swim."

"You never asked."

True. Swimming doesn't sound so bad. I run back to my room to change. The two of us leave to use the indoor pool, seeing as it's still too chilly to use the one outside. Swimming turns out to be more of a competition to stay alive with us constantly dunking each other and the occasional toss into the air. I didn't even know I had enough strength to pick Quinton up, let alone throw him across the water, albeit not far or high. Of course, he returns the favor and smirks smugly upon realizing he had tossed me farther.

I scowl. Leave it to him to turn this into a competition...not that I'm helping with going along with it, but I can't just let him win! My pride would be shattered! Not to mention the idea of Quinton beating me pisses me off. He's already too arrogant as is. I don't wish to make it worse!

"You two look like you're having fun," Mom says, who somehow does not find Quinton holding me beneath the water odd. Instead, she giggles as I thrash and kick about, commenting on how we're 'just too cute.' How is my drowning cute!?

Not to mention, shouldn't she be mentioning to Mrs. Coralline, who is standing directly behind her, that this is not a normal thing? The woman is a snobby little bitch though, so I imagine if she said something, she'd simply shrug it off and insist on speaking about how childish the royal family is. She has this nasty habit of bitching about everything, and I really mean everything. Ok, so mostly about me. In case anyone is wondering, I don't like her. Pretty sure the feeling's mutual too.

I tap Quinton between the legs with enough force to get him to let go. Quinton grunts and stumbles back, hands cupping his probably now throbbing manhood. I come up gasping and glare at his glare. Mom continues giggling. Mrs. Coralline grimaces at the three of us. Her wrinkled mug making the grimace even more noticeable with the way her face stretches. She's like an old leather handbag.

"Do you want something, Mom?" I ask. She isn't in her bathing suit, so obviously she came down here to get us, or maybe to simply check in.

"I wanted to tell you that your father and I would be out for the evening." She gestures to her side to Mrs. Coralline, who has her eyes narrowed on me. I am tempted to narrow mine back at her, but she constantly brings up my 'childish behavior' and that ticks me off. Every time she's over, I am bothered by her. She either comments about my grades, my behavior, anything and everything she nitpicks at it. It is beyond annoying. I am going to be the better person here and simply think about glaring at her wrinkled old face!

"We have some things to discuss with the Corallines and will be back later this evening," Mom finishes.

"All right, be careful and have fun," I say, while pushing myself up far enough out of the pool to place a sloppy kiss on her cheek.

"Oh, we will, we will!" Mom calls as she turns away, leaving us alone with Mrs. Coralline. Quinton and I gaze at the woman who remains still in place even after my mother leaves the swimming area. Her dark brown eyes close in on me, examining me. It's as if she is searching for a weakness and, when I was younger, the look frightened me. Now, I hardly blink. She isn't the only one constantly checking for chinks in my armor for her to wiggle her way through. I've become accustomed to it.

"Is something wrong, Mrs. Coralline?" I ask, doing my best not to show my disgust towards her through my words. Honestly, she has to be aware of it already. I avoid her like the plague.

Mr. Coralline is in charge of our military operations. He is also the Regent, meaning if something were to happen to my father before my coronation, Mr. Coralline would rule. If I were to die before having an heir, it would be the Coralline's who would be next in line for the throne. My parents get along with them, but they are quite cynical about me, seeing as I am the next in line rather than them. I already have parents riding my ass about my grades and what I must accomplish in life. I don't need the Coralline's too.

Mrs. Coralline tilts the corner of her lip up into a haughty smirk and scoffs, "Nothing at all, Your Highness, simply...admiring how nice it must be to have so much time to spare to spend it frolicking in a pool."

"Everyone needs an off day," I hiss back at the woman who dared to make me sound like some type of lazy asshole.

"I suppose they do, some more than others." She does not hide the disgust in her own voice as she turns to walk away. "Good day."

Once gone, I slam my arms angrily against the water, creating waves in every direction. Before I have the chance to get enraged by her words, I flinch when water is splashed in my direction. I cough out what got into my mouth and shout, "Quinton, what the hell?!"

Looking at the boy, I find him ready to continue his attack on me. I don't have the time to be mad when there's a battle to win and something tells me that's exactly why he started our splashing battle. I maneuver myself over to him regardless of the white waves being pushed in my direction. Once near, I reach down for Quinton's leg, effectively knocking him back under the water. Ha! Didn't see that coming, did you?

Not that he doesn't get me back later by running up behind me on the diving board, shocking me so much that I do a rather painful belly smack. Thirty minutes later and my stomach is still red, but I didn't once think of how annoyed Mrs. Coralline made me and that's what's most important, in my mind anyway, but that doesn't mean I won't complain about the belly smack.

"Look at what you did!"

"Technically," Quinton says between spoonfuls of food. "The water did that."

"But it's your fault!" I point an accusing finger at the true perpetrator. Said perpetrator rolls his eyes and eats his dinner as if he hadn't done a thing wrong. Whatever. I'll get my revenge. He'll fall asleep, eventually.

Dinner goes by with me, fighting the urge to start a food fight. Quinton, probably knowing this, smirks throughout the entire dinner, which just adds more fuel to my already roaring fire. He knows how to push my buttons and that bugs me. I should get a trophy because I make it through dinner without wasting any food.

Ok, so I threw one noodle at him. One.

"Do you want to play a game?" I ask after we return to my room. I receive a shrug.

"Put something you want to play in. I'm going to read," he replies. I'm about to complain about how the point of these 2 weeks is for us to hang out when Quinton takes a seat beside me on the bed with a book in hand. I stare, eyes blinking in confusion.

"What?" He asks, flipping through the pages. "Put something in already."

"Ah, you sure?" I feel odd playing while he reads. "Won't it bother you?"

He shakes his head in response, seeming to already be absorbed in some book that I'd probably never understand. I put in a game. Quinton appears to be fine with reading while I play. I sometimes look over at him to see if my occasional shout or constant cursing during fights or losses bothers him, but the boy says nothing and continues on reading. After about a half hour of this, it becomes almost peaceful.

Sitting here like this, far closer than necessary, seeing as my bed is big enough for at least four full-grown people, isn't so bad. Shoulders touching, my leg thrown haphazardly over his and, dare I say this, the occasional nudging of our feet whenever I shout or Quinton comes across something that intrigues him in his reading. It all seems like something that... lovers would do. This content and warm feeling within my chest, just from being within close proximity, is foreign but satisfying. Part of me, my pride, is saying to shove him away and insist that we not be so whatever this is, but another part of me enjoys the silent show of affection.

I like the warmth in my shoulder, the tingling in my chest, the smile on my lips. It feels so normal. This is what normal people do in their normal lives with their normal relationships. I bet this is as normal as anything will ever be for me, and I really like it.

Panic arises in my stomach. Questions like 'what if this is just curiosity for Quinton', 'is he serious about whatever the hell this is we have', maybe I really should ask him what we are? He could easily end this, and that frightens me. He isn't as easy to read as I am. He so clearly states what is on my mind while I desperately search his.

Sometimes, he lets things slip, but I can't survive on that alone. I can't stay like this forever, constantly questioning myself and him and whatever relationship we have between us. What would I do if one day he told me this was all just a game? It's not like we're dating, so he can.

Something warm brushes against my forehead, breaking me from the trance I had lost myself in. Blinking, I see Quinton has pressed the tip of his knuckles to my head. If someone were to see, they would think we were fighting, but I can tell it's nothing more than a concerned gesture, one that worries me. Quinton doesn't show concern, so why is he looking at me with a frown?

"Stop thinking so hard. You'll hurt yourself," he says.

"Funny," I spit and knock his fist from my head. It falls to his side easily. His book now rests in his lap and my controller in mine. "I wasn't thinking of anything."

"I can believe that." I stick my tongue out, to which he rolls his eyes, then points out, "Your character hasn't moved for at least five minutes."

Ah, I look at the screen to see my toon has sat down since I was taking too long. Sighing, I lean back into my pillows. The warmth that was once spreading within me evaporates and my happy thoughts are shattered. Reality hits me hard. I really wish it'd give me a moment to catch my breath. Sometimes I hate how easily my mind can go off track and cause a train wreck within my head. Don't most people have more control over their thoughts?

Can I call for a time out? Let me have a breather or a drink. I got so caught up in whatever the hell Quinton and I are, that I didn't think about if I should bother starting it. I never planned on asking this, but seeing as his answer doesn't even matter.

"What are we doing?" I ask, staring at my TV screen as if it holds the answers. I can't bring myself to look at Quinton. Knowing him, he'd somehow read my mind, freak.

"Excuse me?"

"Us," I swing my hand between the two of us. "What are we? Are we even an us? What is a we or us?"

"I can't follow, dumbass." He narrows his eyes on me in confusion.

It's my turn to roll my eyes. Sighing, I stare at the book he holds in his hands. I watch his fingers that remain still against the pages while I can't keep mine from shaking.

"Are we..." I take a deep breath. "Are we together? Dating?"

Though the answer does not matter since nothing good would come of us dating, somehow I am still shaking uncontrollably. My lips quiver. My heart thumps violently against my ribs in a nervous rage. The silence is killing me. The clock says a minute hasn't even passed, but I swear it's lying. It has to have been ten minutes already but, no-no wait, a minute has passed now. Are you kidding me? I feel like it's taking him ages to answer!

"No," Quinton replies and I am so shocked that the breath leaves my lungs. However, it returns immediately upon hearing the oozing sarcasm in his next sentence. "I jerk guys off in my free time for entertainment."

I huff. "Don't dodge the question."

"Fine then," He sighs so heavily that one would think the question put a physical toll on him. Setting his book aside, the boy looks at me with his signature blank stare and asks. "What do you think?"

A pair of fingers grips my chin; I don't expect it, so he easily uses the hold to bring my face up to get trapped in an eye lock. He's a bastard. My cheeks are on fire while he remains apathetic.

"I asked first," I hiss. Fighting with someone as stubborn as yourself is hard. I'm seeing where my mom comes from when she complains about me. Then again, it's her fault. She's stubborn, so it's clear that I got it from her! DNA doesn't lie!

"I'll answer if you answer," he hisses back.

"Like hell you would." And so the staring contest begins. Neither of us is backing down, even when my gaming console shuts off from no one playing. Growling, I grow more and more annoyed with him. Can't he answer the damn question?

"Whatever!" I finally give in and shove the boy away. I would leave, but seeing as this is my room, I feel it'd be admitting defeat. Where would I go anyway? His room? That's stupid. "Don't answer the fucking question. Not like it matters anyway."

Mouth, can you shut up for like ten seconds and not dig my own grave? I honestly cannot handle all this. My emotional capacity is in overload. I'm about to get up and head towards the bathroom since that's the only place I can go in order to keep some of my pride, but a hand grasping my wrist stops me. I curse as a force brings me back onto the bed, my head bouncing off the mattress. Soon a body hovers over me, hands on my wrists and hips rested between my own to keep me trapped. All his weight is on my chest and I can't leave even if I try.

"You're acting like a child," he says with narrowed eyes.

"Yeah, well, you look like a child." Great comeback, Aron.

Quinton cocks a brow as if to say exactly what I had thought. Shaking his head, he says, "You would say no if I asked."

Huh? Is he answering my question now?

Seeing my confusion, Quinton groans and reiterates, "Dating. Had I asked, you would have said no."

"Oh." True, totally true. I thought this before, but hey..."Shut up, you would have, too!"

"Obviously." See?! He admits it! And I'm about to go on about how this is his problem, but he speaks before I can. "So let's settle this—we're dating."

"Wait, what? What if I don't want to?" Because I so don't. Clearly, I don't. My heart screams, *get over yourself!*

"After that fit you just threw?"

"It wasn't a fit," I hiss, bringing my leg up to knee him in the side. He grunts, then head butts me. What the hell? Who is more childish now?! Freaking jerk.

"You were throwing a tantrum like a five-year-old in a candy store," he declares.

"Because you were being an ass!"

The arguing about my totally not fit continues. The arguing turns into teasing, which eventually leads to making out with the bastard because, honestly, his mouth is only useful for one thing. And I end up not denying our dating status.

CHAPTER FORTY-TWO

S adly, us admitting to dating does not mean everything is well and good. No, it certainly does not because I find myself in a rather odd predicament the very next day with Willow Coralline, daughter of Mr. and Mrs. Coralline.

I say awkward not because I dislike the girl, rather she seems to like me quite a bit. I suppose it isn't entirely her fault. Since birth, it's kind of been engraved into her mind that she marries a noble. Most likely me. As I mentioned before, my parents had an arranged marriage, as did many kings and queens before them. Though it has never been brought up as an option to me before, that does not mean it won't happen. I dread it as much as any other prince or princess would.

However, it isn't at all unusual for a prince or princess to be wed to someone related to the Regent. After all, the Regent is meant as someone to take over should I not be old enough to rule, so there's nothing weird about marriage being involved. It's never been made official, but our parents certainly bring Willow around often enough and hint at the idea to clue us both in on what they would like. I doubt my parents would ever force me into a marriage, but doesn't mean it will never happen.

"Willow," I smile down at the girl who resembles her mother, only young and not a wrinkled old toad. I pray, for her sake, she does not wind up as terrifying looking as her mother. However, unlike her mother, Willow is certainly not cruel. She's a bit prissy, but not in any way cruel.

"Hello, Your Highness, it's great seeing you again," she says with a dazzling smile as she takes a courteous bow.

"Nice to see you, too." But not really, because if you're here, it means the Wicked Witch is still here. Mom didn't mention they were staying for long, but there's no way they left without their daughter.

"Who is this?" Willow asks, looking over my shoulder at Quinton, whose eyes narrow on her whenever she wraps her arm up with my own.

I bite the inside of my cheek to hold back a grin at the obvious hatred that's oozing out of his pores. Wait, obvious hatred? Quinton's emotions are never obvious, and yet as I look at the boy beside me, it is so clear to see that he really dislikes the way Willow is attached to me.

Holy shit. He's jealous! Hold the phone. Someone take a picture. Record this moment in history! Should I call it a miracle or a bad omen?

Who knew Quinton would be the jealous type?! Not that I'm complaining. It's kind of nice seeing the way his eyes burst into flames. For once, I'm not the one losing control over their emotions. Quinton...loses control? Heart, can you stop beating that hard because I'm going to be sick. I can't handle this because I find him oddly attractive like this, and kissing seems like a great idea. No, I'd much rather take him back to the privacy of my room and, well, use your imagination.

"This is my..." Quinton's and my eyes lock for a second, as if he thinks I may spill the beans and no, I wouldn't but, it hurts a bit to say, "My friend from school, Quinton Underwood."

I don't like the sound of that. I hate it, in fact, to the point that my teeth grind. We're officially dating now, right? I'd like to actually introduce him as my boyfriend, even if thinking it is a bit flustering.

"Nice to meet you, Quinton, I'm Willow Coralline." She holds out her hand for him to take. He gives me a look that says how much he hates me for putting him in such a situation. I shrug sheepishly. With a roll of his eyes, he takes the girl's hand and shakes it.

"Nice to meet you," he says listlessly.

"Did the two of you have plans for the day?" Willow asks, her arms still interlocked with my own. I'm currently trying to shake it off without being too rude while Quinton seems to think if he glares hard enough, she'll remove it. Who are you trying to be? Cyclops from X-Men? You can't shoot lasers. For once, I am the one who may say calm your shit!

I shake my head. "No, we were probably just going to mess around. Why?"

"Why don't we go out into town? I'm sure your father won't mind so long as we take an army with us, right?" She giggles, tugging at my arm pleadingly. I look between her and Quinton, the boy seeming too busy glaring at her to even give us a response.

Sighing, I answer, "I don't think that's such a good idea. Quinton would probably end up feeling out of place and, with the paparazzi around, it's rude for him."

Yes, yes, good job Aron. Use Quinton as a way to get out of this!

"I'm sure your friend wouldn't mind, would you?" Now she's peering at Quinton with big puppy dog eyes.

He shoots her down immediately. "I rather not have my face plastered all over the newspapers."

I have to throw my hand over my mouth to hold in my laughter. I thought he may at least try to let her down easy. He could have said 'no' and it would have been equal to what he had just said. He doesn't hide the narrowing of his eyes directly on her.

Willow sighs. "It's not like they'd focus much on you. Seeing Aron and I together would make more of a boom than anything else."

I flinch at the truth of her words. Quinton glares more, if that's possible. If looks could kill, Willow would be six feet under. The obvious annoyance in his gaze makes my chest warm. As much as I'd love to continue seeing his jealous side, I rather not Willow become suspicious of his obvious instant dislike towards her.

"You know how my dad is, Willow," I say to her in order to bring her attention back to me. "He doesn't like sending us out without prior notice. I've already pushed the boundaries enough as it is, so let's stay here for the day."

Willow pouts at me, continuing to plead for about five minutes before giving in. Though we don't rid ourselves of her, it's better for us to be inside rather than Quinton having to fake having an enjoyable time outside the palace with paparazzi around every corner. I can already imagine the headlines showing pictures of Willow and I with an angry Quinton in the corner. The images make me snicker, which gets me an arched brow from the boy at my side, who I shrug at.

"How is school going? I haven't seen or heard much from you since you've left," Willow asks, giving me a disapproving look.

She goes to an all girls' academy, and we used to see each other over her breaks whenever Mr. Coralline would come over for meetings. Since I've started school, I've rarely seen her. Not that I mind. It feels odd being around someone who has always imagined we'd end up together while I've never been interested. She's nice, but there's been nothing there and maybe it is the pressure. I don't know.

I shrug and swiftly brush my hand against Quinton's beside me. The action makes his shoulders relax for a moment before stiffening again. He's kind of hot like this, not that I'd tell him that. He doesn't need to know! He'd never let it go. Then again, I doubt he wants to admit to being jealous. We both would probably pretend it didn't happen, so rather than get into one of our quarrels; I'll keep my mouth shut.

"Better than being home schooled, I guess," I answer.

"You've obviously made some friends," Willow says while looking at Quinton, who has now decided that not looking at her would somehow get rid of her.

I roll my eyes, mentally cheering at not being the 'immature' one for once. Ha! Who is acting childish now? Not me, that's for sure! Freaking hypocrite! Seriously, I need a camera, though. Let me document this. I need proof for future torment.

However, we all know I'd probably be a hell of a lot worse off than him if I ever saw someone crawling over him. The thought makes me bite the insides of my cheeks to keep back a growl. Just thinking about it aggravates me! Stupid chick magnet.

"Friend is such a strong word," I laugh, peering at the demon out of the corner of my eye. "It's more like we tolerate each other."

Quinton snorts. "I would rather say that I simply pity you."

I scowl and go to elbow the boy, who easily takes a step away from me. I go to step closer, but seeing as Willow is attached to my arm, it nearly sends her toppling over. I barely catch us both and glare at Quinton, who is actually shooting laser beams out of his eyes at the connection between Willow and me. I hiss at the boy hoping to get him to stop, which he does, only to continue moping beside me.

I wish I could say that reality took a break with us and stopped there, but sadly, life is cruel and constantly desires to throw back in my face that things are not so simple and life will never be fair.

My parents, along with Willow's, come out of my father's study. The mothers are squawking together like a pack of birds until their eyes land on us. Mrs. Coralline may dislike, or more likely hates me with an unfathomable amount of passion, however, there is no doubt in my mind she doesn't wish for a wedding between Willow and me. After all, if that happened, she'd be mother to the queen, and why wouldn't she want such power?

Mrs. Coralline, along with my mother, smiles upon seeing Willow practically stapled to my arm while I force a crooked smile. Quinton has softened his face enough to return to the apathetic mask that he wears when trying to hide his true feelings; like jealousy. Our fathers are too busy speaking further with one another to notice the women make their way towards us.

"I see you've found Aron! How long has it been since you've seen each other?" my mother coos, waltzing up to me in order to pinch my cheek. I swat her hand away while she laughs.

Willow blushes at the attention and rests her head on my arm. Immediately, my eyes flicker to Quinton who, time and time again, astounds me with his ability to keep such a poker face. However, I've known him too long. I notice he may hide his emotions behind a mask, but his body tells me more than he's willing to admit.

Hearing my mother's words makes his back straight as a board, shoulders so tense that they could probably hold up a truck while his nails dig crescent shapes in his arms. I have the greatest desire to reach out and touch him, but I can't, and that thought alone makes it hard to breathe. I give him credit for keeping a straight face, but part of me wishes he wouldn't, or rather, wishes that he didn't have to.

However, it doesn't stop there and my mother delivers the final blow by facing Quinton in order to ask in a teasing manner, but oh, is it anything but teasing. "Don't you think they'd make such a cute couple?"

His eyes shut. At that moment, I swear the world stops spinning long enough to physically see the hope drain from his face. Though I have to say, the same is probably happening with me.

The world picks up yet again and Quinton re-opens his eyes to show nothing, like he just packed all his feelings away in that single moment and shoved them all into the back of his mind. The vile building up in my stomach is on the verge of shooting up my throat, even more so when Quinton gazes at me from the corner of his eye and replies in a voice cold as ice, "They certainly would."

Willow's squeal is lost to me, as if she's a thousand miles away as I watch Quinton excuse himself with a bow. My mother, totally oblivious to the damage she just did, returns her attention to Willow, who is going on about something I don't care about. All I do is watch on in horror as Quinton walks with as much dignity as he can muster down the hall and away from me...

For a moment, things were good, but yet again, I am reminded of how much of a lost cause our relationship is. My legs shake so badly I can't even bring myself to go after him. Isn't this the part where I'm supposed to build up courage and run after him as if my life depended on it? Isn't this the part where I say some cheesy line full of absolutely naïve shit and make everything better? It is, but I do none of that.

Even if I went after him, what would I say? It's ok? Everything will be alright? I do not have the confidence or the belief in myself to say such a thing. It would be a lie.

"Aron, are you alright, sweetheart? You seem pale," Mom speaks, her hand resting against my forehead wakes me enough to realize that I'm still at Willow's side, staring off into the distance.

"Fine," I lie, putting on a smile. It never hurt to smile before, but right now it feels as if needles are being shoved into my face. "I'm fine, Mom."

"You sure?" She cups my face, inspecting me with eyes that mean no harm, yet she basically picked me up off the ground and shoved me back into the real world.

I want to reassure her. I want to say that I'm fine, but I'm not. I'm not fine. I'm anything but fine. I'm spoiled, that's something everyone can agree on. When I ask for a new game, a new console, some clothes, hell, a car, if I really thought my parents would let me drive it, I get it. I get what I ask for, but that's only to help ease the pain of knowing I will never truly have what I not only want but also need.

I need someone by my side. My parents hope that someone will be Willow while I—I hope it to be a bastard cold as ice, yet has a touch so hot it scorches me down to the bone. I want Quinton, a man, someone of a different world. My parents and the world want a royal, like Willow, and, to be honest, I think we all really know who I will end up with.

It hurts. It hurts to think that, hurts to imagine ten, twenty, or thirty years down the road from now I'll be sitting at my desk, littered with pictures of Willow and I, possibly even the children we'll come to have, rather than having Quinton at my side. Most likely arguing over something stupid, poking fun at one another even at seventy. I much rather have that jackass beside me, helping me through life while teasingly commenting on everything I do.

I wish to go after him, to ease his mind and my own, but...

"Aron, won't you come speak with us for a moment?" Dad calls, gesturing with his hand for me to make my way over to him and Mr. Coralline.

I swallow the bile in my throat. With a forced smile, I make my way over to them, leaving the girls to gossip. I stand before the two of them, Mr. Coralline looking down at me from his towering height. A military man is the best way to describe him: tall, tough, muscular and stern. His face is always set at either annoyance or apathy, unless Willow is around. Willow can get him to do anything.

"Good afternoon, Mr. Coralline," I say with a bow that he returns.

"I hear that you're attending Thorton's now," he says, more than asks.

I nod. "That I am."

"I was hesitant at first, but we wish for our boy to go to college as well, so I guess it was in his best interest," Dad tacks on, smiling regardless of Mr. Coralline's stern expression. Dad is used to him and has become accustomed to his apathetic face. Though he's a bit of a cold man, he is an incredibly intelligent and loyal one.

Obviously, my schooling is not what they wanted to discuss. Instead, they tell me about how, starting at the beginning of summer, I will attend more and more meetings with them. Of course, my attendance is more to learn the ways of the political world, which I know in theory but not necessarily in person. Oh, the joy, what fun it will be, going around people who smile at me yet within are cursing my very existence. How wonderful to meet people that will happily stab me in the back, given the chance. The world I am to go into is a poisonous one.

After informing me of my oncoming doom—I'm sorry, I mean summer plans—my father asks, "Do you have any plans this evening with Willow?"

I see the hope twinkle in his eye, a hope that sends a javelin straight through my chest. It's like my happiness doesn't matter. I know my parents mean no harm, but it simply feels like they're sitting Willow before me while saying 'she's what you're going to get, end of story.' Doesn't matter if she isn't what I want.

With a shake of my head, I answer, "Not really. We just started talking before you called me over."

"Oh, oh, my bad then," he laughs, looking at Mr. Coralline, who actually gives him a smirk. Yeah, even Mr. Coralline is hoping for a wedding between us. I may not be his first choice, but I have power and wealth. Clearly, he wants that for his little girl.

Isn't it wonderful knowing that everyone's favorite thing about you has nothing to do with who you are as a person? It's a great feeling, let me tell you!

"Why don't you two spend the evening together?" Dad asks, nodding his head enthusiastically.

I feel sick as I try to say, without sounding utterly defeated, "What about Quinton? I can't just leave him on his own. I invited him over to hang out."

Dad makes an 'o' with his mouth and nods, seeming to have completely forgotten about him for a moment before snapping his fingers and saying, "I doubt he'll mind."

Oh, but he would. I feel worse for the anger that is pointed towards my parents that mean nothing by it. I just feel like grabbing them and shaking them, you know?

"We will be leaving tomorrow. I am sure Willow would enjoy your company," Mr. Coralline says with a nod of his head that basically seals my fate for the evening.

I want to say no. I want to come up with some bullshit excuse to get out of it, but it's like the world is trying to tell me something. Quinton and I—it's not going to happen.

With a heavy heart, I fake even more smiles and agree to my parents' wishes. With slow footsteps, I walk to Quinton's room, unable to work up the courage to open his door. I dread it. I dread walking in there, seeing his face and the emotions he will do his best to conceal. I dread telling him I have plans with Willow. I dread everything.

Instead of bursting in as I normally do, I knock and wait for his grunt in response that I was actually expecting. As if he'd give me a verbal response when he's clearly not happy. However, he doesn't open the door and part of me is happy he didn't. I don't know if I could handle seeing him.

"Uh, Willow and I," I swallow the lump in my throat, force the vile to stay within my stomach and speak words that leave me feeling hollow. "We're going to watch some movies together. Do…"

Do you mind? I know the answer but can't bring myself to ask. I rest my head against the door, contemplating slamming it a few times just to see if that would somehow knock some sense into me.

"Go ahead," he replies, voice void of any emotion, which somehow tells me exactly what he's feeling—that he's feeling as cold and hollow as I am. I consider requesting he come along, but the idea of forcing Quinton to see Willow anymore than necessary is stomach churning.

I nod, give no verbal response and back away from the door slowly, as if waiting for him to come out and stop me, but he never does.

CHAPTER FORTY-THREE

"I'm so happy that we're spending the evening together!" Willow sings at my side, her arm now once again locked with my own. It kind of hurts, the contact that would normally warm others is leaving a prickling cold feeling.

"Yeah," I force out a laugh, nodding my head at her eager smile. How I wish I could fake such a happy expression. "What would you like to watch?"

She hums when searching through the personal collection we have in our home theater. I make us some popcorn as she does that. If I'm going to be stuck here watching movies, then I am at least getting some delicious junk food. Stuffing my face with food makes me feel better anyways.

She picks a romance movie, which is my least favorite genre alongside psychological horror. I never understand those. Romantic comedies are way better. Some of my favorite movies fall in that genre. At least then I could have a laugh rather than sit here, desperately trying to stay awake.

Actually, scratch that, I'm wide-awake but not because of the movie. I am awake because of the guilt eating away at my insides. Every part of me tingles, as if there's something moving inside me that I desperately wish to rip out regardless of pain and suffering. I feel sick and annoyed and hopeless. It's a foreign feeling that I haven't felt before. Words aren't strong enough to explain it. How can a person feel so much at once without going insane? Perhaps it's the world's way of saying I'm already insane. I could buy that.

To think that this will be my life, pretending to be ok, forcing smiles and laughter in order to hide pain. Now I feel that I understand Quinton a bit more. Doesn't he do this on a daily basis? Didn't he do this earlier? Hasn't he done this since the day he lost his father? Acting as if he's ok with the world and the way it sees him. He may not fake smiles or laughter, but he appears cold and uncaring when I know it's far different than that. He walks away from things as if his world hasn't shattered around him. I have to give credit when credit is due. This is hard.

It's hard making conversation with Willow when the only thing on my mind is Quinton. It's hard acting as if I'm interested in this movie when my only interest is on whether Quinton is feeling as shitty as I am. Part of me hopes so, while another pleads with the universe that he doesn't.

My fingers constantly twitch at my side, bringing out my phone in order to check for a call or a text, half expecting for one from Quinton to be there. There never is and I know there won't be. As if he'd act up, as if he'd try to make me feel guilty for spending time with Willow when we both are probably fully aware that the relationship we have is going to end one day. Whether it's today or tomorrow or ten years from now, it will end because I am to be king one day. I need to be what the nation wishes me to be.

It was dumb of me to ask what our relationship was. It's my fault. I'm the one who brought it up when it shouldn't have been brought up. Perhaps the real reason neither of us brought it up was because we knew—we both knew, deep down, that it's pointless.

"Aron," Willow calls from my side, looking up at me with a pout. "Are you watching?"

"Ah, yeah, sorry, I was just thinking a bit." More like a lot, about a guy who is meant to be my boyfriend yet I'm sitting here with a girl watching movies and feeling like total shit about it. Then again, even if that wasn't the case I still wouldn't be watching because I stand by what I said—romantic comedies are better!

Part of me is also angry that I did this to Quinton. Part of me is angry that he didn't bother trying to stop me. My emotions are conflicting; conflicting enough to bring on a massive headache that gives me the desire to shove my head into a bucket of ice in hopes of numbing it along with my brain's functionality. I'd greatly appreciate it if my thoughts would just shut up for once. I know that's hopeless because my whole life my thoughts have been raging.

I wanted Quinton to stop me. I wanted to stop myself. I don't want to be here. I want to be with Quinton, even if we begin arguing over this or feeling down about it, so long as I'm there and not here. Get what I mean? It's so aggravating. Thoughts like why am I here, why is he not here, and why the hell am I the one who has to put up with all this shit?

It's strange, the sorrow I'm feeling is beginning to dwindle as uncontrollable rage replaces it. I have to take deep breaths to keep my cool, and by cool I mean not flip shit with Willow beside me. I can't even be that mad at the girl who, honestly, means no harm. She's like me, simply someone who is expected to do great things, to marry a noble person, and do exactly what is expected of her.

Speaking of Willow, I look at her, who has always had it shoved into her face that she and I would make a great couple no matter what she thought. Would she think the same if our parents didn't force the matter so much? It's kind of hard to fall for someone else when deep down you know that it'll never happen. Quinton and I are proof of that, how long did I know that I liked him but simply ignored the feelings because it was easier?

"Willow, would you be as interested in me if our parents didn't force it onto you?" I ask before even realizing it.

My eyes widen at my outburst, as do hers whenever she brings herself to look at me. However, now that I've asked it, I wish to know the answer.

"What do you mean?" She asks, sounding confused. She purses her lips to show she does not like interrupting our movie 'date' for a confusing conversation.

"Since we were younger, not only our parents, but basically the world has been saying how much of a great couple we'd be. You and I hardly know each other yet we're paired up by everyone. Say our parents weren't so adamant about it, and say we actually had a choice in the matter, would you still have any interest in me?"

My question stumps her. It stumps me. I'm asking her that when I'm asking myself the same thing. If I had a choice, would I choose Quinton or Willow? My heart screams the answer back at me in a second.

Willow's jaw drops as she gapes like a fish and tries to think the question over. Her brows furrow whenever she removes her arm from me to cross over her chest. At first, she looks angry, but that anger is replaced with confusion, as if she's thinking it over and is unaware of the answer. I don't blame her. I asked out of the blue while I've been considering the question for some time.

"I don't know," she answers with a quivering jaw. "I never really thought about it, about anyone else because Mom and Dad..." She looks at me with wide eyes as if the answer just smacked her in the face. "I can't say that I wouldn't, but I can't say that I would." I feel like I just pushed the girl into a territory she's not entirely comfortable with. She sighs before asking almost too quietly for me to hear, "Aron, do you like someone?"

Quinton. I bite my lip at the automatic reply of my heart.

Willow squirms in her seat in order to face me. "Do you?"

"Does it matter?" I ask, my voice coming out with such sorrow that I flinch.

Willow looks hurt. Her face seems to drop and, I guess, that's to be expected. Part of her probably genuinely likes me, or she just may have been brainwashed to think that way. However, when she raises her voice in order to shout back, "It does!" It shocks me.

"Of course it matters," she huffs, yet her jaw is quivering again, as if she's on the verge of tears. "Your feelings, your real ones—" she jabs a nail into my chest, over my heart as if she thinks she can physically touch it. "—they matter, Aron."

Her words are short, to the point and incredibly sweet, sweet enough to give one cavities. I bite my lip as I try to think up something to say to make her feel better. She's clearly saddened, confused, and uncomfortable after I basically tore down her beliefs. However, she takes a deep breath, holds her hand up to stop me and says, "You've ruined my makeup."

"Me? What, how?" I ask and debate on mentioning how it looks the same to me...until her eyes begin to water. A few stray tears fall to make her eyeliner or mascara, or whichever one she's wearing, run.

"I am going to clean myself up, then go to bed," she states with a firm nod.

Willow stands, brushes off her dress and even grumbles about the popcorn that I had dropped in her lap, to which I try to smile apologetically at her. She pouts, but before leaving, jabs her manicured finger into my nose as she says, "Whoever this person is, you better treat them with care, Aron. If you don't, you'll regret it forever."

With that, she spins on her heels and stomps off, mentioning something about leaving her be from now on. I frown at Willow, who may or may not be heart broken, stomp away. Then again, I could say she almost sounded relieved, as if she's seriously thinking over what I asked and is now contemplating whether or not she can find someone special in her life rather than allowing others to try to find that special someone. Something tells me, I won't be hearing much from her from now on.

However, her words ring true. I'll regret not standing up for myself even if I know that most of my efforts will be futile. Say we don't work out, whatever, every relationship has its problems, right? But I need to face ours, head on! I hate bowing down to the world and its shackles.

I don't want to marry Willow or anyone picked for me for that matter. I don't want to let the world push their beliefs onto me. I'm beginning to think that the universe has had enough fun. I have been thoroughly fucked with enough. If I can stand up to Quinton, who is Satan reincarnate, then I can stand up against the world, right? I've survived his glares, his hateful words, and our fights so there is no way in hell the universe could throw anything worse than that at me!

I don't need to stand for this shit. I may not be able to say with confidence to anyone right now that I am in a relationship with not only another male, but also the biggest asshole to ever walk this earth, but I'm ready to test the waters. We're officially dating now. After all this shit and emotional turmoil, I have survived. We may have to put up with shit like this for a while, expectations shoved onto us by others, but one day, maybe, Quinton and I could be open.

That thought makes my entire body quiver, not with fear but with excitement. Imagining myself standing before the world with Quinton at my side, announcing that I am going to keep the one thing in my life that I really want and need.

I don't want to give up. I don't want to roll over so easily. I need to stop with this half-assed nature of mine!

I get up to leave our theater in order to have either a really heated argument or a nice long talk with my boyfriend. That's right. He's my boyfriend. We're dating and I should be there for him just like he has and will continue to be there for me. I wish to say that everything will be ok, but that would be a lie. Life will continue throwing us curve balls, but it would do that to us even if we were dating girls, so fuck it!

With each step, I pick up speed until I'm bolting down the halls towards Quinton's room. Not sure if I'll find him there, I still eagerly kick open the doors to peer within, finding him lying on his back with his nose buried in a book. I expected nothing else. Somehow seeing him relieves me.

He refuses to give me his attention. No eye contact. No movement. Simply the sound of his voice, muffled by the book yet as clear as crystal to my ringing ears.

"Shouldn't you be with Willow?" Quinton asks, voice hard as stone yet it reveals more than words ever could.

With a flick of my wrist, I lock the door and move swiftly to his bed. What he expects me to do, I don't know, but certainly not this. I push apart his legs in order to rest myself between them, finally catching his attention enough to reveal dead eyes. Dead eyes that hurt me enough to tell me that I hate that look and wish to never see it again. I make a pact with myself to never allow such a look again.

I rip the book away, ridding him of his shield in order to see an apathetic expression to hide pain. It's what I was making earlier before my parents and the Coralline's. It's most likely an expression I will continue to wear for some time. However, I wish to one day rid us both of that expression. Maybe that won't be today or tomorrow, but one day, for sure.

"What are you doing?" He inquires, arching a brow when I lean forward, resting my hands on either side of his head to look him in the eye. I want to see that smug expression again, even if it's annoying. It's a hell of a lot better than the one he has on now.

"I was thinking about jumping my boyfriend, but—" I throw on a teasing smirk. "He's being awfully cranky."

Quinton wrinkles his nose in distaste. "I'm not cranky."

"You look pretty cranky to me," I laugh, now resting on my elbows, allowing my body to lay over his. I'm trying to think how to say this, how to put my feelings into actual words. Are there even any to describe it all? I doubt it, but it's worth a shot.

He grunts at the sudden weight on his chest but doesn't go to push me away or move. Our foreheads press against each other as my hands play with his hair that is surprisingly soft.

"I'm sorry," I whisper, fingers now entangling in the strands wrapped around them. "Earlier, my mom, you know she didn't—"

"I know," he interrupts, eyes softening, certainly not out of relief or happiness, rather in order to show me his anger is not directed towards my mother.

"And I'm sorry about Willow," I add another apology to the list. Something tells me, there will be more added eventually. "I shouldn't have gone or even came to ask you. It was stupid."

Quinton doesn't answer. He actually looks away from me, to keep the sudden narrowing of his eyes off me. I bite my lip at the glare that's meant for me. It really bothered him. I get that. It really bothered me too. I want to take it back.

"I was thinking though—"

"That's a first." He growls at the sudden tugging of his hair. "Childish."

"Childish," I mock, rolling my eyes then continuing what I was saying before I was so rudely interrupted! "I was scared. No, I am scared. I always think how unfair the world is, how I can't have the relationship I really want, but to be honest, we aren't much different from everyone else."

"Is that so?" Quinton asks, allowing his arms to drape over my midsection. He returns his focus to me. I rather not admit aloud that I enjoy physical contact. We all know, if I did, he'd stop because he's a freaking asshole like that. "Do explain," he says.

"Everyone has relationship problems. They come in different forms, at different times and for different reasons. Right now, ours is we can't—we can't tell the world about us just yet, but that doesn't mean our feelings are any less real or—or that we should let it get us down!" My voice rises with each word until Quinton pinches me as if to say 'keep it down.' I smile apologetically, earning me an eye roll from him before he nods his head for me to continue. "I can't promise that things will be ok or everything will be alright because that would be a lie. I can't say that I'm confident enough right now to tell the world about us. I'm scared of how they'll react, what we'll face, and how to overcome it. I need time. I think we both do. The point is, we're going to run into obstacles like everyone else, but we'll get through them together, right?"

I search those black eyes that, with every passing word, lighten until the anger seems to have dissipated completely. Relief washes over his face that was once apathetic and soon the thin line of his lips twitches upwards into a smirk that has me grinning right back.

"I don't know whether I should call you brave or stupid," Quinton says with a shake of his head.

"Brave. I'm definitely brave," I laugh, running my hands through his hair to mess it up. His eyes clench shut at the way my fingers ruffle the jungle atop his head that begins to stick up in odd ways that leave me laughing.

"Definitely stupid," Quinton grunts, but what does that make him? The one who removes his hand from my waist in order to pull me in for a kiss. I'd argue it'd make him the biggest idiot in the world.

"We may be a secret now," I whisper against lips that brush mine with every passing word. "But..." I peer into eyes that I expect to mirror my own, full of stubbornness and the will power to continue on.

Words aren't always needed. Sometimes a kiss is enough to convey what's on someone's mind and I think, by the way his lips hungrily move along with my own, he got the message.

One day, we will tell the world.

CHECK OUT VOLUME TWO FOR THE CONTINUATION OF QUINTON AND ARON'S STORY.

NOTES FROM THE AUTHOR

I wrote this story in 2012, never imagining where it would be in 2022. While I have many issues with the story, I am ultimately very proud of the community it has created and what it has accomplished. I'm forever grateful to readers who have stayed beside me all these years, continuing to read my content and support me in every way they can. This story is for all of you who have desperately wanted opportunities to purchase Speak the Truth as an eBook or physical copy. I hope that the story continues to mean as much to you now as it did all those years ago. Please look forward to the next two volumes!

To those of you who may be new readers, thank you for giving Speak the Truth a try. I know it can get pretty rough. I don't condone writing stories where bullies get with their victims anymore, but I didn't want to change the story that so many readers came to love. I hope Speak the Truth was still enjoyable. Thanks again for the support and I hope you enjoy the continuation of Aron and Quinton's tale, should you decide to stay!

ABOUT THE AUTHOR

Twoony is a queer geek with a love for storytelling in all forms; movies, comics, books, games, and more. They write young adult and adult stories ranging from the always enjoyable teen rom-com to fantasy romances. At the age of twelve, they posted their first story online and have been addicted to sharing ever since. Although Twoony graduated from California University of PA with a Bachelors in Graphics & Multimedia, their true passion has always been writing. After creating original novels and comics on sites like Tapas and Wattpad, amounting over 105k subscribers and 7m+ reads, they have managed to live their dream. They are a full-time writer with three needy cats and not enough bookshelves. If you're interested in their work, they have a completed romantic trilogy called Speak the Truth and a standalone romantasy called Whisper Woods also available on amazon. Otherwise, follow their social media to learn more.

Instagram: twoonyreads
Threads: twoonyreads
Tiktok: twoonyreads
Twitter: Tw00ny
Wattpad: Twoony
Tapas: Twoony
Patreon: Twoony

Made in the USA
Columbia, SC
16 July 2024

38741705R00157